**Praise for #1 *New York Times*
bestselling author**

KRESLEY COLE's

IMMORTALS AFTER DARK

"This is one of the few series that is actually getting better as it progresses. . . . My favorite thing about these books is that Cole lets the characters act like immortals. They are so violent, so cunning and evil. And yet they are hilarious and smart and, of course, amazing in bed."

—*USA Today*

"Stands out as one of the best paranormal series available on the market."

—Examiner.com

"You can trust Cole to always deliver sizzling sexy interludes within a darkly passionate romance."

—*RT Book Reviews*

"Kresley Cole knows what paranormal romance readers crave and superbly delivers on every page."

—*Single Titles*

Turn the page for more reviews of her bestselling novels . . .

LOTHAIRE

"I was amazed at this world Kresley Cole has created . . . a definite favorite."

—*USA Today*

"How do you make the crazy, arrogant, and ruthless archvillain of a series a hero? With great difficulty! Yet Cole pulls it off splendidly."

—*RT Book Reviews*

DREAMS OF A DARK WARRIOR

"The richness of Cole's world and characters make it a fascinating place to visit!"

—*RT Book Reviews*

"Fast-paced, engaging, and captivating. . . . The perfect getaway."

—Examiner.com

DEMON FROM THE DARK

"Intense danger mixes with insatiable desire to create a scorching hot romance that plays out against a fast-paced backdrop of thrilling supernatural adventure. Addictively good reading."

—*Love Vampires*

PLEASURE OF A DARK PRINCE

"There are few authors that can move me to tears. Kresley Cole is one of them."

—*Book Binge*

"Consistent excellence is a Cole standard!"

—*RT Book Reviews*

KRESLEY COLE

MACRIEVE

POCKET BOOKS
New York • London • Toronto • Sydney • New Delhi

Pocket Books
A Division of Simon & Schuster, Inc.
1230 Avenue of the Americas
New York, NY 10020

This book is a work of fiction. Any references to historical events, real people, or real places are used fictitiously. Other names, characters, places, and events are products of the author's imagination, and any resemblance to actual events or places or persons, living or dead, is entirely coincidental.

First Pocket Books paperback edition December 2013

POCKET and colophon are registered trademarks of Simon & Schuster, Inc.

For information about special discounts for bulk purchases, please contact Simon & Schuster Special Sales at 1-866-506-1949 or business@simonandschuster.com.

The Simon & Schuster Speakers Bureau can bring authors to your live event. For more information or to book an event contact the Simon & Schuster Speakers Bureau at 1-866-248-3049 or visit our website at www.simonspeakers.com.

Manufactured in the United States of America

10 9 8 7 6 5 4 3 2

ISBN 978-1-4516-4992-5
ISBN 978-1-4516-4015-1 (ebook)

Warmly dedicated to the Lykae lovers of the Immortals After Dark community. This one's for you. . . .

ACKNOWLEDGMENTS

Many thanks to Belinda and Karen, soccer goddesses, for all your sporty wisdom. You answered many a late-night query, even though you had to be on the pitch in the a.m.

Much appreciation to Dr. Beth, for all her insights into child psychology.

And lastly, thank you to the production team at Simon & Schuster. Chocolate TK.

The Lore

"*. . . and those sentient creatures that are not human shall be united in one stratum, coexisting with, yet secret from, man's.*"

- Most are immortal and can regenerate from injuries, killed only by mystical fire or beheading.
- Their eyes change with intense emotion, often to a breed-specific color.

The Lykae Clan

"*A proud, strapping warrior of the Keltoi People (or Hidden People, later known as Celts) was taken in his prime by a maddened wolf. The warrior rose from the dead, now an immortal, with the spirit of the beast latent within him. He displayed the wolf's traits: the need for touch, an intense loyalty to its kind, an animal craving for the delights of the flesh. Sometimes the beast rises. . . .*"

- Each Lykae possesses the Instinct, an inner guiding force, like a voice whispering in one's mind.
- Mate for life. Over eternity, they seek their fated one above all things, revering matehood as other species do gods.
- Royal seat is Kinevane in the Scottish Highlands.

The Ubus Peoples

"Descendants of demons, reapers of pleasure. Thrice in one's arms, forever enslaved. Separation begets grave sickness, yet only through death can the envenomed be freed."

- Female: succubus. Male: incubus.
- Derive nourishment from the sexual enjoyment of others.
- Possess the ability to sexually madden their victims. A succubus uses *strew*; an incubus *stav*.
- After a third mating, they form a bond with their conquests, a mystical tie called *venom*.

The Accession

"And a time shall come to pass when all immortal beings in the Lore, from the Valkyrie, vampire, Lykae, and demon factions to the witches, shifters, fey, and sirens . . . must fight and destroy each other."

- A kind of mystical checks-and-balances system for an ever-growing population of immortals.
- Two major alliances: the Pravus Rule and the Vertas League.
- Occurs every five hundred years. Or right now . . .

PROLOGUE

Woods of Murk, Scotland
CENTURIES AGO . . .

I n a dark forest, in a dour land, stood an enchanted cottage. Within it, Uilleam MacRieve was about to bicker with his mate, Lady Ruelle.

Yet again.

As the blizzard outside gathered its strength, Will sat on the edge of her bed, wearily preparing for battle.

"Just once more, my love," Ruelle sighed, letting the silk cover dip to reveal her bare breasts.

In the past he'd have stared agog at that generous flesh; now he scowled at her antics. "You know I canna stay." Always with these antics. Could she not tell how deep she'd already drawn from him this eve?

"'Tis hours till dawn." She rose up on her knees to purr at his ear, "I needn't keep you long." Her words were accented with the flavor of distant realms.

In these northern lands of the Lykae, Ruelle was a rarity, a foreign female who dressed in lace and silks and had no skill with a sword. She lived alone here in the Woods of Murk—a place of fairy rings and curses, of portals to different planes and creatures of old that even Lykae feared.

Only a dare from other boys had coaxed Will's feet into that eerie forest the first time.

"Once more?" He rose to wash, doubting that he had another bout in him. Nay, not a bout—that would imply two contenders. "And after that, you'll demand yet another." Even if he was physically capable, he needed to get back to Conall Keep before his family realized he was gone. "Already I've yielded to your wishes."

At her basin, he gazed into her oversize mirror—his Ruelle could be a *tad* bit vain—and spied her behind him. In the firelight, her hair appeared burnished, her cheeks and lips rouged to match, the colors stark against her milk-white skin and gray eyes.

She pouted prettily. Everything she did was pretty, even lovemaking—unlike the trollops his older cousins routinely tupped in the hayloft.

Afterward, those wenches would be heavy-lidded with satisfaction, even as they looked like they'd just gone to war in the hay: faces and chests flushed from exertion, hair and clothing disheveled.

Ruelle never looked like that. With a pang, he admitted to himself that she had never been completely . . . fulfilled when he'd left her.

She often cajoled him to mate her again and again until he was exhausted. "Look at you—who can blame me?" she'd ask, explaining that his kind was like catnip to her, that his face alone made her sigh. One time he'd jested that she was trying to kill him, and she'd grown cross.

Sometimes being with her was like a swim in chill water—enlivening, until the deep threatened to pull you under. On occasion, he struggled to breathe when she had him beneath her, his lungs seeming to shrivel up.

Which was a shameful weakness. Ruelle was beautiful and sensual—any lad would count his blessings to be in her bed. And she was *his* mate. They were both sure of it.

"You could eat again." She waved to indicate the banquet she'd prepared for him, sweets and delicacies that were rarely allowed at his home. He shook his head, had already eaten his fill.

In the beginning, she'd gotten him to glut himself. With a laugh, she'd pinched his slim fingers and declared him underweight.

Now he said, "Ruelle, *nay*. I'm leaving."

"'Tis your own fault for being so tantalizing." She ogled him as he washed thoroughly. Early on, she'd warned him that his family could smell her on him.

"You're the one insisting that we keep this secret. If I could tell my da—"

"No! That's not possible." She paled beneath those tinted cheeks. "They will never accept what's between us."

"Then I must be there for chores." He had work to do at sunrise, and his twin brother, Munro, was already suspicious of Will's sneaking away late every other night.

"You come from one of the richest families in the land—the Sentinels, for gods' sakes—and still your father makes you work like a serf?"

"Da believes it builds character," Will said, pulling his tunic over his head. The garment was tight, hugging his chest and arms. He and his twin were both growing like weeds, too fast for the harried seamstress at Conall.

He gazed at his own reflection and ran a hand over his lean face. *Still no whiskers though?*

"Ah, Dùghlas MacRieve, the great Lord of Conall, says it builds character? Your father is mistaken—your character is already built! And finely too. You are a man in your own right."

"I *know* I'm a man," he averred, while thinking, *I might no' yet be a man.*

Nay, of course he was. Whenever Will and Ruelle quarreled, he comprehended that he was truly maturing—a grown Lykae. Adults bickered; they had concerns and cares that the young did not.

Yet if he was grown, why couldn't he satisfy her? A flare of anger took him by surprise. "If you have call to criticize my da, you should do it the Lykae way: to his face." As soon as the words left his mouth, he regretted them. Her species was made to love, never to fight.

The idea of Ruelle openly criticizing someone so much stronger was laughable.

As if on cue, her gray eyes misted with tears. She even cried prettily. "You know I cannot do that, can never show my face to them. They will kill me, just for what I am."

His parents wouldn't necessarily welcome her into the pack with open arms, but surely Ruelle exaggerated about their reaction. "No Lykae would ever harm another's mate. We revere matehood above all things."

"What if they don't believe what we know to be true?" She pulled the silk covers over her breasts defensively. "Why do you continue to argue with me?"

"Because keeping this secret for so long sits ill." Lately it'd been weighing on him more and more, but he'd at least wait until after his mam gave birth to her bairn before revealing his secret. She was a couple of months along, just starting to show. Her "three braw lads"—as she called her husband, Will, and Munro— all sensed she carried a daughter and were ecstatic about the fact. Mam wanted to call her Isla.

A wee lass to spoil? Even now Will's lips curled with anticipation. He and Munro could scarcely wait until she was old enough to learn how to hunt, to fish.

Aye, his family needed no tumult now. Best to get back. He quickly donned his boots. "We'll speak of this in the future."

"No, we will *not*." Her gray eyes flickered to jade green, usually the only sign that her emotions were running high. "If you can't respect my wishes in something so important, then do not return for four nights."

Will froze. The fire in the hearth crackled. The wind whipped snow against the windows. "You doona mean it."

"I do."

"Four!" he bit out in disbelief. "You'd punish me

thus?" The longest he'd gone was three. He'd barely survived the sickness.

"I wish that you hadn't forced me to."

"*I* forced you?" Everything was always his fault. When he'd panicked during their first time making love and wanted to wait, she was not to be denied—and it was his fault for being "irresistible" to her. He'd wanted to bring home all the gifts she'd given him—mainly to lord them over his twin—but she'd refused: "Your parents will suspect; it's not *my* fault that you were born into a closed-minded family."

And now he was to go the better part of a week without returning. At the thought of the agony he'd soon experience, his Lykae beast stirred. Though his da, uncles, and older cousins were training him to harness that wild force within him, Will unleashed it each time Ruelle mated him.

"One day, Ruelle, you will push me too far."

"Oh? And then what will you do?" she asked with a triumphant look, for they both knew the truth.

He was bound to her for eternity. Doubly so—not just because she was his Lykae mate, but because of the tie he'd willfully borne after three visits to her bed.

He was fettered to her for the rest of his life. Or for the length of hers.

"But before you go, my love, I truly do need once more."

With a painful surge, his exhausted body reacted against his will, readying for her to take. He grimaced, panic setting in, his breaths shallowing. "You told me you'd no' use your strew again!" It was how she'd gotten him to mate her in the beginning. He shuddered to remember those times. A sickly feeling roiled in his gut as he struggled to withstand her, knowing how futile it was.

"Why fight me?" Eyes glowing green, she dropped the sheet. "Any male would kill to be with me." She traipsed over and embraced him, pressing his face against her breast, against scented white flesh.

He couldn't get enough air. "I canna—Ruelle, nay!" Already his beast was rising, protectively.

She pulled back, grasping his chin, hard. "Your eyes turn blue," she said with a satisfied smile. "Your beast and I will take care of everything. Just as we always do."

"You promised me!"

She pressed him down on her bed, then rose above him, the position she chose without fail. "Look at you, my love. Who could possibly blame me?"

And the deep dragged him down. . . .

Conall Keep, Northern Outpost of the Woods of Murk
THREE NIGHTS LATER

All day the sickness had grown worse until Will's body was a mass of pain. By midnight, he felt like his bones were breaking. Outside, the storm gusted winds, but the great Conall Keep was indifferent to them.

He wrapped his arms around himself, rocking over his damp sheets, praying he wouldn't be plagued with hallucinations this time.

No use fighting this. He would go to Ruelle tonight.

The idea of running for leagues through a blizzard in this condition made him shudder. Not to mention that he'd be entering the Woods alone, weak, in the middle of the night.

Fantastical creatures teemed in that forest, bloodthirsty beings from other realms.

Munro stirred in his nearby bed, as if sensing his twin's distress, even in sleep. Will envied Munro, who could remain snug in his bed, warm and safe within the impervious keep of their ancestors.

This place had been built by them for future Sentinels of the Woods, the warriors tasked with making sure the creatures of Murk never strayed beyond its boundaries—and that Lykae never ventured within.

When Will rose to dress, stabbing his legs into trews, Munro roused and sat up. "Where are you going?" He lit a candle, illuminating the room they shared.

"'Tis no concern o' yours."

A flash of hurt flickered in Munro's golden eyes—eyes exactly like his own, only . . . graver. Despite being identical twins, he and Munro had opposing personalities. Will was oft called impetuous like their mother, Munro solemn like their da.

"You used to tell me everything, Will."

Ruelle had warned against that. She'd helped him see Munro's jealous nature. Munro was envious of his twin, simmering with hatred toward his slightly older brother, the heir.

I'm much more mature for my age, and Munro knows it, canna stand it.

In fact, she'd helped Will see the faults in all his friends.

"Are you going into the Woods?" Munro asked, pulling on his own breeches. "To see that female in the odd cottage?"

A stark contrast to the dreary woods, Ruelle's home was brightly painted, with intricate eaves and spindles, as if from a fey's dream. And Munro had never even seen the inside! It was not only fantastical, but *mystical*—she'd told him it had been standing for centuries, immune to decay.

"What do you know of her?" Will asked, struggling to focus his vision as another wave of pain hit. The tunic he'd just donned was already moist with sweat.

"I know the tales surrounding her."

"That she's a hideous old crone who lures youths to their doom? That she fattens them up, then feeds on their flesh? The rumors are false." The fact that Ruelle cooked feasts for him and then used his body for nourishment wasn't lost on Will. "Are you going to tell Da?" Or, gods forbid, their mother. No she-wolf could be fiercer than Ailis MacRieve.

'Twas one thing that Will had found his mate in a different species; 'twas another that he'd been lying to all of them.

"No need," Munro said quietly. "Mam and Da already suspect you've been sneaking out."

"Because you told them!"

Again came that flash of hurt, like a creature kicked in the flank. "You ken I would no' do that, brother."

Will . . . believed him. At these times, when Munro

continued to prove loyal to him, Will couldn't reconcile all the things Ruelle had told him.

His beast was cut from the same soul as Munro's; it longed to run beside his brother's forever. Surely Munro felt the same way?

"What has happened to you, Will? Why do you never talk to me? Why do you never play or laugh anymore?" Munro looked wary and vulnerable—a mere boy.

Do I look so young? "It's complicated. Just let me handle this as I need to, and I'll be back soon." Will finished dressing. "Mayhap we'll talk then."

Without a backward glance, he hastened from the room to descend the main stairs and head out into the blustery night. He'd just felt the first crunch of snow beneath his boots when he heard, "And where might you be off to, Uilleam Andriu MacRieve?"

Mam. *Oh, shite.* He turned to face her, trying to disguise how bad his shakes had gotten.

She emerged from the shadows, joining him under the swirling snow. Her cheeks were pink, her doe-brown eyes narrowed. "You were too ill to come down for meals today—or to do your chores—and now I find you stealing away in the middle of the night?"

He had waited too long, should've made a run for Ruelle's last night. If Mam kept him from her tonight . . . Much longer, and he'd grow crazed. A hallucination danced at the edges of his vision, the dark closing in. He shifted his weight from one leg to the other; both felt like they'd snap at any second.

She tilted her head. "You go to meet a lass, no

doubt. Thirteen is too young, son. Your da will tell you the same."

"I know, Mam. I'm sorry." *Ah, gods, my bones.*

She cupped his clammy face, her eyes going wide. "Ach, my Uilleam, you're burning up!"

"I have to go!" He could almost scent Ruelle's perfumes. Could almost taste the rouge with which she adorned her skin.

He could all but feel her milk-white arms wrapping around him. "Can you no' trust me, Mam?"

"You're sick, no' thinking clearly. You canna be out in the snow; you need to be abed."

"Please, just go back inside and doona worry over this. I'll return anon."

She snatched his arm and yelled over her shoulder, "Dugh! Come out here! *Now.*"

Will heard two sets of footsteps stomping down the stairs into the main hall. Da and Munro.

Desperation boiled up inside him. "I've got to go!" He flung his arm free, shoving against his mother.

Mam tripped, falling down into the hard-packed snow. She gaped up at him, her eyes watering. "Will?"

He was horrified. He would rather die than harm her. "I'm so sorry! Have I hurt you? The babe?"

Her hands went to her belly as if to protect the wee girl. *Protect Isla from me?*

But then Mam's tears dried. Her inner beast began to rise, her eyes turning ice blue. Never, never, a good sign. Shite!

"You've no' hurt me, boy," she growled, her fangs lengthening. "Best worry for your own hide."

Just as Da and Munro made the doorway, she snapped to Will, "Hie your arse inside. Now!"

Da helped Mam to her feet, glancing from her to his son with his jaw slackened. "Have you lost your bluidy mind, Will?"

Aye! Will glanced over his shoulder toward the Woods of Murk, imagining the relief, the end of this pain. He whimpered—

Da's massive hand clamped Will's neck. "In you go!" He squired Will to a seat before Conall's great hearth fire. After getting a better look at his son's face, he added another log to the flames.

With his tall form outlined by the flickering light, Da looked even more intimidating than usual. Will swallowed, darting a glance at his twin.

Munro's slow nod and steady gaze seemed to say, *We'll get through this. Keep your head.* It helped.

Their mother crossed to sit close by her mate. Mam and Da were always near each other, as if their beasts were tethered with an invisible leash.

Her ire was clearly fading as she stared at Will's sweating face. "Dugh, we need to send for a physic."

"I fear I know what's wrong with him." Da turned to him. "Where were you going, son?" He seemed to hold his breath.

Will couldn't lie to his face. And more, he had to trust what he knew of his father's character—and Lykae law—over Ruelle's overwrought predictions. *No Lykae will harm another's mate.* "I was going to see my female, a woman who lives in the Woods."

Silence reigned. His words seemed to hang in the air.

When Da exhaled a stunned breath and Mam looked stricken, a marked unease stole over Will.

Ruelle had predicted that they wouldn't understand; she'd never mentioned that they'd be *disgusted*.

Turning to Da, Mam muttered, "Too young, ah gods, he's too young." She rose unsteadily to gather a blanket. Wrapping it around Will's shoulders, she said, "Warm yourself, lad. You've a long night ahead of you." He noticed with dread that her eyes watered once more.

"*Why* am I too young? Humans wed when they're no' much older than I." Of course, he'd prepared these arguments, fashioning them from those he'd heard Ruelle say.

"Humans must!" Da began to pace. "In these harsh lands, they scarcely live longer than your age! But you, Will, you can potentially *live forever*. In any case, you're far too young to be in the clutches of one like her."

This was his mate they spoke of! Surely she was.

"Do you no' know what she is?" Da spat the words: "She's a *succubus*."

"Ruelle told me this, right off."

"Aye, but do you understand what the word means, what her kind do?"

Will's eyes darted. "It means that we are so connected we'll suffer without each other." After three nights of mating a succubus, a male would take on her essence, her mystical venom, binding himself to her until death.

Mam said, "It means she's a parasite." Her tears

fell. "One who sank her claws into my lad." He'd never seen his mother cry before this eve. "She's envenomed you. 'Tis why you have sickness."

"Then I need to reach her. It's been three days. If I'm feeling this way, then so is she."

Da shook his head. "Unlike you, she can take another. I'd be shocked if she does no' have a stable of lovers. Even in the Woods, she could lure others."

Impossible. Ruelle loved Will alone.

Da finally sank down beside Mam. "How long have you been seeing her?"

Will hesitated.

In a tone brooking no disobedience, Da snapped, "How—long?"

Forcing his shoulders back, Will answered, "I first went to her cottage four years ago."

Da shot back to his feet. His mother pressed the back of her hand against her mouth to stifle a retching sound. Had there been a glimmer of rage in Da's eyes? A glimpse of his beast? Never had Da unleashed it before them.

Should Will be denied his mate just because he and Ruelle were born in differing times? How could his parents react so violently to something that was natural? They were not usually judgmental.

Will hugged the blanket tighter, struggling to hide his shudders. Pain was like a drum inside him, beating him, breaking him. His bones . . .

"My precious lad," Mam choked out, rising to her feet. "'Tis a vile perversion," she told Da. "I doona understand how he survived her hungers when so young! He's far from his immortality."

Survived? Could he have *died*? All Will had done was bed a beautiful woman.

"His beast is stronger than most, a pure alpha," Da said. "Like Munro's. I've spoken of this before."

Will remembered. Da had sounded both proud yet fearful at the same time. The beast could be a blessing and a curse, lending strength but robbing reason.

"Did your beast rise up when you were with her?"

Will absently nodded.

"Otherwise, she would've killed you—a fact she well knew, son."

Nay, 'twas not true. Nothing could make him believe Ruelle had ever jeopardized his life. She could be demanding, pushing him to his limits, but only because he was strong and could take it. He *was* strong for his age. She'd repeatedly said so.

"Look how our son shakes even now. Her venom's work. This must be answered!" Mam declared.

"It *will* be, love. I set out for the Woods at dawn. I'll petition for entry. The Elders will grant it before they let a pup suffer."

Answered? Will still didn't quite comprehend their crime. His older cousins were forever tumbling females, and they'd started when they were not much older than Will was now.

But I started earlier still. He glanced at Munro, seeking an ally. Munro cast him a baffled look.

"Nay, Dùghlas!" Mam's own beast was rising once

more. "I know her kind! She'll be winsome and manip-
ulative, and she'll twist you too. The men of this pack
have said for ages they would run her out of the forest,
and naught comes of it."

"They're no' our woods to patrol!" Da ran his hand
over his face. "And she's never targeted our young
before! She's never envenomed any of our males. Our
lad will be free of this by tomorrow eve. The day after
at the latest. I vow it."

"Free of this?" The only way out was Ruelle's
death. "I-I need to see her. Just tonight." He and his
mate could run.

Leave behind my family?

A lifetime of drowning . . . ?

"Nay!" Mam bared her fangs. "Over my dead body!
You will never see her again!"

Da wrapped his arm around her shoulders. "Take a
moment, love. Just . . . take a moment. Collect yourself.
Think of the babe."

"If I canna protect the bairns I have, I doona
deserve the gods to give me more!"

"Whisht, love! I will talk to him, and tomorrow we
will end this. Go take your tea and calm yourself."

She lurched from the room, casting a look over her
shoulder. The rage in her expression changed to something like . . . pity when she met Will's eyes. "Never one
like *her*, my Uilleam." Then she was gone.

Pity? Realization struck. *I've done wrong. I've hurt Mam.*

Before, he'd wanted to tell the world about Ruelle;
now he felt shame, even though he didn't quite understand *why* he should. He'd been mating a beautiful

female, his female, so why did his skin feel like it was
crawling?

His nose burned, vision blurring. Tears? He was
sick of tears—had shed them aplenty in the first year
he'd been with her. His voice broke as he said, "I dinna
mean to do wrong, Da. Are you angrier about my age
or about what Ruelle is? How old *should* I have been?"

"You are no' there yet, son. And, as your mother
said, *never* with one like her."

"But she's my mate."

His father snapped his fangs, as if Will had blas-
phemed. "No—she's—no'!"

Will had never seen his da this angry. Still he asked,
"How do you know?"

"Because she's sick in the head!" He shoved his fingers through his thick black hair. "If she were yours,
your Instinct would ring loud and clear, telling you that
she was. Has that happened?"

Will's Instinct, the guiding force all Lykae possessed, was usually quiet with her. But it hadn't been
at first, had warned him not to enter the cottage, had
whispered of peril within.

Peril from a delicate beauty like Ruelle? The idea
had struck him as ridiculous.

"Think, son—if she were truly your mate, you
would have felt the overwhelming need to mark her
neck. You would have gotten a babe on her after all
this time. But I know you have no' done either."

Will shook his head, muttering, "Ruelle *must* be
mine for me to feel this way."

"No, she's entranced you—it's their way. Grown

males are swayed by them, trapped by their wiles and their strewing; at your age, you stood no chance."

Da was making her sound like a sorceress or worse, a witch. Just like the rumors . . .

"You have doubts. I see it in your eyes. Do you no' ken, son? When you find your mate, it feels like the hands of gods have reached out to touch you, like your soul's been branded. There is no *doubt*. And there is no way you could willingly part from her, as you've obviously been doing with the succubus for years. Will, heed my words: where your mate goes, you follow."

Will grimaced as a sharper surge of pain hit. Da continued talking, clearly aiming to distract him. He told Will and Munro all about the first time he'd met Mam, a tale they'd heard before. But tonight it highlighted aspects of Will's own meeting with Ruelle.

She'd lured him to her cottage with sweets. He'd been reluctant, half terrified of her, half fascinated. When he'd tentatively entered, she'd lavished gifts on him, complimenting him, as if she were . . . taming him.

Or *trapping* him?

The firelight had just begun to dim when Will's Instinct suddenly commanded —*SAVE HER!*—

Da and Munro must've received the same warning. They shot to their feet.

"Ailis?" Da crossed to the hallway with long strides. "Come join us."

No answer.

"Love?" His father tensed, lifting his face to scent the air. Will and Munro did the same.

Mam was gone. Will didn't scent her anywhere in the keep.

There was only one reason she would have left home in this storm.

Like a shot, Da charged for the front door. Will and Munro followed him out into the blizzard, sprinting through the snow as he tracked Mam's scent and footprints toward the forest.

With each step, Da was turning, his Lykae beast surfacing. His fangs and black claws lengthened, his face angling into a more wolven shape. His muscles burgeoned, the shadow of his inner wolf rising to hover over him: a vicious, towering creature with maddened white-blue eyes.

Will could see his da struggling to keep the feral beast at bay, to think clearly, to reason.

To best protect his mate.

Will and Munro began to lag behind their desperate father's pace. Two young Lykae in the Woods at night. They had not reached their immortality yet, couldn't regenerate from injury.

As the storm strengthened, shadows closed in on them, snow swirling, trees shuddering. The winds howled, disrupting Will's hearing and sense of smell. Gusts brought confusing scents all the way from the sea he hadn't yet beheld.

His teeth clattered. Pain throughout his body had merged until he couldn't distinguish one area of agony from another, his aching bones from his splitting head. . . .

Will squinted through the snow as they ran, barely

making out Da as he closed in on Ruelle's cottage. Between painted shutters, the windows glowed, softly lit and fogged.

Da barreled through the door. Even over the winds, Will heard his roar.

Of anguish.

No! Ruelle couldn't have hurt Mam. Will's mother was a she-wolf in her prime, fierce as this storm. Ruelle was weak and helpless.

The brothers burst through the splintered doorway and froze at the sight before them. With a sheet secured around her, Ruelle stood trembling behind a terrified lad who looked not much older than Will.

—*Vampire.*—

Their natural enemy. Here, this far north? Will had never seen one, just knew he needed to kill the creature.

The leech was brandishing a bloody sword to protect Ruelle against Da—whose beast was completely risen. It shadowed over him, monstrous and shocking even to Will.

No wonder the vampire was terrified. But why was the male half-dressed? Whose blood coated his sword? Where was Mam?

Will edged deeper into the cottage. Behind a settee . . . he saw her.

Part of her.

Shock robbed him of breath and muted his thoughts. Dimly, he wondered, *Where is my mother's head?*

Da roared, shaking the cottage until dust rained from the rafters.

The vampire could have traced away, teleporting to safety in an instant. Yet he seemed bent on protecting Ruelle—as if he loved her. With a broken yell, he attacked, tracing around Da, landing blows that the older immortal didn't seem to feel.

The leech disappeared again and again, until Da predicted where he'd appear next. With one swipe of Da's flared claws, the vampire was no more.

When Da turned on Ruelle, she backed away. As if from a well-pump, her tears flowed at once. "We had n-no choice. She attacked us, had come to destroy me."

As Da stalked her with a murderous look in his ice-blue gaze, Ruelle eyed the vampire's sword, could have reached it; instead she clasped her hands to her breast, pleading to Will, "My love, help me! He will kill me!"

She would forgo a weapon in order to plead?

Will realized she still possessed her most powerful weapon: her guile. She looked fragile, defenseless, and so damned beautiful. Even now, the urge to protect her seized him.

"My love, I beg you! Do something!" Her eyes glowed green.

He was horrified to realize that he was stumbling over his mother's body to reach Ruelle. *I've done wrong.* Though he knew he was no match for his father, Will rose up in front of his female—

Da bared his fangs and backhanded him, connecting with his jaw. As Will reeled to the floor, Da raised his hand once more. With another slash of his claws, he decapitated Ruelle.

Vision swimming, Will watched as her head tumbled. But her body collapsed slowly. Even in this, she was graceful.

With her death, Will's bones instantly ceased to ache, the fever leaving him. His body was free. But his mind . . .

Sorrow, guilt, horror, hatred—all warred within him.

Da dropped to his knees beside their mother's covered body. Munro must've draped a blanket over her.

Will was numb, incapable of moving. *Wrong. Everything's wrong. All my fault.*

Somehow he found the strength to rise. Through watering eyes, Will gazed over his shattered family.

Munro knelt beside Da, squeezing his shoulder, crying openly. Da clumsily patted Mam's limp hand, his beast receding somewhat. In this half state, Da was awkward, his hands too big, his claws too long. Tears streamed down his wolven face. His blue eyes were blank.

He lifted Mam's hand to his face. When it did not lovingly stroke his cheek, as it had thousands of times before, Da roared once more, then whimpered with grief.

Mam had come to this cursed place for Will, to save her son. He didn't know what disgusted him more, his part in all this—or the fact that he grieved Ruelle's death nearly as much as Mam's.

At the thought, he bashed his fists against his head, face twisting. *What is* wrong *with me? Sick, sick!* His beast kept trying to rise, to shield Will from pain. But Will wanted the agony, needed it.

Because of him, all was lost. Their family broken.

Ah, no, the wee babe. Little Isla. He pulled at his hair, falling to his knees beside Munro. *All my fault.*

He wished to every god in the heavens that he could die bloody, die on the spot, could trade his life for his mother's.

Munro turned to him—but instead of the hatred Will expected, Munro's watering eyes flickered over his face with what looked like pity. *I don't deserve pity!* He wished his father had struck him harder, and more. He wished Munro would hit him.

As Will's own tears fell, he and Munro stared at each other. *Hate me, brother! As I hate myself!*

After what felt like hours, Da turned to his sons, emotion burning in his eyes. But it was not the grief Will had expected.

It was *resolve.*

And Will knew his father would be dead within a week. *Where your mate goes, you follow. . . .*

"Fire comes in all intensities. A hotter tongue of flame can devour another. Surely the hottest can sear a man clean."

—UILLEAM ANDRIU MACRIEVE,
CHIEFTAIN OF THE NOVA SCOTIA SETTLEMENT
OF CLAN MACRIEVE

"The right place at the right time never comes to people standing still."

—CHLOE TODD, A.K.A. BABY T-REX,
OLYMPIC HOPEFUL, UNWITTING IMMORTAL

ONE

Starfire Stadium, Seattle,
Women's Soccer League Finals
PRESENT DAY

Yank my jersey again, Todd, and I'll shove my cleat up your vaj," number eleven said.

Wide-eyed, Chloe gasped. "Who told you I like that?" Chloe and her teammates on the Seattle Reign called this player Handbagger, because she hit like a little old lady. "Your cleat should be so lucky, Handbagger." For good measure, Chloe yanked on eleven's jersey again as she jockeyed for position against the much larger girl.

Trash-talking and rough play were all a part of professional soccer. Chloe had the scars—and foul mouth—to prove it.

On the other side of the field, the ball went out of bounds. She took a breather, pulling up the hem of her jersey to wipe her face, rolling her eyes when camera flashes multiplied. She gazed over the stands, saw the line of shirtless fanboys painted with the Reign's colors: royal blue and midnight black. At halftime, they'd sung

"You've Lost That Lovin' Feeling" to her, and yelled, "Marry me, T-Rex," her soccer nickname.

Despite being the league's smallest center striker—traditionally a tall, burly player's position—Chloe was arguably the best and a crowd favorite. Fans liked that she was ferocious on the field, liked that she still had attitude off it.

She ran her fingers through her short hair, analyzing earlier plays. Tonight she'd been unstoppable, seeing openings and lanes as if other players were moving in slo-mo. She'd already scored a brace—two goals—against the Boston Breakers, tying the game. One more goal would earn Chloe a hat trick, not bad for the championships.

Somewhere in the stands, the assistant coach for the Olympic team watched this nail-biter keenly. Even Chloe's dad had carved out time from his constant work travel to be here. He stood off by himself in the corridor beside the VIP seats, giving her hand signals. Her part-time trainer and biggest fan.

Yes, she'd been on fire this game. But she was also seriously on edge. Over the last few days, she'd been going through some . . . changes, as if all her senses were becoming supercharged.

Or, she was going crazy.

She'd see tracers in her vision and hear sounds from much too far away. Even now she swore she could smell the roll of Tums in Coach's pocket.

And the cherry ChapStick one of the fanboys wore.

Each night, she'd been waking up drenched in sweat, fresh from bizarre dreams that left her shaken. . . .

The ref blew the whistle. Ball in play. Uneasiness forgotten. She and Handbagger jockeyed.

"Here comes the boom, bitch," Chloe said as she spun, evading her. She secured a flying pass, did an inside hook turn, and readied the ball for the launch—

Suddenly she stumbled. Above all the noise in the stadium, she'd heard a single cell phone ring, a pinging so loud she winced. Handbagger capitalized, almost snaring the ball, but Chloe passed it behind her with a heel kick; luckily a teammate was right there to collect. It would all look planned.

Only her team would know something was off. Whenever Chloe got the ball within this proximity to the goal, she was lethal—and selfish. As a finisher, she'd been trained to ball-hog in the strike zone.

As Dad liked to say, "You don't hand off to a weaker player, and they're all weaker players. They feed the ball *to you.*"

So why had she botched her shot? Why had she heard one phone above all the rest of the sounds? She glanced at her dad, saw he'd taken a call, pacing the corridor. What the hell was more important than his only daughter's championship game? Sure, he often had work concerns, but if he managed to get to a game, he was *here*.

Across the field, the Breakers' right wing snagged the ball with a clean tackle. Chloe could only wait and hope as the player ran it down the field. The crowd was now deafening, the other team's momentum building.

Yet Chloe could somehow hear her father's voice as if he were just beside her.

"Is the Lykae capture complete?" he asked.

Lykae? Capture? Even weirder than hearing her father was that she could make out bits and pieces— from the caller. She detected tons of background noise, like you'd hear from a war zone on CNN, and a man's voice: *"In progress, sir . . . not going down without a fight . . . tranqued him . . . matter of time now, Commander."*

Had he just called Dad "Commander"? Of freaking what?

"How much damage?" Dad asked.

". . . threw our own tank at us, sir."

Dad scrubbed his hand over his salt-and-pepper buzz cut. "I warned you against targeting a wolf without Magister Chase present."

Magister. Wolf. Lykae. Tank-throwing. What the hell?

Her dad was ex-army, now sold computer systems to military installations. Dustin Todd was, in essence, a tech guy. The driest, most *un*fanciful man ever to live. He simply didn't talk about paranormal stuff, much less riff with some guy like they were Dungeons and Dragons fanatics.

She grew light-headed, the moment surreal. How could this be possible?

"I still don't understand the soothsayer's insistence with this one," Dad said. "What's the tactical value of one werewolf? Did she say?"

Dear God, her dad was talking about a mythological monster and a psychic.

"No, sir . . . left as soon as we'd laid the . . . wolf's going down at last. They're moving in . . . I'll confirm the capture."

Apparently, her dad was having some kind of psychotic break.

Maybe she was too. She couldn't actually be hearing him. She was losing her sanity and—equally important—this game.

"T-Rex!"

Chloe jerked her head around. She had missed a pass, missed the entire tide of the game changing. And now Handbagger had the ball, charging across the midfield, about to pass to her own striker. . . .

Eyes narrowed, Chloe ran down the woman, giving her a two-foot slide, tackling the living hell out of her from behind.

"You twat!" Handbagger screeched, just as the ref blew the whistle.

Dirty tackle. Yellow-carded. *Shit!*

Coach went ballistic on the sidelines; Handbagger got a free kick in scoring range.

As the woman positioned the ball, Chloe told herself she couldn't fix her dad's breakdown right now—all she could do was finish the few minutes left of this future-making game.

Dad was the one who'd taught her to focus, to stand her ground and see things through when the going got tough.

The keeper snagged Handbagger's missile—*aww, too bad*—then punted it into Breaker territory.

One of her midfielders fed Chloe a hospital ball, a pass that would likely result in injury.

She charged for it anyway with Handbagger breathing down her neck. The bitch slid, knocking Chloe off the ball and onto her ass. Chloe's ankle twisted. Hand-bagger couldn't resist a late hit, a nice elbow to the throat.

No whistle? As Chloe scrambled up, she raised her hands in a WTF gesture. Tied game, two minutes left in regulation—she didn't have *time* for this shit. The crowd booed, but the ref gazed on stonily.

Trying to shake it off, Chloe trotted to position, wincing as her ankle began swelling up like a balloon.

She ignored the pain, repeating to herself, *Rub some dirt on it.*

For all of Chloe's life, coaches had been telling her that in response to everything from a skinned knee to a concussion. It was coach-speak for *Grin and bear it, or I'll send in second string.*

The saying had become her life view. Bad practice? Rub some dirt on it. Fender bender? Rub some dirt on it. It'd turned into an optimistic catchphrase that allowed her to grit her teeth at any obstacle, and muster an *I'm just happy to be here, Coach* smile. It made her hunt hard for an upside.

Her dad going loco was hovering outside the realm of dirt rubbing. There was no upside. He was all the family she had in the world.

Concentrate, Chlo. Focus.

But just as she finally settled in and got her head back in the game, from the other end of her dad's phone call came a . . . *roar*—the most terrifying animal roar she'd ever imagined. Chills breaking out on her sweating skin, she swung her head toward her father.

Then stood there, in the middle of the field with thousands of spectators, gaping in shock.

Because when Dad had heard that sound, he'd *smiled*—

A toe-kicked ball took her square in the face like a cannon shot. Her body was sent airborne. Pitched onto her back, she lay there dazed, watching the stadium lights swirl above her as the crowd grew quiet.

Rub some dirt on it. Upside? She now had her dad's full attention, his call disconnected, and the wolf's haunting roar was no more.

TWO

Orleans Parish, Louisiana
ONE HOUR EARLIER

N ever let it be said that you doona drive like an ace," Will told the three-thousand-year-old mad Valkyrie in the driver's seat beside him, "but if we're in a hurry, perhaps driving *in reverse* is no' the best solution?"

Nïx the Ever-Knowing was doing about twenty miles per hour in the left lane on the Lake Pontchartrain bridge section of I-10. Backward.

She was slinking along with the flow of traffic, somewhat, but the headlights of her abused Bentley were beaming the driver following them.

To navigate, she used the rear-view mirror—and bloody foresight, for all he knew.

Though vehicles were backed up for miles behind her, she seemed oblivious. Cars would pass, their bellowing drivers shooting her the bird—until they got a look-see at the hot mess that was Nucking-Futs Nïx.

She was preternaturally beautiful but vacant-eyed,

with a tangled mane of wild raven hair. She wore a neon pink T-shirt with big bold letters: S L U T

In smaller text below that: SEXUALLY LIBERATED UNINHIBITED TART.

Atop her shoulder? A live bat.

The soothsayer was fairly much crazed, losing track of time, of reality. Understandable, since she'd been seeing the future for millennia.

With a wrist slung over the wheel and Jay-Z on the radio, she said, "It's ridiculous that a car this expensive doesn't have cruise control for reverse."

"You want me to drive, then?"

She'd called his private number, divining the digits he supposed, wanting to meet alone. She'd made him vow to tell no one about their "rendezvous," not even Munro. Will had already asked why she'd wanted to meet him (answer: blank stare) and if he could do anything for her (answer: blanker stare).

"Mayhap I should call one of your sisters? You're looking a wee bit tired, Valkyrie."

"I'm fine," she said absently. "I have Bertil with me."

Oh. The bat. Will decided that if Nucking-Futs Nïx wanted to drive backward and answer none of his questions, to hell with it.

He had nothing better to do than enjoy the ride, so he relaxed back in the plush seat, proud of his nonchalance. Though he didn't like surprises and loathed it when females pressured him to keep secrets, he was managing his unease tonight.

Mayhap he'd finally—finally—started to turn the corner.

Just then, Nïx glanced at Will, blinking in surprise, her expression saying, *Well, how'd you get in here, fellow?*

Her face brightened. "Hot of the Hot and Hotter Twins!" she said in greeting. "Or are you Hotter? I can never tell you apart—both of you with those smoldering golden eyes and dreamy features. Perhaps one of you has slightly longer hair?"

He and Munro hated it when females called them Hot and Hotter, as if they were interchangeable cogs in a joke. "Nïx. It's good to see you," he said, for the second time tonight.

At least she was interesting to be around. And most would consider a meeting with her to be priceless. She could help a Lore creature get out of whatever predicament he found himself in.

No present predicaments for Will. Unless Nïx could send him back in time or make him forget the past, he'd keep idling.

For the last few centuries, he and Munro had lived in Bheinnrose, a colony they'd founded in Nova Scotia. Will was the leader of that arm of Clan MacRieve, but for fuck's sake, who couldn't do that job? All he did was sign a lot of forms. Customarily after Munro read them.

Without a nice grisly war to occupy them—or missions from their king—the brothers had headed south to Louisiana, looking for a change of pace. During an Accession, something was always happening near a Lore hot spot like New Orleans. Such as a meeting with Nïx.

Plus, Will had burned through all the available

nymphs in the North, since he never slept with the same female twice.

Usually by mutual agreement.

A big-rig driver pulled abreast of the Bentley and blasted his horn so loud the car vibrated.

"Mortals," Nïx sighed. "So what did you want to talk to me about, Oolay-ahhhm?"

He frowned at the slaughtered pronunciation of his first name, but thought he caught a twinkle in her eye. "Just call me MacRieve. As for the meeting, you rang me, remember? I assumed you wanted to talk about Munro."

"Umm, no."

Awkward silence. Well, as long as he had a soothsayer here . . . "Mayhap you want to give me the goods on where to find his mate." One of a Lykae's most compelling drives was to find his fated one, and Nïx had helped three members of the clan locate and win theirs—against all odds—during this Accession alone.

"You ask about his before your own?"

"Munro craves his." He needed that female in order to get the bairns he was keen to have. He longed for offspring more than a mother hen did. Already his brother was fostering two Lykae lads in their house.

Yet Munro had best be careful what he wished for; an old oracle had once predicted he'd be cursed with a "harridan" for his mate.

"And you don't crave yours? Spill to Nïxie. I won't tell anyone anything. This night is *our little secret.*"

As if those words weren't disturbing enough to Will, Nïx's bat chose that moment to climb down her front, unfurling its wings to span her collarbones, its wee talons embedded in her shirt.

"It's complicated." He'd once thought he'd possessed his mate. *What a bluidy fool you were.*

"Don't make me turn this car around, wolf."

He raised a brow. "Verra well. I've envied other males who've found theirs. But I'm no' in a good place right now." He pulled on his collar. Understatement. *Hi then, I'm MacRieve, and this is my Lykae beast. Get used to him, because you'll be seeing a lot of him.*

Even so, he couldn't stop himself from asking, "Have you foreseen mine, then?"

"Oh! Here's my exit!" With expert precision, Nïx cut across the second lane of traffic to an off-ramp. They turned, still in reverse, onto a smaller country road.

Before he could repeat his question, Nïx asked, "So what are you going to wear to the apocalypse? I'm thinking something sparkly and transfixing."

"Apocalypse?"

"We all must band together, enemies and allies, gods and men. Or *they* will win."

"And who would *they* be, Valkyrie?"

"The Møriør. Bringers of Doom. By the time I even foresee them, it's already too late."

Ominous words. "You can't drop a line like that without unpacking it."

"Just did, *You-Lame*!"

"It's MacRieve!"

"Where?" she gasped, jerking a glance toward the side of the road. She swerved sharply before righting the car. They collected another horn honk.

"Nïx, answer me."

She faced him again, waving that away. "Let's just put it this way: smoke 'em if you got 'em."

Will tried to muster the appropriate apocalyptic concern. But if you'd lived as long—and as badly—as he had, impending end-of-world scenarios lost their bite.

Nïx's expression perked up. "Here's our turn."

He finally twisted in his seat to glance over his shoulder. It was a dirt road overgrown with banana trees and kudzu. As they wound deeper into a gloomy, fog-laden swamp, Will again felt sorry for this Bentley.

After bottoming out—backward—for a fourth time, Nïx pulled into a small clearing and parked. "Oh. We ended up being early."

"For what?" Did she want to show him something out here? "Where are we?"

"Our destination. Consider it a waypoint."

"Why? Am I going somewhere else?" he asked, the hair on the back of his neck rising. Was there a threat? He scented nothing, and his Instinct remained quiet.

But then, these days it was usually quiet.

In any case, Nïx would have foreseen any trouble, and she'd specifically driven to this place.

She turned to face him, giving him the full view of her crazy. The bat's placement on her T-shirt made it seem like Bertil had been captioned SEXUALLY LIBER-ATED UNINHIBITED TART.

Nïx was so lovely and so . . . damaged.

"Let's talk a sec, just you and me. Relax, don't you trust me?" she asked in a playful tone.

"Face it, Valkyrie. There are few in the Lore that I trust, and you're one of them." She was a tested and true ally of the clan.

"How sweet, Ahllomeam—"

"*MacRieve,* Nïx." Just because she was trusted didn't mean she couldn't be a pain in the arse. "Could you call me MacRieve? Or wolf, or prick, or anything but my given name? Now, back to my mate. When will I find her?"

"Before Munro finds his."

"That tells me nothing. Are we talking decades, centuries?"

"How boorish of me, divulging all while you're divulging nothing." She leaned in closer to him. "Look into my eyes. Let me see your history."

History? Not just foresight? "I doona know about this—"

"Ruelle did a number on you," she said softly. "But I already knew that."

He jerked his head back. "And what have you heard, then?" Whisperings of his shameful time with the succubus had passed among the older Lykae of the clan.

Had other factions learned of that?

"Not *heard*, wolf. Seen . . ."

He swallowed. Could Nïx see that he'd wiped out most of his family by succumbing to that parasite? Could this Valkyrie see that Ruelle still seemed to control his mind and body even from beyond the grave?

When he had been not yet double-digits in age, that bitch had gotten her claws into him. *And I've borne them in one way or another ever since.*

She'd ruined the boy he'd been and perverted the man he would become.

Nïx gazed at him with pity, and he knew she could see. Gods, he *despised* the pitying looks. Had received them all his miserable life! Was he truly so pitiable? *Just because I hate myself and have no control of my beast?*

"Yes, wolf, I see *all*. And by all, I mean *some*."

Sweat dotted his upper lip.

"What is it the nymphs say about you? I remember! You're all 'good and fucked up,' 'dark and twisted.' But they don't know *why*."

They called him Bucket List, one to do before they died—because they knew they wouldn't be getting vanilla.

He had nothing to give *but* dark and twisted.

Suddenly, he had difficulty catching his breath, as if a weight pressed on his chest. As if Ruelle pressed on his chest.

He wanted away from the soothsayer, from this car, this swamp, this bloody state. His earlier nonchalance had vanished. Mayhap it was time to return to the North—

"And then, as if Ruelle wasn't bad enough," Nïx said sadly, "you had to endure Dr. Dixon's tortures."

Will froze. He didn't know this person. "Never heard of a Dr. Dixon."

"The psychotic mortal scientist? From the Order's island prison?" At his confounded look, she said, "Surely you must remember all those experiments she performed on you when you were captured by humans? Electrocutions, beatings, weapons testing, vivisection? How could you forget when she cracked open your chest with a rib separator and sliced out your still-beating heart? She beamed proudly as she showed it to you. Of course, she was only following Webb's orders, but she did seem to take a sick interest in you."

The hair on the back of his neck stood up. "Nïx, these things have no' happened to me. I've never met this Dixon woman or anyone named Webb."

The Valkyrie looked puzzled. "You don't remember being blasted with electricity, then trapped like an animal for weeks? After the prison overthrow, when everything was pandemonium and death, you organized the Vertas shifters, saving them from wholesale slaughter! That's one of the reasons a wisewoman dispatched you there."

"You are unnerving the hell out of me, Valkyrie."

"Oh." She frowned, petting her bat fitfully. "I must have misread the future for the past." She shrugged. "It happens."

"The future?" He swallowed. "You're saying these things are *going* to happen to me?"

"Yes, wolf." Nïx's face abruptly went cold. "And all because you were betrayed by a soothsayer."

Spotlights blazed around the car, temporarily blinding him. They were suddenly surrounded—by mortals with weapons.

"How? I scented nothing! What the bluidy hell is this, Nïx?"

"You need to rebreak that bone." She casually gestured at *all* of him. "It didn't set right. . . ."

THREE

Time to call out some crazy.

Not long after the end of the game, Chloe was back at home in the McMansion she shared with her dad outside of Seattle proper.

Hoping to catch him before he went on the road again, she'd cut out early from the team celebration. Their next Reign practice wasn't for months. What was she going to do without her teammates for that long?

Oh, yeah, figure out what was happening to her, heal up, and hopefully try out for the Olympics.

After showering and securing her ankle in a well-used air cast, she limped from her room, meandering around an array of athletic gear: a snowboard, a basketball, a softball bat—all tokens of sports that could never sway her devotion to soccer.

On the landing, she passed the wall of framed jerseys that her dad had proudly hung, then hopped down the stairs.

Inside his study, one banker's light was on, the rest of the room dark. He was stuffing files from a cabinet into his go bag.

"Heading out of town?" she asked as she dropped into a seat. His travel schedule was one of the reasons she still lived at home at the age of twenty-four. They got along great, and there was a lot of house between them. Besides, it wasn't like she dated or anything.

Dad nodded. "I'm thirty minutes late."

For another capture? She gazed away from him, surveying the study's ego wall—covered with her high school and college diplomas and his many commendations.

"Do you have any explanation for what happened out there tonight, Chlo?"

She turned back to him. How to put this? *Either you're nuts . . .*

Or I am.

At least her weirdness could possibly be explained. She figured that since her super-senses ability was physical, there must be a physiological reason behind it. Maybe she had a brain tumor that was heightening everything! Like in that Travolta movie.

Her mom had died of cancer just after Chloe was born. Wasn't the Big C genetic? Her dad must believe so; he'd insisted that Chloe have her blood tested routinely.

From the few pictures she'd seen of her mom, she knew she favored Fiore Todd's looks. What were the odds that Chloe had inherited more than Fiore's tawny hair and strange hazel eyes?

"Talk to me, Chlo." Though Dad never looked his age—was fitter than most thirty-year-olds—tonight he appeared exhausted, wearing every one of his fifty-five years. Despite his age and salt-and-pepper hair, her teammates all thought he was hot, with his even features and muscular build. Which was too gross to even contemplate.

"It's hard to explain, Dad." She peered at the Newton's cradle on his desk, wondering if she'd ever seen the silver balls moving.

"What happened to your focus? You've been one hundred percent scope-locked on the game since you dribbled your first ball. Hell, since you *saw* your first ball."

Chloe had been five when she'd watched the first women's Olympic soccer game on TV, and the entire course of her life had changed. Later Dad would laughingly tell friends that she'd been glued to the screen like a dog watching bacon commercials.

Instead of telling him, "I'd like to play that," or even "That's what I'm going to do when I grow up," she'd informed him, "That's *my* sport."

Unfortunately, she'd had no natural aptitude for the game, tripping over her own feet. But she hadn't let that get in her way.

Dad had helped her train, ball-gophering over and over as she'd learned to punt, running with her to increase her dismal speed and endurance. She'd declared the sport her own, then followed up with nearly two decades of hard work to claim it.

When Dad had spread out brochures for all the

best colleges with soccer programs, she'd pointed out Stanford: "That's *my* school." When a women's professional team had come to Seattle, she'd said, "That's *my* team. . . ."

Dad snagged another file. "A lot of eyes were on that game. Your play tonight—and your injury—might have affected your invitation to tryouts."

Just for a shot at the Olympic roster, a potential had to be invited to the grueling two-week training camp/tryouts down in Florida.

"I'll be healed by then." It was next month; she had time to get fit.

"I've never seen you choke like that. Ever."

She raised her chin. "I pulled it out in the end." She still didn't know *how*, but in the last seven seconds of the game, she'd done a flying reverse kick to score the winning goal, landing on her back just as the ball shot past the keeper's fingertips. She'd been blinded by the camera flashes. "All anyone's going to remember was that last score for the hat trick."

She'd channeled freaking Pele to make that shot. It was an *SI* cover moment. "I'll get my invitation, and then I'll claim my spot." One of twenty-two players, headed to Madrid.

"Well, I like your confidence, at least." Dad's phone buzzed. "You'd think they could manage without me for one day." *Yeah, one would think.* He checked the ID, declined the call. His phone immediately rang again, but he ignored it. "Look, I know something's going on with you. Before I leave, I need you to tell me what it is. We don't keep secrets from each other."

Don't we, Commander?

When he took his pistol from his desk and holstered it, she wondered if his consulting job was ever dangerous.

Wait—one thing would explain that mysterious conversation of his. With dawning realization, she breathed, "You're a spy." He'd been using code words! *Lykae* would mean *insurgent* or something.

"Why would you think this?" he asked, sounding amused.

Shit. She'd really been hoping he was a spy! "Your hours, your travel, your evasiveness about your job. I don't really know what you do. And you always wear a gun."

"No, Chlo. I am not a spy. I'm just ex-mil. Have you been worrying about this? Is that what affected your play?"

"I heard a conversation of yours. It made no sense."

He paused his packing. "And when was this?"

"I know this is going to sound crazy, but I . . . I heard you on the phone. During the game. I don't know how, but I did."

Instead of pointing out how ridiculous this was, he adjusted the framed picture sitting atop his desk with precise movements. She didn't know why he kept that photo of her mother there. Whenever he looked at it, his lips would thin with anger. Chloe figured some part of him must irrationally feel like Fiore had abandoned him. "And what did you hear?" he said.

"You were talking to some guy, and the topic of discussion was a *werewolf*. He called you 'Commander.'"

Dad narrowed his eyes. He would now tell her that she was crazy, having imagined all that. *Chlo, you've done one too many headers.*

He cleared his throat. "Has anything else happened physically?"

She reluctantly nodded, having no intention of telling him about her more embarrassing changes.

"I've noticed you haven't been eating as much."

"My appetite's totally off. Have to force myself to eat. I'm not sleeping more than a few hours a night, but I'm never tired."

"I s-see." With a dazed look on his face, he stood and crossed to his wall safe, placing his thumb on the sensor to unlock it. "I have to go out of town for a week, perhaps two, to service some . . . international accounts." He retrieved an aged book from inside. "While I'm gone, I want you to read this. Once you've finished it, we'll speak again."

When she'd gotten her period at thirteen, he'd given her a copy of *The Care and Keeping of You*. He'd been red-faced, gruffly saying, "Here. I'm sure you'll put all this together."

So what kind of life transition was she undergoing now? Instead of being red-faced, he was pale.

He handed the tome to her; a chill took her, and the tiny hairs on her nape stood up. *The Living Book of Lore?*

"What is this?" A slip of paper jutted from its edge, so she opened the book there. The pages were filled with archaic text, but the paper marking the spot was ruled, with her father's handwriting on it:

The Order will stop the abominations walking among humans, the detrus—those immortal creatures of darkness filled with untold malice toward mankind. Detrus are a perversion of the natural order, spreading their deathless numbers uncontrollably, a foul plague upon man that must be eradicated through any means necessary.

Capture them, study them, exterminate them. . . .

"Dad, I-I don't understand. Are you part of this Order? Do you believe creatures of darkness exist?" Like werewolves? Had one of them made that animal roar? This was so insane! She flipped through the book, spying countless entries, all bogeymen and myths. Some she recognized, most she didn't.

When his phone buzzed yet again, Dad collected his bag, still seeming dazed. Ex-mil and old-school, her father was usually a master of self-control. *He of the stiff upper lip.* Dad simply didn't demonstrate raw emotions, yet right now, he looked like he'd been coldcocked.

"For twenty-four years, I've debated with myself whether or not you would ever see this book. You're such a tomboy, well, I'd really thought we were home free." He placed his palm on her head. But when she looked up, he wouldn't meet her eyes. "Each blood test that came back, I held my breath. For so long, I . . . believed."

"My blood was tested for cancer. That's what you told me!"

As if he couldn't hear her, he said, "Just know that you're my daughter. No matter what you are—I'll always love and protect you." Then he turned toward the door.

"Wait! You can't leave like this!" Book in hand, she hobbled after him, but he kept walking. "What *am* I? What's happening to me? Am I a . . . detrus?"

"I'm not prepared to discuss this tonight." His voice was shaky. She'd never heard him like this, had never seen Dustin Todd *losing it*. "I won't be until I return."

"If you think I'm a detrus, then what does that make you? Are you even my real father?" she demanded, though they had too much in common for him not to be.

Over his shoulder, he said, "You know I am, Chlo."

Her eyes went wide. "Then you think Mom was one of those things?"

Had his step faltered slightly? "There won't be more changes in you without a . . . triggering event. Just hold tight. Stick to your normal routine. I'll be back soon." He opened the front door. A tinted-window sedan awaited him in the drive. "If for some reason I'm not back in two weeks, do not go to the authorities."

"What *is* this?" she cried. "What's happening?"

"It's secret. And you must keep it that way."

She grabbed his arm. "Dad, I'm about to freak out here."

His brows drew together. "Are you scared?"

With all his wilderness survival trips, shooting lessons, and self-defense camps, her fear response had been numbed. Staring down bigger players for almost two decades had nearly stamped it out. In fact, she had only one fear, an irrational one: *dating*. "No. I just need to know, but I'm not scared."

"After you read that book, I'll expect you to be."

He was truly going to leave her like this, leave her in turmoil. "Daddy, *please*."

Finally he met her gaze, staring at her like he was memorizing her face. "Ah, Chlo, I really thought we were home free. . . ."

FOUR

Glenrial, the Lykae Compound Outside of New Orleans
SEVERAL WEEKS LATER

Will was asleep, knew he was, but he dreamed life-like scenes, all his senses engaged. The sounds of screams in the Order's prison, the scent of death, the bloodcurdling sight of five starving succubae stalking him through wards filled with fire and dismembered corpses . . .

He wore a mystical collar that deadened his strength and speed to those of a mere mortal, and he was still weak from Dixon's experiments, but the succubae were desperate to feed.

If they caught him, he wouldn't be able to defend himself like this. As he loped down winding corridors, he tore at the collar, even knowing it was indestructible.

He prayed for his Instinct to guide him. But since his capture, that comforting force had gone from quiet—to silent.

Losing one's Instinct was like losing one's soul.

The five drew closer, need making them swift. He took off in a sprint, felt like he was running through mud, so slow. So *human*.

And still he was surprised that they caught him, stunned when numerous hands seized his limbs. With their unfettered strength, they threw him against the wall, bringing him to the ground. They easily shook off his blows, soon pinning him.

In their frenzy to claw off his clothes, they tore at his flesh, bombarding him with their strew. They flailed atop him, their limbs tangled, their dresses smothering him like a shroud.

He was suffocating, as if there were no air left on earth because only their scent remained. He fought them bitterly, but they were too frantic, too strong.

Succubae coaxed and poisoned, never attacking, yet these were mindless with hunger. Though their eyes glowed jade green, their gazes were vacant.

And at that moment when he knew they would win, the strongest one looked exactly like . . .

Ruelle.

She gripped his face, murmuring down at him, "Just look at you. Can you blame us, my love?"

His eyes shot open; he jerked upright from a spot on his bedroom floor, and promptly vomited the whiskey he'd imbibed before passing out.

A pair of fifths. What a waste.

There he sat on the cold wooden floor, covered in sweat, shuddering next to a pool of his own sick.

This should disgust him, the squalor of his suite

should, but he was too far gone to care. He rubbed his palm over his bare chest, could still feel their claws ripping through his skin. Their scent lingered in his consciousness.

This was his worst nightmare—and over the weeks since he'd escaped the Order, he'd had it whenever he slept.

Another half-empty bottle on his desk called to him. He rose unsteadily, shuffling through the layer of clothes and trash covering his floor to reach it.

Also calling to him? In the top drawer was his open-ended ticket to Hungary. There, in a hidden pocket of forest, was the lair of the Fyre Dragán, a pit of unnatural flames hot enough to kill even a Lorean.

Otherwise known in the Lore as Where Immortals Go to Die. For Will, no other option was as tempting.

When a Lykae's Instinct grew silent, it was time for him to take a bow. A pack was only as strong as its weakest member.

Me.

Will knew his brother sensed he wasn't long for this world. Munro was out doggedly chasing down former Order prisoners—captives at the same time Will had been taken—to learn more about his brother's ordeal and help him "beat" it. *Fuckin' fixer.*

Will had refused to talk about what happened to him, saying only, "The last three weeks ripped the scab off a festering wound." For all these centuries, he'd been riddled with guilt and self-hatred. Now he'd comprehended that only the hottest of flames could scour him clean.

They'd fought about Munro's leaving, coming to blows as they so often did. They were two alphas who'd never separated in nine centuries; they fought routinely.

"Let me deal with this!" Will had roared. "I'll have my revenge, and then we'll put this to rest!"

Munro had roared back, "I see you drinking every day, staring at nothing, lingering in your beast state longer and longer. My Instinct tells me that you are *dying*. We're no' just twins, we're cut from the same beast, and we've lived together for our entire lives. If you feel something, I feel it too. And this is bluidy agonizing!"

How could Will tell his twin that the only reason he'd fought to survive on that island was so he could mete out revenge and then die?

Yet today Will had accepted that there would be no revenge. His enemies were all out of reach in one way or another.

He glanced at the ticket to Hungary, imagining the scouring purity of such a fire. If he couldn't have a clean life, he could seize a clean death. That was within reach.

Suicide. *Just like Da* . . .

He lurched toward the bathroom. After rinsing his mouth, he drank water from the tap, then peered into the mirror at the same reflection he'd seen for nearly a millennium.

His hair was more black than brown, and when he'd turned immortal, it'd been chin-length. He could cut it, but it would always grow out into that exact length, yet never longer. The stubble covering his broad jaw would never grow into a beard.

This face is the ruination of me. Ruelle had told him his features looked as if they'd been carved by a sculptor, his golden eyes tinted by an imaginative painter.

How he wished he could see the evidence of his continuous benders and hard living. Anything to alter his looks. To *not* look like the Uilleam MacRieve who'd gotten his family killed.

Will hated his own face. Which meant he sometimes hated Munro's.

He scented his brother's return just then. Speak of the devil.

Will had meant to be gone by the time Munro returned. He crept to his bedroom's thick oak door. Even outside his room, the lodge reeked. Stale pizza and old beer.

This home away from home was a proud eight-room hunting lodge, complementing the main Glenrial residence of Prince Garreth. Inside, it resembled a fraternity house on Sunday morning.

Their two younger wards weren't the tidiest of males either.

He heard Munro talking to them. "You two ever heard of a broom? Mayhap a trash bag?"

Rónan, the youngest at fifteen, yawned as if he'd just woken up; it was ten at night. "I'm no' cleaning if the others will no' lift a finger. Face it, cousin, Head Case is no' exactly a stellar role model."

Head Case? The blunt-spoken lad was a regular pain in Will's arse.

"What happened to the cleaning crew I hired?" Munro asked.

"He scared them off."

Will recalled that he'd been less than sober, his beast right on the edge.

He heard the refrigerator door open . . . promptly close. Meager offerings?

Rónan continued, "One of the girls tried to throw away a nearly empty bottle of whiskey. He roared, flashing his beast out there for all to see. No' even trying to keep it down."

I did try. *At least a little.*

The boy's older brother, Benneit, said, "He's only getting worse." Twenty-three-year-old Benneit was also known as Big Ben, a giant even among Lykae. He was as quiet and unassuming as Rónan was brash and mouthy.

The two lads were fosters—Rónan because of his age, and Ben because he hadn't yet mastered the Lykae beast inside him. When the boys had lost the rest of their family six months ago, Ben had fairly much lost any control he'd once garnered.

Will understood. Sometimes it was just easier to let the beast take over. Like a drug. Any time he was under duress, it surfaced, raring to take the pain for him.

He cast another glance at his plane ticket. It was one-way, of course.

"Where is he?" Munro asked.

"Where he usually is these days—passed out drunk," Rónan seemed to delight in saying. "He has no' left the lodge all week."

Nor the Glenrial compound, not a single time since his return from hell.

"No' that I'm complaining about Head Case," Rónan said. "I like this foster family. The level of supervision here clearly benefits us all."

Ben asked, "What did you learn on your trip?"

Aye, Munro, what news? Would he have learned all about the notoriously bloody prison break? All about the unspeakable things the mortals did to their captives?

"It's as bad as the rumors milling around."

Rónan said, "He was . . . vivisected?"

Dissected while still conscious. Will's hand went to his chest, his claws digging into his skin.

"Some prisoners believe he was."

Dr. Dixon, the Order's head surgeon/researcher/ psychopath, customarily opened up her chosen victim, then removed all his or her organs. While the being was aware.

A clammy sweat dotted his skin.

Ben said, "How could humans have captured him in the first place?"

"They have advanced concealment techniques and weaponry. He was likely electrocuted, then collared with a band that controlled his strength."

Correct and correct. The humans had been clever, forcing each inmate into that mystical collar, a "torque" to neutralize the immortals' abilities.

"His beast could no' overpower this?" Rónan asked.

My beast could no' rise. The collar had prevented it for

the weeks Will had been imprisoned, the longest he'd ever gone since Ruelle.

Munro must've shaken his head in answer, because Ben said, "There's more you're no' telling us?"

Munro hesitated. "The prison break . . . left all our allies there at a disadvantage," he said, hedging. *Oh, aye, Munro knows much.*

In the melee that followed the escape, amid the chaos and fighting and explosions, some immortals had been able to remove their torques—the most evil ones.

Like the succubae.

Will's worst nightmare was indeed running through a hellish maze of fire and blood while a pack of ravenous seed-feeders hunted him.

Only it'd happened. Except for Ruelle's appearance, it had all happened.

The bottle of whiskey shook when he turned it up. How hard he'd fought not to be gang-raped in full view of a throng of Loreans. . . .

Munro finally answered, "Let's just say that Will has every right to be in his current state. Does no' mean we're going to allow it any longer."

Allow it? *You should no' even know about this, you nosy, self-righteous prick!*

Ben said, "If he could just get revenge, he could beat this."

"The ones responsible are out of our reach," Munro said.

Utterly out of reach. Dixon had already been taken care of. Commander Webb—the mortal leading the

Order—couldn't be located, not even by the most powerful witches, wizards, oracles, or Sorceri. Magister Chase, a.k.a. the Blademan, who'd run the prison, had changed sides, now protected by powerful Loreans.

Nïx was untouchable.

When Will had gone to call her out over shafting him, she'd nonchalantly reminded him that he'd vowed not to tell anyone about their meeting. When he'd accused her of working with Webb, she'd coolly replied, "I use every means at my disposal to shape fate. The Order is a powerful shaping tool."

And then she'd told him why he couldn't exact vengeance against the Blademan. *A verra disturbing reason why.*

"I'm going to confront him with what I've learned," Munro said. "If we come to blows, do no' get between us, no matter what occurs." The lads were still vulnerable to harm. "Why do you no' go for a run?"

Just as Will heard Munro at the stairs, Rónan called, "Probably bad timing and all, but I wanted to give you a *yo!* concerning Head Case. While you were gone, I had some expenses I had to peg to his credit card. I put it right back into his wallet."

That little prat came into my room and stole my card. At the thought of Rónan seeing him passed out, the back of Will's neck heated. Which might've been a remnant of . . . shame.

Munro called, "Could give a shite, Rónan."

"Beauty!"

With each of his brother's steps, Will grew more

enraged. *Confront me, Munro?* His beast was rising. His claws sank into his palms. If Munro cast him a pitying expression, he'd flay his brother. He'd whip his arse—

Munro entered. They shared a look between them.

With an *"Oh, you sodding, self-righteous prick!"* Will attacked.

FIVE

Someone's in the house with me.

Chloe's eyes shot open. She'd just awakened in her bed to the sense that she wasn't alone.

Her hearing had leveled off at last—it was still revved up but not insanely so—yet she detected nothing unusual. Just the windstorm outside.

Paranoia? Was the book getting to her?

If someone had managed to break in . . . She sighed. After the last few weeks she'd had, she could almost feel sorry for the burglar.

Her dad hadn't returned, hadn't contacted her or answered her numerous calls in more than a month. Yesterday, his number had been disconnected.

Still, she didn't think he was actually in danger. He was capable, smart, and, with a gun at his side, deadly. Plus, he'd given her instructions in case he didn't return soon for a reason—because he'd been expecting, even planning *not* to.

She felt in her bones that he was alive. Which meant her emotions had vacillated from fear that he was in some kind of trouble, to sadness that he might have abandoned her, to anger that he'd skipped out after leaving her with so many questions.

She was pissed that he couldn't spare a single call to his only child. *Hey, Pop, not only did I survive the Florida training camp, I'm going to be an Olympian! Thanks for calling in for an update. . . .*

Fear, sadness, anger. Rinse and repeat. Her emotions spun as wildly as a roulette wheel.

She'd long since taken stock of her situation, trying to get a sense of her life, her overall field position. She'd come up with three truths.

One: her dad was almost certainly part of that Order. Two: she'd told him she was changing, and he'd given her that *Living Book of Lore*, an encyclopedia of myths, for a reason. He must believe *she* was one of those detrus that shouldn't be allowed to live.

Three: he still loved her. . . .

She'd dutifully read every page of that book, perusing thousands of entries from Amazons and kobolds to witches and Valkyries. Did Chloe believe that yard gnomes, fairies, Shreks, and Edwards roamed the earth?

Um, *not quite*. Believing in those creatures meant she had to believe in her own looming transition—you couldn't have one without the other. If they existed, then Dad wasn't crazy. If Dad wasn't crazy, then she was an undetonated detrus.

So she'd decided to hold out on accepting an

entirely new world for as long as possible. Still, for shits and giggles, she'd tried to match up her new symptoms to a species.

No appetite? Maybe Valkyrie. Superhuman senses? Most of them.

Supercharged sex drive? *All* of them.

In the past, her libido had been so dormant that even countless hours watching RedTube.com couldn't spark it to life. Yet now she kept dreaming of a faceless man doing things to her, wicked things.

Sometimes he'd coax his erect penis between her lips, making her moan with satisfaction as she began to suck. Other times she'd feel the weight of his body pressing down on hers, his shaft sliding in and out of her until he treated her to the burning heat of his semen.

She would wake up throbbing with lust.

Chloe had brought herself to come before now, of course, but her orgasms had been so lackluster, so, well, *anticlimactic*, that she'd wondered what all the hubbub was about. There was a reason she hadn't done more than kiss a boy; she'd never believed that overcoming her dread of dating was even worth it.

Now? She was getting an idea about all the hubbub.

She seemed to be developing a new sensibility toward men, an appreciation of them. When passing some guy on the street, a prominent Adam's apple or a wide jaw or developed chest would draw her eye. She'd caught herself checking out asses—and assets.

It was like her own sex drive was coming online for the first time, a process she'd come to think of as *awakening.*

All she knew for certain was that the next chance she had to score with a halfway decent guy, she was taking it to the net.

Her awakening wasn't the only change in her. She couldn't sleep more than three or four hours a night. Despite having zero appetite and barely eating, she hadn't lost an ounce of weight. In fact, her jeans were tighter.

Even stranger? Whenever she did manage to choke down a meal, the food seemed to stave off the awakening, blunting her sex drive.

All her life, she'd controlled her training, her heart rate, the shape and condition of her body—now everything was beyond her, and the transformation seemed to be escalating. . . .

Over the last week since she'd returned from Florida, she'd stared at her mother's picture, trying to decide if Fiore *looked* immortal. She'd agonized over that trigger Dad had spoken of. How to avoid something if she didn't know what it was?

In two weeks, she was supposed to fly to Madrid for a last training camp with the finalized team before the Games commenced. If she couldn't figure out what was happening to her, she feared she'd have to give up her spot.

She felt like she'd go insane if she didn't get to talk to Dad. She played offense—not defense—and she was on something of a clock here. So she'd searched his office for clues, surprised by how many cabinets were locked.

Finding nothing, Chloe had taken to driving the

streets of her neighborhood, passing by his frequent haunts. She'd cruise through drizzle, hypnotized by the windshield wipers, feeling more lonely than she ever had before.

At first she'd attributed that pang in her chest to her transition, just another of her symptoms. But really, her loneliness arose from *circumstance*. She was used to being around a team of women, playing in front of fans, talking to her dad at least every other day. This solitude was gut-wrenching—

There. Finally a sound. It was coming from Dad's study.

Her eyes widened. He'd returned!

Dashing out of bed, she hastened to her chest-o-drawers. She dragged on a pair of sweatpants over boy-short panties and a baggy jersey over a cami bra. At her doorway, she paused. Just in case it *wasn't* Dad, she snagged her aluminum softball bat. Silently, she slipped down the stairs.

At the door to his study, she took a deep breath, feeling silly about the bat. But she didn't put it down as she entered.

A creature stood at the desk, rifling through Dad's belongings. It had to be eight feet tall, wearing a cloak. Horns jutted up past the material of the hood.

Horns?

Though she hadn't made a sound, it glanced up, its face shaded. All she could see were two eyes—they were black as night, yet they seemed to glow.

A creature from the book. The book was real. Or this was some kind of prank. Yes! A prank. Even faced with this sight, her mind resisted believing in the supernatural. It'd take anyone time to say, *Hey, scratch what I know, the world really was flat all along.*

The thing moved around the desk with lumbering steps, the claws of its bare feet scrabbling across the hardwood floor.

Chloe's stomach clenched. *The world is flat.* Shit! She raised the bat. "D-don't come closer, asshole."

"Mortal?" it grated, still stalking toward her. It sounded like an animal imitating human speech.

She sensed she shouldn't run, feared it would just provoke this creature. "I s-said no closer."

When it kept coming, she took her at-bat, swinging for the goddamned stars.

She connected with its shoulder. As if she'd hit a tree, the bat reverberated in her hands, sending pain up her arms.

With a hiss, the thing seized the bat, crushing it like a soda can with its meaty hands.

She screamed, sprinting all-out for the front door. *Get outside, into the neighborhood. Evacuate the house, evacuate. . . .*

Almost to the door, to the outside, to safety.

She reached the front door and fumbled with the dead bolt. That thing was coming; she heard those claws. She gave a cry, cursing her clumsiness.

Finally, open! *Consider this house motherfucking evacuated.* She took one step. The welcome mat was gone, the *stoop* was gone.

She plummeted into an abyss.

SIX

Will had taken one look at Munro's pitying expression and lunged for his brother, raining blows.

Rage seethed. *Fucking hate pity!*

"What the hell is wrong with you?" Munro bellowed as he blocked hits.

"You could no' leave it alone! Had to dig and dig." All his shame laid bare. "If I'd wanted you to know, I'd have told you!" His beast was rising to punish, and Will was about to let it out of its cage.

"Calm yourself—I doona want to fight you!"

"But you will!" Whipping his brother's arse was all that was left to him. Fangs bared, he snatched Munro's neck in a choke hold, pounding his fist up into his face.

"Damn you, Will! Why do you *always* go for the face?" When Munro thrashed against him, grappling to get free, they tripped on refuse. Boots, food containers, bottles.

"Why do you always bluidy pry?"

"I needed to know the truth!" Munro wrenched free, throwing a fist like a sledgehammer, connecting with Will's nose.

Bone shattered; blood spurted. They faced off.

In a thick voice, Will said, "The truth?" *Try this on for size: I am twisted. I am good and fucked up.* His Instinct, quiet before his capture, was now silent. His beast had been uncontrollable during sex; now it constantly prowled inside him, right at the edge of rising, a danger to everyone around.

Will might have been able to tolerate "normal" torture. In fact, over the centuries, he had done so bravely.

But those sick experiments and the succubae attack . . . everything had brought him full circle. Always back to Ruelle. That bitch had hovered over him, harvesting his seed; Dixon had stood over him, harvesting his goddamned insides.

Oh, aye, Nïx, she showed me my beating heart.

With a roar, he barreled into Munro, sending them hurtling through the doorway, across the landing, and over the banister. They plummeted into the great room below, landing atop the coffee table, demolishing it. Wood exploded from the impact.

The brothers scrambled up, kept fighting.

"Did they test weapons on you?" Punch.

Counter. *Their sirens at unimaginable decibels . . .* "Oh, aye, things designed to take out my hearing, my senses." There'd been a reason those mortals had gone undetected just before his capture. "Good bluidy times!"

With a sharp jab, Munro tagged him in the kidney, a particularly painful spot for both of them.

Only problem with fighting your twin: you both shared the same weaknesses.

"Were you vivisected?"

The word made Will flinch more than the punch had. So he launched another fist. "Chest cracked open, organs plucked, then stapled back up? The prisoners called it a zipper in the chest." A big seeping Y from belly to collarbones—something on the outside to keep you occupied while regenerating your insides.

"This was done to you, *bràthair*?" Brother. Now Munro seethed.

"And I canna get vengeance!" No outlet to vent this rage.

Will couldn't decide which of his four enemies he hated more: the soothsayer who'd betrayed him, the Blademan who'd caged him, the scientist who'd tormented him, or the one who'd set it all in motion: Preston Webb.

He lunged for Munro again, pummeling his brother, pissed because he knew Munro was holding back. His eyes had scarcely flickered, his beast as firmly leashed as usual.

To hell with it. Will's knuckles stung, his face throbbed. At some point in the last ten minutes, he'd begun to crave whiskey more than hitting Munro. With a final halfhearted blow, Will released him. As quickly as the fight had started, he ended it. They were both breathing heavily, both bloodied.

At the same instant that Munro swiped his sleeve

over his lacerated forehead, Will did the same over his shattered nose.

Then he turned toward the liquor cabinet to root for a fifth. Ah, Macallan. Fine whiskey, expensive. He chugged it like water. The liquid stung his lips, swirling around temporarily loosened teeth. He couldn't quite taste it with his nose full of blood.

But Munro wouldn't let this drop. "And what about the doctor I heard tell of?"

Will clenched the bottle neck so hard it broke, shards digging into his palm while the bottom half fell and shattered all over the floor. "She took a special interest in me." Her eyes wide behind oversize glasses, she'd softly queried, "Why should Chase be the only one with an immortal plaything?"

Will had made her pay—but too late. The experiments and torture had dredged up all his memories. *I'd thought I was doing so well.*

"Do you know where Dixon is?" Munro asked. "No one in the Lore can find her."

"I made sure she was conscious as I ripped her limb from limb." And he wished to the gods that he could do it again, leisurely. He dared his brother to say aught about that.

Munro didn't. "Someone saw succubae tracking you through the prison."

To avoid Munro's gaze, Will dug up another bottle. "They wanted Lykae for dinner. As usual." Ruelle had been right. Werewolves *were* sodding catnip for those parasites.

New bottle in hand, Will staggered back against the wall, overwhelmed by the memories. His hatred of succubae burned afresh, until it choked him of breath, threatening to suffocate him.

If a man hated for this long, would there soon be nothing left of him?

Mayhap that was why the Instinct had left him. Because he was halfway to the grave already.

"And did they . . . feed?" Munro seemed to be bracing for the worst.

"They dinna." But it'd been so damned close. "They would have if no' for the Valkyrie Regin the Radiant and her cellmate." With their help, he'd been able to behead all five succubae. He often replayed that memory, the seed-feeders' screams, their *surprise*.

"Regin is the Blademan's woman, and she helped save you from a hellish fate," Munro said. "Is that why you have no' targeted her male?"

The man had overseen security on the island and had bludgeoned Will for an escape attempt. Thought to be human, the Blademan was actually a berserker. "That's one reason." Another? Nïx had told him that their future lines would entwine. *No' if I'm dead, Nïx!*

Munro snapped his fingers for the whiskey. "Give over."

Will cradled his bottle in the crook of his elbow, handing Munro his own. "Are we done now? Can we never speak of this again?"

Munro raised his brows, the slash on his forehead making him wince. "We have to do something."

Will took another long draw. "I canna target Chase.

I canna find Webb." *Canna target Nix.* "There's nothing to be done." Never had his future seemed so hopeless. Not even when he'd inadvertently killed both of his parents and his unborn sister. At least then he'd naively thought that time healed all wounds, that one day his pain would lessen.

What a crock of bullshite. Time multiplied all wounds. "And if I see one more pitying look, I'll give you a proper hiding, I swear to gods."

"I know about the plane ticket," Munro said simply, but so much was going on behind those eyes.

Will's time in that prison had made him realize how ridiculous it was to keep struggling, to keep living as if he had reason to. Nine hundred plus years was plenty. And only an idiot would continue constructing a building on such a bollixed foundation. "Wanted a change of pace."

"Doona lie to me! You think I doona know what you're contemplating? You interrogated Bowen about the Pit of the Fyre Dragán."

Last year, their cousin Bowen had been trapped in that lair before escaping. When Will had heard of the place, he'd perked the hell up. It was all well and good to be suicidal, but an immortal had practicalities to deal with. Namely: unless you could cut off your own head, you couldn't kill yourself.

As my father knew . . .

So Will had planned to take a dip in the Pit.

"And then," Munro continued, "you bought a one-way ticket to a place nicknamed Where Immortals Go to Die."

The whiskey was loosening Will's tongue, coaxing him to admit the truth. "When I was young, I got . . . twisted. Now I'm no' right. There it is, there's nothing to be done for it." He shrugged. "If there were, it would have happened by now."

Munro's eyes were widening as if he was chilled by Will's casual demeanor.

"Gods, man, I've had so many centuries," Will said. "I've lived long enough." Nïx had been right about one thing—the bone hadn't set right. *Now pulverized, never to knit.* "The prison was just a hint, brother."

"Did you never consider how I'd feel to lose the last of my family?"

"Oh, aye." He'd debated it, deciding Munro would be better off. Since he was revealing all, Will might as well round out the tale. "My Instinct was quiet before the prison. Now it's gone."

Munro's jaw slackened, as if he could scarcely imagine this loss. The Instinct was part of what made a Lykae who he was.

Will drank deep, then said, "Hell, that means I'm halfway dead already. I've no Instinct and little control of my beast. I'm a liability. I will no' be a burden to this pack." *To you.*

Munro had said he didn't pity Will. *But I pity him.* In one fell swoop, Munro had lost two incredible parents and a baby sister, and gained a burden for life.

Will had been waiting centuries for Munro to wake the hell up and realize he hated his brother. "The only reason I'm no' already dead is because I craved retribution first."

"We'll find your mate. She can heal you. We'll call Nïx and ask her to search—"

"Doona say that Valkyrie's name to me again!"

Munro raised his brows. "Yet another secret?"

Rónan and Ben burst into the lodge then, gazing at all the destruction, the blood. Rónan looked impressed, but Ben's eyes began to flicker blue, his beast stirring from just the evidence of violence.

Hair trigger. I've been there. I am there.

"Easy, Ben," Munro said. "Get control of it."

Ben inhaled deeply, clenching and unclenching his fists.

Once Ben's eyes finally cleared, Rónan waved a computer printout. "We've got a present for you, Head Case."

Will glowered at him. "I want nothing you have," he said, still unsure how the two had ended up here. What was the clan thinking, foisting lads on the twins? Aye, their orphan situation was similar to Will and Munro's—and their lines were closely related, with only about forty or so generations between them. But for fuck's sake, if the boys needed to learn how to control their beasts, you didn't send them to Crazy Uncle Will's.

He suspected fixer Munro had lobbied to take them in.

"The clan just got a message at the den," Rónan said. "A Lore-wide alert. There's to be an auction at the demon crossroads at midnight, hosted by the House of Witches."

Witches. Devious creatures.

Rónan read from the paper: *"Members of the Pravus Rule and the Vertas League are both welcome to bid on this capture, a female who will have tactical value against a common enemy."*

Wide-eyed, Will exclaimed, "Someone was captured? No shite? Wonder what that's like!"

Munro asked, "Who's the female?"

Rónan raised his brows. *"The highest wire transfer will win that which all the Lore covets. . . ."*

⁂

"Chillin' by the fire while we eatin' fondue," crooned Justin Bieber. *"I dunno about me but I know about you. . . ."*

About an hour ago, Chloe had awakened on the floor of an RV to the tunes of J.B.—with a strip of cloth gagging her mouth and shackles around her wrists and ankles. The RV was strewn with Mardi Gras beads and the air outside smelled of marsh and jasmine. She was definitely no longer in Seattle.

Because her front doorstep had been replaced with a trapdoor to hell.

Three teenage girls were inside the RV with her, listening to the music, doing their makeup, stepping over Chloe with little regard. For the most part they looked human. One was a Scandi-looking blonde, one a pale brunette, one a willowy Asian—all pretty, like postmodern Charlie's Angels.

But Chloe sensed something was *off* about this trio. There was an eerie grace to their movements, and their eyes seemed to flicker under different lights.

Once she'd roused, two realizations had struck Chloe: Detrus were totally real. And she was about to suffer at their hands. She'd started struggling against her bonds, trying to squeeze her contorted hand through one manacle.

Earlier the three had cracked open wine coolers to celebrate their catch. "We are the tanda of twenty-thirteen!" the brunette said.

Tanda?

"This is our year!" the Asian beauty said. "Our auction will be talked about for eternity!"

Was Chloe about to be . . . auctioned?

"Long live the House of Witches!" They all clinked bottles.

Witches. *Going to vomit.* The *Book of Lore* said that Wiccae were mystical mercenaries, obsessed with amassing wealth. They sold their spells and tonics—and apparently, they weren't above human trafficking.

But then, Chloe wasn't quite human, was she?

Rub some dirt on it, rub some dirt on it. She realized that her optimism had gotten benched tonight, and might never return to the game.

She could only conclude that the Order was real, her dad's mission was real, and he'd made some immortal enemies carrying it out. Having met some of these detrus, Chloe wished Dad all the success in the world with his extermination endeavor.

Except she was one. That house of cards had come tumbling down. *Time to face facts, Chlo.* If detrus existed, then she was transforming into one of them.

Because her mom had been one. Chloe's eyes

widened. Her mother could never have passed away from cancer! That had been just a cover story. So how *had* she died?

I need answers! Filled with impotent frustration, she yelled against her gag, "Ey! Elp a itch out! Ake is ag ov!"

The witches ignored her, turning up the stereo. She cringed when yet another Bieber song pumped away. Great, she'd been captured by fucking Beliebers.

They planned to sell her at auction? When "Beauty and a B'eat" played for the fifth time, Chloe decided she was ready for the block.

With a huff, she renewed her struggles. If she could get free, she could yank up that removable table—the one with all the old wads of teenage-witch gum stuck to the underside—and use it as a weapon.

The RV door opened, revealing a young black-haired female with luminous brown eyes. Definitely not human; no one's hair could possibly be that glossy without Photoshop.

She had a clipboard in hand, a walkie-talkie attached to her belt, and a backpack slung over her shoulders. The others greeted her with a chorus of "Belee!"

At the sight of the wine coolers, this Belee's shoulders stiffened and a weird electricity began to fill the air. "Drinking on the job?" The RV briefly shook as the other girls scrambled to dump their drinks.

Alpha-bitch alert. If this was a team, Chloe had just met the playmaker.

Belee's walkie-talkie hissed. *"Bee, you said there might be a few hundred people here tonight,"* another girl's voice said.

An audible swallow sounded over the line. *"We've got about five thousand, and they're still filing in. What are we going to do?"*

Five. Thousand.

"Hellooo, then start charging for admission," Belee snapped. "You're acting like this is your first rodeo."

"It is. We're worried. If Mari and Carrow find out, they'll bring the heat," she added in a *Mom and Dad'll bust the party* tone. *"Maybe I shouldn't have added that last part to the auction announcement."*

"What last part?" Belee asked.

"That they had to forward the message to ten other people or something bad would happen to them."

Chloe rolled her eyes. *You have got to be kidding me.*

Belee pursed her lips. "Mari and Carrow are deep in the bush, offplane for all we know. They'll find out *after* we've staged this coup! Belee out."

The walkie-talkie continued transmitting. Two girls spoke:

"Belee scares me."

"All the transfer students from Blåkulla do. What do you think that coven must be like?"

Blåkulla? Chloe had never read about that.

Belee radioed: "Your transmitter's still on, idiot!" After gazing up at the ceiling for patience, she turned to Chloe, telling no one in particular, "The package isn't displayed as well as it could be."

I'm the package? Kill her!

From her backpack, the witch produced a white, nearly transparent nightgown.

Chloe preferred to wear loose jerseys, looser shorts. Now she was supposed to wear a see-through gown?

Belee appraised her with a critical eye. "Pretty face."

Chloe wanted to spit in hers.

"Shame to cover it up, but . . ." From her pack, Belee also drew out a black silk bag. "We need to remind everyone why we're here, Daughter of Webb."

"At's no mi na!"

"It *is* your name. You just didn't know it. Your father, Dustin Todd, is also known as Preston Webb. The commander of the Order. You're the daughter of the most hated man in all the Lore. . . ."

SEVEN

I never scented him," Will muttered with a chin jerk toward a centaur in the distance, past row after row of parked cars at the demon crossroads. Centaurs aligned with the Pravus, the evil side of the Lore.

"Probably because I dialed down your nose," Munro said, his mood improved. Tonight they'd received a lead on Webb, a daughter of his for sale. Which meant there was *possibility*, after weeks of nothing.

Munro had a bloody spring in his step.

The centaur in question had a nymph pressed up against the side of a sports car and was rutting her with zero-to-sixty thrusts.

The ride was a Mustang. Fitting.

"We're no' to fight them," Munro said. "From the sound of it, there's an honest-to-gods truce going on tonight." Not far in the distance, they heard scores of immortals peaceably milling.

As they strode by the couple, Munro muttered in Gaelic, "Did one—or both—of us do that nymph?"

"Odds are," Will said casually, though he made a point of remembering, so that he never bedded the same one twice.

Twice was too close to three times, and to this day, he had a phobia about that.

Munro's question was answered when the nymph waved happily at the brothers; the centaur shot them killing looks and thrust more aggressively. Between his angry shoves, she gasped: "Hi, guys . . . unh, see you . . . unh, later?"

"Ah, sure thing, sweet," Munro said.

Nymphs were easy and pleasant bed sport, seeking nothing but mutual pleasure. Unlike seed-feeding succubae.

Munro told Will, "Perhaps a comely nymph is just what you need to get back in the saddle? I know it's been weeks for you."

Try months.

"You could burn off some . . . aggression?"

Munro also knew all about Will's many sexual hang-ups and peculiarities. Though Will had long since recognized his "relationship" with Ruelle for what it was—a violation of a young mind and body, a nightmare—the scars remained.

"I've no time for that. Come on, we're late." Will had taken scant seconds to change, plucking clothes from his floor, an array of garments that appeared less worn/dirty than others. "It's nearly midnight."

Munro had driven his brand-new Range Rover

turbo here, topping the thing out on old Louisiana county roads. "Does no' matter if we're late," he said. "I doubt we can win this auction. I could only drum up a million-dollar wire on such short notice. And the lowest number on the witches' *bidding app*—I shite you no'—was one mil."

"What good is it to be rich if we canna scrape up the scratch to buy a political prisoner on a whim?"

Past a line of pecan trees lay a wide-open field packed with Loreans. Understandable. Webb had upended countless lives, and this capture was the first lead on him since the prison break.

As Will and Munro strode into the crowd, they saw all manner of immortal species, even a few gypsy and berserker humans who lived on the fringe of the Lore.

Most immortals here belonged to one of the two major alliances, Pravus and Vertas. Amazingly, the temporary truce between them *was* holding. But then, they had a common enemy: the Order.

The brothers passed a group of young Vertas shifters—fox, wolverine, and cheetah—that Will recognized from the island. While the Pravus shifters were predominantly reptilian, the Vertas were most often mammalian.

One of these pups called out, "Mr. MacRieve!" and they all turned and gazed at Will as if he were some goddamned hero. He scowled at them and turned away. He might have organized them and saved their lives—as Nïx had predicted—but only to save his own arse.

He'd fought to live solely for revenge.

Aside from the alliances, there were the neutral factions like the nymphs, who were likely only present to scope out new bedmates—from both sides. A gaggle of them cooed, "Hot and Hotter!" to Will and Munro, trying to get their attention.

Will muttered, "I really fuckin' hate that." He crossed his arms over his chest, found a new hole in his shirt.

Munro nodded. "Hate it—beyond the telling of it. But you do know I'm Hotter, right?"

"No' even on your best day, *bràthair.*"

They spotted a few more Vertas allies: the fey, Furies, Valkyries, and behorned members from some of the solid demonarchies.

There were at least as many Pravus members: soldiers from dark demonarchies, Sorceri, nearly two dozen centaurs, and countless Cerunnos—giant snake-like humanoids that were as fast as lightning and just as deadly. Crocodilae and viper shifters abounded.

Will followed Munro, surveying the sea of Loreans for succubae. What if they were here tonight? Seed-feeders were Pravus as well.

Then I'll be jeopardizing this truce directly. Because nothing would stop him from killing any he came across. Just as he'd done for all his life. To date, he'd ended twenty-four.

When a witch passed close by him, his hackles rose. There were several scurrying around with headsets, as if they were on a trading floor. "Phone bidders?" Will glowered in one's direction. If his Instinct were intact, it'd warn: *—Guard yourself.—*

Their cousin Bowe might have married Mariketa the Awaited, the leader of the grand mercenary House of Witches; didn't mean the rest of the clan had overcome the Instinct's constant cautions against Wiccae.

Will spotted Malkom Slaine, a vemon they knew, walking in the direction of the stage. The vampire/demon had been in the same prison as Will.

They greeted Malkom, falling in step beside him.

Munro said, "Demon, you're no' often seen without Carrow." Another local witch, also a former capture.

Though Malkom had been born a demon in some far-off, archaic demonarchy, he'd been turned part vampire—into a rare vemon, a creature even stronger than a Lykae. But he still identified as a demon, hating leeches.

Like most of us. Just last year, Will and Munro had been ordered to storm a vampire stronghold to search for King Lachlain's mate—not to spy, not to monitor, but to bloody *engage.* Just before they'd reached the perimeter, when Will had been shaking with anticipation, already imagining the havoc he'd wreak, they'd been called off.

How different things might have been for Will—how much improved—if only a goddamned war had broken out.

In thickly accented English, Malkom said, "Carrow, Mariketa, and some Valkyries are out collecting Order orphans—the offspring of immortals who died on the island."

Will understood why Malkom hadn't been invited.

He was an intimidating male, taller even than Will's towering height, with lethal-looking horns. He would scare the hell out of the tots. "So if Carrow and Mariketa are no' here, who's running this show?"

"Some teen witches. They think Carrow and Mari don't know. I'm supposed to watch out for them and make sure they don't get killed by the Pravus."

"The witches are Vertas," Munro pointed out. "Why no' keep the prize for our side?"

Mayhap because they're all bent for the dollar, each and every one of them? Eerie bluidy witches . . .

Malkom just shrugged.

"So what do you know about this prisoner?" Munro asked. "How'd she get caught?"

"The witches cast some kind of surveillance and capture spell."

"Is the daughter with the Order?" Will asked.

"We don't believe so," Malkom said. "From what we know, Webb disappeared after the prison escape. His daughter had no idea where he was, had been searching for him. My guess is that Webb kept the Order part of his life secret. It makes sense. I'll not tell my daughter many of the things I've done."

"Wait." Will frowned. "If she was searching for Webb, then she does no' have his location. What's her tactical value if she knows nothing about the Lore and does no' have a twenty on her dear ole sire?"

"Bait," Malkom said. "Surely she'll lure Webb in."

Will imagined possessing the female, using her to trap that bastard. Gods, the satisfaction . . .

"The Vertas won't win her, though," Malkom continued. "While the Pravus have pooled their money and mystical goods, most of our factions are going to bid against each other. We're supposed to be allied with the fey? Their king is phone-bidding through that juvenile witch right there. Millions in Draik gold. The witch beside her is bidding for Nereus the sea god. All we're going to do is drive up the price."

Will turned to Munro. "Then she truly canna be won by us?"

Munro shook his head. "Look, we'll stalk whoever gets her. We'll lie in wait for Webb. This is no' over."

Why couldn't Will get one break? All he wanted was one bloody, viscera-coated moment of revenge. Then he'd find peace in death.

Filled with frustration, he pinched his nose, none-too-gently manipulating the bone back in place. Ah, that was better. He inhaled deeply, suddenly bombarded by new scents, tens of thousands of them—

One stood out.

Something so sublime he was thunderstruck, nearly put to his knees.

Disbelieving what he'd smelled, Will tentatively raised his head for another hit of that beautiful thread. For the first time in months, he heard his Instinct. And, gods, it rang loud and clear.

—*Yours.*—

He swallowed, had to clear his throat before he could mutter, "It's . . . happened."

"Excuse us, Malkom," Munro said as he dragged Will away.

"My Instinct . . . it said . . ." Will could barely form words.

"I scented her too," Munro said, excitement filling his expression.

Excitement? A blind rage suffused Will. Before he could swing, Munro snapped, "While your Instinct is clamoring about her being *yours*, mine is saying *sister*."

"Oh." Will gazed around, desperate to see her, to know what kind of creature could possibly smell that luscious. He'd been wary of finding her before, but now . . .

"Is it like Da said?" Munro asked.

Will briefly closed his eyes, inhaling deeply. "The hands of gods," he breathed. "Aye."

"Then let's find her."

Sudden doubt hammered at Will, and he hesitated.

Munro said, "Look, I ken you're in pain, but you've waited ages for your mate. You'll never get another one."

He shook his head. "I'm fit for no one."

"She can help you heal if you just let her. Besides, you've taken her scent into you. There's no letting her go now. No' without trying first."

"I can still walk away," he said, even as her scent beckoned.

"Are you no' about to die of curiosity, man? I bluidy am, and she's no' even mine!"

No, doona get too excited. Will tried to tamp it down. "What if I'm no' ready for this?" *Good and fucked up.* "I canna tell what she is, but I sense she's no' Lykae." There was a fifty-fifty chance she was Pravus. With

Will's luck, they could just go ahead and round that up to absolute certainty.

"Will, do you no' understand—it's happened for you. After nine hundred years. What I wouldn't give . . ." Munro grabbed his shoulders. "It's *happened.*"

A shocked look between them.

"Brother, give the lass a chance."

With grim intent, Will started toward the source of the scent, Munro following. Wherever she was, she remained stationary.

Lesser beings took one look at Will's face—a Lykae in his prime, hell-bent on something—and cowered from him.

Before, he'd been ambivalent about his mate. Now he had to experience her scent for just a touch longer. He had to see her face. Would she be tall or petite? Would her locks be long or cropped? Her personality lighthearted or serious?

And since she wasn't a Lykae, would she even want him in return? Mayhap his cursed looks would finally come in handy. He scrubbed a hand down his face, surprised to find thick stubble and bruised skin. "I might've shaved today, huh?"

"Might've." Munro yanked his clean, nice shirt over his head, motioning for Will to trade his faded, ratty one. Without missing a step, they swapped shirts; nymphs squealed at the bare-chested brothers striding past them.

Once they'd changed, Munro gestured to indicate *all* of Will. "It is what it is."

Nïx had made that same gesture, the night she'd

betrayed him. As Will took unfaltering steps toward his mate, realization hit him. This was all according to plan. If he hadn't been on the island, he never would have come to this auction tonight. Nïx had set this in motion.

To what end, soothsayer?

"We'll find her," Munro assured him as they pushed through crowds of immortals.

"And then what?"

"Then nature takes over."

The throng around them began booing at the stage. Catcalls and jeers followed. They must've led Daughter of Webb out.

The sound of someone blowing into a hot mic pinged Will's sensitive ears, dredging up memories of torture. What didn't remind him of the island? *Shake it off.*

"Welcome to the House of Witches auction night," a female announcer said into the mic. "My name is Belee, and I'll be hosting this eve. Up for grabs is Chloe Todd, the verified Daughter of Webb. Age of twenty-four. Excellent health. Tonight's her first time ever to see immortals. So let's give her a big welcome to the Lore."

The crowd booed louder.

Though Will was curious to see the spawn of his enemy, he was enthralled by his new mate's scent.

To go to sleep awash in it? To wake to it? Resisting the call felt impossible.

"The bidding will begin at one million U.S. dollars or equivalent." As Munro had predicted. "Who would like to open?"

—*"One million in Draik gold pieces from the king of Draiksulia."*

—*"One point five from the Accord of the Valkyries and the Furiae—plus the Brisingamen Chain."*

More bids came in, and still the brothers hadn't reached her. A line of centaurs blocked their way; just as Will bared his teeth, about to plow through them, Munro yanked him around. "Keep your head."

Will's Instinct was now screaming —*YOURS!*—

In the background, the auction continued at a furious pace.

—*"The last of the Banemen Godslayers bid a dieumort, a god-killer."*

—*"The Pravus Rule bids two million as well as a barely used Bridefinder talisman."*

—*"Rodrigo Gamboa bids two tankers full of Colombian marching dust."*

Will dimly wondered if that last one was a joke.

The bidding reached eight digits, yet he and Munro still hadn't found her. They followed her scent toward the front, now shoving creatures out of the way.

Will drew deep of her once more and nearly stumbled. "Munro, did you catch that scent? She's—"

"Human," Munro finished, the word like a death knell.

"If I canna control my beast . . ." Bucket List Will. *It'd be best for her no' to know me. Let her go.* "I would kill a mortal."

"We'll figure it out. Will, I'll help you through this. I vow it. But for now, we just need to find her."

They were closing in on the stage when a last flurry

of bids came through. Soon everyone would leave—and then how would he find her? Will scrubbed his hand over his face, casting a confused glance at Munro. "Where the hell is she?" Then he turned, frowning at the small female coming into view.

The one on the stage. The one strung up against a pole—with a black bag over her head. She wore a filmy gown over a pink bra and black panties. She was petite, with tanned skin and the most incredible legs he'd ever seen on a female. Her heart was racing.

Daughter of Webb. They both drew up short.

The sublime scent was coming . . . from her.

This couldn't be possible. After waiting lifetimes for her, he'd found his mate in the offspring of a male so vile Will couldn't say his name without rage bubbling up inside him. "That fiend's daughter is my eternal mate?"

Munro uttered his thoughts, words that Will knew he regretted the second they'd left his tongue: *"This is so fucked."*

Will couldn't even process all that he was feeling. Disgust was there, along with the deepest welling of disappointment he'd ever experienced.

"Why did they black-bag her?" Munro bit out in Gaelic, sounding outraged.

"Because that's what was done to the Order's prisoners. To *me*!" When the breeze blew her white frock up above her knees, Will noted more of her shapely thighs, his predator's gaze locking on them. He reacted, hating himself.

"Will, it does no' matter who she is—you have

nothing to lose with her. I'll put it simply: she canna be worse than a pit of mystical flames. And that's your only other option on the table."

The witch announced, "The bidding is concluded! Congratulations, Pravus Rule, you have purchased Daughter of Webb. Thank you to everyone for attending this House of Witches—tee-em—production, and be on the lookout this week for our service questionnaire. Pravus, please claim your prize."

At that, the mortal's heart sped up even more. She screamed, but she sounded gagged under that bag. He thought she'd yelled, "Let me go, you sick pricks!" And then she started struggling.

Hard. Her wrists were bound, looped over a spike above her head. She thrashed to free herself.

"I should leave her arse to the Pravus." Even as Will said this, his body readied to fight for her. His Instinct was clamoring for him to save her, to cherish her. His beast prowled inside him, frantic to protect her. Will's claws lengthened along with his fangs, his muscles increasing in size. —*YOURS!*—

Two centaurs leapt atop the stage. One said, "I'm Lord Velees of the Centaureans, and I claim her for the Pravus."

Claim her? The fuck that would be happening!

A Cerunno slithered up to the pole. "I undersssstood that we would have her firsssst."

"Then you misunderstood." Velees unhooked her bound wrists from the spike. Immediately she flailed against him, kicking at the centaur. Blood began dripping from beneath her wrist shackles.

—*Protect!*—

When he gazed up at her little mortal form, fighting so bravely—even in the face of her fear—he found himself a bit . . . awed.

"Will, your female is a terrified girl not twenty feet from you. Her name is Chloe. Gods, man, she's so bluidy young."

Chloe.

"Right now, brother, she's losing a fight that is *yours* to win for her."

Not for long. Will's beast was uncontrollable on the best of days; now, for the first time in Will's existence, he had a mate to protect. It would rise up like horror embodied against anyone or anything that kept him from his female.

Munro clamped his shoulder. "I assume you're going to steal her from the Pravus first and ask questions later?"

He couldn't answer, already turning. When his beast clawed at its cage, Will was happy to let it free.

EIGHT

When Chloe had heard the word "purchased," something in her snapped.

This Velees guy gripped her around her waist, lifting her off her feet, tucking her against his bare chest. Still she fought and kicked. "Don u tou ee!" she screamed into her gag, thrashing against him with all her might. "Leh ee o!"

Screaming, thrashing—

Her foot struck what felt like the barrel chest of a horse. Her mind denied this—the man who had her was simply riding a horse, like a cowboy. A shirtless cowboy, of course.

Even over her frenzied fight, she heard people close to the stage gasp. Murmurs arose, *cries*. She could see nothing.

Then came the unholy roar of some beast.

A *familiar* roar. She'd heard one like it the night of the championships. Just as before, chills raced through her.

Silence fell over the crowd. After an extended moment, what sounded like chaos erupted.

—*"Run! The Lykae's turning!"*

—*"Ah, gods, don't get between them!"*

—*"She's MacRieve's mate!"*

Mate? Lykae? What had she read about them? Each had a beast housed inside—and each one sought its fated mate *above all things*. And she was this one's female? Hysterical laughter threatened, until she heard a low, feral growl.

The ground shook as people fled. What the hell was happening?

Velees snapped to some unseen person, "Mind yourself, wolf." But he was backing away, with Chloe clamped tightly against his body. Hooves stamped the stage.

"I'll snap this mortal's neck." Velees continued his steady retreat. "Another step closer, and she's dead!"

In a beastly, grating voice, the Lykae answered: *"Mine."*

That one word had Velees yanking her into his side and leaping off the back of the stage to hit the ground running—as if for his life. He yelled, "Cover me from the wolf!"

At that, she heard the clomping of hooves, a herd of them. As what sounded like a brutal fight broke out, a man yelled back, "Cerunnos attacking from the south!"

Were these beings now going to battle over her? The Lykae howled as if fighting his way closer.

Velees abruptly turned in another direction, flinging her with him. She thrashed to get the bag off her head, but it was tied on. *Can't see . . . can't see!*

Some being was just beside them; she heard its breaths. Then came a hissing sound, a gurgle, and suddenly she and Velees were falling, falling . . .

With another gurgle, Velees heaved her upward, pitching her body into the air, like a chipped pass—

Someone caught her in midair, wrapping a palm around her right arm and dragging her against his upper body. Another one of the cowboys? Damn it, there was no denying it—a centaur had her!

He held her as if she weighed nothing, yelling to the others, "The wolf comes for her! Kill him!"

Coming for her. *Because I'm its . . . mate.* Oh, man, that couldn't be good. She wanted this centaur to get her far away from that wolf! She screamed against her gag, "Moo ur ass! Hu-y!"

"Silence." Centaur gave her a shake, dislocating her shoulder with a pop. Pain flared, and she couldn't bite back a scream.

The wolf gave an enraged howl from some distance behind them.

She whimpered. *He's gaining.* Every gallop made fresh pain shoot through her arm and shoulder.

When some creature hissed beside them, Centaur yelled, "Nooo!"

No? No *what*—

She heard a solid thud, felt a teeth-jarring impact, heard bone snap. Centaur was flung onto his side. As that wolf roared in fury, still nearing, she and Centaur crashed to the ground. His hold loosened; he fumbled for her, but she'd already gone careening along his horse body, over its flank. She bounced over something metallic and sharp—*a sword?*—and pain sliced into her.

She hit the ground with a thud, the air wrenched from her lungs. Her side was slashed, pouring blood. She'd just sucked in her first hectic gasp when she got scooped up like a goalie save by some being that undulated over the ground.

Her mind fought recognition with this new captor, even as chills broke out over her skin. Some subconscious awareness within her screamed: *Snake!*

With a wet hiss to the sky, the creature increased its unfathomable speed. It sounded like others of its kind were flanking them. They were flying across the ground so fast that bugs pelted Chloe's black bag like a windshield. Then the being began zigzagging around trees, limbs swatting her legs.

Surely nothing could catch this creature? Not even a wolf . . .

As soon as the thought arose, she heard something crashing through the woods nearby, matching even this thing's fantastical speed.

※※※※※※

They have my mate.

Will's thoughts were murky, his beast in control, Instinct ruling him.

The need to protect her . . . he'd never felt a more primal drive.

In the distance, he heard a war zone, his brother wolf roaring, fighting to reach him; closer, he heard his female.

His heart seemed to stop each time she screamed. How much could she withstand? Her scent was just as loud to him. *Her fear. Her blood.*

He'd left dead, twitching centaurs in his wake, could still taste their throats, could feel their flesh embedded under his claws.

Now Cerunnos. So many of them, their scaly bodies whipping around trees. When the terrain became an open field, he gained. But another forest loomed.

He heard her cries, her frantic heartbeat. Beating, beating, beating.

Cypress, broken leaves. Somehow he ran faster, lungs heaving. He was upon them! *Kill them all.*

Slashing claws, snapping jaws. Warm blood rained down.

One remained, her captor. To take it down—without harming her? He sank his claws into its tail, snatching it up short. The momentum sent the girl flying. Will hurtled into the air.

Got her. He cradled her protectively, his arms closing around his trembling mate for the first time.

The last Cerunno coiled to strike. Will roared, baring his bloody fangs. *Try to take her from me!*

Taking his measure with slitted eyes, it hesitated. Will licked his fangs; with a hiss, the snake wisely began to slither a retreat.

Will threw back his head and howled with triumph.

Now to put the beast back in its cage. . . .

NINE

Field position? Chloe's life had never been so offsides before. She still couldn't see and doubted she would believe her eyes anyway.

She was severely injured, with a mythological creature holding her secure in his brawny arms.

Though explosions were blasting in the distance, shaking the ground, in the immediate area all she heard was this male's deep breaths. Inhale, exhale.

Even under her bag, she could detect his scent: evergreen, copper, and . . . male. His arms were unyielding around her, but still gentle. She thought they'd finally stopped running.

He howled once more, like an animal, paining her ears. When an answering howl sounded, the being seemed to relax a measure.

"Ey," Chloe weakly murmured against her gag. "Ake is ov?"

Instead of taking the bag off, he reached under it

for her gag. It felt too private, like he was reaching under her shirt. He pulled only the gag free.

She licked her dry lips, then worked her jaw back and forth. She had no reserves of strength left, was freezing cold, shaking from blood loss. And his body felt so hot against her. Still . . . "I-I need you to release me." *Just give me a second.*

"Canna do that." His voice was deep, beastly, and accented. He sounded like a Scot.

According to the book, the Highlands were Lykae territory. "Are you gonna hurt me?"

Silence. He was hesitating to answer? "You kill immortals like your sire? Or did the witch speak truths?"

"I've never seen immortals before tonight. Didn't think they existed."

"If no' one among the Order, then what are you?"

"Center forward."

"Doona follow."

"I play soccer. That's all I do. I-I don't know how I got mixed up in all this. I just . . . I chase a ball for a living."

"Chase a ball."

That must've been the exact right thing to tell a werewolf, because he released a gust of breath. "I will no' hurt you. I'll see you well."

Had she lucked into the one creature who wouldn't harm her? Of course, the crowd of detrus had screamed at the sight of this one, had scattered because Chloe *was his mate.*

He'd frightened even other monsters. And she was

utterly under this one's power. Though Chloe was first and foremost a fighter, she wasn't above making allies. Her foggy brain tried to recall more from the book's Lykae entry.

The bond between mates was the ultimate for them—revered by them as others did gods. Each Lykae only ever had one, so it followed that they would fight anything that tried to separate them. *Such as auctioneers and other bidders?* "Am I really your . . . mate?"

Another hesitation. "Aye."

She relaxed slightly. She didn't see how that was possible, but as long as *he* believed it, he wouldn't hurt her. "Th-thank you for saving me back there."

He stiffened against her. "Dinna have a choice." He might think she was his, but that didn't mean he was happy about it. He must hate her because she was human, because she was *Daughter of Webb.*

Dustin Todd was Commander Preston Webb. Not just a member of the Order, but a leader.

She exhaled with confusion, the movement making her wound sing. Her dizziness increased—probably because she was light a few pints of blood.

"Freeing you." He slashed through the chains binding her wrists.

She swallowed. *Slashed that metal with what?*

"Doona fight me."

With effort, she raised one hand to the bag to draw it away, but he stayed her arm. "No' yet."

"Why not?" Rain began to mist over them.

"You've had enough . . . frights for the night."

Exactly how hideous was he?

He started feeling her head through the silk bag. Checking for injuries? Finding none on her head, he gently swept his hands over her ankles, her calves, even up her thighs. She tensed but was too weak to resist him.

He hissed out a curse when he got to her left shoulder. Dislocated. He wrapped his hand around her upper arm. Then, seeming to think better of it, he adjusted his grip to what felt like his thumb and forefinger. With just two fingers and the tiniest movement, he jerked down. She gritted her teeth as her shoulder popped back into place.

When the sharp pain receded to a dull ache, she exhaled in relief, her eyelids growing heavy. "Th-thank you." Was that *her* slurred voice? How much blood had she lost? Why couldn't she think?

"Brave," he rasped.

When he lifted the skirt of her gown, sodden with her blood, she couldn't fight him, had to believe he was only checking her injury anyway. It was deep, excruciating.

He shuddered against her. At the sight of it? She could only imagine what it must look like.

She thought he was drawing off his shirt. A rip sounded. After a second she realized he was securing his balled-up shirt against her wound with a sleeve tied tightly around her waist. Smart.

But was it too little, too late? Without a hospital and a transfusion . . . "You think I'm about to eat it? Be honest."

He froze. "What?"

The mist turned to pounding rain, soaking her. "Pretty sure . . . I'm bleeding out."

"Dying? Nay. *Nay*." Without warning, he cupped the back of her head with one massive hand and her bottom with the other. She tried to muster the strength to resist, but then this man began to rock with her—as if it was the most natural thing in the world. "I've got you," he grated. "You will no' die."

She might be wary of him; her body wasn't. It melted against his.

"That's it, my lass." He pulled her closer.

"You're s-so warm." Despite all her turmoil and all her fear, she knew she was about to black out in this stranger's embrace.

When he said, "Rest, Chloe, everything'll be all right," she was too exhausted to doubt him.

Blackness was clawing at her. "You'll keep me safe?"

The last thing she heard before she passed out: "No one will ever hurt you again."

TEN

Will had tried—he'd truly tried—to hate her just for who she was.

None doing. When his brother's SUV skidded to a stop just feet from him, Will was cradling the unconscious girl as if she were the most treasured thing in the universe.

She'd been so brave, barely whimpering when he'd forced her arm back into its socket. She'd *thanked* him.

And then she'd uttered the most chilling words he'd ever heard: *I think I'm bleeding out.*

"How bad is she?" Munro asked as he drove them away, speeding toward the city.

"Bluidy bad!" Will had stopped the blood flow, but she was pale and cold. He reached for the heater control, blasting warm air over her damp skin. "I had to get past a dozen centaurs and ten Cerunnos to seize her. They were no' exactly gentle with her!"

She'd been passed among the centaurs and then to

the Cerunnos like a sodding rugby ball. Each time she'd changed hands, he'd experienced fear as never before.

He inhaled, still struggling to rein in his beast. He'd always heard that nothing made it rise up like a mate in peril.

If she woke and saw him like this, the mortal would probably stroke out before he could ever get her to a healer. Their immortal enemies cowered in the face of the beast. A young human might never recover from the sight.

He'd leave the bag on for now.

"And where the hell were you?" Will snapped at his brother. Right before Will had taken off after his mate, Munro had told him to meet in the woods if they got separated.

"Fighting my way out of a war to rescue you!" It was only then that Will noticed Munro was covered in blood and gore as well. "It's pandemonium back there. You were the spark on a powder keg. When the Vertas realized you were stealing the girl, they rose up and battled the Pravus back. Kind of like a real alliance—who knew we had it in us? By the by, remind me never to tangle with Malkom Slaine." He whistled low.

Chloe began shivering even harder. "We need to get to a witch healer. Drive to Andoain." Will couldn't believe that he was demanding his brother take them to Louisiana's infamous coven, the bloody H.O.W.

"We just cost them a serious loss of face. They'll hex us on sight."

They both shuddered.

"Besides, others will be waiting for us there. Brother, you ken this girl's the most valuable asset in the Lore right now? They're no' going to just forget about her."

Because she was Webb's daughter. The beast inside him didn't seem to give a fuck about that. Will's newly recovered Instinct didn't.

Munro asked, "What about a mortal hospital?"

"They'll be expecting us to go there. Besides, I doona trust mortal quacks. Sawbones, all of them."

"They've come a long way in the last century, Will."

"She might be past their reach. As much as I hate to say this, she needs mystical means. We head to Loa's." Loa was a voodoo priestess with a curiosity shop in the Quarter. "She sells witch potions. She might have a healing tonic."

Munro sighed. "Music to my ears." Loa was a comely one, with abundant curves and coffee-and-cream skin. She tended to show off both in revealing garments. He cast Will a sidelong glance. "You've had a change of heart about your mate?"

"When I realized who her father was, I imagined her to be like him, but I think she's . . . good. She talked about being a soccer player."

"Football, huh? Is that how your female got those scars?" She had surgical scars on one wrist, an ankle, and her right knee.

"Doona be looking at her legs!" Will yanked her frock down, accidentally ripping the lower half clean away, leaving her in only the top of her gown, the makeshift bandage, and her sleek black underwear. He took deep breaths to tamp down his beast. Inhale. Exhale. Precarious moments passed.

"Good man. You got control, heading back to normal. Well, relatively. I think you can risk taking her bag off. You must be dying to see what she looks like."

I'm going to behold my mate's face for the first time. He nervously clawed through the bag's tie.

With a shaking hand, he began to draw the material away . . . revealing her face.

While Will worked to catch his breath, Munro glanced over. "Ach, and there she is. You lucky sod."

Her damp hair was sun-streaked, cropped close to her head. Her lips were plump. She sported freckles across her nose and cheeks. Her cheekbones were prominent, like a model's might be, but with her pointed chin, bee-stung mouth, and short locks, she looked like a wee pixie.

He felt one corner of his lips curl. —*Yours.*— Had his arms closed more tightly around her?

Munro said, "Her timing is impeccable. She's your lucky penny."

Will's grip loosened, his excitement dimming. "Just look at her. She's too . . . too . . ." Too everything he could ever dream. "You *know* something's inherently wrong with her. She must be shallow, vapid, dim. Webb must've left his mark on her."

"She's also *young*, Will. Whatever damage Webb might've done can be righted if you're patient with her."

"Why would fate give me a human to protect? Especially this human?" When he was raw with rage toward her father?

"Because, brother, you can handle it."

Will's Instinct was pushing, his beast stirring for her; resisting her pull was harder than the tortures he'd recently endured. He gazed down at her, rubbing his thumb over her bottom lip. It was plush like a little pillow. The lower edge went straight across before curving up at the corners, a soft bracket. Gods, she was a pretty thing.

—*Yours.*—

Mayhap she *was* his reward? *To help me get over torture, help me understand my past.* "Looks like I'll have to handle it."

"Where do we take her after Loa's?" Munro asked. "My first thought is Bheinnrose. We'd be isolated up in Nova Scotia, away from all this commotion."

"I say we stay in Louisiana, at Glenrial. Strategically, it's easier to defend." Though the compound consisted of hundreds of acres, it was completely walled in, with a trained watch stationed at intervals. The place was simply too close to the homes of myriad other factions not to be guarded like a vault.

"Aye then, I'll make the call." Munro briefly spoke to Madadh, Glenrial's master of the watch, explaining all that had happened, telling him to get the clan prepared for anything. Munro hung up once they'd made the Quarter, concentrating on driving.

The maze of one-way streets was filled with drunken tourists, mounted police, and rolling Lucky Dog stands.

Will gazed down at Chloe. Were her breaths shallowing? —*Protect!*— Another jolt of fear hit him. *I canna lose her, just when I've found her.* "Faster, Munro."

With his lips thinned, Munro made a sharp left, heading the wrong way down a one-way street. "I'll get us there—just have your credit card ready. Loa will be pissed that we're no' there to flirt with her."

ELEVEN

Candles, taxidermy, incense, cannabis.

As ever, Will's senses were overloaded by the cacophony of scents inside Loa's store.

The bell above the door was still ringing as he and Munro barged into the candlelit interior, Will with Chloe wrapped securely in his arms. He called, "Loa!" The scuffed wood floor creaked beneath his feet, but there was no answer.

Whereas the front of the shop was a touristy affair—with fake voodoo charms and dolls, shelves of tarot card decks and black candles—the back was an authentic Lore establishment, filled with mystical wares. A Lore-mart.

Munro entered the concealed doorway first, Will right behind him.

Loa was seated at a counter, reading some tome with *Geopolitical* in the title. Her smile was broad as she called, "Hot and Hotter?" It dimmed when she caught sight of their battle-worn appearances—and Will's bloody female. "Is that who them spirits are talkin' 'bout?" she said with her islander accent. "The auction prize?"

"Aye, and she's injured," Will said.

"My business how?" she said, adding sarcastically, "You buyin' a *witch* healing potion?"

Will slapped his credit card on the counter. "Aye."

She raised her eyebrows. "*Lykae* seekin' witchcraft. The apocalypse truly is here."

"We doona have time for this!"

With a shrug, she said, "Aisle five. But they only heal non-lethal wounds."

Another jolt of fear. Couldn't be a lethal wound. As they charged toward five, Will read the overhead signs: CONTRACEPTION, GLAMOURS, CONJURINGS, APOCALYPSE PREPARATION . . . then HEALING ARTS.

At last! But the shelf was chock-full of confusing vials and jars. "Which one, Munro?"

Munro yelled over his shoulder, "A little help, Loa?"

"Look at the prices," she called back. "You want the most expensive one."

Will spotted a stoppered vial of lime-green liquid for three hundred and fifty thousand. Surely that cost the most?

None doing. That was the cheapest.

Munro rifled through the rest, grabbing a lever-top jar filled with a tarlike paste for twice that.

"Instructions come with?" Will asked as they barreled up to the counter.

Loa arched a brow at him. "Your credit card nuh irie."

"What does that mean? It's limitless."

"Alternative payment requested. And I'm tackin' on a sanitation fee—she's drippin' blood."

Munro was already rooting for his wallet. "Damn, Loa, you know we're good for it." To Will, he said, "You might talk to Rónan—he mentioned making some charges. Had no idea he was talking about card-killing purchases."

Could give a shite right now. "Loa, how do we administer this?"

"Quickly, if you'd like her to live. See the sale table over there? What you want to do is use one arm to sweep all the goods to the floor. At cost. Once you've laid her down, clean her wounds with a case of Mount Doom Springs, then smear the paste on. Oh, and you must keep her warm with a one-of-a-kind dragon-silk quilt." She handed him a soft white blanket, bilking him thoroughly.

Uncaring, he lunged for the table, sweeping merchandise to the ground. As basilisk piggy banks, Rothkalina snow globes, and Horn-of-Fame castings shattered, Loa's cash register sang *ka-ching.*

Laying Chloe down, he covered her lower half with the blanket. Munro had already retrieved the water and a beach towel.

"What else can I do?" Munro asked.

Will answered, "Guard the door. Others might suspect we've come here."

When Munro jogged off, Loa sauntered over, studying Chloe's face. She nodded as if Will had said something to her, then turned to light black candles in a circle around the table.

"Oh, now you're going to help?" He poured water over Chloe's wound, then assessed it: redder, more inflamed than before—and much deeper than he'd thought.

Gods, she was so small and pale. So . . . human.

"The spirits like her. Not many pure hearts pass through our doors."

Pure of heart? "You ken who she is. Why would they think that of her?"

"She's *of* Webb. She hasn't followed his path."

"How can they tell?" Will already believed this, felt in his gut that she was good.

"Violence and hatred leave marks the spirits can see. You're riddled with them."

You have no idea.

"This one is not. Plus she doesn't have them deep, dark secrets like you and Munro." When she began chanting to "Li Grand Zombie," Will's hackles rose. He'd once heard the priestess explain the difference between her magic and the magic of a typical witch: "Mine is darker. And while theirs is based on life, mine is steeped in death."

Loa gave a half-grin, as if someone had said something amusing. Creepy, mystical bullshite—Lykae hated it!

Then, in a singsong voice, she called, "Here, Boa! Come, my sweetheart!"

Summoning a pet? "Loa and Boa? You dicking with me?"

"I'm not jesting, if that's what you mean."

The lights began flickering, the candles fluttering. An ominous air stifled the room.

"There you are," she cooed—to the *boa constrictor* slithering from a hole in the floor.

A big hole in the floor.

"Ah, fuck me." It must weigh a hundred and fifty pounds. His Instinct was screaming at him to get Chloe away from the snake—and Loa. "Put that thing *back* in the motherfuckin' hole, Loa!"

As if Chloe sensed the snake, she turned her face into Will's palm.

Unperturbed, Loa said, "Boa keeps death away. And your female has lost a lot of blood. Do you want us to save her or not?"

Eventually, he gave a curt nod. But when the boa began to climb Loa's leg like a jungle gym, he almost lost his nerve.

From her pocket, the priestess drew a pinch of dust, blowing it over Chloe's face. Again the lights flickered, the candle flames dancing.

"What the hell was that?"

"A narcotic. Something for the pain." At his look, she said, "Relax. Your new mate will just be a touch bamcocked."

"What?"

"Buzzed."

Chloe moaned then, and her lids fluttered open to reveal the bonniest hazel eyes he'd ever seen. "Hi," she murmured, blinking up at him. She raised one hand, evidently to press it to her forehead, but ending up missing.

He swallowed, voice gone hoarse as he answered, "Hi, yourself." *You're my mate. I'm gazing down at my female, at her mesmerizing eyes.* Her irises seemed to hold every color, like when sunset burns across the sea: golds, bronzes, greens, blues.

The moment began to feel surreal, as if he were going to wake any minute, hungover and choking on rage as usual.

"Feel funny. Um, I'm stoned. I think."

"We're getting you patched up, sweet." He brushed her light brown hair off her forehead. Her tresses were drying into sun-streaked tawny curls that felt soft as gossamer.

She sighed. "You look different than I imagined."

The obligatory gushing would follow: *You're so hot, you're gorgeous, you're sexy—*

"You have kind eyes."

"Do I, then?" Again, his voice was hoarse. "Chloe, I need you to be strong and get well."

"Because I'm your, um, mate?"

"And mayhap because I fancy you. I want to know you better."

She motioned haphazardly at her side. "Rub some dirt on it. S'll be fine."

"Rub some dirt, then?" he repeated, unable to keep the amusement from his tone. "I like your attitude, lass."

When she grinned crookedly, his heart thudded. *I think I'm bluidy in love.*

Gods, he was so eager for this, too eager, running headlong. Experience told him to slow down, but this girl was rousing feelings in him he'd never experienced before. They were so different from anything he'd ever known that he wanted to seize these feelings with ten claws. "Doona worry, I'll take care of you." He grasped her hand in his. "You're going to be all right."

Chloe's gaze drifted to Loa. "That a snake?"

Loa said, "She keeps death away."

Chloe blinked those big eyes up at him and whispered, "Wish that was the weirdest thing . . . I've heard tonight."

Loa popped open the medicine jar, handed it to him. He took a whiff. Licorice? With a grimace, he stuck two fingers into the witchy paste, pulling out a generous dollop. He murmured to the priestess, "Is this going to work?"

She nodded. "Between that, me, and Boa, you're in good hands."

He told Chloe, "Going to put some medicine on your wound." While Loa chanted, he smeared the stuff over the gash. It bubbled like hydrogen peroxide, making Chloe wince. Sweat dotted her brow as she clenched her jaw against the pain, not making a sound. Fierce wee thing. "There's my brave lass."

Loa murmured, "Distract her, wolf."

"Oh, aye. Uh, who do you play football for?"

She grated, "You're looking . . . at the Seattle Reign's . . . playmaker."

He almost grinned at her cocky tone. His mate was a professional footballer. Who would've thought?

Then his brows drew together. She'd said she was a center forward? Without a doubt, it was the most hazardous position, bound to leave those scars. She'd been getting her arse kicked out on a field. "Are you no' a bit wee to play football in the big leagues?"

At once, her eyes narrowed, her stubborn chin jutting. "It's *soccer*. And I made the Olympic team, asshole."

Bluidy—in—love. He solemnly raised a palm. "My apologies."

She mumbled, "Uh-huh. Don't forget it."

Gods, she couldn't be more appealing to him.

When her lids slid closed and she went limp once more, he said, "Wait, Chloe, stay with me!"

The priestess said, "No, let her rest."

"I canna lose her, Loa." Because already he *needed* her. In the short span since he'd found her, changes had been occurring inside him, things clicking into place.

He now had a purpose. He was her protector. There'd be no more idling. No more benders.

Everyone in the clan spoke of how rewarding it felt to protect a mate, but he'd never imagined that it would be . . . life-changing.

Munro ducked in from the front to find Will clutching Chloe's hand in both of his. Will briefly glanced up, not bothering to hide what he was feeling.

Munro's brows drew together. With a nod of understanding, he turned back to guard the entrance.

"Just let the medicine do its job," Loa said. "And remember, Boa's here."

While the paste continued to fizzle, Will wetted the towel and washed off the worst of the blood covering his mate.

Loa brought him a Saints T-shirt to dress her in. A gentleman wouldn't have looked at Chloe in her underthings. *So no' a problem for me.*

Peeling off what remained of her frock, he discovered that her figure was as bonny as her face. She wore a tiny bra over full, pert breasts. Her panties covered a lot, but they also highlighted how narrow her waist was, how toned her legs. He could tell she was an athlete, yet she still had curves in all the right places.

Women's football—*excuse me, women's soccer*—was officially his favorite sport.

By the time he was ready to apply a bandage, the paste on her wound had dried into a hard shell. And he could've sworn Chloe's color was already better. "Is the shell thing normal?" he asked, beginning to bandage her.

Loa nodded. "She's going to be fine." She looked confident, but tired. This must've taken something out of her.

"Thank you, priestess. I'm in your debt."

"Wait until you see your bill. You'll find we're even."

As he bundled Chloe in the blanket, Loa said, "You cared for her well and trusted the spirits. They ended up liking you. They want you to make a wish."

He scooped Chloe up in his arms, already thinking of getting her home. "That's easy. I wish that this lass was immortal."

TWELVE

L et's see Daughter of Webb!" Rónan exclaimed
  when Will and Munro stormed into the lodge—
covered in dried blood and with company.

"I suppose everyone knows?" Will said, adjusting
his bundled mate in his arms.

"We saw the forces mustering to protect her," Ben
quietly said. "Got Madadh to tell us what was going on."

One phone call had mobilized hundreds of Lykae
at the wall and outside their lodge. It wasn't every day
that a member of the clan found a mate, especially not
one in such danger.

Getting through the handful of enemies who'd
gathered on the other side of the wall hadn't proved
too challenging. A centaur had attempted to ram them,
which had only resulted in it decorating the Range
Rover's grille for precious, thrilling seconds.

But Will knew they'd keep coming, increasing their
numbers.

Rónan said, "I thought you two would come home hours from now, reeking of nymph perfume and covered in grass stains. Now you've got a mate? Is Daughter of Webb drunk?" In a deadpan tone, he added, "Like seeks like, huh? But I'm no' judging."

Smart-arse.

Will gazed down at Chloe's pretty face, again thinking that her color was returning. Could she rebound from blood loss this quickly? "She's no' drunk. She was injured tonight. And she has a name—*Chloe MacRieve*." Had his shoulders gone back? Bloody hell, they had.

"Well, it's your lucky day, gentlemen," Rónan said. "Because I just had a sweet protection spell installed on the lodge. No one who means us harm can enter."

Munro crossed to the window, raising his hand against it. "I sense something's here."

"What?" Will hugged Chloe tighter. "We doona use spells and magic," he snapped, well aware that he'd just used spells and magic.

But not *here*. And never again. Slippery slope and all that.

Munro said, "The spell might help us. At least the Pravus won't be able to simply trace inside and steal her."

"I purchased it from this young, beautemous witch." Rónan sighed. "Ach, you would too if you saw her. Legs for miles, goes by the name of Belee. She sells spells door-to-door like Girl Scout cookies. Put me down for five thousand boxes of Thin Mints, you know what I mean?"

Munro narrowed his eyes. "*Witchcraft* is what you used Will's credit card for?"

When Chloe stirred against him, Will turned

toward the stairs, keen to put her in his bed for the first time. Munro followed, the boys hurrying up the stairs behind them.

On the way up, Will remembered the hazmat condition of his room. The squalor. For the second time tonight, his neck heated.

He couldn't stand the idea of laying her on those sheets. Where to take her? The guest rooms were directly beside the boys', which wouldn't do. He could swap rooms with Munro, as they had shirts, or use the smaller room adjoining this one—but the wolf in him wanted *his* mate in *his* bed.

As they approached the thick oak door, Will braced himself—

His room was . . . spotless? He swung his head around to his brother.

"What?" Munro leaned against the doorway, looking like the Godfather. "I made a call from Loa's. You still have to get Chloe to like you. Saw no reason to load the dice against you from the outset."

Always having his back. "Appreciated." Will laid Chloe on the bed, covering her with another blanket.

"Now, get yourself cleaned up too," Munro said. "I'll watch her."

Will hesitated to leave her for even a second, but he had blood all over him. "Aye, then." He raced for the shower, ripped off his pants, then sloshed cold water over himself until the worst was removed. Less than two minutes later, he returned in a towel.

Munro motioned to Will's closet. "Clean clothes in there."

Will rooted for garments. He'd never cared about looking good; all his clothes were worn. He selected his least-frayed pair of jeans and his nicest button-down.

Rónan asked, "So is this a *like-father, like-daughter* situation? Is she also into slicing and dicing Lykae?"

From inside the closet, Will answered, "She dinna know about the Lore, has never harmed any immortals."

"Beauty."

Once dressed—*it is what it is*—he returned to the bed and sat beside her. "When she wakes, we need to ease her into this." Will stared down both of the boys. "If I so much as spy a *hint* of your beast . . ." He trailed off, the threat clear.

"*You* are worried about *us* beast-wise? Good one, Head Case." Rónan sat on the opposite side of the bed to study Chloe. "I have to say, well done, chief. If being cute were a crime, she'd get the chair. Is she going to be doing the cooking and cleaning? Man, I hope she can cook."

Ben smacked him on the back of the head. "Mayhap you should be more concerned about whether she'll recover or no'?"

"She'll be fine," Will quickly said. "She's on the mend." Aye, her color *was* better. In fact, her skin now looked sun-kissed. From days spent on the field?

Now that the worst of his worry had faded, he had new ones to contend with, namely those sexual hang-ups of his. The most unusual? Will unleashed his beast whenever he fucked—something no Lykae did outside of a mate's bed on the night of a full moon.

If any Lorean female ever wondered what it was like to be a wolf's fated one, to be taken by the beast under the light of the moon, Will had showed them. The girlfriend experience? Try the mate experience.

Or at least, he'd shown them a brutal, debauched rendition of it.

Ruelle had molded Will to have sex a certain way, and in nine hundred years, he'd never been able to refashion himself. For Will, every night was the night of the full moon.

If he took Chloe in that state, she wouldn't survive the size and strength of his body, his rising beast. She wouldn't survive his Lykae claiming bite. Much less all of that together. . . .

He gazed up at Munro, who must have sensed his disquiet. His brother's slow nod and steady gaze said, *We'll get through this. Keep your head.*

As ever, it helped.

Rónan leaned down until he was almost nose to nose with Chloe. "I'd even go so far as saying she's as pretty as Belee. Though this one's got more of an I-eat-testicles-for-breakfast kind of rock-star look about her. Hey, speaking of hot arse, now that you've got a woman, can I inherit the pornucopia I found stashed in here—"

Chloe head-butted Rónan, who howled with pain.

Before Will could register his surprise, she'd darted to her feet and sprinted away from them.

THIRTEEN

Chloe charged toward a door, struggling to keep her balance. Her equilibrium was shot. Weapon, she needed a weapon—

She'd run into a bathroom. Trapped. Shit!

She heard males talking in a foreign language, words underscored with urgency. A door opened . . . closed.

When she warily exited the bathroom, one man was standing alone in the center of the bedroom, with his palms raised. "Easy, lass."

She backed into a corner. The room was large, tastefully decorated, but definitely a man's domain. *This* man's.

The most handsome male she'd ever seen.

Molten gold eyes and chiseled features. Thick, dark hair that couldn't decide if it wanted to be brown or black. Broad shoulders on a muscle-packed frame. He had to be more than six and half feet tall. "Who are you? Where am I?"

"Do you no' remember me from earlier?"

As she might a dream. Hazy memories arose of him stroking her hair, murmuring how brave she was. She remembered opening her eyes, seeing flickering lights around her. His face had been shadowed, but she recalled his brilliant colored eyes. And his voice.

His sexy, sexy voice. It was deep and gravelly, shiver-inducing.

That feeling of awakening multiplied until she almost winced.

Ignore him, evaluate your field position! Though her head ached and she was dizzy from the sudden movement, she assessed every detail of her surroundings, scouting for exits, weapons, resources.

"You're safe, lass," he said. When she didn't relax her guard, he added, "None of us would ever harm you."

She swallowed. "Who are you?"

"My name's Uilleam MacRieve, but you can just call me MacRieve."

His Scottish accent was bone-meltingly hot. *Lord help me.* What'd he say his name was? It sounded like Ooh-lum. When she tried to pronounce it back, he cut her off.

"I said to just call me MacRieve."

She could swear he was disappointed by this. The gorgeous Scot with amber eyes was disappointed in her.

"And you're Chloe. You look like a Chloe."

"What does that look like?"

The corners of his lips curled. "Cute."

Merely looking at his smile made her heart thud.

He glanced at her chest, as if he could hear it, and his smile deepened.

Like all immortals, Lykae had superhuman senses. *He* can *hear it!* Face flaming, she glanced away. "What do you want with me? What happened when I was unconscious?"

He sat on the edge of the bed and rested his elbows on his knees. She noticed then that he had on battered jeans but wore a nice black shirt. "After I saved you from witches, centaurs, and Cerunnos, I got you patched up, then brought you back to the house I share with my brother and two young punks who doona understand the concept of rent."

His tone sounded so *normal.*

Wait. "Patched up?" She'd been injured in the melee. So why did she feel no pain in her side? Oh, God, what if she'd been out for days? And how could it possibly itch this bad? "That was tonight?"

"Aye. I took you to a healer of sorts."

Memories began to filter into her consciousness: his admitting she was his mate, blood pouring from her side as the rain came down, the . . . voodoo? She squeezed her forehead, vaguely remembering a sexpot with a pet boa constrictor. "Did you take me to a voodoo woman?"

"A priestess." He grinned with perfect white teeth, adding, "We rubbed some dirt on it."

That grin. Again she reacted physically, her heart speeding up. Had she ever beheld such kissable lips? Though she could count on one hand the number of guys she'd kissed, she could imagine, in detail, licking this one's lips, sucking on the bottom one.

Inner shake. "Wh-why am I in different clothes?" Someone had changed her into a Saints T-shirt that went down to her knees.

"Because your frock was toast."

Frock? "Not mine. They put me in that." God, her side itched. When she gave it a scratch, she found something hard underneath a bandage, something she desperately wanted *off.*

"You had blood all over you from your wound."

"So you took it upon yourself to wash and change me?"

"Hardly looked down a'tall," he answered with a shameless wink.

A man had been looking at her undressed. The first one. And he wasn't even apologetic. Chloe didn't have time for this. She needed to figure out what she was, what she soon would be. She needed to find her dad before the Lore did. "I appreciate everything you've done, but I've got to be on my way. Do you have any clothes I can borrow?"

His face fell. "You want to . . . leave me?"

She didn't figure this happened to the guy very often. Gorgeous did not begin to describe him.

"You're safe here, Chloe. Just stay for one night. You can leave once you've recovered more."

She did feel safe with him, probably because Mac-Rieve had saved her repeatedly. He'd gotten her healed, just as he'd promised. *I'll see you well.*

Starting out tomorrow, when she was rested, made the most sense. But this situation was riddled with so many unknowns. "Do you have any, well, expectations of me? Since I'm your . . . mate?"

"I expect you to let me protect you," he said. "Nothing more than that."

Was he being truthful? Was this guy too good to be true?

"You canna leave without a game plan. Those creatures will be searching for you."

"Creatures." Her life was a shit storm. And that itching was driving her crazy!

Maybe MacRieve could answer all her questions. "Okay, I'll stay tonight." Maybe *he* could figure out what was happening to her.

"Chloe, we need to speak about what's going on so I can better protect you. But first, are you hungry, thirsty, cold? Are you in pain?"

She didn't have pain in her side, just itching. She hadn't eaten all day; she wasn't hungry in the least. *You're changing, Chloe.* "I am a little cold," she admitted.

He hastened to grab a blanket off the bed, rushing back to drape it around her shoulders. Then he motioned to a pair of chairs in front of a fireplace. "I'll start a fire."

As she took a seat, he set to work; soon flames were warming away the last of her chill.

When he joined her, he asked, "Do you know where Webb is?"

She wouldn't divulge anything unnecessarily about her dad, but admitting she knew nothing about all this seemed reasonable. "I have no idea. He's been missing for weeks."

"He has no' tried to contact you?"

She was embarrassed to admit the truth: "Not a peep. Do *you* have any idea where he is?"

"I doona. Word has it that he went into hiding. No one in the Lore can find him."

Hiding? Then why hadn't he taken her with him? Maybe he hadn't wanted to interrupt her life.

And *maybe* he shouldn't have left her ass so vulnerable!

The roulette wheel of her emotions spun wildly. Anger, fear, sadness, anger, fear, sadness . . .

As if he read her mind, MacRieve said, "He left you at home, open to attack? You're lucky to be alive."

"How did the Lore find out about me all of a sudden? Two different species were after me in one night. And that was *before* the auction."

"What do you mean by two?"

"Earlier tonight, back at my house, I thought I heard something downstairs. I figured my dad had finally returned. Instead there was an eight-foot-tall, horned guy."

"A demon, then."

"Well, when I hit him with my baseball bat, that demon crushed it like a tin can."

MacRieve raised his brows like he was impressed. "You swung on an eight-foot-tall demon? You've got some fight in you, no?"

She shrugged. "For all the good it did. When I ran from him, I fell through a trapdoor and woke up with witches all around me."

"Loathe witches." His amber eyes flickered to an otherworldly ice-blue. "They must have found out about your existence and scried for you. Mayhap the demon caught wind of their plans. Those witches are detestable creatures. Do you ken what they are?"

She nodded. "I remember. They're mystical mercenaries."

His gaze narrowed. "I thought you dinna know about the Lore."

"I know all about it. I just never knew it was real." At his frown, she said, "I read the *Book of Lore*. Before tonight, I thought it was fiction."

"Who gave you the book?"

"My dad. But we never got a chance to talk about it before he went missing. I still have a hard time believing detrus are real."

"Watch your tongue, lass." Again MacRieve's eyes flickered. "No one likes to be called a 'vilest abomination.'"

"I-I thought it was a catchall for, uh, mythological creatures."

"*Loreans.* Go with that word."

"Um, okay." Great. She'd insulted the one person in this entire Lore world who'd been decent to her.

"Did you read about Lykae?"

"I did. But I still have questions." Dozens of them. When he waved her on, she asked, "Do you have a pack? How many of you are there?" Did she pass them on the street each day? "Are there alphas and betas?"

"We have a pack, but most Lykae belong in some way to the MacRieve clan. It's a kingdom as well."

"Kinevane is the royal seat."

He nodded. "And, aye, there are alphas and betas.

You're looking at one of the former. Lykae number in the hundreds of thousands."

Her lips parted. So many? "So you're a . . . werewolf." And an alpha to boot.

"We doona shift into wolves. No' like in the movies. We each have the spirit of a wolf inside us. We call it our beast; sometimes it rises and takes us over. *A'leigeil a'mhadaidh fa sgaoil.*"

"What does that mean?"

"'Letting the beast out of its cage.' Once it's fully risen, then you can see it."

"What does it look like?"

"When a Lykae turns, it overshadows him—or her. He also grows fangs and claws, and his face changes a wee bit. He gets . . . bigger."

Bigger? He already dwarfed her five-three height. "It doesn't sound so bad. So why did those other Loreans scream at the sight of you?"

He scrubbed a palm over his face, looking uncomfortable. "It takes some getting used to."

"What makes it rise?"

His eyes shifted away from hers as he said, "For most, it's an infrequent occurrence. In mated Lykae, it rises each full moon. Otherwise it remains dormant, unless a mate or pup is in jeopardy. Something along those lines."

"How do you know I'm your mate?" Again, she believed that *he* believed this. Didn't mean it was fact. If it was . . . *I'd be freaking out right now.*

"Lykae have an Instinct—a guiding force, yet it's *verra* developed, more so than with other shifters.

When I scented you, the Instinct told me you were mine," he said, but she got the impression that he was simplifying his answer for her—or holding a lot back. "I've waited my entire life to know that scent."

"Exactly how old are you?"

His discomfort seemed to deepen. "I've got some years on me. A few lifetimes. But I stopped aging at thirty-two, no' much older than your twenty-four years."

She wondered how he knew her age, then remembered it'd been announced at the auction. "What would those creatures have done with me if you hadn't saved me?"

He hesitated, as if weighing the pros and cons of what he was about to say.

"Please. I need to know."

"Rape and torture. Once they found Webb, they would have killed you."

Nausea churned. "Because of my father's involvement with immortals?"

"Aye. He's a commander in the Order, a mortal organization that seeks to capture and study immortals so that they can better exterminate us. We believe it has ties to the military."

"Exterminate." Just like the note in that book. Had her dad left *her* because she was becoming an immortal? A vile abomination?

Anger, fear, sadness, anger, fear, sadness . . .

"Chloe, your father's a killer."

"He's been an adoring dad to me. Supportive and loving." She pinched the bridge of her nose. "So he kills snake creatures and centaurs who would rape his daughter? He kills witches who would auction her off? No offense, but I'm not seeing a problem."

"Your father seeks to wipe us *all* out, even though Lykae doona harm humans. Nor do the members of my alliance. No' like Pravus immortals do. Have you heard of them?"

"Yes. They won the bidding."

"They're the monsters of myth. Unfortunately, the Order does no' discriminate between us and them."

That gave her pause. "My dad isn't narrow-minded or prejudiced with humans—why would he be with immortals?" She clung to the idea that this was all a misunderstanding.

"Doona know. But he had his henchmen do things that canna be forgiven. Families were torn apart. Bairns orphaned, some captured themselves." MacRieve's eyes flickered once more and sweat beaded his upper lip. "Order scientists tortured captives in sick ways, vivisecting them while they were conscious."

"You're saying my father was responsible for all that?"

"He still is. There were five prisons. Four remain. I vow to the Lore that what I'm saying is true—and that's a vow few Loreans can break."

Should she believe this stranger? When she recalled that slip of paper in the *Book of Lore*, Chloe realized that she couldn't dismiss what this Lykae was telling her.

But she also couldn't accept that her dad would hurt children, no matter their species.

"The people at the auction wanted to use you to

draw out your father," MacRieve said. "You're the only lead in the Lore, it seems. No one can find him, and so verra many crave vengeance. No' to mention the locations of the other prisons. They want their offspring and mates back, their siblings and friends."

She glanced up. "Then why were you at the auction?"

He parted his lips, but said nothing.

"Oh. Oh, no! Did you lose family? Children?" *Say no, say no.*

"I canna have bairns with any save for my mate." His golden gaze pinned her. "With *you.*"

She swallowed. This whole mate thing was unnerving. "You didn't answer the question."

"I lost no one, but I will no' lie to you—I'm among those seeking revenge. I have as much call for it as any of them."

"What happened to you? Were you in one of those prisons?"

The bleakness in his expression rocked her. "That's a discussion for another night."

He was! Dear God, she might have heard his capture. She'd thought that his furious roar had sounded familiar. If he hadn't lost anybody and he wanted revenge, then he'd been tortured. Her father might be responsible for the torture of this male.

The one who'd saved her life.

If there was one thing Chloe believed, it was that there were exceptions to every rule. She herself was an exception. While the rest of her teammates had long legs like gazelles, Chloe was a short badger, not exactly playmaker material. But she'd worked ten times as hard as they had, and she'd prevailed.

If other Lykae were evil enough to be . . . exterminated, then she'd just found the exception in Mac-Rieve. And for that matter, Chloe wasn't evil, yet her dad had shown her the book—had shown her hand-written words like *foul plague* and *abomination*.

Obviously the Order was flawed.

"You knew nothing of what your father was doing?"

"God, no! And if I had, I never would have stood for it!"

At her words, he exhaled a pent-up breath. "So you will no' hate us just because Webb does?"

"I can make up my own mind."

His expression lightened. "Dinna know if you would want my head on a platter just for what I am."

"And how are you handling the fact that I'm *Daughter of Webb*? Seems like you would want my head on a platter just for what I am."

"That might have been true once. No longer."

"Will you hurt me to get back at him?"

"Nay!" He gave her a look as if the very idea was ludicrous. "Never hurt you."

"And him?"

"Chloe, it's complicated." He stabbed his fingers through his thick hair. "Things have changed—I ken that—but I need to think on this for longer than hours. For now, let me enjoy being with you." He rose, then closed in on her. "Been waiting a long time for you."

She stood as well. She could feel the heat coming

off his body, could luxuriate in his masculine scent.

"We'll figure out all of this in the morning." He eased closer still. "I've other things on my mind just now."

The Scottish god was flirting with her? She felt flustered for the first time in her life. *Awakening!*

Before, whenever she'd felt attracted to a guy and thought about acting on it, she'd been filled with dread. She'd never told another, had never been able to understand it, but just the idea of talking to a hot boy had terrified her—as if she were about to embark on a trip from which there was no return. Like there should be a neon sign blinking over each guy's head: HERE BE DRAGONS!

She'd never dated, giving in to her fear like a coward. But now she felt zero dread, more anticipation, like maybe those dreams of hers might come true. "Other things on your mind?"

"Like kissing you for the first time. Ah, Chloe, your heart speeds up when you look at my lips."

Her face flushed with embarrassment.

Right when she was about to make a smart-ass remark, he said, "My heart has no' slowed since I first saw you."

She found herself wetting her lips. But after so many celibate years and such wariness with men, this easy acceptance was as bewildering as the dread. "I-I need a shower," she blurted, scrambling away from him.

He raised his brows. "I'm in need of one myself. And we like to conserve water around here."

FOURTEEN

MacRieve dogged her heels as she strode toward the bathroom. After his comment, all she could think about was showering with him. Soaping his big body . . .

At the doorway, she faced him. "Can I get some privacy?"

He blinked at her, and she got the sense that she'd asked for something he considered *odd*.

"Out, MacRieve! Shoo."

He refused to budge. "You lost pints today. What if you grow dizzy and slip?" Then he flashed a look of realization. "That could actually *kill* you. Fuck me. You could die from a shower fall!"

Though she often cussed like it was going out of style—how else was she supposed to trash-talk opponents?—she was unused to men doing it around her.

"You must keep the door open, Chloe."

Did she dare risk it? The shower stall was as big as

a room, with a screen at least six feet high. He wouldn't be able to see her. Her wound was itching like crazy, and her hair was dirty, with real particles of dirt. "Fine. As long as you don't come in."

"I will no'." He leaned his back against the doorjamb and crossed his arms over his massive chest.

Once she managed to stop staring at it, she turned toward the shower. In the stall she removed her T-shirt, underwear, and bandage, frowning to find a hard black shell over her side.

When she stepped under the water, she groaned with pleasure.

"Lass?" he called.

"Nothing."

As steam filled the room, the itchy shell on her side loosened until she was able to peel it off like papier-mâché. She gaped at what was revealed, sagging against the wall. "Oh, my God."

"What is it?" His voice was panicked—and it was coming from inside the bathroom.

"Get out!"

He didn't come closer, but he wouldn't leave. "No' until you tell me."

"My wound—it's completely healed." With a nice new scar.

"Huh. Dinna think it would heal that quick. What about your other injuries?"

She rolled her shoulders. No pain. She surveyed for bruises, found none. "They're all better."

"Then I saw you well, just as I promised. So mayhap you can start trusting me a little?"

"It's not necessarily that I don't trust you. I just don't want you to look."

"My mate's a bashful one then?" His husky words accompanied a spray of water over her breasts.

Bashful? Hardly. But God, just the way he said *my mate* had her heart speeding up again. "Are you one hundred percent sure I'm . . . yours? I mean, when you scent me, don't you just smell a run-of-the-mill human?"

"Aye, you're mortal."

It followed that she would remain so, transforming only to a certain degree—right up until her *trigger*. "Is it normal for a Lykae to have a mortal mate? Or does that mean I have Lykae somewhere in my line?"

"You doona have to be a Lykae to be mated to one. My cousin wed a witch. Our queen is a vampire."

So Lykae mates ran the gamut? Maybe she was, in fact, his. Didn't mean *he*'d be *hers*. "Any Pravus mates? Or do you kill every one of them you come across?" she said lightly.

He didn't match her tone. "I endeavor to," he said in all seriousness.

"Oh." If she was turning into one of those, would he kill her too? *Self-preservation, Chlo.* Okay, she would *not* be asking him about her symptoms. "So how often do mortals and immortals hook up?"

"No' that often. But it's no' unheard of," he quickly added.

"I understand that you feel a connection to me, but if I'm not a Lykae . . . should I be expecting some kind of compulsion to like you too?" Though she didn't feel compelled, this sudden disappearance of her customary dread puzzled her.

"Nay. I'll be winning you with my own charms."

Of which there were so very many. Hey, hadn't she promised herself if she got close to the net, she'd score?

No, bad idea! What was she thinking? She hardly knew this guy. "Is that so?"

"Oh, aye, and I *will* be winning you, my Chloe. It's no' every day that a sexy Olympian falls into my lap."

Olympian. Tonight she'd all but accepted that she had some kind of immortal blood. Were the Games beyond her reach forever? The soap slipped from her limp hand when it dawned on her how much she'd lose.

Family, a potential medal, friends.

She'd had her future planned out. She'd been making six figures, with Olympic sponsorships on the horizon. Dad was supposed to be there cheering in the front row as her team seized gold.

She cringed, recalling all that punishing training she'd endured down in Florida. Header after header until her forehead swelled. Ice numbing her joints while burning her skin. Sweat stinging her eyes. Hiding her lack of appetite from a team of women, from eagle-eyed coaches and physicians.

All for nothing.

Rub some dirt on it. Though her situation seemed grim, there was an upside. She'd thought she was going to die earlier; now she was completely healed. In fact, aside from being sleepy, she felt great physically. She'd been so wretchedly lonely before; now a Scottish god of a man couldn't seem to get close enough to her.

He'd saved her life, had fought for her against monsters.

"I'm going to fetch you a T-shirt. Doona get yourself killed while I'm away, mortal."

She almost smiled. Was he being serious or teasing her? She sensed a playfulness inside him. She supposed she'd find out soon enough.

Two seconds later, he said, "How'd we do while I was gone?"

"A few close calls."

He chuckled. "I'm getting the feeling that you might be a smart-arse. But I like it."

The water sluiced over her. His voice poured over her. How could his mere voice call to mind those wicked dreams so readily? What if she stepped out, and he kissed her with his gorgeous lips?

Don't think about the faceless man . . . don't think . . .

Too late. Her lust surged. She placed her palms against the wall, her fingers curling. Maybe he *was* the faceless male who would do delicious things to her.

"Uh, Chloe, is everything all right?" he asked, his voice rumbling.

"Of c-course!" Oh, God, he might be able to smell her! She dumped half a bottle of shampoo over her head, letting it coat her all the way down.

※※※※※※

When Will scented her arousal, his body shot tight with tension, his shaft readying for her.

She must be feeling better. And, lords, she must be a lusty one.

He inwardly groaned. *But I canna do anything about it.* Not without his beast rising. The harder he got, the more it would claw him inside, the two eternally linked. He scrubbed his palm over his face. By the time he was ready to rut, it'd be fully at the fore.

His beast was already stirring, roused by her scent. If Will lost control for a second, he could kill her.

Inhale, exhale. *Rein it in, Will.* Once he'd garnered a measure of control again, the peculiarity of this situation hit him. He was licking his chops over the daughter of a man he despised, one he longed to destroy. But without Webb, there would be no Chloe.

Will would never have received his mate.

Chloe had asked him earlier if he would hurt Webb. His eyes narrowed. If Will could take her, he would get revenge. Nothing could destroy Webb like the knowledge that his beloved daughter had been compromised by a *detrus.* Will hated to think in this vein, but there it was.

Turning off the water, Chloe reached through the steam for the towel. He lunged forward to hand it to her.

"MacRieve!" She'd already turned her back, yanking the towel to her body, quickly wrapping it around herself.

"Just being of assistance." *And copping a look at my woman.*

He'd only caught the merest glimpse of her arse: pert, generous, the kind of arse that would still be mov-

ing for a breathtaking split second after she'd stilled.
Or after it'd been spanked.

He nearly groaned at the thought. Gods, soccer
had done her right.

He'd seen just enough to render him mind-blown
and hard as rock. Which meant his beast was now
prowling within him.

No, Will hadn't been able to refashion himself after
Ruelle. He gazed at his mate. *But then, I've never had a
real reason to before now.* "Come, Chloe, are you always so
shy?" She was still standing in the shower stall.

"No, I'm not. I'm the chick who walks around
naked in the locker room."

A wolven chuff escaped his lips as he imagined
that. If he hadn't been sprung before . . . In a strangled
voice, he said, "Next you'll tell me you like to pillow-
fight in the nude."

As if he hadn't spoken, she continued, "*However*,
just because I'm not shy, that doesn't mean I'm going
to streak in front of you."

"No' yet." His lips curled. "Are you going to stay in
there all night?"

"Depends on what *your* plans are."

"Do you no' want a clean T-shirt?" He dangled it
enticingly.

Lips thinned, wary as prey, she stepped out in her
towel.

Aye, her color had returned. Her skin was tanned,
with sexy little strap lines over her shoulders. He
wanted to taste her skin. Just one fleeting taste of her.
And then I'll be good.

A drop trickled down her neck; he followed it with his eyes. She noticed, shivering in reaction. So sensitive, his mate.

Before he could stop himself, he'd swooped in and pressed his opened lips to the drop, licking it up. At her ear, he said, "You doona need a towel, no' when you have me around. I'll tend to every inch of you."

When he drew back, she was panting shallow breaths, her pupils dilated. The honeyed scent of her arousal filled his senses.

She was about to go off, and he couldn't do a damned thing about it without risking disaster.

Then she seemed to wake up. Her vivid eyes flashed with embarrassment. The smooth skin of her cheeks blushed red.

She was so fucking adorable, it hurt him. He tilted his head at her. Might his Chloe be a virgin?

A delicate, mortal virgin? He backed up a step. "You tempt me, sweet. Gods, you tempt me. But you've been injured. You need to be abed."

"And if I hadn't been injured?"

"Then *we* would be abed right now," he lied, handing her the shirt. When she raised her brows, he turned around for her to change.

But even once she'd dressed and he'd led her to his bed, she still looked a bit dazed. As he pulled down the covers and clean sheets—*bless you, brother*—she asked, "How are *you* handling this, MacRieve?"

"What do you mean?"

She crawled under the covers, flashing toned thighs. *Mercy.*

"This must be a shock to you too. You were just minding your own business, and all of a sudden—*wham!*—you've got a mate."

She was worried about how *he* was taking this? "You're what we consider Other. And I think you might be the first Other female who's ever asked how a male Lykae was taking all this."

He recalled his cousins who had non-Lykae mates. Each of those females had panicked at the mere idea. Garreth's had even shot him. "I'm handling this just fine," he said, surprised to find that was the truth.

Because you're my lifeline. He could see it so clearly now. She *was* his lucky penny, found right when he'd needed her most.

Everything was falling into place. His Instinct had returned. There was hope.

But if Chloe was his cure, Nïx was the cause. At the auction, he'd recognized what the Valkyrie had done for him. Now he realized what she'd done *for Chloe.*

If not for Nïx, centaurs would be raping Chloe right now. And they would use their own healers on her so they could do it again and again. At the thought, bile rose in his throat.

Once they'd captured Webb, they might've allowed her to die.

A gust of breath left him. *Nïx, you beautiful bitch.*

He wanted to grab that Valkyrie and kiss her, then ask her why she couldn't have just texted him to be there.

No matter; he'd have gone through that torture a thousand times over to spare Chloe a fate like that.

"MacRieve, I appreciate all you've done for me. You saved my life."

And you saved mine. He couldn't wait to tear up his plane ticket. As he gazed down at her lovely face, he felt shamed to have bought it.

"But if I stay here, I could be bringing these Pravus creatures down on your head. What about the other people who live here?"

Worried for them? He couldn't believe he'd feared this girl would be like her father.

She deserved better than Will, someone not so jaded, someone who could make love to her. Someone . . . mortal. *Fit for no one.* He had the passing thought that he should let her go.

Yet who could protect her more fiercely than Will?

Not a damn soul. "Shh, Chloe. My clan is ready for anything. You're safe here. Now my wee mortal needs sleep to finish healing."

He tucked her in, about to howl from the rightness of seeing her in his bed. *Hell no, I'll no' give her up.* Finally, a relationship he could be proud of.

"Sleep, lass. Heal. We'll work all this out tomorrow." He leaned in to gently press his lips to hers, and she let him, even sighing.

His first kiss in centuries. In Gaelic, he told her, "Our last first kiss."

Her lids slid shut, and her breaths deepened. Just before she slipped into sleep, she murmured, "I could get used to you."

FIFTEEN

When Chloe woke, she found MacRieve seated in a chair beside the bed, elbows on his knees.

Staring at her.

"Been waiting for you to wake. You always sleep this much?" He flashed her that grin. He looked rested and was clean-shaven, dressed in another pair of jeans, a black long-sleeve T-shirt that hugged his chest muscles, and expensive-looking hiking boots.

In other words, he was even more gorgeous than he'd been last night.

She sat up, ran her fingers through her hair, discovered a tangled mess. "How long was I out?" With a start, she noticed how hard her nipples were beneath the white T-shirt, and raised the sheet to conceal them.

She'd been engulfed by those wicked dreams. Only now the man had a face—MacRieve's. In those scenes, she'd explored what might've happened if she'd let him take off that towel and bare her body. If she'd let him lick the water from her skin . . .

Think of something else, or he'll know!

"You were out all morning. Still as death."

"And you've just been sitting there, watching me? That's not creepy at all."

"What else would I do?" he asked in genuine puzzlement. "Of course, you had me pacing whenever your dreams changed." He stood and did so now. "It was everything I could do no' to fall upon you in that bed."

She swallowed. "How did you know what I was dreaming?"

"Your heart rate and breaths."

She raised her chin. "Could've been a nightmare."

He stopped to face her, his lids gone heavy. "And your scent."

Her cheeks burned with embarrassment. "I need to get dressed. Can I borrow some more clothes?"

"We canvassed the clan for some. I've put everything in that wardrobe." He pointed to an immense oak piece that she didn't remember seeing last night. "Just until I can buy you new, naturally."

Buy her new? "MacRieve, I appreciate your . . . hospitality, but I can't stay here any longer."

He gazed at her with a half grin, as if she were jesting.

"I'm dead serious. What if my dad shows up here? You'd kill him. I'm not going to sit here and act as bait."

"Is that your only objection?"

"I have things I need to do," she said. "A life of my own. And I don't want to endanger anyone else."

"You should get dressed, so I can show you something."

"What?"

"The obstacles to you leaving."

At the side of the bed, she hesitated. He seemed to be waiting keenly for a view of her legs, eyes locked on that edge of the comforter.

"Um, privacy?"

He snapped his head up. "You want that?" At her exasperated look, he sighed. "Aye, then. Privacy. From *me*." He crossed to her and pressed a kiss to her head, inhaling the scent of her hair. "You're adorable, you ken that? Meet me in the kitchen for breakfast."

Once he was gone, the room seemed bigger. And more . . . boring.

Dimmer.

If she wasn't careful, she could grow smitten with him. Which was a bad idea on so many levels. First, he and her father would kill each other on sight. Second, he was a Lorean. And third, she didn't know *what* she was.

She scuffed to the wardrobe, found expensive garments, many of them clearly never worn. There were several pairs of shoes and some toiletries as well.

Lacy underwear with the tags still on filled a silk-lined drawer. A far cry from her sports bras and Under Armour panties.

Wait. *He* had been the one to fill the wardrobe? The thought of him handling panties he intended for her made Chloe's face flush. With embarrassment? Or that weird awakening . . . ?

After showering again and brushing her teeth, she dragged on a pair of jeans that fitted a bit too tightly over her ass and a peasant blouse that showed more cleavage than she was accustomed to. Slip-on sandals rounded out the ensemble.

In front of the mirror, she ran her fingers through her wet hair—the closest she ever came to styling it— and appraised her appearance.

The outfit looked classy but much more feminine than her usual apparel. For most of the year, she wore cleats, soccer shorts, and workout tees.

An outfit like this seemed to demand makeup, which she couldn't be bothered with. In concession, she pinched her cheeks, testing a smile.

Though she deemed herself *cute*, just as MacRieve had called her last night, he was in the league of leggy supermodels who would live forever with him. Yet this male couldn't seem to take his eyes off *Chloe*, a.k.a. Baby T-Rex, a runtling soccer player with no feminine wiles.

She knew what his tie to her was: he was compelled by his instinct to want her. Was MacRieve's marked interest in her fueling Chloe's own infatuation?

When she descended the stairs and entered the kitchen, his face lit up, as if she were a beauty queen modeling an evening gown.

"What do you like to eat?"

Before her recent decline in appetite, she'd been a big eater. She opened her mouth to list all her favorite training foods, only to remember there might never be training again. If she didn't make it to Madrid in time . . . if her immortality was triggered . . .

MacRieve had pronounced her human the night before. The question was, how to stay that way? Was it possible to find her dad and learn what her trigger was before the Games?

"I'll just take a cup of coffee," she muttered, though she rarely drank caffeinated drinks. Her voice had wavered, so she jutted her chin.

"Hey, hey, lass. Come here. What troubles you?"

When he reached for her and she realized how very badly she wanted to be enfolded in those arms, she made herself back up a step.

At that moment, two younger guys entered the kitchen.

"This is Rónan and Benneit," MacRieve said. "They live here. Lads, this is Chloe."

Ben was even taller than MacRieve, duck-under-the-doorway tall. He was also handsome, with thick black hair that hung over one eye. His face heated as he gave her a wave, and she realized he was really shy.

The younger one, a cute rangy blond, had no such problem. "So what're we having for breakfast, sweetling?"

She hated it when people assumed she could cook just because she had a vagina. "Whatever your happy ass makes—for yourself."

Ben cracked a grin. Rónan cast her a measuring glance.

MacRieve laughed. "Ah, lass, you're going to do just fine here."

"What'd I miss?" asked another male from the doorway.

Chloe blinked. And again. "You didn't tell me you had an identical twin." An excruciatingly handsome one.

"I'm Munro, and I'm pleased to have you here, Chloe." He seemed like he was about to say more, only to stop himself.

"Thank you, Munro." She realized she was still staring, and blushed. "Wow, you really do look alike." When he stood next to MacRieve, she could tell they weren't quite identical. MacRieve looked a little more . . . worn, his hair longer. She also noticed that neither of them had laugh lines.

Rónan said, "Female Loreans call them Hot and Hotter. I doona see it."

I'll bet they do. A flare of jealousy took her by surprise. For most of her life, she hadn't been interested in men, much less jealous over them.

MacRieve quipped something in Gaelic, making his brother grin, then handed her a mug. "Come on, I've much to show you." When he squired her through a set of french doors, the afternoon sun illuminated his face.

His eyes were the color of a gold medal struck by sunlight. She told herself it was the zing of caffeine that caused her head to rush—not the sight of his brilliant gaze. He was jaw-droppingly fine, and apparently he got told that all the time. Having had fanboys, she'd sworn never to be a fangirl. She wouldn't start now.

She dragged her gaze away, making a study of the outside of his home. The lodge was constructed of brick, with exposed wood beams. The arched roof was covered in slate tiles. "It's beautiful." After growing up in a house that looked exactly like every other McMansion in the neighborhood, she'd always wanted to live in a home with character, something unique.

When MacRieve smiled, her skin grew flushed. She didn't like the effect he had on her or how quickly all this was moving. He kept her off balance, like she was running with a cleat on one foot and a climbing boot on the other.

She groped for something to talk about. "So if you and Munro are twins, how does the whole alpha thing work?"

"The wolf that created our line was an alpha, so most Lykae males have alpha tendencies, just waiting to come out. In my and Munro's case, his beast is cut from the same soul as mine, so we're definitely both alphas. Let's just put it this way—we brawl. A lot." He steered her onto another path.

"Where are we headed?"

"The main house of the compound."

She rolled her eyes. "Of course I'm at a *compound*. Great. If I see any fourteen-year-olds, should I congratulate them on their nuptials?"

"No' that kind of compound. You'll enjoy it here. It's like a big team. And this property is like a locker room."

"You expect me to sign on?"

"Our facilities are top-notch, and we're *all* starters."

"I need to get back to the team I've already joined. I have a life of my own." And questions that had to be answered. Not just about her father.

Now that she'd confirmed immortals existed, she

kept wondering what species her mom could've been, and what her ultimate fate was. Dad had told Chloe that Mom had no relations. What if that statement was as false as the terminal cancer lie?

"What do you have to get back to?" MacRieve asked. "Your season's over with your team, is it no'? Your father is no longer there. Is this about the Olympics? They're no' out of reach, Chloe. I will move heaven and earth to get you there."

Part of her wanted so badly to confide in him about her symptoms. Again that sense of self-preservation held her tongue. "I don't want to talk about it."

"Ach, you should know that a Lykae's curiosity is a powerful thing." He said this like it was an understatement. Suddenly, his gaze narrowed. "Do you have a lover back there, then?" His tone was nonchalant, but his eyes were blazing blue. "Some bloke in Seattle?"

"I'm one hundred percent committed to sports." In the past, she'd tried to convince herself that she hadn't dated because of training demands. But other players had managed to balance a love life and a career. She'd heard the locker room talk. "I haven't had time for dating." Or for the dread that inevitably accompanied it.

Her answer appeared to delight him. She could perceive him relaxing.

In fact, she was very in tune with him, her senses seemingly heightened by him. She was abundantly *aware* of him at every second. Merely walking beside him, she could feel the heat radiating from his skin.

What if she did fall for a werewolf like MacRieve? Dad would hate her. He might already.

No, she refused to believe that.

"Here's the main house," MacRieve said, gesturing toward what looked like a millionaire's hunting lodge, decorated by a manly man. "We call it the den. It's well-loved, lots of claw marks. And a Valkyrie threw a car on the roof no' too long ago."

"They're *that* strong?" So cool! Maybe Fiore was a Valkyrie?

"Aye. But that's a drop in the bucket compared to a Lykae's strength." He opened a heavy wooden door for her, taking her hand to lead her inside.

His was hot and rough against her own, yet the contact was electric; Chloe shivered, and stared in puzzlement at the spot where their skin touched. He too seemed affected, his brows drawing together.

This *was* some kind of connection—the kind she'd read about in books, the kind she'd decided was just a stupid myth.

Apparently all myths were real.

With his brogue thicker than she'd ever heard it, he said, "Ah, Chloe, lass, I just need tae . . ." He leaned in, looking for all the world like he was about to kiss her.

She found herself captivated by the prospect. *Awakening!* She'd had far too few kisses in her life.

But then she heard the murmur of conversation from a nearby room. Would someone come upon her and MacRieve? "Y-you said something about obstacles?" Her voice was as breathy as a porn star's.

Looking suddenly troubled, he straightened. "Aye, then. This way to our security area." They headed into a dimmed room.

There was a giant computer screen, like a movie backdrop, with dozens of camera feeds stacked and labeled: WALL 1, WALL 2, WALL 3 . . . all the way to WALL 50.

One Lykae manned the desk.

"Here's Madadh, our Master of the Watch. Madadh, this is my mate, Chloe."

The colossal man stood, towering over her, as tall as MacRieve with bulkier muscles. He had a straight scar that ran through his eyebrow and down his face, making him look dangerous. He seemed to be simmering with aggression. But his expression was neutral.

"Pretty big wall you've got here," she said.

"Aye. It surrounds hundreds of acres." With a polite nod, Madadh said, "I'll leave you to it, MacRieve."

Once he'd exited the room, she got a better look at the feeds, and her jaw slackened. Nightmare creatures teemed outside the fence, hundreds of them, with more arriving in droves.

All here for me?

SIXTEEN

Chloe hadn't taken her eyes off the screens; Will hadn't taken his eyes off her.

Ach, she was a bonny thing. Now that her hair was drying, it curled into fetching disarray, glossy little spikes framing her pixie features. Her changeable eyes gleamed with intelligence.

Bonny *and* brave. Though her heart beat with fear, you couldn't tell by her stoic demeanor.

"This is what you saved me from?" she asked with hardly a tremor in her voice. "What I would've seen last night? I'm glad of the bag now. Can those things breach the wall?"

"No' many have the stones to invade a Lykae stronghold when we're all a hair-trigger away from turning. We protect our own, lass. Understand me, I will slaughter anyone who gets near you."

"You must have a secret way out."

Why was she so sodding eager to go? Females

usually tripped all over themselves to get near him. Why was this one not bonding to him? "You canna leave. Chloe, as I said, these creatures will no' kill you at first. You would no' be so fortunate as that."

She bit her bottom lip. "I can hide . . ." She trailed off when he shook his head.

"You lost a lot of blood at the crossroads last night. They can use it to track you. I vow to the Lore that they would find you within minutes, and that they would torture and abuse you." By the way she gazed at his eyes, he knew they'd flickered blue. "I canna let you be hurt."

"How long will this siege last?"

"Likely until your father is found."

"Why can't they track him?"

"No blood. And he's probably camouflaging his location with mystical means anyway. He uses aspects of the Lore when it suits him." For decades, Will's former prison had been concealed through magic; the other prisons still were. The Order's torques were mystically reinforced and empowered. Webb had even used a soothsayer's help, though Nïx had clearly been furthering her own ends.

"Maybe I can get some mystical means?"

"So desperate to leave?" His face tightened. "You could purchase a concealment talisman from the witches for hundreds of thousands of dollars—oh, wait, they're the ones who kidnapped and sold you!"

Her lips thinned. "If my dad showed up here, what would happen to him? MacRieve, I can't let him be hurt. My mom died when I was a baby, and he was all I had. He's been a great dad, kind and supportive. My biggest complaint is that he always travels way too much."

"And guess what he's been doing on those trips," he said, hating the stricken look on her face, hating that he'd caused it.

In a softer tone, she asked, "What did my father do to you?"

Will avoided her eyes. "I canna speak of it. No' yet."

He could tell she wanted to press, but to her credit, she didn't. "You'll tell me when you're ready, I guess."

"In any case, you're safest here."

She started to pace. "So here I'll be staying?"

"Could you sound more put out? It's no' so bad here. *I* am no' so bad. Why are you so averse to me? I know you're attracted to me." Mayhap that was the way to get her to bond—by using her lust against her. Lykae were notoriously brutal warriors, but they could also be sly tricksters, able to coax and maneuver their prey as expertly as they could seize it.

She straightened. "You can't know that."

"I scented you in the shower last night. And then there's the matter of your dreams. Mayhap they included me?"

Her blush said *bingo*. Satisfaction filled him.

She pursed her lips. "Attraction is involuntary. But if I had control over it, I wouldn't be attracted to you."

"Why no'?" he asked, his mood gone surly just like that.

"I don't have time. I need to find my dad, Mac-

Rieve. We left things unsaid between us. Not to mention that you want to murder him. Plus, if you must know, I'm due at Olympic training camp in Europe in less than two weeks."

That soon? Still, he was determined to get her there. He'd figure it out later. For now, he needed some kind of bond with her to soothe this feral restlessness he felt. While he'd been running headlong toward her, she'd been looking for the exit. "I will no' speak of any of this today."

"Why?"

"Today is my day to convince you to accept me as yours. You will give it to me." When he moved in even closer, she backed up until her arse met the desk.

Before she could say a word, he'd lifted her on top of it, easing his hips between her knees. He caught a peek down her blouse, was thrilled to spy the black bra he'd put in the wardrobe last night, the one he'd imagined molded over her plump breasts.

She moistened her lips, her breaths shallowing, her body already trembling with lust.

The way to bind her to him was obviously through sex; sex was impossible. *Gods, I wish I was . . . right.*

But then, he didn't have to take *them* all the way, just *her.* All he had to do was give Chloe a mind-scrambling orgasm while keeping his beast in check.

Two problems. That bastard might slip the leash. And Will had never set out to pleasure a female.

For all these centuries, his beast hadn't strayed from perfunctory sex in one animalistic position. It got a release, the nymph made her conquest, all was well.

Will hadn't heard any complaints. Of course, he hadn't exactly stuck around afterward.

Kissing, oral sex, foreplay, these things were foreign to him.

I'll figure it the hell out.

When he imagined delving his tongue between Chloe's thighs, he shot hard as steel, and his beast stirred. He gritted his teeth, struggling to keep it caged.

Chloe tilted her head. "And why would I give you this day?"

"We're going to make a wager, you and I. At the end of today, if you still want to leave me, I'll try to get you a concealment talisman from the witches."

"Truly?"

"Aye." He was such a twatting liar. But his ploy was working. She'd begun to relax—because she thought she was heading out tomorrow on her doomed quest to find her father.

At least she was loyal. Along with touch, sex, and food, Lykae revered loyalty. "If you give me a *sporting* chance to win you over, and I fail, then I'll help you leave."

Her gaze was on his lips when she murmured, "What would one day hurt?" Then she blinked up at him as if her own words had shocked her.

"Verra well." This close, he could see her long lashes were tipped with the tiniest fringe of blond. "We start now."

"Do one of those vows to the Lore first."

He froze. How to word this? "If you truly give yourself up to this day, enjoying everything I have to give you"—*orgasms*—"and still want to leave, I will help you"—*for a total of two minutes before tossing you over my shoulder and dragging you back.*

Having played soccer all her life, Chloe could recognize when another player was aiming to score. MacRieve planned on luring her to stay with sex! And it might work!

No, no, no.

Yes. Yes. Yes. She'd promised herself. And who better to lose her virginity with than a male like this? She could only imagine how experienced an immortal would be. She'd keep her heart closed off, sate some of these pressing urges, then be on her way tomorrow. "Okay, you have a deal."

"Good." He backed up, allowing her to hop off the desk. "I've something else to show you. My favorite spot on the entire property." Well, his mood had certainly improved. His grin was about the sexiest thing she'd ever seen.

At the front entrance, when he opened the door for her, she said, "Why are your nails black?" She'd noticed last night.

"They're claws."

When he briefly flared them, she swallowed. "Any other anatomical differences between you and a standard-issue human?"

He bit his full bottom lip. "Aye, there's a major one. It's definitely something you've never seen before."

"Oh, God, what?"

"Better if I just show you." With a grave look, he started on the top button of his jeans.

Right when she was about to scream/faint/smile with delight, she realized he was janking her.

"MacRieve!" She swatted his hip, and he chuckled.

Now he was going to have a sense of humor on top of everything else?

"No other anatomical differences. Though you might term what you'll find in my jeans *superhuman*."

She knew he had to be kidding, but now he'd gotten her *thinking* about it.

They started down a new path. "As per the terms of our deal," he continued, "you're to give yourself up to this for a day, which means you should act like my mate."

"What do mates do?"

"Hold my hand." He took hers in his. "Look up at me adoringly."

So not a problem.

Though they'd barely passed anyone earlier, now more people were out. He'd initially tried to avoid them, but then MacRieve seemed to get caught up, introducing her as his mate with his shoulders back and his chin lifted.

His cockiness was breathtaking.

Everyone she met was kind to her, seeming just like regular folks. Well, except for the fact that they were uniformly good-looking. The women all looked the same age, and possessed an earthy type of sensuality. The males? She'd yet to see one that her team wouldn't catcall from their bus.

They must be braver than normal as well. If any of them were freaked out by an immortal army gathering outside their gate, they didn't show it.

After a while Chloe got used to MacRieve calling her *his*. She might even have liked it. What girl could resist the look of utter pride in his eyes?

She realized she was feeling excitement—and optimism—for the first time since this nightmare had begun. Her loneliness had ebbed until it had all but disappeared. She was in no immediate danger, she was uninjured, and her weeks-long dejection over her transition was lifting.

At least there were *some* high points to the Lore. Sexy Highlander high points . . .

When he squeezed her hand unexpectedly, she found herself grinning up at him. And he was already grinning down at her, like they were conspirators who'd pulled off some coup.

After they met yet another couple who gushed about how happy they were that she'd arrived, Chloe asked, "Why are they so friendly to me? You'd think they'd hate me like all the others out there."

He began leading her toward a forest of cypresses, oaks, and pines. "You're now a part of this pack. This is your clan too, Chloe. And anyone here would protect you with his or her life."

"My clan? So I'm already part of the team?"

"Oh, aye, we're always recruiting playmakers." Though clouds were rolling in, he didn't head back toward the lodge, just continued into the woods. "So how did you get started playing soccer?"

"I saw an Olympic match when I was five. After that, the game was all I could think about. When I was in college, I majored in soccer first." Yes, she'd earned her degree, but only by the skin of her teeth. "Do you have a career?" Her eyes widened. "I didn't even think to ask if you would miss work because of all this!"

That clearly amused him. "No nine-to-five for me, lass. I'm head of the Nova Scotia branch of the clan, and I serve my king however he needs me. But mainly, I'm a soldier. There have been no wars in some time, so I guess you could say I've been waiting for a new season to start."

"Have you been in a lot of wars?"

"Oh, aye. I used to search them out, especially against vampires. They're our natural enemies. But I will no longer seek out conflict."

"No?"

"I've got a mate now. That changes everything."

She stopped. "You seem very confident about winning me over today. What if I resist those charms of yours?"

He curled his finger under her chin. "If you're feeling a fraction of what I'm feeling, then your pretty arse is *mine*." His eyes narrowed with intent. With possessiveness.

She swallowed. Still no dread? Just anticipation. For the first time, she allowed herself to entertain a startling thought: what if she and MacRieve *were* fated?

What if she'd dreaded being with another—because she'd been waiting for this Lykae to come into her life?

Taking her hand back in his, he started deeper into the woods. When they reached a river, he said, "Almost there. It's just past the opposite bank."

She gazed around for a bridge—

He pulled her into his arms, and leapt over the water.

In midair, she screeched, *"What are you doing?"*

When he landed, as easily as if he'd hopped from one step to the next instead of twenty feet across the water, he kept his arm under her ass, their faces close. "Ach, even your freckles are sexy."

Her heart skipped a beat.

After long moments, he released her. "We're here."

She turned away from him to get her bearings— and found an idyllic scene. In a clearing, a smaller rivulet wound through swaying grasses. Atop a slight rise to her left, a majestic tree rained white blossoms over a field of clover. The sky above was opaque. A warm drizzle had just begun to fall.

"We call this place the glade. Decades ago, when the Lykae first settled here, that tree was planted from seed. It's a sera cherry tree, from a different realm. They live for thousands of years."

"There are truly other realms?"

He nodded. "Most of the time, they're just cubbyholes in our landscape. You reach them through portals."

How much she could learn from him. Too bad she had to leave him. "It's beautiful, MacRieve. Thanks for bringing me here."

He frowned. "You never need to say thanks to me again."

"Why not?"

"Because it pleases me to do nice things for you. Makes me feel . . . good." As he cupped her elbow and started for cover, she thought she heard him mutter, "For once."

Beneath the boughs of the cherry tree, she asked, "So other than holding your hand and looking adoringly at you, what else does matehood entail?" *Any weird mating rituals?*

He brushed his knuckles over her cheek. "It means that I will protect you and provide for you. I'll give you anything you've ever wanted. I doona have a career, but I've money to spoil you. I crave to."

His words were brimming with his typical confidence. Yet she sensed an underlying . . . nervousness?

He drew in even closer, again looking like he was going to kiss her. The mere idea sent her awakening into overdrive. Her face flushed, her nipples hardening. She stared at his lips, imagining how they would feel on hers, how they'd taste. Up close, she could see the bottom one had the faintest crease in the middle. She wanted to lick it.

"You've pointed out a lot of pros," she said absently. "So what's the downside?"

SEVENTEEN

Downside? *I canna bed you, even though you dearly need me to.*

When Chloe had gone soft with desire in the security room, it'd taken every ounce of Will's self-control not to tup her on the desk. Even now the delectable scent of her arousal filled his senses.

"I've got to control myself with you. If my beast rose, I could hurt you." What would be a teeth-clattering rush for a Lorean female would be bone-crushing for Chloe. "You're verra . . . mortal."

"What would make it rise?"

"If you were in danger. Or if I bedded you. That's why I canna take you today. Even though I think you would receive me."

Her cheeks bloomed with color and her gaze darted away: *bingo.* He nearly groaned with loss. *Why can I no' be right?*

Earlier, when Chloe had said she'd been completely

committed to sports, he'd grown more convinced that she was innocent. He had wanted to howl with satisfaction that he would be the one to introduce her to lovemaking.

Then he'd reminded himself, *You doona make love. Doona even know how to.*

Now, as then, misgivings swamped him. His plan to give her release, while remaining detached and in control, seemed impossible.

"I don't understand," she said.

"If I get too excited, it surfaces. It takes me over completely."

"What's that like?"

A crutch. "I'm still there, yet everything feels altered. It's kind of like a drug. Though I'd experience pleasure and I'd remember anything that occurred between us, I would have zero control over its actions."

"Actions?"

"It'd want to take you hard, Chloe."

Her breath hitched, but she didn't glance away. In fact, he saw *interest* in her vivid gaze. That look heated his blood, hardening his cock until it throbbed, waking the beast he warned of.

Will leaned down to say at her ear, "It'd want you on your hands and knees as it fucked you from behind."

She bit her lip, almost quelling a soft whimper.

The sound made his shaft pulse. She was getting aroused by his talk? "Ah, lass, you're needful, are you no?" The wind began to comb the tree, loosing petals like snowfall.

She didn't seem to notice them. "Yes . . . needful."

He laid his hand on her cheek. It shook as he cupped her face. "You doona know how much I want to pleasure you." This was his mate, and from the scent of her, he'd find her nice and wet. But he was too screwed up to see to her?

His gaze narrowed with realization. His beast should be nigh risen now. It roared inside him; it seethed.

It remained caged.

His Instinct spoke, pinging his mind, jolting his body. . . .

—*Your female aches. Tend to her.*—

The Instinct was infallible. And it was telling him to touch Chloe. "Do you ache?"

She gazed up at him, nodding helplessly.

"What color are my eyes? Are they blue?"

She shook her head. "Flickering a little."

He knew he couldn't claim her, but mayhap it *was* possible to tend to her. "If I said I'd ease your ache, would you let me? Just that and nothing more?" He captured her hand, raising her wrist to his lips. A grazing kiss across her rapid pulse-point made her gasp. Then he used her arm to draw her closer, so he could run his lips up her neck.

She sighed, "Yes."

<hr/>

This was probably a bad idea, but at that moment, Chloe couldn't recall a single reason why. If he stopped this, she was fairly certain she'd slide-tackle him.

He didn't stop. His lips were hot on her, scorching a line up her neck.

Excitement drummed through her, her dread completely absent, her senses overloaded. She smelled the rain, the blossoms, his heady scent. How could he possibly smell so good?

When his clever tongue flicked rain from her damp skin, she wondered, *Why fight this?*

She was as eager as she'd been during her first pro soccer game. She hadn't let anything stand in her way that day, just surrendered completely to the thrill, the adrenaline, the driving need to experience everything.

She would do the same with this. *Don't be a coward. See where this path leads you.*

So far this path was making her question how she'd been living without MacRieve her entire life.

Not living. Simply existing from one game to the next.

He looped an arm around her, dragging her body tight against his, then gently took her earlobe between his teeth. Her knees went weak.

Just as she wondered if he could feel her nipples pressing against his torso, he murmured at her ear, "If this is how you react to a kiss along your neck, I wonder what will happen when I set my mouth to those pretty nipples."

She gasped, as much from his words as from the burst of lust they caused. She couldn't think. How did one answer a statement like that? Her mind cried: *With a kiss!*

He read her thoughts, kissing across her cheek, the

corner of her lips, then fully on her mouth. When she parted her lips in surprise, still so unused to all this, he took the opportunity to flick his tongue between them.

Her hands flew to his shoulders, squeezing with delight. Those muscles moved sinuously beneath her fingertips, giving her a preview of what she'd see if he removed his shirt.

With his palm tenderly cradling the entire back of her head, he eased his tongue into her mouth, carnally sweeping it against hers. When she moaned, he did it again. And again. He was teasing her to distraction.

But then he drew back, gazing down at her with a look of . . . longing?

"Why'd y-you stop?" If her sex drive had been ramping up for weeks, now it was suddenly *exploding*.

Why wasn't he making more moves? Shouldn't he be trying to feel her boobs or something? Girls in the locker room often described guys with octopus hands.

She wanted MacRieve touching her in eight places at once!

He'd told her he'd ease her ache. She preferred he do it this century. How to initiate this? She struggled for something to say. *I need to lick you.* No. *My hand would be happier in your pants.* No!

Maybe he hesitated because he was still afraid of hurting her. "I'm, uh, tougher than I look."

He swallowed audibly. "Ah, my lass, that's good to know."

My lass. In that brogue. Stifled shudder. Near orgasm.

She almost wished she'd been with other guys when she'd had the chance, so she'd know what to do in this situation. There were soccer team fan clubs, guy boosters who made the girls gifts and held parties for them. There'd been some cute ones too. "I've never done anything like this before."

He smiled that bone-melting smile. Wolfish and *pleased*. "My Chloe's a virgin?"

Her cheeks felt like they were on fire. "Yes. Which means I don't really know the rules of this game."

He grazed the backs of his fingers over her blushing face. "The only rule you need to know is that nothing is out of bounds between us. Nothing."

"Then why are you hesitating?"

"I'm savoring. I've been waiting my whole life—"

She buried her face against *his* neck, gave his skin a lick.

He bit out, "Verra well, I've savored enough." He grabbed the hem of his shirt, yanking it up and over his head to bare a glorious sight.

Wide shoulders, rock-hard pecs, a drool-worthy eight-pack. Damp, tanned skin. An ink black goody trail disappearing into his jeans.

His *bulging* jeans. She could see the outline of his thick erection stretching to his right hip.

There'd been pinups in the locker room; this guy made those physique models look like wannabes.

And he desired *her*. It was stamped on his face, in every line of his magnificent body.

Chloe knew well what it took for a man to have muscles like that, and she wanted to show him how much she appreciated this view of perfection. But she didn't know how.

Luckily, he took charge. He spread his shirt on the clover-covered hill beneath the cherry tree. "Down you go, baby." He easily swooped her up and laid her upon it.

"Can anyone see us?"

He knelt beside her. "I would scent anyone who got close. It's just us." With a pained expression, he adjusted his shaft until it pointed up, the head and a few inches emerging past the waist of his jeans.

She sucked in a breath at the sight, squeezing her thighs together. Her mind momentarily blanked to just one thought: *big, too big.*

Superhuman? Oh, yeah. The crown was broad and taut, moistened across the slit. Veins swelled just beneath that flaring head. She was desperate to see more, to touch it. To taste it.

She wanted to twirl her tongue around it like a candy cane.

"Off with this." He pulled her shirt from her, tossing it away. "I'm hankering to see those breasts of yours."

She arched her back when he reached for her bra clasp.

Once he'd bared her, he stared with such hunger that her breasts seemed to swell for him, aching for his big rough hands to cover them. At the thought, she whimpered, thrusting them out.

He bit out something in Gaelic that sounded like a curse. His shaft pulsed, more moisture beading the head. Voice hoarse, he said, "You're a vision, love."

She got the impression that he was making an effort to remember to talk to her. What did he usually do in these kinds of situations? Again, she sensed that he was nervous, as if he was trying to remember a thousand things as he went about this.

He peeled her damp jeans off her, lifting her to tug them past her ass, leaving her in black lace panties.

More staring.

"Am I . . ."—she swallowed—"am I what you were hoping for? After all this time?"

His brows were drawn tight. He had to clear his throat before he could say, "Much more than that. And my hopes were sky-fucking-high." His gaze was so fixed on her straining nipples, she could almost feel it. She wanted to ask him to lick her there, to suck on her.

"Is this, um, different from what you normally do with women?" She might've expected a shade more . . . smoothness.

"Verra different. You could say night and day." Then he tensed. "Why would you ask that? You doona like how I am with you?" So much was going on behind his closed expression, but she couldn't decipher any of it.

"You seem a little nervous."

His tension eased. "I've only one day to convince you to stay, remember?"

"That so?" She impatiently arched her back. "The game clock's ticking, MacRieve."

With a groan, he straddled his arms on either side of her waist and lowered his head. He pressed kisses over the mounds of her breasts, circling licks up to her stiff nipples.

Her breaths shallowed. This was so much better than dreams! When his tongue finally dragged over one nipple, she cried out, shivering with bliss. She laced her fingers through his hair, tugging his head closer, earning a harsh growl around a peak.

Yet when his hand slipped into her panties, she tensed. Not because she didn't want his touch—her body was screaming for it—but because this was unfamiliar to her.

"Relax, baby." He nuzzled one breast. "I will no' hurt you." He petted the hair down there. "Have you ever had a man kiss you here . . . ?"

EIGHTEEN

N o. Am I about to?" Chloe asked, her eyes flashing with excitement.

"Oh, aye," Will said, nipping at her breast. With her
head slightly raised against the hill's slope, she could
look down at him, seeing everything. "I'm goin' tae lick
you between your pretty thighs till you scream for me."

His hand shook in her tiny panties as he inched
his fingers lower. *My mate, just before me, my mouth at her
breasts.* Lower. Will could scarcely believe it. Lower.
The afternoon had taken on a dreamlike quality.

His fingers discovered plump, wet folds. Her cunny
was weeping for him. "Gods almighty, woman." He
cupped her possessively. Wetness soaked his hand,
making his cock pulse. Pre-cum gathered on the head,
drawing her heavy-lidded gaze.

As he began to fondle her, she moaned, her eyes
locked on his shaft. "Ah, lass, you're looking at my cock
like you want tae give it a suck."

Another blush answered him. She bloody did! He shuddered to imagine her reddened lips wrapped around his length.

Control! *Must keep control.* . . . For her, he could do this. In the future, they'd figure out something; for now, he just wanted to pleasure her. To have this afternoon between them. "I would dearly love tae feel that! And soon I'll let you have your fill of it. But my beast and I are dancing the razor's edge today."

"You're not getting undressed?"

Keep the beast in check. "I canna get too carried away, love." He hooked his forefingers under the sides of her panties, tugging them down . . . revealing a trim thatch of tawny curls that made his mouth water.

When he had her completely unclothed, he gazed with disbelief. Had he called her *cute?*

Try *exquisite.*

Her skin was smooth and golden, a fascinating shade against her unusual multicolored eyes and sun-streaked hair. Falling cherry blossoms kissed her flat belly, her breasts, her lips.

She sighed, "I can feel them," as her lids slid shut.

He watched in awe as slick, white petals slipped down her body. One hugged the curve of her left breast.

Her right nipple was capped with a fragile petal, white against swollen-with-need red.

But her scent called to him. He turned to the silken petals between her thighs, jaw slackening at the sight of her glistening flesh. "You could no' be lovelier, lass. The things I plan tae do tae you . . ." As he moved between her knees, he licked his lips, feeling like a slavering beast about to ravish a beauty.

The beauty said only, *"Please."*

He lowered his head and set in. With his first lick, she moaned low; he nearly ejaculated in his pants. Her taste was the most delectable he'd ever had upon his tongue. "Chloe! Gods, you're like honey tae me." Like silk dipped in honey, then drizzled upon his ready tongue.

Perfection. He lapped her up. "Been waiting forever for this."

When he rubbed his tongue over her budding little clitoris, she cried, "Oh, God! Please don't stop that."

No' a chance of it. His cock strained against the waistband of his jeans, about to rip them. The beast clawed at him. To stay present in this, Will would claw back. He spread her thighs wider, covering her clit with his mouth, rolling his tongue over it again and again.

He realized he was growling against her when she said, "What are you *doing* to me?"

He drew back. "Do you no' like it?"

"I love it!" Yet then she fretted her bottom lip. "A-are you okay? Your eyes are blue."

Looking into *her* eyes centered him, focused him. Without breaking his stare, he licked lower, delving at her honeyed entrance. To his amazement, the beast was standing down, appeased with this, as if fed a particularly toothsome treat. *In this, beast, we agree.* Against her flesh, Will said, "I'm no' going anywhere."

"Are you sure, MacRieve?"

"And miss my Chloe coming for the first time with me?"

She shyly said, "First time with anyone," and his heart thudded.

"I'll make this good for you. I swear it." He wanted to torment her with pleasure, to make her never want to leave the source of it.

She ran her fingers through his hair, watching every lick.

"Lusty little mate." He was discovering so much about her, what pushed her buttons. He'd learned that she liked his dirty talk. He'd learned that she had so much fight in her, but not when needful—and not against him. For Will, she surrendered her fire so sweetly. "You like my tongue on you, lass?"

"Yes!"

"In you?" He parted her with his thumbs and fucked her with his stiffened tongue; she melted, giving a strangled scream.

"You want more?"

"I *need* more! I *want* it. . . ." When she moaned, undulating wildly to his tongue, his cock pulsed so hard it ripped the top button of his jeans open. His zipper was no match for his length. So he shoved his pants down to his knees.

But even when his hand found his throbbing cock and began to masturbate, the beast didn't rise. Will was dripping with pre-cum, harder than he'd ever been, yet the beast was *thrumming* with delight inside him.

Will fully comprehended that he was in control. And more, he was *good* at this. She was going crazy. Her head thrashed above the edge of his shirt, her tawny locks bright against the clover.

All he had to do was feast on her as he and the beast needed to, and she would come against his mouth.

He'd been discovering much about her sexually—but also *about him*. Will could satisfy her, could even tease her. Which meant she was at his mercy.

Suddenly, he felt very powerful.

He grinned against her wet flesh. And very, very wicked.

Shivers danced all over Chloe's naked skin. She'd never felt such lust, knew she was seconds from orgasming for a man she'd only known a day.

He'd released his erection from his jeans, was stroking it. When she saw that thick length, she grew wetter in a rush, and he licked greedily, snarling against her. God, his penis was amazing, pulsing and rigid—larger than anything she'd seen on RedTube. *And it's all mine.*

He was hers. All she had to do was say yes to him.

She'd sensed he was on the precipice of that wild beast nature inside him, and it excited her. When she gazed down at his feral, predatory look, her heart beat erratically.

"No more talk of leaving," he rasped. "You need this, do you no'? You're burning inside; you ken you need me tae tend your fire." He ran his tongue along her folds with a long, slow, sensuous stroke.

"I-I can't think. Just keep doing it."

"Doing *what*?" He tongued at her opening.

She arched sharply. "L-licking me!"

"What if I want tae do this?" He gave a light suck on her clit.

"Oh my God, oh my God—"

"You want more?"

"Yes! Ah, yes. . . ."

"Then in turn, you'll give me a week tae convince you that you're mine." His brogue was so thick. "Each day I'll do this tae you."

"What?" She couldn't think, felt drugged. Each day, really? "I don't . . . you're bargaining with me?"

"Aye. And, baby, right now I hold *all* the cards." Another brief, sweet suck.

Desperate to come, she gripped his head and rocked her hips to get his mouth back on her. He growled, heaving his breaths against her dripping flesh, but he wouldn't budge.

"Surrender tae me, Chloe. We both know you want tae."

What could one week hurt? "O-okay. Seven days. And you have to do this on every one of them."

He gave a half-laugh, half-groan against her. "Consider it done." A last light suck before he pulled his mouth back. "Vow tae stay with me."

She stamped her feet with frustration. "Fine! I vow it."

When he lowered his head once more, she felt him grinning against her, a wolfish smile. Then came his sinful tongue again—and she knew she'd made the better bargain.

Yet just when she was about to tip over the edge, he grated, *"Leamsa."*.

Fearing he'd tease her again, she hastily said, "You!"

"Then tell me." He suckled her clit again, flicking his tongue at the same time. . . .

So close. She burned, she ached. Gone shameless with lust, she arched her back, cupping her breasts. As her orgasm swept her up, she cried, *"I belong to you!"*

The rapture was scorching.

Wickeder than dreams.

Addictive.

When it finally subsided, she had to push his head away, shivering as he growled, *"I taste it, baby. I fuckin' taste you."*

She lay dazed, dimly aware that she was naked in the woods with a Scottish sex god—one who still needed to come.

He rose up on his knees, jeans shoved down his flexing thighs. His big hand squeezed his engorged length as he masturbated. She'd never imagined that a guy's erection could be so delectable-looking—thick, hot, pulsating. Again came that overwhelming urge to take it in her mouth.

She gazed up from his bobbing fist to his rippling torso muscles and bulging biceps. The straining tendons in his neck protruded. His expression was agonized with the need to come—but it was still MacRieve.

"You didn't hurt me. You stayed with me."

He stroked faster, faster. "Wanted tae see you come for me." He licked his lips, groaning . . . from

She didn't understand. "Um, whichever way you prefer?"

He leaned forward, placing his hand over her neck—not squeezing, just making a cage of fingers over her throat. A cage that said, *Lie back and stay.* "I want my seed marking your soft flesh," he bit out between gritted teeth. "I want my seed on you, my *scent* on you. I want no one tae mistake who you belong tae."

At his words, she helplessly arched up to be marked by him. In his eyes, she saw *yearning*, a brows-drawn vulnerability. Whatever he needed, she was ready to give.

Her surrender? For this brief window in time, he had it. She saw his fangs growing longer, but he only looked wilder. *Savagely seductive.*

He growled, "Feel me. Take it upon your flesh."

She squirmed in anticipation.

He gave a bellow of pleasure when the first jet erupted from the crown, spurting across one breast and aching nipple. He aimed another lash to take her other breast.

She gasped, stunned by how hot his semen was. How heavily those creamy ribbons landed upon her. How she did feel *marked.*

Bucking violently at his fist, he threw his head back to roar, *"Chloe!"* On and on it continued while he yelled to the sky, his hips jerking above her. . . .

When he was finally spent, he surveyed her. She sensed a fierce masculine satisfaction in him as he said, lass should look.

She plucked green from her hair, shrugging with a smile.

Before he collapsed next to her and pulled her to his chest, she thought she'd seen his eyes misted wet.

NINETEEN

*F*ood."

With MacRieve's one word, their interlude earlier this afternoon had been sidetracked.

Before that, he'd leisurely—and proudly?—wiped her off with his shirt so she could get dressed. Then he'd lain back with a crooked arm behind his head, his demeanor all king-of-the-castle and domineering as he'd watched her body moving.

Even she might've been embarrassed to be buck naked and scrambling for clothes, but his look of utter contentment had made her want to prolong the process.

He'd all but grunted *"Leamsa"* again, and it'd sunk in that she *was* his—for at least a week.

Yet then he'd suddenly sprung up like an animal on the verge of attack. "I smell a bounty. At the den. Sizzling food, sizzling *meat.*" He'd reached for her with that wolfish grin, dragging her close. "And, gods, ass, a slap that made her breath catch for some reason.

By the time they'd reached the den, the drizzle had ended, the sun beginning to shine. Sure enough, the other members of the clan were preparing a feast, Lykae-style. In an impressive outdoor kitchen, folks were barbecuing ribs and bone-in filets the size of soccer balls.

"It's a celebration to welcome you to the clan," MacRieve had told her.

So she'd showered and changed into a clean blouse, a skirt, and heels, dressing up a little, making an effort to show her appreciation. Skirts and heels, for the record, sucked.

Once she and MacRieve had returned to the group, she'd gotten the impression that the festivity was also the Lykae's way of thumbing their noses at the creatures besieging the compound. Things had still been howling, hissing, and stomping outside the wall. . . .

Chloe's offers to help with preparation had all been declined. The clan members only wanted her to relax, enjoy, and eat. Over the course of the meal, she'd at least managed the first two.

As soon as they'd finished, MacRieve dragged her into his lap, in front of everyone at the long banquet table. No one blinked an eye.

She'd noticed that all mated couples were constantly in contact, touching each other, feeding each other. According to the *Book of Lore*, Lykae needed—really needed—to touch.

"I could barely coax you to eat anything," Mac-Rieve told her, adding in a murmur, "An arse like yours does no' maintain itself, Chloe."

He seemed obsessed with her ass. Actually, with all parts of her. Under the cherry tree, he'd kissed across her nose, across her freckles, telling her, *"I'll count every one. . . ."*

"I think I've filled up on barley and hops," she answered. When she'd admitted earlier that she'd never drunk alcohol, MacRieve had been aghast.

"No' even a taste?" he'd said. "That's criminal, lass." While almost all of the adults drank whiskey, MacRieve had provided beer for himself and her.

She'd looked at the label. "Voodoo Beer?"

"In honor of Loa and Boa for chasing away death."

"That was a big snake, wasn't it?"

"It was a seriously large snake. . . ."

Despite her lack of appetite, the dinner had been truly enjoyable. Everyone in the clan had proved welcoming and funny. There was no way Chloe would sit back and accept that these warmhearted people were all evil and needed to be destroyed by any *Order*.

"I canna get you to eat more?" MacRieve asked, concern in his expression.

"I'm good." To change the subject, she said, "So how many times did I breach Lykae etiquette?" She'd learned that couples were expected to share one big trencher. She'd been looking for her own plate, earning a grin from MacRieve.

her ear, he said, "You pleasured me thoroughly. Then all through dinner, you looked at me with adoration."

She tapped her chin. "Funny, I was going to say the exact same thing about you."

He gave a laugh. She suddenly sensed all eyes on them. Sitting in his lap didn't earn a raised brow, but MacRieve laughing did?

He leaned in again to say at her ear, "I like your fire, lass. I like that you surrender it for me to tend to when you're needful. And *only* then. You were heaven-sent for me." He nipped her earlobe, and she sucked in a breath. "All that beautiful fight becomes mine."

Some of the males rose from the table then, making noise about a rugby rematch. MacRieve tensed, but didn't join them.

When a couple of the men said things in Gaelic, their tones taunting, she asked, "Are they trash-talking you?"

"Oh, aye. According to them, I'm the veriest pussy. Already mate-whipped."

"You need to go lower the boom on them. *Now.*"

He laughed again. "Fierce wee creature. You'll have me in brawls for eternity."

He clearly didn't want to leave her side, but she was feeling a little overwhelmed by everything. Had she really promised seven days of her life to this man? Worst decision ever? *Best* decision? She wouldn't mind some space to sort through the day.

Besides, she wanted to see if he had any moves.

He transferred her from his lap back to the bench, then shot to his feet. "Prepare to be awed."

Because he'd done it to her, she slapped his ass. He flashed her a smoldering look over his shoulder, his eyes saying, *You're going to pay for that.*

As he loped off to the field, he pulled his shirt over his head; he was on the skins team—hallelujah for that. His brother Munro was on the same team—double hallelujah.

Two muscular, manly specimens, exuding strength and vitality.

One of the females in the clan, a tall beauty named Cassandra, snapped her fingers in front of Chloe's star-struck eyes. With a smile, she said, "You've got a little something here"—she patted the back of her hand against her own mouth—"mayhap drool? Munro and MacRieve have that effect on females."

"They get that reaction all the time?" *Hot and Hotter.* She pictured MacRieve kissing some supernaturally beautiful Lorean, and her fists clenched.

"Oh, aye. They have since they were just boys." She bit her lip, as if she'd said something she shouldn't have.

"Why is MacRieve called by his last name?"

"He's the chieftain of the Nova Scotian Lykae, so it's a title. He's considered the MacRieve there. Plus, Sassenach have been slaughtering his given name for centuries." She spelled it for Chloe. "I suppose it got old. Only his twin calls him Will. For the rest of us, it's MacRieve."

Cassandra said, "You just enjoy the show."

The game started with a barn burner of a drive. Chloe had never really paid attention to rugby—if a particular sport had no women's league, then she wasn't much of a fan. Yet after a few plays, she noted similarities to both soccer and football.

All of the males were fast, but MacRieve's speed down the field was blistering. A good thing. Considering the way these men tackled, she would've been doing anything possible not to get caught with the ball.

His chest sheening with sweat, his eyes focused, he and Munro passed the ball back and forth, eluding defenders, seeming to know exactly where the other brother would be.

A twin thing? Or just lots of practice?

Oh, yeah, did MacRieve have moves on the field. *And off it.* Whenever she recalled what he'd done to her, her face would flush scarlet.

He was so domineering. And a dirty talker. Apparently, she liked both. A lot.

He'd said that she'd surrendered to him, and she supposed she had. But in her mind, sex was a new sport she'd never played, while he was a seasoned pro. Of course she was going to let him take the lead, submitting to what he wanted, because sex was his home turf.

Was it any wonder she'd promised to stay with him? Yet even though she'd been under duress, how could she have just blown off trying to leave this compound, to find her dad?

ing—or how to get past a freaking siege. But she played offense. *So what gives?*

Was some dark part of her convinced she'd already forfeited the Games by having an immortal mother? Was some darker part of her relieved?

If she was triggered and became immortal, then this worry would be gone. She'd have more strength to defend herself from all the Loreans that wanted to abduct and torture her. She'd never get sick or die.

And she'd get to be with MacRieve.

The more she liked him, the more out of touch she felt. Her old existence was slipping away. Her dreams, her goals, her training—all gone. Yet when she was with him, she didn't feel the pang of loss.

Shouldn't she? Maybe she didn't because she'd suspected for weeks that her life as she'd known it was over?

You're not human.

Instead of devastation, at that moment, she experienced a sense of foreboding, like the other shoe was about to drop. It couldn't possibly be worse than the one that had already penalty-kicked the shit out of her life. Between the enemies at the gate and not knowing what was happening with her own body, how could she *not* feel foreboding?

Rónan slid into the seat next to hers, patting his belly. "Okay, lass, I've decided to forgive you for no' cooking breakfast. Just so long as it never happens again."

"Lucky me." Since she'd probably be this kid's

get to know him. He looked about fifteen, so she said, "You're nineteen, right?"

Shoulders back, he said, "Just turned fifteen. But I get that all the time."

She checked a grin. "So what grade are you in?"

"We doona have *grades*." He rolled his clear gray eyes. "Doona go to human school. We learn from parents, then we pick up everything we need."

"Pick up?"

"Lykae spot details others can't see, and then our curiosity drives us to investigate them. Our superior intellects mean we retain most of what we learn."

This kid had attitude. But then, Chloe had always liked attitude.

He popped a new beer for her—because she'd finished hers.

"Thanks. Why have I never discovered beer before?" Then she frowned to see a bottle in Rónan's underage paw. "They let you drink?"

"It's no' like I'm a lightweight human who canna handle my liquor."

"Ooh, *burn*." To be fair, she was already buzzed.

He chuckled, and she joined him—until a particularly high-pitched shriek sounded from over the wall.

"It doesn't freak you out that those things are out there?" she said.

"You've never seen a turned Lykae. There's a reason those creatures have no' braved an attack."

So she kept hearing. Which made her wonder how terrifying a turned Lykae truly was.

bow to his opponents. He ran his arm over his fore-head, and all the sweat-slicked muscles in his torso contracted. His body was even larger from exertion, his corded thighs pressing against the legs of his jeans.

When *un*turned, MacRieve was hotter than flames. As if he sensed her eyes were glued to him, he turned to wink at her. She resisted the urge to fan her face. Casting about for a subject, she said to Rónan, "This must be a fun place to grow up." Underage drinking and no school.

"I guess. I'm new here. For the most part, Glenrial is the dreck dump."

"The what?"

"Our clan originates from Kinevane, Scotland. And then we have an official colony in Nova Scotia called Bheinnrose. The twins founded it, carving that place from scratch in the wilds up there. But here? This is where the fuckups come, the ones who doona fit in elsewhere."

"Like who?"

"Our prince, Garreth—a.k.a. the Dark Prince—lived here before he met his mate. And see Cassandra over there?" He subtly pointed with his beer. "She's in love with our king, but Lachlain's happily mated, so she's taking a hiatus from Kinevane. And Madadh? They call him Mad Dog, 'cause once he loses his temper, he nigh goes insane."

Though she'd met Madadh in the security area, she gazed at the man anew. That scar on his face made him

Since he was a Lykae, that just meant he looked like a dangerous, *hot* thug. Still, she never, ever wanted to see him lose his temper.

She asked Rónan, "So why are you here then?"

"Ben and I are orphans. It's no' exactly common to lose immortal parents at our age, so no one knows what to do with us."

"What happened?"

"Ghoul attack. Fuckers got two members of our family."

"I'm so sorry, Rónan."

Plainly uncomfortable, he nodded toward Mac-Rieve. "The twins were orphaned too. They lost their folks at thirteen."

Oh, God, that must've been awful. "How did their parents die?"

"Their mother was killed by a vampire." No wonder MacRieve hated vampires so much. "Their da followed."

"Followed?"

"Most Lykae males will no' live on without their mates. Let's put it to you this way: only our mother and sister died in the ghoul attack. Our da offed himself directly."

For a place full of immortality, the Lore seemed to be rife with loss.

What if Chloe was never triggered? Would Mac-Rieve end himself when she finished her mortal life?

She'd agreed to his week, but now she vacillated.

don't fit in, then why are the twins here? They were gorgeous and powerful. "Shouldn't they be in Nova Scotia?"

Nymphs. Chloe remembered reading about that species. They were preternaturally stunning, with a driving need to give and receive sexual pleasure.

She saw red at the thought of MacRieve having sex with one of those creatures—no, not *one*. Evidently he'd gone through an entire Canuck population of them.

She gazed over at him. MacRieve was barefooted, shirtless, magnificent, laughing at something Munro had said.

No more nymphs for him. That's my *man.*

As soon as the thought arose, her breath left her. In the past, whenever she'd made a snap determination— *that's my sport, my school, my team*—she'd never wavered.

Was MacRieve hers as well? No, no, the intensity of the situation was getting to her. That was all. She downed her beer, muffling a burp.

Another bottle slid in front of her. She glanced at Rónan, who gave her an innocent look. "So you're really going to play in the Olympics?"

MacRieve kept bragging to everyone that she was an Olympian, crushing her a little inside. "I was chosen to represent the U.S.," she said, and took another chug of beer. Maybe with MacRieve's help, it would still be doable.

Could she reveal her transition to him? After the day she'd had, she was so tempted.

A chorus of yells on the field interrupted her thoughts. "Why aren't you playing?" she asked Rónan. Though she relished watching MacRieve, on the whole, spectating with no chance of playing blew goats. She felt like she'd been benched, riding the pine like second string.

"Canna play with adults. They'd steamroll me. No' until I'm an immortal and can regenerate."

"How does that work?"

"When I reach the age where I'm strongest, I'll freeze there and never grow older. Usually happens in our thirties."

"When did MacRieve do his freeze?"

"Nine centuries ago."

She choked on her beer. "Nine *hundred* years." How could a freaking crypt keeper look that hot?

"Roughly." His gazed darted. "Head Case dinna tell you? He'll whip my arse for this."

"I won't tell him. Well, not if you tell me why you call him Head Case."

He picked at the label on his beer. "Uh, he was no' doing so well after he got back from the prison."

"What happened to him there?"

Rónan leaned in, whispering, "The Order tortured him for weeks. He came home all kinds of wrong."

She gazed up to see MacRieve running the field, happily tackling another player. That proud male had been tortured by her father's henchmen. And some-

MacRieve caught her gaze just then, gave her a sexy lift of his chin, as if just checking on her. She raised her bottle toward him, and he grinned.

As soon as he turned away, she told Rónan, "Spill. Everything you know."

"Shite, Chloe, I canna."

"Start talking or I do. To MacRieve."

Churlish, Rónan said, "They vivisected him, okay? Took out his organs while he was forced to watch."

Nausea roiled. No wonder MacRieve couldn't talk about it. He'd been tortured in unimaginable ways. "When did they capture him?" She rattled off the date of her championship game, asking, "Does that sound right?"

"Aye, that's it exactly. I recall because it was the night I met this knockout witch, my soon-to-be girlfriend."

Chloe *had* heard MacRieve captured. She'd seen her father's smile. Feeling violently protective of MacRieve, she squeezed her bottle. How could her dad have signed off on this?

"The Order abducts Loreans my age, and younger too. Kids everywhere are scared. No' *me*, of course," Rónan said, his eyes darting again. "There are others who have nightmares. But *no'* me."

My father's the bogeyman to these people.

Dad must have a blinding hatred toward immortals. Enough to blind a father to his daughter? Conflict churned inside her. On the one hand, she remembered

When he'd told her he loved her no matter what she was, he hadn't been able to meet her eyes.

Yet he'd memorized her face. *The roulette wheel spins and spins. . . .*

TWENTY

Look at you, brother!" Munro slapped Will on the back during a break. "Cracking a smile for the first time in ages. This is just what you need."

"Well, it does no' suck." Today had been the best day of Will's life. And Chloe didn't even know it. His Instinct had been strong, his beast had behaved, and the clan had welcomed her with open arms.

At the cooler, fifths of whiskey chilled for all the players: Lykae-ade. But Will took a beer instead. He planned a repeat of his earlier encounter with Chloe and needed to stay sharp.

Keeping her in sight, he and Munro meandered off from the others.

"I'm seeing things in you that I've no' seen in memory," Munro said.

"Like what?"

"You're laughing," Munro answered. "You joked earlier."

Expression turning serious, Munro said, "When we were young, you were so fun-loving and jovial, always playing pranks and teasing. Then overnight, you seemed to grow up, into a sullen-eyed, closed-lipped lad. That's when I knew something was wrong."

Because Ruelle had cut Will's boyhood short. He remembered little of what it was like to be a child. He knew he must have played with Munro before meeting Ruelle, but couldn't recall an instance.

Strange, he could remember every precise detail of what had happened in that cottage. How she had repeatedly pinned him down and used him, ignoring his alpha tendencies while forcing him to release his beast.

And worse, up until the very end, he'd convinced himself that it was his *responsibility* to feed her. No wonder he'd been so fucked up.

That cottage still stood today in the Woods of Murk, a constant reminder of his weakness.

"Ruelle took much from me," he said, the understatement obvious.

"But now you've a future to look forward to," Munro said. "Everyone likes your mate. She fits in—even with wolves. That's no' something just any mortal can boast of."

"Everything feels different now that she's in my life. Munro, I think I can bed Chloe." He'd kept his beast on the leash, hadn't wanted to miss—or rush through—a single second of her first orgasm.

could take Chloe like a normal man, Ruelle would finally lose.

"You *think* you can bed her?" Munro looked uncomfortable. "You'd best be sure. If your beast rose . . . it would be a horrific way for a mortal to die."

"We were"—Will gazed around—"intimate. And I kept the beast in its cage. With her, I can."

"But the risk!"

He exhaled a gust of breath. "Aye, I know. You're right. Wishful thinking on my part. I would never jeopardize her." He took a swig of his beer. "Hey, dinna Garreth get a talisman from the witches to curb his beast?"

Munro nodded. "Doona know all the details. Just know he would *no'* recommend the H.O.W. in matters of the beast."

"I canna believe I'm about to say this, but I wish I had my goddamned torque." As soon as Will had been freed of it, he'd flung it into the ocean.

Though hated, that collar had taught him much about himself. He'd realized how much he depended on his beast, how much it defined him.

"You'd wear it once more?"

"For her? Oh, aye." After the day he'd had with Chloe, Will was shamed to have confused what he'd felt for Ruelle with a mate's bond. Already he was experiencing a soul-deep need for Chloe, stronger than he'd ever imagined. Chest bowed out, he said, "She's bluidy perfect for me, brother. Aside from her family, I love everything about her."

Chloe had yanked Will back from the brink. It made sense that he'd now be falling backward, falling for her. Will shrugged. "When you know, you know."

The more he learned about her, the more fascinated he became. She'd never had a nip of alcohol, because she'd been so serious about training. She was a smart-arse with a clever wit, and a tomboy uneasy in the girly clothes the clan had brought her. She was constantly fiddling with her skirt, and when she'd caught him glancing down her billowy blouse, she'd been startled, as if she'd forgotten she was showing skin. Will figured his lass was most accustomed to a jersey and cleats.

At his earliest opportunity, he would take her past the wall and buy her a new wardrobe of whatever she fancied. He didn't give a damn what she wore—as long as she came naked to their bed.

These discoveries came on the heels of what he'd learned in the glade today. Though innocent, his mate was lusty and sexually curious. The hungry way she'd stared at his cock . . . He scrubbed his hand over his face, stifling a groan. His Chloe had wanted to suck it.

He couldn't remember the last blow job he'd received. They'd been short-lived, because his beast would rise without fail. And the beast had no patience for them, would always turn the female on her hands and knees for a crude and brutal rutting.

If Will could seize control from his beast, he could look forward to a thousand new experiences with Chloe.

So tell me what it's like to *love everything about her.*

Munro drank his whiskey. "Is this no' the way of it? The attraction to a mate?"

"Nay, I've discovered something. I always thought you were compelled to like things about your female *because* she was your mate. The truth is, she's my mate because I like everything about her."

Munro looked a shade skeptical.

Will couldn't tell him how well they'd meshed sexually, not without admitting how badly he'd needed a woman to look into his eyes and trust that *he* would take her where she needed to go. So he said, "She's fierce as a wee Lykae. And nothing like Webb. Was outraged over the things I told her about her father. She actually wanted to know how *I* was doing after finding my mate."

"You're taking the piss."

"Nay! And she likes me just as well. Has agreed to stay with me for a week, to give us a shot."

"Even though you plan to kill her father?"

Will was conflicted on this, knowing he probably oughtn't to kill his mate's sire, no matter the circumstances. "Hell, it's likely someone else will get to him before I do."

"What are you going to do about her mortality?"

"I've got to find a way to turn her." All day, the more he recognized how perfect she was for him, the more he'd dreaded her mortality.

Theoretically, Chloe could be turned into a Lorean, but the catalyst for the transformation was death.

have to bite her—then kill her. If she managed to survive, the beast would rise up in her so strong that she wouldn't be able to control it for years. If ever. Vampires had much more success at turning humans than Lykae did.

Transforming her into the type of creature who'd killed their mother?

Even these grim options had to be considered. He gazed over at her companionably sipping beers with Rónan. Will sighed when she tugged at her wee skirt.

"What about the Olympics?" Munro asked.

Again, Will felt a flare of pride for his mate, shockingly strong. Pride was not an emotion he was accustomed to these days. "I wouldn't turn her until after the Games. I doona know how that will work out, but I'll figure out some way to get her there." The only way to take the heat off her would be to find Webb, feed him to the Pravus. Which he hadn't been able to do before—and there was scant time left before she was due in Europe.

"Speaking from experience, I suggest turning her sooner rather than later. Mortals . . . they perish so *readily*," Munro said as a flash of sorrow crossed his expression. He had his own past tragedies as well. "What species were you considering? Vampire? Demon?" He took a slug of whiskey. "Nïx would know."

Will had already put in a call to the soothsayer. "I've contacted her."

Munro nodded. "In the meantime, the full moon's in eight days. We can do as we did with Garreth."

from his mate when the moon was full, Garreth had ordered them to break his legs repeatedly—so he couldn't reach his spooked female.

"Aye," Will said easily. "Anything to keep her safe." Had Chloe just rubbed her forehead? Will stalked off without another word, hurrying toward her. She probably had a headache. Judging by commercials, mortals got splitting headaches all the sodding time.

"What's wrong?" he asked when he stood before her. "Is Rónan pestering you? Do you have a headache?"

"No, not at all." Her words were slurring. "Feel *great*."

His gaze flickered over her face, and his lips curled. "Aye, 'cause you're drunk."

She blinked up at him. "I am?"

"You've had a dram too much. I should no' have let you drink this soon after your injury. But you look so healthy, your color so good, I forgot." He swung her up in his arms, and she laughed. Ach, the sound of it! "My mortal needs sleep. Off to bed, love."

She gazed up at him like she was half in love with him already. *Feeling's mutual, little mate.* How could one woman be so fucking adorable and sexy at the same time?

As he carried her inside, she said, "So about your first name . . ."

"It's a sore subject," he answered in a dry tone.

She grinned. "It's Gaelic for William?"

"Aye. Like Uilleam Uallas."

"Can I call you Will?"

Will was what his family had called him. Yes, Chloe was his mate, but the name reminded him of his past.

Hell, he'd figure all this out tomorrow. "Mayhap." He ran up the stairs three at a time, making her laugh again. "If you're verra good."

In their room, he laid her on the bed. Any hopes of doing more with her were dashed when he saw her yawning. "You need to rest." He slipped her heels from her wee feet, then reached for her skirt. She swallowed, turning those big hazel eyes up toward him.

"Just getting you ready for bed." He couldn't tell if she was happy about that or not. Once he'd tucked her in, he said, "Need to go shower off."

This shower was slightly slower than the one he'd raced through the night before. Towel wrapped around his waist, he swiftly hunted for a pair of worn jeans and another T-shirt.

When he returned, her mood had turned more somber.

"What happens to you if I die?"

He sat beside her on the bed, stroking her hair from her forehead. "I'm going to find a way to make you immortal, lass."

"You want that?"

"It must be so."

"MacRieve, I . . ." She trailed off, as if she had too many things to tell him at once. "There's something you need to know."

"What? You can tell me anything."

She bit her lip. "Um, I really appreciate all you've done for me."

Clearly not what she'd been about to say, but he didn't press. They had time.

"I had a lot of fun with you today." She traced the sheet with her forefinger. "There were a couple of times . . . when I found myself grinning up at you and you were already smiling at me. And it felt like we'd pulled off some kind of coup. Just the two of us."

"We did. Simply by finding each other. And I'm glad to hear you enjoyed the day, since this has been the best one I've *ever* had."

She frowned. "You don't have to say that."

"You asked me how old I am. I was born roughly nine centuries ago. I've lived for more than three hundred thousand days. And you made this one my favorite one of all."

"Really?"

"Oh, aye. And I vow to you, Chloe, somehow, someway, we're going to have an eternity more of them."

Just then, one of the creatures beyond the wall gave a particularly loud screech.

"Talking about the future?" She gazed away. "Mine is a bit in flux." She seemed to be sobering up. "You said you'd move heaven and earth to get me to the Olympics, but even if you got a talisman, I'd still be in public. Those things would find me."

When he said nothing, she asked, "Have you ever worked for something—giving everything, sacrificing all you could—only to have it snatched away?"

He'd helped in the search for their king when Lachlain had been captured by vampires. For decades, they'd searched only to fail.

Lachlain had escaped on his own.

"I want verra badly to give you the chance to play," Will finally said. "But there's only one way to ensure your safety."

She read his tight expression. "By giving them my father."

"It would erase all our problems."

She shook her head, tawny curls bouncing. "I could never let that happen."

He exhaled. "What can I do to make you believe that he's a villain?"

"Nothing. There is nothing you can do. I've known you for only twenty-four hours. I've known him for twenty-four years. I just need to talk to him."

"I bet you're telling yourself this is all a big misunderstanding. It's no'. People were hurt." His voice was rough as he recalled being strapped down on Dixon's operating table, a chest-cracker poised above him. He'd never wanted anything more than to free himself. To deny her what she sought . . .

Chloe's gaze dropped. Only then did he notice that his hand was pressed over his chest, as if guarding his heart, his claws digging into his skin.

By the look on her face, she comprehended his reaction. So Rónan had told her. Only a matter of time before she found out in the compound.

"*I* was hurt," he said brusquely, letting her know he wouldn't discuss this further.

She sat up, laying her small hand on his forearm. "I am so sorry, MacRieve. I wish that you hadn't been. But for all my life my dad was the guy who picked me up when I fell, who taught me to be strong. If it wasn't for him, I probably would've cracked at that auction. I can't forget all he's done for me. I just can't. In my position, you wouldn't be able to either."

And on top of everything, she was loyal. *Just to the wrong man.* "Nay, I would no'. But I fear for you, lass. One day you will learn what he's done; one day it will grieve you."

"If only I could see him."

"As I said, no one in the Lore can find him."

"Maybe if you helped me past the wall, he would make contact with me."

Will cupped her nape. "You vowed seven days with me, Chloe. Could you leave me behind so easily? Even after today?"

"I'm not going to lie to you—I feel some kind of connection to you that's different from any I've ever felt with another. It's . . . staggering to me." She squeezed her temples, clearly bewildered. "For weeks, I've been so confused and lonely. And something about you feels right." Turning watering eyes up to him, she clutched his free hand and squeezed it hard. "You're the only thing in my life that makes sense right now."

"You're the only thing that makes sense *to me.*" *You're going to bring me peace.* Finally, after so long of feeling nothing but guilt and self-hatred.

"This is really intense." Her gaze darted. "I just

feel like I should watch myself." She looked utterly spooked.

As Munro had said, this was moving fast even by matehood standards. She must be overwhelmed. "We'll figure this out in the morning. I'm going to help you however you need me to. All will be well. For now, lie with me."

If any part of his body below his waist touched any part of hers, he'd lose control. So he lay beside her on the outside of the cover. But then she looked hungrily at his arms, like she wanted to be within them. He chucked off his shirt and reached for her. Cradling her head to him, he reclined back.

She laid her palm over the center of his chest, then stiffened and drew it away. Oh, aye, she knew what had happened to him. Did she think he was still injured? Or that he wouldn't want her to touch him there? He bloody *craved* her touch there—

She leaned her head down to his chest. He felt her fluttery breaths; he didn't breathe at all.

She pressed a single soft kiss over his heart, having no idea he'd just given it to her.

TWENTY-ONE

C hloe was adrift in that stage between wakefulness and sleep when a scent tickled her nose.

What is that smell? Masculine, crisp, intoxicating. Her heart began beating faster, her skin heating.

She turned toward the source and found her head resting on a man's bare chest. *Her* man. She lazily smiled.

He was asleep beside her in the dimmed room. Pale sunlight tried to steal in through a crack in the heavy curtains. Morning?

Though she was tucked beneath the covers, he lay atop them—no doubt to keep control for her. Because he was generous and protective.

And athletic, sexy, fun, smart, sexy, cocky, and sexy. Realization struck her. She could look for lifetimes and never find anyone who fit her so well.

She watched him sleeping. His firm lips were parted, stubble shadowing his rugged jaw and stubborn chin. Her gaze swept lower to his muscle-packed chest and the indentations of his stomach muscles.

That line of hair descending from his navel to his low-slung jeans.

On the outside, he was physical perfection. But inside . . . he'd been hurt and still bore the mental scars. Last night, he'd unconsciously covered his heart when thinking about his torture, confirming what Rónan had told her.

MacRieve had realized that she knew. He'd accepted that. And after she'd kissed his chest, he'd clasped her in his arms so tightly she'd feared he would break her.

Then, as if he'd been waiting for ages to sleep, he'd seemed to pass out. She'd missed the opportunity to tell him of her fears, to ask for his help in discovering what she was.

Today, she decided. She'd talk to him today. Because she *did* want this thing between them.

For now, she reveled in his scent and heat. Yes, she'd realized she could get used to him. Waking up with him like this made her wonder again if she was exactly where she was meant to be.

Fated to this man.

He'd told her that he'd lived for more than three hundred thousand days. Yet yesterday had been his favorite of all of them?

She decided that today would be his new personal best.

No more cowardice. She would boldly explore this thing between them. When she nuzzled him, her lips skimming one of his flat nipples, he woke.

"Chloe?" He inhaled, muscles tensing. "You needin' me, lass?" he asked in that rumbling brogue.

"Mm-hmm."

She watched his penis begin to stiffen, caught within his straining jeans. With a groan, he adjusted himself, and his length distended once more, jutting into view.

Her fingers curled as the urge to seize him arose. The more she stared, the more she wanted to kiss it. She licked her lips for it. "Yesterday, I thought about something." Her hips had begun rocking against her will. *Literally.*

"What's that?"

Her fingers walked down his torso to the bulge between his legs, caressing him there. "About kissing you."

His hoarse voice broke lower as he said, "Were you then?"

"Kissing you"—she rubbed her thumb across the head—"here."

His hands flew to his pants, snatching them down his body so he could kick them off with a growl. "Well then, if you *must.* . . ."

His body was laid out like a bounty before her. Broad shoulders, narrow hips. That glorious shaft continued to harden.

"I've never done it before," she said absently as she moved between his legs.

He spread them, beckoning her, that big rod pulsing up and down. "I'm honored you're starting—and ending—with me. But do it so I can see that little body of yours."

She gave him a businesslike nod, as if he'd just told her to drop and give him twenty. Yet once she'd gotten her shirt off, she hesitated at her bra.

"Show me those bonny breasts, Chloe."

His home turf. She might've been shy in front of this man, but baring herself to him felt so . . . *right.* So she did, following with her panties.

As his gaze raked over her, he spoke to her in Gaelic, words she knew were praise. Remembering himself, he added in English, "Ach, this will no' last long for me."

"How do I go about it?"

"What do you feel like doing?"

Gaze locked on his mouthwatering erection, she murmured, "Lick it like a candy cane."

"Gods have mercy," he hissed as more moisture beaded the head. He took his shaft in hand, holding it for her like an offering. "Come have a taste."

This felt natural to her, like she was *supposed* to be here, with him, about to do . . . that. So she leaned down and gave the head a long lick. As she gazed up to gauge his reaction—utter bliss—she tasted the delectable bite of his seed. An almost electrical sense of pleasure flooded through her. She moaned, "I think I'm going to love this." One thought repeated itself: *Need more.*

Another lap made his shaft pulse again, giving up more moisture, providing another hit of sensation. If hints of seed were making her feel like this, she couldn't imagine what his orgasm would do to her. She eagerly licked each new bead, like she was racing a melting ice cream cone.

A growl rumbled from his chest. "I need . . . I need your eyes on mine."

For him to keep control. Gaze locked on his, she descended once more, circling the crown with her tongue. As she loved him with her tongue and lips, she recognized that something was clicking into place inside her, like some kind of womanly intuition was emerging. She kissed down the side of his length so he'd move his hand and let her drive.

"There, my lass," he rasped, "that's it."

This intuition guided her, until she seemed to know exactly how to kiss him. She knew he needed her to take him deeper into the heat of her mouth. She knew he craved her hand tight around the base of his shaft, pumping him at the same time. She knew his balls would be aching for her to fondle them in her rolling fingers.

Her ears twitched at his every groan or growl, at the way the timbre of his voice changed as he neared his peak.

According to her new intuition, she needed to take him to the edge. And then maybe to let him linger there. . . .

<hr />

Two nights ago, Will had mused, "I think I'm bluidy in love."

As Chloe took his cock between those plump reddened lips, he thought, *I* know *I am*.

She moaned and the scent of her arousal deepened. The sweetest, most alluring scent. She was enjoying this.

Lucky man, Will! He was hard as stone and randy as a lad, excited like one.

He could tell Chloe was unpracticed with this—she'd hesitate before trying something new. Yet she was figuring it out handily.

He relaxed back, stroking her hair as she explored him with her soft lips and seeking tongue. But then his beast began to stir with more aggression. It clawed inside him, and again, Will clawed back.

This was Chloe, giving her first blow job. If he didn't get control, he could ruin this forever. She was so young, so eagerly doing this. *Don't ruin it.* He released her, clamping the headboard. If he had to white-knuckle his way through it, he would.

When she moaned and pulled on his length, he arched his back. *This is* mine *to enjoy, beast.* He was harder than he'd ever been without it rising, sweating with pleasure.

Yet an underlying uneasiness arose. He was worried about his beast, but also about how utterly perfect this felt. He'd woken to her nuzzling him after he'd slept with nary a nightmare. Will MacRieve simply didn't get mornings like this. "Head case" took on a totally different meaning.

When she began using her hand to pump him as she sucked him deep, he knew it was only a matter of time. "You're sucking it so good, lass. Can you feel my seed rising up my cock?"

She squeezed her hand around the swollen ring, making him buck to be free of that semen.

Just when he was about to come, was opening his

mouth to tell her, she eased off, leaving him hanging at the edge. His claws dug deeper into the wood. The intensity was mind-numbing. Biting back a curse, he reminded himself that she was exploring him. *Let her play.*

When her hot little tongue tucked against his sensitive ballocks, he gave a shout. "Chloe!"

She set in with her hand and mouth once more—until he was shuddering with the need to ejaculate—only to ease off again.

"Finish me!" he grated between breaths.

She licked the slit of his cock, then pursed her lips to blow on it.

"*Ah!* Merciless woman!"

She worked him steadily until the pressure was unbearable, until he'd reached the point of no return.

Have to warn her. "You've got me in a bad way! I'm goin' tae come a river."

She drew back, gazing up under those long lashes. "Okay." She played with his laden ballocks, grazing her nails behind them.

He tried to speak. Couldn't. Tried again: "*Okay? How do you want it, then? Have care, or it'll come right upon your tongue.*"

She lovingly rubbed his shaft against her cheek . . . such a sweet gesture amidst all her hot and dirty sucking—his mind was blown as thoroughly as his dick.

"I want it *now.*" She returned to her kiss, taking him even deeper, pumping him faster.

He drew his knees up beside her, thrusting hard to her lips. His claws dug into the headboard as his eyes rolled back in his head.

TWENTY-TWO

MacRieve's head thrashed, sweat slicking all his tightened muscles. His legs quaked around her ears as that bulge of seed in his shaft climbed all the way to the top.

She'd rendered him this way. This was *her* doing. Pride and arousal warred inside her, along with a tenderness for this man that shocked her in its strength. *He's mine.*

When his hips bucked too wildly, Chloe's nails sank into them, holding him still.

"Fuck, fuck! You want me tae come harder than I ever have?" His accent was so thick. "Then doona stop, baby, just doona—*ahhh!*" His back bowed.

Heat spurted into her mouth as he roared her name. She jerked at her first taste, as if lightning had struck. How could anything be this delicious? She felt as if she'd waited forever to taste him. When she swallowed his semen down, energy seemed to fill her, like currents racing through her veins.

Panting around the head, nearly delirious, she drew even deeper. *My man, my man . . . mine.*

Her scalp began to tingle. She saw tracers in her vision. Shivers danced over her damp skin.

His heartbeat thundered like earthquakes in her sensitive ears.

And when he was spent, he put his palm atop her head to stay her. But she was reluctant to end an experience like this, kept tonguing him.

Though he shuddered violently with each of her lingering licks, he didn't stop her. "I think I'm in a dream." He reached out his straightened arms, cupping her face. "Just came till my eyes rolled back in my head, and my mate is lapping at me like a kitten with cream."

He was grinning. Her heart twisted in her chest. He was the most handsome male she'd ever seen. A golden-eyed Scottish sex god. And he wanted her. Forever.

She grinned back, excitement seizing her. Because she suspected she would come to want him for just as long.

Again they were smiling at each other like they'd pulled off some kind of coup.

At that moment, she thought, *Why would I ever let him go?*

⁂

Will lay stupefied, legs sprawled around her body.

Chloe had just sucked him till he'd seen stars, and

now his beautiful mate was licking him clean. As he gazed down in awe, she continued to kiss and nuzzle until he was hardening again.

Never had he been pleasured so profoundly. Which was something for a nine-hundred-year-old to recognize. He was proud of his control—and completely enamored with his mate. "Looks like we've found something Chloe genuinely enjoys."

"I loved it."

"And it loved you, *mo chridhe*."

"What did you call me?"

"My heart. Now for your turn."

"Hmmm?" she murmured against the tip, her breaths tickling him. When he drew her away, she cried, "Hey, I wasn't finished."

"It's no' going anywhere, love." He turned her over on her back, spreading her legs. Found her gaze locked on his mouth. "Ah, Chloe, your heart speeds up when you look at my mouth. Because you know what I'm about tae do with it." *She's mine. And I'll take her.* Just not completely. *Keep the beast in check.*

"I'm goin' tae make you come till you ride my tongue like a wanton. Because that's what you are."

"What does that mean?" she asked in a throaty voice that sent blood rushing to his shaft again.

"It means you were *made* for me." He started kissing down her neck, intending to blaze a trail all the way to her toes and back.

Suddenly he stilled.

"MacRieve? Is this more of your teasing? I'm already about to die!"

Another scent was now coursing through his consciousness. He gave himself an inward shake. Flashback? Memory of a nightmare?

Chloe was rocking her hips against his torso when he scented something he'd hoped never to smell again.

Succubae. Close. He inhaled deeply, the scent getting stronger and stronger. *Gods, they've gotten inside the wall!* Were they here for revenge? Or to steal Chloe for the Pravus?

With a bitter curse, he dove for his pants, snatching them up over his cock. "Get dressed now!" He tossed his shirt to her.

"What?" She pulled it over her head. "What's going on, MacRieve?"

Dressed enough! He grabbed her, securing her in his arms as he lunged for the bedroom door—

He froze, all his muscles tensing. He slowly drew back to stare down at her eyes. They . . . glowed green. Her hair was lengthening by the second. Claws tipped each of her fingers.

"No, *no.* This is no' happening."

"Why are you looking at me like that?"

This was no mortal in his arms; she was a succubus. *My mate . . . my mate is one of their ilk.*

Bile rose in his throat. She'd just *fed.* Off of him!

Though he'd vowed to the gods that he would rather die than feed one of those vile creatures again, he'd allowed this parasite to play him, seduce him, then harvest his seed.

Canna do this, canna handle this—

The beast rose, roaring free.

TWENTY-THREE

MacRieve, you're scaring me!" Chloe cried. He was staring at her with unmistakable revulsion, his face twisted. When he began shaking her, she screamed, *"Let me go!"*

His fists tightened around her upper arms with such force that she thought they'd break. His eyes turned ice blue and glowed. Fangs protruded from his mouth. Black claws lengthened from the tips of his fingers.

"No' you, no' you!" He lifted her until her feet were dangling, then drew her in close, those huge fangs inches from her lips. His feral gaze bored into hers.

She turned her head away, whimpering with fear. With a roar, he flung her to the bed. She scrambled to the floor with startling speed. Confusion roiled as she backed into a corner.

He swung around to pound his palms against the wood-paneled wall, then slashed those claws straight down. Splinters arced across the room.

When he faced her once more, it wasn't him. *Not human,* her mind dimly recalled. *He's not human.* She was looking at his . . . beast. A monster. In its white-blue gaze, she saw madness—and animal cunning.

She shook so hard her head bobbed.

He slashed down the wall again, roaring at the ceiling, "I fuckin' give up! YOU BLUIDY WIN!"

Munro charged into the room. He looked like MacRieve had just moments ago.

Before and after.

"Will? What's set you off?"

MacRieve growled, "Get her out of my sight!"

"What is wrong with you?" Munro gazed at Chloe huddled in the corner, shaking. "Do you want her to die of fright?"

He roared back: *"YES!"*

Munro's eyes began glowing blue as well. "That's my *deirfiúr.* I will no' let you hurt her."

"She's a goddamned succubus! A seed-feeder!"

Chloe gasped. "Succubus?" She'd read about them. They derived nourishment from . . . *sex.*

MacRieve's twin scented the air, went motionless. He gazed at her with his brows drawn. "Dear gods."

Chloe was an immortal? A Lorean?

She must've been *triggered.*

Munro quickly recovered, shoving a snarling Mac-Rieve toward the door. "Outside!" Over his shoulder, Munro told her, "If you value your life, doona leave this room." The door slammed.

She sat dazed. She didn't know what terrified her most: MacRieve's true self—or the revelation of hers.

Succubus.

By the way these two males had reacted, she figured succubae weren't exactly universally beloved. And her mother had been one?

Somehow Chloe managed to rise, then stumble into the bathroom. Her reflection stunned her. Her face was softer, her hair now curling past her shoulders and still growing.

Her irises were glowing a rich green. She'd read that all Lore creatures had eyes that changed with emotion. *Me, a Lore creature.* So when would they change back?

She pinched up the hem of MacRieve's shirt, flashing the mirror, and found her hips were rounder, her breasts plumper. She dropped the hem, grasping the basin for support, noticing her new claws. They were pink like her nails but had tapered tips and sharp edges.

Freaking *claws.*

And even more gut-wrenching than what she'd gained was what she'd lost.

All her scars were gone.

She supposed most girls would be delighted; Chloe was *pissed.* She'd *earned* those marks, every one of them, like merit badges.

The one on her ankle had reminded her of the big Brazilian midfielder who'd two-footed Chloe right into the hospital—and how, the next season, that girl had paid.

Now Chloe saw that her knees were smooth, the arthroscopic scar on the right one gone. That type of surgery was like a rite of passage. Even the scar from last night, the one that would've reminded her of all that she'd survived, was missing.

Her badges. Gone.

With a yell, she shot her fist out, breaking the mirror. She gaped down at her lacerated hand. Stupid, stupid. She needed to be figuring out a way to escape this place before MacRieve returned to finish her off. The hatred in his eyes . . .

How could he treat her like this? After what they'd just shared?

All those promises he'd made, all lies! She was furious that he'd been hiding that beast part of himself. Yes, he'd mentioned something in the glade, but she'd thought he was talking metaphorically.

She hadn't known what *she* was—but he'd known fully what *he* was. There was a part of him so monstrous that she shook just to recall it. She was glad she had seen it so soon, before she'd fallen for him completely.

The nymphs could have him! At the thought, a pang of loss battled her fury.

That bewildering pang hurt worse than her new wound.

She turned on the water, wincing as she ran her hand under it. As the blood washed away, she saw that her skin had already begun regenerating. *Because I am an immortal.* She grabbed a small towel and knotted it around her hand.

She'd known something was happening. Little by little, she'd been changing. *This shouldn't be such a shock, Chlo.* Not like the shock that had hammered her with her first look at the real MacRieve. He was disgusted with her? Mutual. He'd been repulsive. Her beautiful Scot had masked a monster.

Deciding that the creatures at the wall weren't as bad as the thing she'd just been in bed with, she picked out a shard from the mirror, coiling a washcloth around it.

If she ran into that wolf-monster again—such as on her way out—she'd gut it. She knew it was kill or be killed.

And she was no victim.

She hastily dressed, tucking the shard in her back pocket, concealing it with a long sweater. She didn't hear anyone outside the door, so she turned the knob, found it locked. Frustrated, she yanked on it.

It broke off in her hand.

She stared down at it in wonderment. Exactly how strong was she?

Desperate to escape, she used her *claws* to jimmy open the door, then eased out onto the landing. Downstairs in the great room, Rónan and Ben sat stiffly on the couch.

Rónan flashed her a confused look.

Ben shook his head slowly in clear warning. "Chloe, you need to wait up there for Munro. You canna be near Will."

She faded back into the room. *Looks like I'm going out the window.*

"If you kill her, you canna ever get her back. . . ."

After an unavoidable exchange of blows with Munro, Will tore through the woods, his brother's parting words replaying in Will's disordered mind.

Munro seemed to think Will *shouldn't* murder the parasite who had wormed her way into their home and lives. She was lucky his beast had risen. Otherwise she'd likely be dead.

Will had been maddened with rage—yet his beast had accepted Chloe as his, had been tempering *Will's* actions. Even as Will had craved to kill her, his Instinct had been commanding him —*Protect, provide.*—

He wondered if his Instinct understood that providing for her meant jeopardizing his entire existence and risking her venom bond.

A succubus just fed off my body. Hatred seethed inside him, so thick he thought he'd choke on it. This couldn't be happening. He'd bloody liked Chloe, relishing her passion, her spirit. He'd thought his life was finally turning around.

I thought I could refashion myself. Now, impossible.

Though he could normally run leagues without getting winded, he couldn't catch his breath. He stumbled, then leaned over, palms on his knees, sucking in air.

Suffocating. The deep pulling him down. Chloe had fed off him. Just like Ruelle.

Her claws had dug into his hips as she sucked him, fed, then teed him up for another round. For another feeding. Because she would never be satisfied.

Why did this keep happening to him? He was right back to Hungary.

No, first he would punish Webb. Now he would have no qualms about using Chloe—

Realization struck. Webb had to have known what she was. He'd found out she was changing, and he'd washed his hands of her. Chloe had been looking for her father because the man had abandoned her. Of course.

He stilled. She would have put that together herself by now. Was she devastated by the betrayal? Stricken? Had she cried?

He roared, slashing through a tree. The need to protect her still assailed him.

Her entire life had been upended. He pictured how she'd been in his room earlier, stunned, defenseless. Aye, she'd been defenseless. Just like Ruelle. Will wondered if he would climb over his mother's corpse to protect this succubus as well. At the thought, he banged his head against a stalwart pine, cracking it, bloodying himself.

Felt good. Necessary. Like that blow his father had delivered. So Will rammed his head over and over.

He'd believed that he had a true connection with Chloe, that she was as aroused by him as he was by her. Instead, she'd been coldly serving him up.

Ruelle must be laughing in her grave.

"Ahhh!" he bellowed, swinging his arm, ripping his flared claws through another tree.

He watched it topple. Felled.

Just like me.

TWENTY-FOUR

For the second time in three days, Munro climbed the stairs to his brother's room with a heavy heart. *I'm going to lose him.*

When he and Will had fought moments ago, Munro had come up with many reasons why Will shouldn't kill Chloe. But anticipating Will's rebuttal of each, he'd voiced none of them.

For instance, if Munro had pointed out that Will could only have bairns with Chloe, Will would have comprehended that his offspring would be part incubus or succubus.

Heap yet another worry into this situation, then slow boil.

Munro too had call to hate Chloe's kind. He'd lost his mother and father, and on some dark days, he feared he'd lost his brother that night as well.

But Munro's Instinct was telling him to protect Chloe, his *deirfiúr*, his sister. According to fate, according to all the Lykae believed, this female was Will's future. She was Munro's family.

Make no decisions. He would talk to her, discover more about her. He'd decided that one of the two brothers had to approach this rationally. Straightening his shoulders, he knocked on the door.

She didn't answer. After a hesitation, he entered.

She was sitting at the window, staring out. At the guard Munro had posted below?

Her looks were altered. Her hair was wavy and longer, shining in the morning light. Her curves were more accentuated. Her biological imperative was to feed off men; in a rush of changes, she'd become even more attractive to them.

He frowned at the bloody towel wrapped around her hand. "What happened?" he asked, even as he deduced the answer. "You dinna like your new reflection."

She remained silent, watchful. Probably fearing all Lykae after Will had revealed his beast.

Even Munro had been shocked by the sight. With his ice-blue irises glowing in the darkened room, Will had looked so much like their father had in those last hours. . . . "I'm nö' going to hurt you, Chloe. Do you understand me?"

"Why should I trust you? You're twin to that thing out there. Are you like that too?"

"Well, almost exactly."

"You know what I mean. A monster."

"When I lose control over my emotions or my aggression, I would look like that."

She shuddered again. "Is what he said true? Am I a succubus?"

"Aye. That's your scent. I doona know why you've changed. You were human last night. Mayhap you reached a certain age and transitioned. I canna say."

She finally faced him. "Am I immortal?"

"Can I see your hand?"

She unwrapped the towel. The lacerations were already healing.

He exhaled with relief. "It's regenerating. Quickly. You're immortal. That's one less worry, at least." He well knew what it was like to dread a human's fragility.

She gazed up from under a lock of her now-flowing hair. "Why are you being nice to me? I saw the look on your face when you scented what I am."

"Did Will explain what our Instinct is?" When she nodded, he said, "His Instinct tells him you're his mate. Mine is telling me you're my sister. That has no' changed for me, no matter what you are."

"There's that phrase—no matter what you are."

"Has someone else said it?" When she remained silent, he said, "You can trust me. I will help you with this."

"How can I trust you? Obviously, your kind hates . . . mine."

"My family has had a bitter history with succubae. A tragic one."

"Like what?"

"That's no' my story to tell," he said cautiously. "It's complicated. Just know that this is difficult for everyone involved."

"Difficult." She gave a harsh laugh. "Did you almost just die at the hands of a monster? 'Cause that was *difficult*." She stood. "I've gotta get ghost from this place. I'd rather risk the snake men than see that beast again."

"Will's beast will no' hurt you."

"No? You didn't see, but it was bellowing at me, shaking me."

"Unfortunately, that was all Will. His beast rose up to *protect* you." When she appeared disbelieving, he said, "Can I level with you, Chloe? Those beings beyond the wall would rape you without cease, and you would pray you were still mortal so you could die from it. Here, no one will touch you."

"Not even your brother?"

"Especially no' him. Come take a walk with me, and I'll tell you what I know about your kind." When he waved her toward the door, she hesitated. "Are you no' curious?"

With a grudging look, she complied.

Downstairs, they passed the boys. Rónan, never shy, said, "You really a seed-feeder?"

Munro scolded, "Language, Rónan!"

The boy couldn't use that word, but MacRieve could call her that to her face? "Apparently I am."

"What does that mean?"

"Beats the hell out of me, kid."

Munro opened a french door for her, saying over his shoulder, "If Will returns, tell him we went out for a spell."

Outside, they walked in silence past a couple holding hands. When the pair turned to stare at Chloe, Munro wondered if Rónan had already made the rounds, telling everyone that Will's mate was a succubus.

Chloe gave a humorless laugh. "Yesterday they were all smiles and waves. Now I've got a scarlet *S* on my chest. That puts things into perspective, doesn't it? They'll accept the daughter of someone they hate like Webb, but not a succubus?"

"They doona know how to react. Lykae doona naturally revile succubae, no' unless they've call to."

"And your brother does? Come on, I can recognize utter hatred when I see it."

"Did you know this was going to happen?" he asked, deflecting the subject.

She narrowed her eyes, but allowed it. "I knew something was off inside me. My senses went haywire a few weeks ago."

"That's common for transitioning halflings."

"I told my dad about it. He said I needed to avoid a trigger, but didn't tell me what it was. He hinted that my mom was an immortal, but again, wouldn't tell me what kind."

"A trigger? It must have been when you and Will had sex."

She whipped her head up. "We didn't. Not all the way. We just fooled around."

Differently than they had yesterday? *Oh.* Munro could deduce what the trigger had been. She'd . . . fed for the first time.

Judging by Chloe's blushing, she'd deduced it as

well. "Your father dinna tell you no' to be with men . . . that way? I would think he'd do anything to keep you from turning."

"He probably didn't think he had anything to worry about. I never had much interest in guys."

"I see. It's no' unheard of for a halfling's powers or . . . appetites to be dormant until some catalyst. I've heard of a human halfling becoming a Valkyrie after a lightning strike."

"I had no idea about any of that. Dad just plopped the *Book of Lore* in my lap and took off on a business trip. He told me we'd talk when he returned. He . . . he never did. His phone was disconnected." Her voice wavered, which clearly aggravated her. "The next thing I know, I've got Lore creatures in my house and I'm getting kidnapped."

"I'm sorry, Chloe." Munro couldn't even imagine her confusion and fear. Again that protectiveness surged within him. "Considering his hatred of immortals, your father probably believed his actions merciful."

She shrugged, feigning indifference. "So spill about succubae. Give it to me straight. I'm a big girl."

He only had vague reports from others to draw from, and his brother's bitter recollections of Ruelle. "You're a cambion—a human and succubus halfling, which makes you part of the Ubus Peoples. They hail from the Ubus Realm, located on a hidden plane. Males are incubi, females are succubae. No' much is known about your kind. Some say males can fly and females can turn invisible. All we know for certain is that your species draws nourishment from a partner's sexual release."

"So when MacRieve called me a seed-feeder, was that . . . literal?"

Munro pulled at his collar, as uncomfortable with this as she clearly was. It was like explaining the birds and the bees—to his brother's mate. "Some say there's a mystical energy with release, and your species can convert it to a life force." Could this be any more awkward? "In that case, seed could be just an attractant of sorts, kind of the icing on the . . ." He trailed off. "Any metaphor I come up with at this point is just going to sound perverted."

Her cheeks flushed even brighter red. "I get it."

"Others say, well, that the physical, uh, result is what gets converted." He coughed into his fist. "I do know it can be from intercourse or oral sex." Will had once revealed that though Ruelle could feed both ways, she'd never deigned to perform oral sex and had no interest in it herself.

"How often do I have to do that? Months? Weeks?"

"Since you're young, you'll need it more often. I'd guess every day. Mayhap every other."

Her face paled. "That much?" she cried. "What happens if I don't?"

"For a cambion, I doona rightly know. But for a succubus, the longer she goes, the more intense her desire for a male grows. By a certain point, she becomes mindless and animalistic with need." Like the succubae who'd stalked Will, intent on raping him.

Gods, mayhap this *was* far too much to ask of him. "Great. Anything else?"

"If you have intercourse with the same male more than three times, you can bind him to you, envenoming him—"

"Like venom out of fangs?" She was aghast.

"No, no, it's a *mystical* bond. Once that tie is formed, he'll sicken without you." He recalled Will rocking in his bed, covered in sweat. "I understand that it's like heroin withdrawal, but it never gets better."

She gave him an incredulous look. "Then why would anyone have sex with a succubus in the first place?"

"You're bonny. And you can emit chemicals that make males crazed. It's called strewing."

"*How* do I emit them?"

"From what I understand, it comes from your verra breath. It's scentless, so it's impossible to detect until the result is felt. Even an unwilling male would find it difficult to resist, if no' impossible. Mated males are thought to be immune."

She stopped. "So my new feeding m.o. is to roofie men, then get them hooked on me like heroin, so they'll keep coming back to the dealer? That's just messed up."

He couldn't disagree. He remained silent, giving her time to work through all the angles.

"I'm going to be dependent on guys, *really* dependent on them, for the rest of my life?" She looked like she was about to be sick. More to herself, she said, "I was making a great living. I had my future planned out." Another group passed them, casting her hesitant looks. "What are you gawking at?" she snapped.

Munro told her, "News spreads fast around here, I'm afraid."

"Well, they need to keep their eyes in their heads."

Before, she'd appeared woeful. With each second that she grew accustomed to all these surprises, her expression grew more mutinous.

Succubae were known to be fawning. They coaxed and beguiled men wherever they went. Chloe looked like she was on the verge of head-butting unsuspecting bystanders.

Munro tilted his head, a flare of hope rising. This female acted like a wee bruiser. She'd made a living as a professional athlete, about the least likely career Munro could imagine for a succubus.

His own innate wariness toward her was fading. Just because she was a halfling succubus didn't mean she'd be anything like Ruelle.

There was a spark in Chloe's eyes, a toughness in her demeanor that was so radically different from Munro's memories of that other creature, so different from any succubae he'd encountered over his long life.

Which meant Munro still believed her a fitting match for Will.

"What about pregnancy?" she asked.

"Full succubae have a few cycles of fertility in a year. I doona know what will happen with you. There's a soothsayer we can contact to determine more, but it will likely take time."

"I'm going to wake up, and this will all be a bad dream." She rubbed her temples. "Is there *any* upside here?"

"You're immortal now. You could live forever."

"Live forever as an out-of-work, roofie-dispensing, drug-dealing skank? If that's my upside . . ."

"You'll be stronger. You'll regenerate from any wound. Other than decapitation, of course."

She perked up. "Stronger?"

"Take a swing at me." He patted his upper arm.

She shrugged, then launched her good fist.

He gritted his teeth, saying, "Aye. Stronger." The pain was pleasant to him. It meant his newfound sister might survive in the Lore.

She frowned at her other hand. "It's healing really fast."

He rubbed his nape. "You and Will, uh, your morning together would help that along."

Her skin flushed again. "What would happen if I never did that again? I'm a halfling. Maybe I could still exist on food. It used to stave off the worst of my symptoms."

"It might be possible."

She narrowed her gaze. "If it's even *remotely* possible, I'll make it work." Her hazel eyes flickered then gleamed green with determination. "If I want something bad enough, it'll happen."

Chloe was like the anti-Ruelle. Suddenly, this didn't feel like a tragedy in the making. This might be . . . *workable.*

At that moment, they heard an agonized roar from the woods. Trees crashed down.

Will. Sorting out his issues.

※※※※※

Chloe gazed up at MacRieve's twin. "That's him, isn't it?" As if she could ever forget that horrifying sound.

"Aye," Munro said, surprising her by telling the truth.

She'd sensed he was well-meaning. And at least he wasn't violent. A huge improvement over the other one.

She still couldn't believe the way this morning had gone to hell. Before that monster had showed—talking to her like it was from Aesop's fucking Fables—she'd been happy, feeling desire and being desired. She'd *liked* MacRieve, had found him to be a sexy, exciting lover.

I lost everything today. Her dad had freaked at the *possibility* of her transition. How would he feel about his detrus daughter now? Olympics? Forever out of reach. She'd been paranoid about her drug tests in Florida; now she could only imagine how wonky they would be. Not to mention her newfound strength and glowing eyes.

She wanted to blame MacRieve for all this—he deserved nothing less—but now she realized how inevitable her change had been. Considering the nature of her dreams and her awareness of men, sooner or later she would've found a guy and been triggered—with or without MacRieve.

"Are there any succubae I can talk to about all this?" To say it was a lot to take in . . .

At least now she knew why she'd felt that sense of dread each time she'd even considered embarking on a flirtation. Because, evidently, her first boyfriend could've triggered her with his semen.

Maybe her human half had tried to keep her from going down that path? Chloe was brave, physically at least. But she'd been too cowardly to explore her dread, to try and overcome it. It'd been easier to make excuses.

Too busy. Too driven. Too committed.

So why hadn't she felt dread with MacRieve?

"Chloe, any succubae I've ever encountered have proven to be evil and malicious," Munro said. "I would no' recommend reaching out to them."

She frowned. "So my mom was evil?"

If possible, Munro looked even more uncomfortable about that question than he'd been about the sex talk. "I canna say."

If Dad hated Loreans, why would he ever be with one? "Maybe my dad hates immortals *because* he was hurt by my mom?" She recalled how he'd peered at that picture of Fiore. Had Chloe's mother *forced* him to love her?

"It's possible. Though it's more likely that he was already a member of the Order. From what we understand, your father has been at this for decades."

What if her mom had been his prisoner? As usual, her feelings toward her father were in turmoil. Last night she'd been outraged that anyone would want to hurt people like MacRieve and Rónan and other Lore kids.

This morning she'd realized why MacRieve was a danger to society. Had her mother been one as well?

Hunt for the upside, Chlo. After lifelong blood tests, she no longer had to worry about the big C. No, she could potentially live forever.

She grimaced. She was an independent female, yet she was now expected to depend on males to survive—not just for one lifetime, but for *eternity*.

Another thought struck her. Those "womanly instincts" she'd experienced earlier . . . they were *succubus* instincts, instructing her how to land the best score. Ugh!

The idea of living forever like that appealed to her not at all.

"We should get you back," Munro said. "My brother will no' like that you're gone."

"He'll be angry? Wonder what that'll be like!"

"Again, he will no' harm you." Munro raked his fingers through his dark hair, reminding her of how handsome the twins were. *And* what lurked beneath.

"What makes you so certain?"

"He would've already. I have no' seen him so out of control in memory. I think it's much worse because of the timing, coming on the heels of his torture in an Order prison. He's no' been right since he returned."

"He was vivisected, right?" She recalled last night when MacRieve's shaking hand had covered his heart. As she'd kissed his chest, she'd vowed to herself that she'd never let anyone hurt him again. How much had changed so quickly. "He was tortured by my dad's people?"

Golden eyes flickering, Munro admitted, "One doctor showed him his beating heart."

She pressed the back of her hand over her mouth. Even after everything, she felt sympathy for MacRieve. God, she'd never been so confused in her life. After seeing MacRieve's beast, she understood why the Order feared Lykae. But then she gazed up at Munro—serious, grave Munro—and couldn't imagine anyone harming him. "So your brother could get past *that* to be with me, but my transition makes him want to kill me? You need to tell me why that is."

Munro's expression was stark. "Chloe, it's—"

"Complicated. Got it." She sighed, tempering her tone. None of this was Munro's fault. He was just trying to be helpful. "Look, I can't stay here. There has to be a way for me to get past those creatures at the wall."

"I'm sorry. That's no' possible right now."

"Okay, I might be stuck in this compound, but that doesn't mean I need to be staying at his house. I'm not *living* with him!"

"No one else would take you in."

"Because I'm a succubus?"

"Because you're Will's mate. His Instinct will demand he keep you close. Even if he hates it at the time."

She'd been as good as abducted again. From the witches' clutches to the Lykae's.

As her situation sank in, Chloe repeated to herself,

Rub some dirt on it, rub some dirt on it. But this was so far beyond the realm of *I'm just happy to be here.*

Some things she knew for certain?

She couldn't change what she was, so to be punished for it by that werewolf wasn't happening.

She'd be planning to escape as soon as possible. In the meantime, she didn't have to live by their rules at ye olde compound.

She refused to be afraid of MacRieve. All her life, she'd faced bigger opponents. When they'd attacked, barreling down upon her on a field, she'd trained herself to stand her ground. Once she'd mastered that, she'd trained herself to strike back. She'd marched into myriad stadiums all over the world, turning herself into a fucking gladiator. Even knowing what horror roiled inside MacRieve, Chloe would not falter.

And finally, she'd starve to death before she ever "fed" off him again.

"Munro, you've been decent to me, so I'm going to level with you. I'm not planning to brave that wall by myself." Yet. "And I understand that my lodging choices are limited. But I also don't plan on putting up with any more wolven bullshit from your brother. He pulls any stunts like this morning, and I'm going to shiv him with the shard of mirror I'm carrying."

He looked startled, then . . . heartened?

"I'm not kidding," she insisted. "Somehow, someway, I'll nail his balls to that wall."

Munro's golden eyes widened. "I think that's a great idea—no reason to tamp down any ferocity, now, is there?"

Um, okay. "And another thing. I want a matehood divorce. I want no tie to your brother."

Munro's delighted look faded. "He'll change your mind once he's recovered from the shock."

I wouldn't take that to the bookie, Munro. . . .

She glanced up; clouds were moving in, just as they had yesterday afternoon. They reminded her of the idyllic time spent with MacRieve. Which made bitterness churn inside her.

As they approached the lodge, she spied MacRieve at the entrance, gripping the doorframe with outstretched arms. His claws sank into the wood, his body seeming to take up the entire width of the doorway.

His eyes were still that icy blue, but there was no shadow of his beast. He appeared on the ragged edge of control.

His bare chest was splashed with mud, heaving from his deep breaths. His face was streaked with *blood.*

She noticed passersby slowing near the lodge. Loitering to see the show? If MacRieve screwed with her, she'd give them a show worthy of a stadium.

Without a look at her, MacRieve lunged toward his brother. "Where the hell were you?" he snapped, bowing up to Munro. "You took her from here?"

Just like Munro had said. Chloe rolled her eyes and continued on toward the house, passing Rónan and Benneit, who gave her a wide berth.

While they were all outside pissing on each other for dominance, or whatever they did in times like these, she would move her things out of MacRieve's room, then raid the kitchen. As she'd told Munro, she fully intended to eat like a human.

She had to believe it was possible.

Munro said, "I just got her out of the house for a walk."

"You doona take her out without my permission!"

Chloe stopped in her tracks, turning on them. "Whoa, hold on! I'm *Chloe*; I'm not *Pop's motorcycle*. Nobody's giving permission or receiving permission to do anything with me!"

Her four new roomies frowned at her, as if surprised she'd even address them. They were in for a lot of surprises.

Every word booming louder, MacRieve said, "You'd do well to get the *fuck out of my sight, succubus*!"

"And you'd do well to shut your whore mouth!"

He lunged forward—like the biggest, baddest fullback she'd ever imagined. Picturing him like that enabled her to hold her ground.

His eyes narrowed, his voice vibrating with rage. "I beheaded the last five succubae I encountered. Keep talking shite, and you'll be the sixth!"

TWENTY-FIVE

Me a sixth?" the bitch queried with a raised brow. "I'm going to have to say no to that plan, dickwad. What else you got?"

Will grabbed her upper arm. "You rile me at your own peril—"

"Fuck your peril! Beat feet, MacRieve!" she yelled at the top of her lungs, flinging her arm away, which surprised him enough to release her. "Get out of my face!"

"You have no idea what you provoke! Doona forget your fear when you saw my beast revealed."

Reminded of that horror, she would cast her eyes down, attempt to placate him—

Her chin went up and her shoulders went back. "For the record, asshole, I wasn't *scared*. I was *startled*. There's a difference. And now that I know what's lurking inside you, I won't be startled again." She turned toward the house.

Filled with fury, he stormed after her. When he snatched her arm again, she whirled around, kicking the side of his knee.

She'd definitely gotten stronger. Because she was a goddamned succubus.

Perhaps all the Lore needed to know what she really was. He turned toward the wall, his grip on her tightening until she cried out.

"Where are you taking me?"

"You were so keen to leave, mayhap I'll toss your arse over the wall."

Her heart pounded with fear, like a drum sounding within him. He might be the first Lykae to purposely frighten his mate; his Instinct was not having it.

—*You harm what you've been given?*—

—*PROTECT.*—

Munro chased after them. In Gaelic, he said, "Are you insane? Treating her like this? I just got through assuring her that you would never hurt her."

Will answered in the same language, "Then you're a bluidy liar!" He swung her forward as she flailed against his hold.

"What are you going to do to her?" Munro dogged his heels. "She's no' as you think her."

"We're going to go have a peek at the wall. Mayhap I'll lob her over to the other side where she belongs!"

"Have you lost your mind? She's your *mate*, brother."

Over his shoulder, Will said, "I doona recognize her as such! Do you remember what Mam's last words were to me? 'Never one like her, my Uilleam.'"

Chloe thrashed harder.

"But this girl's no' a full succubus," Munro said. "She's a halfling."

"Aye," Will grated, "and her other half is WEBB!"

"I thought you were going to get past that."

"Canna. No' now. Just another example of how wrong she is."

"I heard your wish at Loa's. You wanted your mate to be made immortal. You've got your wish—her wounds regenerate. I saw them. You can claim her, man!"

"I'd rather she be mortal with a day left to live!"

"You speak so easily of a human dying? To *me*?" Munro snapped, past pain tingeing his words. "I'll no' let you harm my sister. You might no' want her, but I do." Then in a clearly desperate move, Munro said, "You owe her to me."

Will bared his fangs at his brother. "You bring that up now? Here?"

Munro was resolute. "I've waited a long time for her too, Will. And I like her, think she would make you a fine mate if you would only give her a chance."

Will gazed down at her struggling to keep up with his strides. Her eyes glowed succubus green. "Never. Happening."

Munro stopped. Just when Will thought he'd given up, Munro called, "She was discarded like trash by her father. That's why she was searching for him. She told him something was wrong, but the bastard revealed nothing to her, leaving her in misery for weeks—with no idea how to live as an immortal. Your young mate was *abandoned* by her only family."

Will's beast howled with rage. She'd been defenseless, vulnerable to the entire Lore. Kidnapped by witches! That this had happened to his mate—

Nay, nay, I should do worse *to her!* She deserved nothing less.

He slowed as realization dawned. There'd be no revenge. Webb wouldn't give a shite about who was defiling his daughter—because he didn't give a shite about his succubus offspring.

Chloe used the opportunity to resume kicking him. When she stomped her shoe directly atop his bare foot, he gave her a shake.

With a "You prick!" she kicked harder.

"Look at her!" Munro jogged up to them, still speaking in Gaelic. "She's no' like any succubus I've ever seen. She's no' changed. Like you said, she's fierce as a Lykae."

She had seemed fierce. But then, she'd also seemed *human.*

When Chloe sank her teeth into his arm, Will growled, "She has no' settled into her new role." He gave her another shake, loosing her bite. "Give her time, and she'll become the devious, selfish succubus she was born to be."

"You're no' thinking clearly."

"Nay, *you* are no'. You truly want me to be mated to a female who will take over my body and poison me? Who fed from me this verra morning?" He drew his lips back from his fangs. "She could be related to Ruelle, could be her granddaughter or niece or cousin! There are no' that many of them on this plane. Did you think of that possibility?"

That shut Munro up.

Will couldn't catch his breath. *Ruelle laughing from beyond.*

When they neared the wall, Chloe fought even harder. "Don't, MacRieve! I'm warning you!"

Switching back to English, he sneered, "Do you no' want to see your new allies—"

Suddenly a sharp pain pierced his flank.

He gaped down at a shard of glass protruding from his side. Chloe's green eyes were slitted, her teeth bared.

"You stabbed me?" He yanked the shard out, tossing it away. "I should return that to you in kind! Mayhap you're more like your father than your mother."

Munro snapped in Gaelic, "If she's harmed, you and I will no' come back from it! Do you want my hatred?"

"Brother, I've been awaiting it for centuries." Will clasped the back of her neck, forcing her up the stairs toward the watchtower.

She twisted back to cast Munro a look. Seeking Munro's goddamned protection? His brother told her in English, "He will no' harm you. I trust this."

Then Munro was vastly more confident than Will.

Atop the tower, he and Chloe passed a shocked Madadh. "What are you about, MacRieve?"

"Out of my way!" Will dragged her onto a platform overlooking the wall. Beings teemed directly below them, like a cesspool.

They fell silent at the sight of Chloe. She'd stopped struggling, gaze darting over the crowd. Though her heart skipped with fear, she put her shoulders back, as bold as a queen.

So much fire. How much he'd already come to crave it. How out of place in a simpering succubus.

Her looks had already been altered; her personality would transform as well.

That fire in her would soon ebb to ash.

***

"You all wait here," MacRieve addressed the mass of creatures, "for the chance to take this female from me. Yet she knows nothing about the Lore. She has no idea how to find her father or the other Order prisons."

His grip on Chloe's nape was like a vise. She was trapped here in front of these beings. Munro might trust MacRieve, but she didn't.

A centaur called, "Don't give a damn. She'll make good bait."

MacRieve cast him a cruel smile, flashing white fangs. "You all assume Webb will want his darling daughter back. He might have. Except for the fact that she's turned into a succubus."

That got the crowd talking. Then a female with cold eyes and golden antlers cried, "You seek to deceive deceivers? Her scent was human at the auction!"

"But it's no' now, is it? Looks like the commander got a succubus pregnant. His daughter seemed human, so Webb accepted her. Up until the minute she began to turn. Then he disposed of her like garbage."

Chloe was about to yell that that wasn't true. Surely

it wasn't. But she knew she'd be safer if these creatures believed it.

Was MacRieve telling them this to get rid of this gathering—or simply to humiliate her?

"He will no' want the refuse he's discarded, much less risk capture to rescue her. Just be glad you saved yourselves a Bridefinder."

Hisses and mutters sounded as the monsters discussed this new turn of events.

"Why should we believe you?" asked one woman who looked human, although she was dressed in a scanty outfit made mostly of metal pieces and an elaborate mask.

"I vow to the Lore that she was betrayed by her own father. I vow to you that she's worthless in regard to him. And I vow that you could no' be more disappointed than me."

Chloe stiffened against him, muttering, "And I couldn't hate you more."

The masked woman laid her hand flat against the wall. Smoke rose as she burned her handprint into it. "If Daughter of Webb crosses this boundary, we'll know it."

MacRieve ignored her, telling the crowd: "Go away, you sodding fools. Do you really think he'll fight to reclaim a creature he's ashamed of?"

At that, some did start to depart. Others remained, unconvinced, or perhaps out of spite.

Two females toward the back of the crowd caught Chloe's attention. They stood in the shadows of a distant tree. One had black hair, the other chestnut brown; both were clad in flowing gowns, their shining locks intricately styled. The brunette spoke, hardly above a whisper, yet Chloe could hear her say, "She's of our kind, Lykae. You've no claim to her. Send her past the wall."

Their kind! Chloe was drawn to the women, wanting to go to them, wanting to be anywhere but here. They didn't look malicious or evil. They appeared concerned for her. She thrashed against MacRieve, reaching her hand toward the two. Would they have known Fiore?

He grated at her ear, "Look at them all you like. Long for them. But you will never, *never* be with them."

TWENTY-SIX

T he succubus was pacing inside the adjoining guest room. Will could hear her, could sense her anger. *She* was angry with *him*?

Her scent was still that luscious, ethereal smell, but now it was underscored with the faint scent of her species, the one other males found irresistible.

Will was at once attracted to her scent—and plagued by it.

Earlier when he'd taken her from the wall, he'd shoved her into that room. "Your new accommodations."

"Why do I have to stay so close to you?" she'd asked. "Clearly I disgust you, and you repulse me. So why keep me nearby?"

He'd had no ready answer, still shocked by her attack with the shard—and shocked by the appearance of those succubae, the first two he'd encountered that he hadn't killed. Twenty-four had died by his hand—

the same number as Chloe's age. "I dinna repulse you this morning when you were sucking my rod like a straw," he'd told her.

Face gone red, she'd answered, "That was before I saw what you really are."

Now questions arose within Will, one after the other. Had she known what she was turning into? What was she thinking as she paced? Plotting an escape, no doubt.

When would she grow hungry again? A day or two? Some twisted part of him could hardly wait. He'd make her plead to be fed.

She'd be at his mercy.

Unless she could strew. Then he'd be at hers. The self-control he'd celebrated yesterday would be wrested from him yet again.

He had responded nigh violently to the scent of her arousal; he could only imagine what her strew would do to him. . . .

Munro had been trying to talk to him all afternoon. Light raps on his door had turned to openpalmed hits. In Gaelic, he'd said, "Mayhap succubae are taught to behave the way they do. Mayhap it's no' innate. I remember that night too, Will. I remember Ruelle eyeing that sword, thinking about seizing it, then begging for your help instead. Chloe would've dived for the sword and bared it along with her teeth. She *stabbed* you today. Which means she is no' like the others."

Munro's words had set Will to prowling his room, aching for that to be true, like a drowning man who thought he'd glimpsed land. But just because Chloe was one way now didn't mean she wouldn't transform, becoming more like her kind.

Toadying, ingratiating, seductive.

Weak.

Downstairs, Will could hear Munro and the lads watching TV, what sounded like a ball game. How nice life must be for them, drinking beer and watching sports without a care in the world.

Then he frowned. He could have sworn he'd just heard spectators yelling, *"Chloe!"*

He bounded down the stairs into the great room, stopping short when he saw his mate in a clip splashed across the big-screen TV. She was in a blue jersey, running down the field in front of an audience of thousands. "What the hell is this?"

"Seattle Reign clips of Chloe," Munro said. "Rónan found them on a site run by some fanboys."

Fanboys?

The website background was a collage of still shots of her in action. Her stats were listed on the side of the screen, along with a section for "Chloe Todd Trivia." Nickname: Baby T-Rex. Soccer style: Misdirection and sheer ferocity. School: Stanford. Likes: Eighties music and movies. Dislikes: Pushy fanboys.

Ferocity? And they'd never seen her with a shiv! He turned toward the liquor cabinet, grabbed a fifth. *Doona give a shite about her.* The last thing he'd be doing was checking out her games.

But why hadn't she told him she'd gone to Stanford? Not that he cared—

Rónan, Ben, and Munro simultaneously groaned, as if they'd all been kneed in the ballocks.

Despite himself, Will turned to the TV. Chloe had just gotten steamrolled by a six-foot-tall player.

He despised the succubus; he should be enjoying this. "If the runtling plays with the big girls, she's going to get hurt."

In a pissy tone, Rónan said, "We're trying to watch here."

When Chloe got to her feet and dusted herself off, the much larger Amazon shoved her again. Chloe shoved back, not giving up an inch.

When the Amazon yanked Chloe's ponytail so hard it looked like her neck had snapped, Will found himself growling. The others glanced over at him.

No wonder she'd shorn her hair. Yet now it had grown out with her change.

He drank his whiskey, but damn if he could take his eyes off the screen. The site had clip after clip of her exploiting weak coverage and scoring with clever, unexpected shots.

He casually sank down on one of the couches. "Playing against humans? Where's the sport in that?" he asked, even while he knew she'd been mortal during those games. There were clips of her limping as she ran for a penalty kick or spitting blood after being kneed in the mouth.

Which meant she'd been that good because of training—not because she'd been on the cusp of immortality. She appeared to have earned her skill.

When she had the ball, it was like a part of her;

her body was constantly moving, as if in a dance of misdirection.

She would use her arms to telegraph a strike to the right, only to tuck the ball in to her left, slipping past a flummoxed player. He could never predict whether she'd push the ball with her inner left foot or outer right or vice versa. Always something different.

It was dizzying—jaw-dropping. When he could momentarily forget what she was, she spellbound him.

In one game in the cold, her breasts had pressed against her sweat-dampened jersey, her nipples hard against the material. Had the others noticed that? He recalled how those tight points had tasted—of rain and cherries.

He drew deep of his bottle, seeking numbness.

One clip showed her taking the ball down the field, sprinting all-out, leaving her guard in the dust—until another player clotheslined her, sending Chloe crashing to her back.

Will shot to his fweet. —*PROTECT.*—

Had any Lykae ever sat back and watched his mate get beaten like this? His Instinct didn't know the difference between televised history and the present.

But Chloe hadn't needed any protection. She'd waited until later in the game, spotting her chance. The one who'd clotheslined her had been *sidelined*. Rónan cheered. "I think I'm in love!"

Will sat back down. She was like a mouse with a lion's roar, a wee warrioress.

Munro flashed him an *I told you so* look.

A succubus warrior? There was no such thing.

Even the ones who'd attacked him in the prison had behaved out of character by using force.

Chloe didn't seem to communicate in any language other than force. But now she would begin changing, transitioning into a good little succubus. The ones he'd encountered before her had all been physically flawless, possessing innate talents to lure males into their clutches. Singing, dancing, cooking, and so forth.

Chloe had already become physically flawless. Thinking back, he realized that the scars on her ankle and knee had disappeared. Her new mane of tawny hair would draw male gazes like a flame amid moths.

Soon she'd be using her newly acquired arsenal of skills. The female in these games was gone forever. . . .

His claws sank into his palms when he realized some of the clips weren't even of her playing. In one, she did nothing but wipe her face with her jersey, exposing her flat stomach and the bottom of her bra. Who were these pricks who'd put together this site?

—Males covet your unmarked mate.—

As if she'd been conjured, he heard her emerge from her room. She appeared at the top of the stairs, her shoulders squared, eyes narrowed and watchful.

Will now recognized that look. It was the same one she wore in the seconds before kickoff.

As she descended the stairs, his predator's gaze was locked on her. Forever she would look this way. He allowed himself to stare, to assess the changes in her.

She'd already sheared off the length of her hair, leaving curling tousles jutting all about her face. From

the looks of it, she'd used a knife or even another mirror shard. He wondered if she knew it would grow
back in a day.

Though her scars had disappeared, her skin remained
tanned, and she still had those freckles on her nose. Her
figure was a touch curvier, but she'd retained her athletic
shape. Anyone who saw her would know she'd been
honed by sports.

For Will, she was a fantasy made flesh—and a
nightmare.

Munro rose, as if a lady had entered. "Do you need
anything, Chloe?"

"Just going to make myself some dinner."

Will gave a harsh laugh. "Did you no' get the memo,
man-eater? What your kind dines on canna be found in
a kitchen."

She pointedly ignored him. Stalking into the kitchen,
she perused the meager offerings of the fridge, then
took out bread, butter, and cheese.

In short order, Chloe scorched the butter, burned
the sandwich, then plopped the resulting brick onto a
plate. "Does anyone else want one?" she asked sweetly.

She might not be able to cook, but that wouldn't
stop her from ingratiating herself with males, a succubus's m.o.

Rónan raised his hand. "I do." At Will's scowl, he
said, "What? I like them burned."

"Okay," she said in a bright tone. "Then I won't
clean up. Everything'll be right here when you need it."

Crestfallen, Rónan muttered, "That's my trick."

Plate in hand, she started back toward her room.

She'd have to walk past Will again. Already she swerved closer to him. *She's helpless no' to want me.* Catnip.

Soon enough those claws would come out, and finally everyone would understand what they were dealing with. Strange that she wasn't *looking* at him—Ruelle had hardly taken her eyes off him.

Never missing a step, Chloe reached down to the side table next to him and stole his whiskey bottle.

Will's jaw slackened as he watched her trot up the stairs. When she entered her room, he turned to the others. The lads were flabbergasted. Munro stifled a grin.

Ben said, "She's no' scared of you at all. Even after she saw your beast."

I could show it to her again. She was immortal, could withstand even the beast's stiff fucking. At the thought of taking her, lust hit Will like a punch in the gut, making him growl once more. *I could be inside her right now.*

Her succubus allure was already working on him.

"He's growling for her?" Rónan asked. "His mate walks by, and he does no' touch her? Or pull her into his lap? It's no' natural! And it's starting to freak me out."

"I canna be with her as I would with a fitting mate," Will said. "She comes from a diabolical species. You have to be constantly on guard."

"Can someone please tell me why succubae are so bad?" Rónan said, quickly adding, "Ben does no' understand this either."

Munro answered, "They do have powers over men. The *evil* ones"—glower at Will—"can emit chemicals to make you want them against your will."

"She's Head Case's mate; he's going to want her anyway. Besides, it's no' like she needs any chemicals. She's smokin' hot."

Another growl from Will. A defiant look from Rónan.

"Succubae form a mystical connection with their bed partners called a venom bond," Munro said. "Once the male takes it into him, he's bound to her until she dies."

"Again, she's his mate. They're already bound."

Munro raised his palms: *I've got nothing.*

Will took up the cause. "They *feed* off you, boy."

"So do vampires, but that dinna stop our king from making one his queen," Rónan pointed out. "Does it hurt?"

"If you doona do it enough, it'll hurt." As if it'd been yesterday, he could remember how his bones had felt like they were shattering, over and over again.

"So let me get this straight. Your smokin' hot mate might use chemicals to make you want to do her. Except you already want to, so it's wasted chemicals. Then once you start having sex with her, you're going to keep wanting to, which would likely have happened anyway, because like I said, she's totally hot."

"And like *I* said, there's pain involved if you doona."

"Is there no' always? It's called blue ballocks. Mayhap you've forgotten what it's like to be in your teens—"

"That female has the power to *enslave* men." Will was growing exasperated.

Rónan seemed even more so. "Doona they all?"

Again Munro raised his hands: *Pup's got a point.*

"It's a violation!"

Ben cast a wary glance at Will. "Just leave it, Rónan. It's no' for us to understand." He rose, squiring his brother away.

But the lad wasn't finished with Will. "I'll never understand this. You're supposed to hunt and provide for your mate. All you have to do is nut with her? What is wrong with you people?" As they walked off, Rónan told Ben, "If she was no' his mate, then I could see, but she is. And she's never done anything to us—except for refusing to cook—and he's threatening to behead her and shite." In a quieter, even more confused tone, he asked, "Are all the old ones this prejudiced?"

"Fairly much, aye."

When they were gone, Will sat back, filled with fury. "She's already started working on the dunderheaded pup. He'll be infatuated soon."

Munro quietly said, "I feel the same way."

"She got to you too!"

"Nay! I agree with all his points."

"You know they're sympathetic—they make you feel sorry for them, to want to protect them. I faced off against my own *father* to protect Ruelle." *Why did he no' hit me harder? I'd just gotten his beloved mate killed.*

Done discussing this, Will stood.

"Where are you going?" Munro asked.

"To make sure our new houseguest understands the rules. . . ."

TWENTY-SEVEN

It's just like reps, Chlo.

She figured there were about a dozen bites of sandwich that she had to get down. Then she could reward herself with whiskey, possibly getting drunk like last night and passing out.

Anything to end this day.

First bite. She used to love burned grilled cheeses. Second bite. *Tastes like cardboard.* Third. She could do this!

It wasn't just her utter lack of appetite that was freaking her out. If MacRieve hated her so much—and he'd just made that clear yet again—then why keep her here? This compound was huge, but he'd ordered her to stay here with one wall between them. She'd locked the adjoining door, for all the good that would do.

He should've let her go with those two succubae at the wall. How badly Chloe wanted to talk to someone of her own . . . species. To discover how to control her powers and her new strength. To determine a way around having to *feed*.

To find out about her mother and ancestors.

Until Chloe was able to escape this place, she'd have no answers. She set her plate aside and tilted her head at her room's TV. If it was connected to the internet, could she get a message out?

To who? Her friends on the team? She'd never involve them in this. With a start, she realized she might never see them again—

The adjoining door to MacRieve's room burst open, the lock broken. "You doona *ever* lock a door against me." His expression was enraged. "Understand me? And why the hell would you take my whiskey?"

She was presently experiencing the worst day of her life; she didn't need any more of his shit! "Because I want to get drunk and act like the last two days never happened."

He seemed confused that she was glaring at him. "What reason do you have to look at me like that? You're the one who hid what you were!"

"I didn't *know* what I was!"

"How could you no' sense something was wrong?"

"I believed there was a chance I was becoming immortal, but I didn't know what kind. Yet you *knew* you had a freaking monster in you just waiting to surface."

"I told you that."

"You said you might get *a wee bit bigger*, or some bullshit. Everything you say is bullshit!" And she'd bought his every line—believing herself halfway in love with him. "I might be a succubus, but at least I'm not a liar."

MacRieve was bristling. "What the hell are you talking about?"

"You told me I was part of the clan, that I was one of you. You told me you'd protect me, treasure me, and that no one would ever hurt me again. You told me we'd have eternity together, like a freaking Hallmark card! And at the first opportunity you were hauling my ass to the wall, threatening to cut off my head."

"I would have kept those promises—if you had no' transformed."

"That's why promises are made, asshole! To be kept no matter the situation."

"No' to *your* kind," he said simply, as if explaining a new truth to her.

"No, you usually kill my kind. Just like you kill all Pravus creatures you come across," she said, her voice rising with each word. "Oh, and vampires too! Exactly how is this different from what you're accusing my dad of?"

"You dare compare me to him?"

"Yeah, I just did. After the way you've treated me, I'm beginning to see his side of things. You're *teaching* me to see things his way!" She was one decibel shy of screeching.

"I war with evil creatures. Those that like to murder, rape, and torment—"

"I'm a succubus, and I'm not evil!"

"Mayhap no' yet. You're still playing at being human." He cast a cruel smirk at her half-eaten sandwich. "Trying to choke it down?"

"I don't have a choice—because I refuse to feed off another. The idea is *horrifying* to me."

She thought she saw a flash of surprise on his face before he disguised it. "You'll come to crave it soon enough. Your kind enjoys nothing more than feeding. Parasites, every one of you. And doona forget that your eyes were rolling back in your head this morning when you drank me down."

She shuddered. "That's all in the past. Now that I know what I'm up against, I'll prevail."

"You canna change what you are. As young as you are, you'll start strewing soon, emitting your chemicals. You're a ticking time bomb."

"I won't. I'll figure out a way to control it."

"You get hungry enough, there will no' be control. You'll get so aroused, reason will leave your brain. Your claws will flare, and you'll want to sink them into whatever luckless bastard happens to be close by. This is your life now; best accept the realities."

A life without soccer or friends or a dad.

MacRieve seemed to take great relish in reminding her, "There'll be no Olympics for you. Doubt you'd pass a piss test. Since you canna piss."

Her lips parted.

"Aye, that's right. Like the vampires, you've no bodily functions. Just another example of how *wrong* you are. No wonder your father abandoned you."

MacRieve was *enjoying* this, tearing her down little by little. Like he was getting revenge against her—when she'd never done anything to him. Enough. "Good to know, *Head Case*." How apropos of Rónan. "Now, as much as you're clearly getting off on dishing out pain to me, I'm done accepting it. Find someone else to spank, because the only thing I've done wrong with you is to trust all your mate bullshit." She reached for the TV remote, ignoring MacRieve as she might an aggressive fanboy.

"You doona seek to curry favor with me? Your life is in my hands, and yet you are defiant?"

Get used to it, dickwad.

But MacRieve was not to be ignored. "Look at me." Before she could blink, he'd leapt atop her, pinning her arms over her head. "I said to look at me."

The weight of his body was crushing, his erection like a steel beam pressing against her. Despite her hatred of him, she felt herself responding.

Why couldn't she turn off this arousal? Was it a succubus thing? Or a *MacRieve* thing? After all, the traits that had attracted her before remained unchanged— his sigh-worthy body, his golden eyes, his firm lips . . . his talented tongue.

A flash memory of his mouth between her legs made her heart thud and her nipples go hard. *Don't think about that!*

"When you get hungry enough, you'll come crawling to me."

She refused to look away. "Never. You disgust me." His treatment of her did.

He inhaled deeply. "Nay, disgust is no' what you're feeling. I can scent how much you want me inside you."

Her cheeks flamed, because it was true. She was *aching* for something to fill her. "What's the difference between that scent and strew?"

He seemed surprised by her question. "A mate's arousal would make a Lykae desperate to get her somewhere alone to tup. Strew would make a male rip off a succubus's clothes to rut her on the spot. Would no' matter if the entire clan was watching."

Would *he* do that if she strewed? "Like I said, I'll eat regular food. Then there'll be no need for any strew. We don't ever have to touch again."

With an angry shove, he thrust his erection over her again. "You think you'll be able to keep your hands off me?"

She couldn't deny her physical reaction to him. But she would make sure he understood exactly what was going on. "Say I do get turned on by you—even though I despise you. What's the difference between what you're doing to me, and what you think I'll do to you?"

He scowled. "What are you talking about?"

"If you make me want you against my will, then who's the succubus? Your *looks* are your strew. Explain to me the difference."

A troubled expression flashed over his face before his hatred blazed through once more. "I would never use my looks to rape others."

She shoved at him. Even with her new strength, she couldn't budge him. "You don't have to fear that from me, MacRieve. I'd rather starve to death. I'd look forward to it, before I ever fed from you."

He released her and rose, gave her a withering look. "I'll remember that when you're pleading with me to fuck you. And when I deny you again and again. . . ."

TWENTY-EIGHT

"**P**ass the ball, Ben!" Chloe yelled.

She was playing a pickup soccer game with him, Rónan, Madadh, and six others. It'd been four days since she'd seen MacRieve's beast, but she still found it freaky that all the Lykae around her had a similar wolf thing inside them.

Rónan was guarding her, and she was tooling him with her new immortal strength and speed. As the self-proclaimed clan athletic director, she'd started working drills with him. Alas, moves like hers took time to perfect.

She'd decided to put herself out there as clan AD because she needed something to occupy her time or she'd go crazy—and because she needed Rónan's help to escape. . . .

MacRieve sat next to an oak on the sidelines, as he usually did. For someone who hated her so much, he was always watching her, silent and brooding, as if just waiting for her to drop trou and "plead for it."

Fortunately for her, she was halfling enough not to suffer those urges. Much. Hardly at all, if she kept herself busy and her stomach full of food.

She'd ignored him for the most part. Okay, he was fairly impossible to ignore. She sensed his presence if he was nearby, sensed his gaze on her across the field. She would wonder if he was recalling their day together. "Best day of my life," he'd said. She must be a glutton for abuse, because whenever she replayed that day, she still felt a pang in her heart. . . .

Amazingly, MacRieve's stunt at the wall had worked. The creatures had departed, but he still wouldn't release her. Even Munro was against her leaving the compound, insisting that she could be tracked without the proper precautions.

Like a camouflage talisman.

She'd assessed her field position and concluded that she didn't want to be near MacRieve; nor did she want to be kidnapped by centaurs again. Chloe remembered that burned handprint on the wall. Would the Pravus get an email alert if she crossed the boundary? A talisman was the only solution, which meant it had become the championship trophy in her mind.

Rónan had told her of his friendship with certain witches—including those who'd kidnapped her—so she'd asked him to help her make a purchase.

"Sorry, T-Rex," the kid had told her. "The House of Witches always demands payment up front."

"No lease with option to purchase?" she'd asked. "Layaway?"

"No such thing as Wicca credit." He'd laughed at

the idea. "If you knew any witches, you'd understand why your questions are kind of funny."

She constantly thought about that talisman. She'd lie in bed, imagining ways to get hundreds of thousands of dollars.

Until such time, she was stuck. To be fair, it wasn't as bad now that she was starting to get the hang of this immortal business.

The afternoon of her change, Rónan had knocked on her bedroom door. She'd been staring at the ceiling, still agitated from her last interaction with MacRieve. "Go away, kid. I'm busy."

"You canna stay in there forever. You want to play soccer?"

She'd shot up in bed. She could hear . . . yes, he was kneeing a ball into the air.

Out on the field that first day, Chloe had found that she was faster and tougher. Or else Lykae pups were pussies.

Her improvement was bittersweet. Yes, flying down the field at revved-up speeds was amazing; but she'd also recognized that she had probably been super-charged because of MacRieve. And his *nourishment*.

Which made her want to strangle something. . . .

Rónan was a big help, keeping her mind occupied. In exchange for coaching, he'd given her his old iPod and all the T-shirts and soccer shorts she could possibly wear. He'd even coughed up an old pair of cleats. They were too big, but she managed with them.

The kid had also been showing her what she could do as an immortal. "Climb up on the tower roof and jump off," he'd said, pointing to a nearby lookout that was easily five stories high.

Recalling how quickly her hand had healed, she'd eventually succumbed to his double-dog dares. The second time down, she was laughing all the way.

Munro was helping her settle in as well. He didn't say much, but he would ask if she needed anything. He'd given her a laptop, and she suspected he was the one making sure there was always food in the house, silently supporting her efforts.

The clan had warmed up to her once more, as if to make up for how unreasonable MacRieve was being.

When she could block out the shit show of her life, she'd actually begun enjoying some parts. She'd settled into a routine. Every morning, she woke and lopped off her hair, taking the length from mid-back to boy cut. Then she would force herself to choke down a minimum number of calories. After breakfast, she, Rónan, and Ben would run over the compound, from one wall to the other, what must be dozens of miles. She never lost her breath. All afternoon, they played sports. At night, she and Rónan drank beer.

Rise and repeat. Until today.

She'd awakened nauseated, suffering waves of it all morning. When she'd grown increasingly weak, her first thought was that she had a stomach virus. But according to Munro, she was immune to such ailments.

Which meant she was losing the battle to stay on food. It made sense. What else could explain how she could still desire MacRieve, even when she hated him? Her succubus half must be clamoring for dinner. *Ugh!*

If she replayed their encounters, her libido would spike, sending her diving for crackers or a banana, anything to quash it—

Her stomach rumbled now, another surge of nausea taking her. So what would happen if her breakfast didn't stay down? All she knew was that if she had to feed—she furtively gazed over at MacRieve—she'd do anything possible to avoid a Big Mac.

Escape, she thought for the thousandth time. *I've got to get ghost.*

⁂

She's no' becoming the succubus she was meant to be, Will thought as he watched Chloe playing soccer.

She was supposed to obsess about her looks, always putting herself in the most desirable light; Chloe wore Rónan's shorts, somebody's wife-beater, and borrowed cleats. They were too big, so she'd duct-taped them to fit her wee feet.

She was supposed to be a talented singer, dancer, cook; he'd discovered Chloe's voice was horrendous—and she used it to belt out eighties power ballads as she jogged the grounds with the lads.

She was supposed to be irresistibly attracted to Will; for four days, she'd avoided him, never looking at him if he placed himself in her proximity.

Such as now. Not even a glance over. He could swear he almost . . . missed her, already grown used to having her by his side. Or mayhap she was simply a succubus who could make him feel things he didn't want to.

Hell, even Webb hadn't been able to resist her mother. *What hope have I?*

So there Will sat, drinking whiskey, dangerously close to bloody pining for her, even while applauding himself for his control. *My will is my own.*

He was so caught up watching her play that he barely noticed Munro joining him under the oak.

"You look like hell."

"Have no' slept much." After that peaceful night with Chloe, his nightmares had returned with a vengeance, alternating between Ruelle and his torture.

His time in that prison still haunted him. Which made sense. Will had gone from being one among the most powerful creatures in the Lore—a warrior honed by battle—to a victim who could do nothing more than take his torments.

Just as he'd been unable to do anything but take Ruelle's feedings.

In each nightmare, he powerlessly surrendered something—his seed, his lifeblood, even his fucking heart. And always his pride. He'd wake, unable to breathe, experiencing that unmistakable feeling of suffocation.

The deep dragging him down.

So he rarely closed his eyes. He would stay awake watching those clips of Chloe, punishing himself with imaginings of what could have been. When he saw her on the field, his perfect mate, he yearned for her. He . . . grieved her, as if those clips were playing at a wake.

Soon she would change; but he could fantasize that

this girl from before was his. Instead of surrendering and ceding, he imagined conquering and claiming her.

"Chloe's been settling in nicely," Munro said.

She played on the field like a pro—and off the field like a kid, taking dares and giving them, exploring the compound, trash-talking Ben and Rónan. "Doona give a shite how she's settling."

"Then why are you always watching her?"

"Because she's dangerous, a ticking time bomb. Even if I canna get anyone to believe that, I know it." Though no one in the clan knew quite what to do about this situation, it was clear they all liked her. Of course, they had no idea what she was truly capable of.

No' like I do.

Munro said, "Chloe's still trying to eat food. Mayhap she can continue."

"If no', have the witches returned your calls?" He'd gotten Munro to ask for a potion to make them immune to strew.

Turning to the witches? Obviously Will was desperate. But this was one of his last hopes. His other was that Chloe could continue to eat normally, that her human half could rule her in this.

Will had also asked if the witches could scry for Webb using Chloe's blood.

Munro said, "I just heard back from Mariketa the Awaited."

If Will could ever bring himself to trust a witch, he supposed it'd be that one.

"She does no' have high hopes for an immunity

potion. She said she'd try when she got back to town—but at the verra least, she needs a sample to base it on."

"A sample? By then it'll be too late." There went that hope.

"The witches had already used Chloe's blood to scry for Webb," Munro continued. "They've said their results were 'puzzling.' In short, they canna locate him. The Lore's back to square one with that."

Why could nothing work out for Will? What had he done to deserve his fate? Daughter of Webb *and* a succubus. Who the hell had Will pissed off?

Munro gazed out at the field, scrutinizing another scoring drive. "I doona want to say Chloe's unlady-like, but she does no' remind me of *Lady* Ruelle at all."

"They're more alike than you know," Will insisted, though he couldn't quite come up with an instance. "Just trust me on this."

At that moment, Rónan accidentally elbowed Chloe in the face, then looked horrified to have walloped a girl. "Chloe, I'm sorry!"

Ruelle would've cried prettily, milking sympathy for all she was worth.

Chloe just shrugged, though her lip was now bleeding. "We're in the middle of a game, Rónan." As she signaled for the ball with one hand, she absently spat blood, then evaded Madadh with a clever spin move. She took it the length of the field and scored.

Rónan jogged up to her. "Your lip and cheek really look bad."

She rolled her eyes. "Rónan, I'm *fine*. Now, why

don't you shove in a manpon and tug up your manties and PLAY SOCCER."

"Oh, aye," Munro began in a mocking tone. "She's *just* like Ruelle. They could be sisters."

Will scowled.

"Chloe's fierce, a fighter who does no' give a damn about her looks," Munro persisted.

Ruelle had been weak, cowardly, obsessed with her own beauty. Never a hair out of place, not even when she was feeding.

Chloe's attitude toward her own appearance could best be described as *See me, love me, motherfucker.* Even now her hair looked like she'd hacked it off with a knife. *And it still bluidy looks good.*

You'd never know the heavenly arse on that female because it was always hidden by loose men's shorts, and he could swear she wore more than one bra, just to conceal the size of her perfect breasts.

No, the two succubae were not alike. But if Will ever allowed himself to believe that Chloe wouldn't transform into a facsimile of Ruelle, and then she did . . .

I would no' recover.

Munro continued, "No' to mention that Chloe's no child molester."

Will gazed around wildly. "Doona ever say that again!" he sputtered, though that was precisely what Ruelle had been.

She'd poisoned him to make him do things his young mind couldn't understand—and his body hadn't been ready for—as if he'd been a puppet. It'd been terrifying to him. He remembered how she'd rise over him, her green eyes alight, smothering him with perfumed white flesh.

Even when his beast had risen, Ruelle—a fully grown immortal—had still been able to overpower him, a child.

"I'm tired of this, *bràthair*." Munro scrubbed his hand over his chin. "We've tiptoed around the subject for centuries. We need to talk about this if we're ever going to get past it."

A flash memory of Nïx arose. *You need to rebreak that bone. It didn't set right.* Was this all a part of her plan? Was she trying to get Will right with himself?

The more he'd thought about how he'd come to possess Chloe, the more he detected Nïx's interference. He'd realized the soothsayer had gotten him to the auction; now he suspected she'd gotten Chloe there as well.

After twenty-four years, two factions had found Daughter of Webb on the same night? *Dropped a dime to the witches about her existence, did you, soothsayer?*

Munro said, "I keep thinking back to that night, Will. There were two females in Ruelle's cottage, and Chloe is more like Mam than she'll ever be like that succubus."

"Doona dare compare her to our mother!"

They fell silent, both gazing at Chloe. The sun flashed through clouds, prisms of light cascading over her. Her skin was beginning to bruise from the corner of her busted lip past her cheekbone. Looking pale, she abruptly ran for the woods. Will tensed, uneasy when she left his sight. Then he heard her throwing up.

She returned moments later, paler, heading straight for the cooler. She swished beer into her mouth, then spat it out.

Munro exhaled. "She's lost her breakfast, then."

"Aye. There went my second hope."

By the end of the game, her bruise had blackened her eye as well. And she'd hurt her ankle. When she put weight on it, she winced, then cast Munro a questioning glance.

He gave her a grave one in response.

Turned to Munro instead of me. *My mate. Mine!*

Munro said, "She's stopped healing. She'll need to feed soon."

"What do you expect me to do about it?" Chloe's black eye was as glaring as an accusation; he might as well have given it to her. "I'm no' eager to take on her venomous bond. To be tied to her forever." *To discover that I canna satisfy her either.* He'd never been able to feed Ruelle enough. And if she'd come during sex, he had no memory of it. No wonder she'd taken a vampire lover in addition to Will.

Munro gaped at him. "You could heal your eternal mate with one tup. Do you *want* me to be ashamed of you? Your choices are verra simple. Either you bed her or you allow another to feed her."

"I'll kill any who touch her!"

Munro raised his brows at Will's outburst. "Then you either bed her or watch her die."

Or I die. As soon as the thought occurred, he knew that path was closed to him. His newly returned Instinct would never allow him to harm himself, not while he had a mate who'd be left alone in the world, unprotected.

Munro pulled a stalk of grass, twirling it in his fingers. "When you were manhandling Chloe to the wall, you repeated the last words Mam said to you. What do you think she and Da would react to most: the fact that your mate is one among a hated species? Or that you're no' protecting or providing for her? Fate made a decision, and now you're to abide by it. They raised us to believe in fate as our faith, Will. They raised us better than this."

Will stabbed his fingers through his hair, then admitted a shaming truth. "I doona know if I *could* tup her. Physically. Even if I wanted to." Sex with a succubus was different from sex with other females; even after her partner had come, emptying himself, a succubus could pull a last mind-numbing spasm.

When he was young, he'd always thought that last pull would kill him. Would Chloe be as greedy?

Merely imagining it made his breaths shallow. "She would likely *have* to use her strew on me."

"And if she does, how will the others here resist it? How long do we have before she begins to?"

Were the lads following Chloe with their gazes? They'd ended the game and were setting up drills. Ben was helping her, placing cones, positioning balls, being overly solicitous.

Will's Instinct had been cautioning him for days.

—*Other males, near your unmarked mate.*—

Ben could barely control his beast in the best of conditions. Add a succubus's chemicals to the mix . . .

Munro pressed on. "We have to think of the lads,

of the entire pack. Your beast will kill any who try to bed her. You must take her from the compound. Especially with the full moon to rise in three nights."

At length, Will said, "Verra well. I'll ready to leave. Go back to the witches. Ask for a talisman to hide her."

"Easy enough, with the right funds. They spoke of a simple bracelet that would do the trick. But where will you go? It must be hidden from the Lore."

At his brother's considering look, Will said, "Oh, no, no! I will no' take her there."

"She's still target number one," Munro said. "If we have to borrow a place, others will know of it. Information like that spreads like wildfire. Yet no one knows of Conall any longer. The Woods were cleared. It's a forgotten land."

Will hadn't been back there since the late Middle Ages, but he knew the impervious keep was still standing strong, would forever. The ashes of their ancestors had been baked into the bricks, warding off time—as well as any enemies.

"The Woods were no' *completely* cleared." Though Will, Munro, and their men had burned all other structures—the Cerunno nests, the centaur halls—Will had ordered Ruelle's cottage untouched. He still recalled Munro's questioning glance and his own explanation: he needed it to remember.

Munro had asked, "Could you ever truly forget?"

Apparently so. Because Will was considering feeding one of Ruelle's kind.

Munro said, "I had the keep modernized a few years ago. Brought in sheep again."

"Why did I no' know about that?"

He shrugged. "It's no' exactly your favorite subject. There's a caretaker looking after it. I'll have him ready everything for you."

"If I take Chloe there, I'd be consigning myself to bedding her. She'd be consigned to accepting me." Traveling to Scotland would be like a gallows march across the world.

Munro gave him a bemused look. "Brother, you are *already* consigned."

Consigned. Which was another way of saying, *I have no choice.* So this was a done deal, then? He was to claim Chloe.

Some traitorous part of him quickened at the idea. Words left his lips: "I'll do it."

"I'll take care of the bracelet and transportation directly. Give me an hour. You'd best let Chloe know she's soon to leave. No' that she'll need much time packing her things."

A subtle jab at Will—who hadn't provided her with jewels, luxuries, or even additional clothes, as a mate should.

Will stood. "I've one last thing to ask from the witches. A second hex for that bracelet."

When Will told him, Munro cast him a look that was disappointed—but not at all surprised.

TWENTY-NINE

MacRieve strode directly through Chloe's obstacle course, ignoring Rónan's drill. "Pack your men's clothes, succubus," he told her. "We're leaving."

Chloe waved the kid on. "You need to clear that in under a minute."

Rónan nodded, giving MacRieve a glare, then continued his practice.

"Leaving? Let me guess, a prison transfer?" She wasn't going anywhere with Head Case. "I'm going to have to say no to that plan, crypt keeper. What else you got?"

He scowled at her new nickname for him.

She could make fun of his age all she wanted, but that wouldn't change how physically attractive he was. Even if she hated him, she could admire his looks. He stood so tall, still drool-worthy. Still obviously a douche.

After a figurative ass-kicking, Chloe was usually

pretty good at picking herself up and dusting off her pants. But then, she'd never been quite as crushed as with him—so why did she still feel that *connection* to him?

Though he smelled like whiskey, she could detect that addictive masculine scent of his. With her stomach now empty, she was feeling a completely different kind of hunger. Her claws sprouted. She hid them behind her back. Sweat beaded her forehead. She needed to get away from him and nosh another round of food.

"We depart in an hour for Scotland."

One of the few European countries she'd never played in. As much as she'd wanted to leave before, now she was suspicious. "No can do, MacRieve. You see, I'm currently employed as the clan AD—"

"AD?"

"Athletic director. Some of us actually have a job to do. Besides, why would I ever go anywhere with you?"

"Because your shortsighted plan to eat like a normal person dinna work out. I know you threw up."

She swiped her arm over her forehead. "I've just been running too hard. That's nothing definitive. I'm about to go eat again."

He flicked his gaze over her face and eye, then scowled. Rónan had told her it was bruising. And more, her bad ankle was killing her. So much for immortality.

"You will no' regenerate like this."

She gazed away, then back. "I'll continue to get worse?" Until what? She died?

A curt nod. "You need to feed. Resign yourself to this fact."

Every time he used the word *feed*, her mind was cast back to their last encounter—when her claws had sunk into his lean hips as she'd swallowed him down. The most delectable taste she'd ever imagined.

Her claws were now *aching* to pierce his skin. Her nipples hardened under her shirt, until even two sports bras couldn't conceal the taut points.

"Gods, woman, I can scent your arousal," he said, voice gone hoarse. "Others will soon enough."

How embarrassing! Her gaze darted to the lodge. *Need an apple. And a shower.* And perhaps an orgasm of her own, to release some pressure. "I can handle this. Eating food tamps that down."

He shook his head. "It's only a matter of time before you start strewing. And if I doona take you somewhere isolated, every unmated male around will fight to mate you."

"If I say no to them—"

"Then they'll fight to rape you."

"Every male?" She shielded her eyes against the sun, watching Rónan dribbling around cones. Ben was practicing punting. Presently he could kick the ball about two miles. With her help, he could achieve three.

MacRieve followed her gaze. "Ben would be first in line." His harsh voice drew her attention. She noted his fists were clenched. "Probably after killing his little brother for the pleasure."

"I don't *want* to emit chemicals. There has to be a way for me to control it. If you would just let me speak to one of my own kind! We could find those two who were outside the wall—"

"*Never.* This is my decision. You'll abide by it."

So arrogant! She longed to put him to the ground, to slide-tackle him till he ate turf. "I thought I couldn't leave the compound. That the Pravus would find me through burning handprints or whatever."

"We're acquiring a talisman. Remember the mystical means I talked about?"

He was offering a . . . talisman? Holy shit! This would be her chance to escape! She knew he could detect any changes in her voice, could hear her heart speeding up. *Calm yo tits, Chlo.* "Oh? Is that so?" she said in a bored tone. "Wow, you're going to spend that much money on me—and you plan to do business with my kidnappers. I *hate* your world."

"And it hates you."

"Your clan likes me well enough."

With utter confidence, he said, "Because they doona *know* you."

Bite your tongue. "I don't have my passport with me."

"We'll travel through private Lore airports."

All she heard was *private escape-ports.* "So when do I get this alleged camouflage doo-thingy?"

He narrowed his gaze. "Ah, look at the wee succubus making plans to flee. Your heart races. You truly think you can get away from me? Lykae *hunt.* It would no' even be sporting."

"I have nothing to lose by trying." She gave him a long look. "Except for werewolf dead weight."

"I should just let you walk out of here with your little hobo stick filled with men's clothing."

"Yes. You should."

"You've been told that the Pravus males will gang rape you, and still you seek to leave. Mayhap you crave it from them?" He turned and strode away.

"Prick!" She lined up two balls. Taking aim, she reared back and kicked the first as hard as she could. The second followed in quick succession.

As planned, the first took him in the back of the head. When he spun around, the second nailed him in the testicles.

"What . . . the . . . fuck?" He gritted his teeth, but remained standing.

As others tried to hide their laughter, she shrugged. "Penalty."

He bared his fangs at her, stalking off to the sound of Rónan singing the soccer anthem, *"Oléeee, olé, olé, oléeee. . . ."*

THIRTY

Scottish Highlands

With every mile of forest and dirt track closer to Conall, the isolation weighed on Will. He drummed his fingers on the wheel of his new truck.

With each mile closer, his future became clearer. There would be no other for Chloe. It was down to him. And he was alternately disgusted and aroused by the idea of claiming her. Never had he felt such conflict within him.

She was oblivious to his turmoil, currently fast asleep in the passenger seat. Unless seriously weakened, most immortals needed only a few hours a day. The food she'd been trying to keep down might temporarily douse her arousal, but it did nothing to sustain her energy or heal her injuries.

He tried to concentrate on the road, on the scenery. Despite visiting Kinevane, he hadn't been this close to Conall in centuries. He'd had no reason to return, making his home in Nova Scotia. He'd nearly forgotten the beauty of this region. Cloud shadows roamed over

bronze mountains and mirror-smooth lochs like giant
phantoms. Breathtaking.

He frowned at Chloe. She was missing everything.
But then, did he care?

Mayhap? Should he wake her up? He decided
against it. Their daylong journey had only fatigued her
more. . . .

After giving Chloe a simple silver talisman bracelet,
Munro had driven them to the Loreport, where a jet
awaited. They'd hired a demon pilot who already had a
mate, just in case Chloe began strewing at forty thousand feet.

Munro had taken each of them aside in turn for a
few private words. "Have a care with my *deirfiúr*," he'd
told Will. "And I suggest you inform her what else her
talisman does."

Chloe had been standing at a little distance, clearly
weighing her chances of escaping. She'd fiddled with
her new bracelet, having no idea it had a second critical
function.

Munro's parting words to Will: "Even now, your
mate suffers because you deny her. You were ill-used in
the past, but if you take it out on her, then you become
the *slaoightear*." The villain.

Whatever Munro had told Chloe had left her
equally shaken.

On the plane, she'd scuffed to the back cabin and
fallen atop the bed, sleeping for most of the trip. He'd
crept into the cabin, stretching his body out beside
hers. Again he'd thought, *I'm looking down at my mate.* So
lovely. Deceptively delicate. —*Yours.*—

Part of him still hated her for becoming a succubus, for pulling him from the brink only to shove him right back. But now it was too late. He knew it as well as he knew his reflection.

My soul's been branded. Which was yet another way of saying, *I have no choice.*

—*Claim her. Protect. Provide.*—

He'd been tempted to provide right there on the plane. When he'd scented her renewed arousal and spied her stiffened nipples, he'd trailed his hand down her body to cup her between her legs, fondling her over her jeans. She'd woken with a gasp.

Her thighs had spread so obediently, and she'd rocked her sex into his palm as a good mate would. *Acquiescing already?*

Then she'd seemed to rouse fully. Her knees had slammed shut. "Get away from me, asshole."

With a blistering curse, he'd obliged, pacing the plane for hours. Restless, miserable.

Even if he wanted to claim her—even if he *could*—she wouldn't receive him. As she'd put it, she was repulsed to see his beast.

Sequestered at Conall, she wouldn't have a lot of choices. She'd start strewing, and his beast would be helpless not to take her, whether she wanted it or not. If he had to hate-fuck his mate to keep her fed, then so be it.

They'd landed on a private strip in the Highlands, with a three-hour drive to Conall still ahead of them. When Will had picked up his new SUV, she'd frowned. "I don't know about you driving. What if your beast

comes out? I don't think he's got a driver's permit."
In a weird voice, she said, " 'He don't even have his
license, Lisa.' "

"Who's Lisa?"

She'd blinked at him. "*Weird Science*? Never mind,
crypt keeper. I'll shoot you a YouTube sometime,
through this thing we youngsters like to call 'electronic
mail.' "

Now they crossed a bridge over the river that
marked the eastern edge of Conall property. *I'm on my
family's land.* At the thought, his uneasiness increased.

He was returning to the place of his origins with
his mate in tow. A mate who was sound asleep from
exhaustion, favoring one leg, sporting a bruised face,
and suffering the effects of malnutrition. She'd brought
one of Rónan's old gym bags, and all the belongings
she had in the world hadn't filled it.

His brother had given her the one piece of jewelry
she owned.

The back of Will's neck heated. He shouldn't give
a damn. He reminded himself that she was *lucky* to be
with him, fortunate that he'd been prepared to make
sacrifices for her.

He was about to bring one of her kind within those
hallowed walls of Conall, defiling his home. He was
about to feed her, healing her.

But those were his limits. His gaze fell on her
bracelet. As per his orders, that talisman would keep
her hidden—and keep her from conceiving. Just the
idea of Ubus spawn was ballock-shriveling for him. If
he and Chloe had incubi sons and succubae daughters,

he would have to withdraw his offspring from the clan, could never let his line prey on others.

Again he drummed impatiently at the wheel, every mile cranking up the tension within him. And the more anxious he became, the more his Instinct told him to take comfort in his mate.

Just when his hand was reaching for her of its own volition, she woke, blinking at her surroundings. Now that he'd slowed their speed on a dirt road, she rolled down her window, laying her head on the door.

The scents of the Highlands swept him up, easing some of his tension. He gazed over at her. The late-afternoon sun flickered through trees, reflecting off the silver cuff on her wrist and bathing the smooth skin of her unmarred cheek. Over the course of their journey, her hair had grown out to nearly shoulder-length, shiny waves streaming in the wind.

She's so bluidy bonny.

As he took in her heavy-lidded eyes and drowsy smile, the urge to stroke her face was nigh undeniable.

He needed to tell her that he found her beautiful, that he would give her anything she desired. Gods, he felt as if he'd die if he didn't kiss her—

Comprehension.

As the keep came into view, it was not a moment too soon.

Because Chloe was beginning her first strew.

THIRTY-ONE

*L*ifestyles of the Rich and Famous* meets *Medieval Times,*" Chloe said casually as she stepped out of the SUV, making an effort to mask her amazement at the sight before her. She wouldn't give Mac-Rieve the satisfaction, not when he'd just grated, "Out *now.*"

Conall Keep was jaw-dropping, like it belonged on a postcard. The main part of the building was a squared-off, three-story structure built of cream-colored stone. Wings sprawled on either side, each framed with towering trees. Smoke plumes curled up from two chimneys, promising warmth, a welcome sight as dusk neared and a chill set in.

A real-life babbling brook coursed nearby, with its own water wheel and everything. The front yard consisted of miles of green hills dotted with fluffy white sheep. Beyond them lay a distant forest.

When MacRieve slammed out of the truck, she

wondered what had crawled up his ass. Ever since they'd closed in on this place, he'd grown even more surly—yet on the plane, the bastard had made a move on her.

She'd woken to find his rough palm covering her crotch completely, the heat of his skin seeping through her jeans. She'd barely rebuffed him, almost calling him back. Then she'd discovered the snacks on the plane, choking down peanuts and a Coke.

Yes, food could dull her arousal, but it provided zero energy. Though she'd been excited about being in Scotland for the first time and eager to escape, her body hadn't cooperated. She'd dozed off on the way here.

Way to pay attention so you can flee, Chlo. And more? She would kill for a nap right now. She planned to shower, sleep, force herself to eat whatever was available—then plot her exit strategy.

As she and MacRieve approached the wide front doors, it fully sank in that she was alone with a man in a remote location. She'd never even been on a date before MacRieve, so this all felt momentous. She tried to fill the silence. "I, um, dig your place."

He paused with his key in the front door, narrowing his eyes at her. Sweat dotted his upper lip. His voice was strained as he said, "This is my ancestral home. I doona give a damn if a succubus *digs it*."

Before she'd left Glenrial, Munro had explained that Conall was where they'd grown up, and that MacRieve held it sacred. The fact that he was bringing her there was important.

Maybe, but he was blatantly unhappy about it.

"How's this place still standing?"

In a put-out tone, MacRieve answered, "The bricks were made with the ashes of those who came before us. They ward away time—and any who would do us harm."

"Your cremated ancestors are part of the bricks? I *hate* the Lore," she said, even as her gaze was drawn down to her new silver bracelet, imbued with Lorean camouflage mojo.

When he pushed open one of the front doors for her, she gamely trudged inside.

The foyer was stately, with a grand curving stairway that looked like it'd been carved from the keep itself. The tiled floor gleamed. The air smelled faintly of beeswax.

In an adjoining library, book-filled shelves covered walls from floor to ceiling. The antique furnishings were finely crafted. Oil paintings and tapestries accented the decor. Yet as she passed a second room, a lushly arranged sitting area, she noted that there was no hint that children had once lived here, no hint that this place had belonged to a family.

But then, it wasn't like there'd be grade-school pictures to hang—because her travel companion was really freaking old. Like he'd call rock-n-roll *that infernal racket* old. Like when-dinosaurs-ruled-the-earth old. God, this was so messed up.

She turned when she realized he wasn't behind her. He stood at the threshold, hesitating to enter, his big frame silhouetted in the doorway.

An ancient immortal had returned to his boyhood home. So why this hesitation?

Something was seriously wrong here. His brows were drawn tight, his muscles tensed.

Even after everything, she had the impulse to soothe whatever was hurting him, to smooth away his lost expression.

She found her feet taking her back toward this man. . . .

＊＊＊＊＊＊＊＊

Will had made it through the first wave of her strew without whipping out his dick and falling on her. *Good on you, man.*

His self-congratulations were short-lived when faced with Conall. Every detail of this place made memories erupt in Will's mind, keeping him on edge.

Though Munro had brought in plumbing and electricity, the furniture and tapestries had remained largely the same. Like a time capsule.

When Chloe turned back with a quizzical look on her face, he brusquely pushed past her, that slight contact making him ache for her.

But he remained in control. Mayhap her strew was weak since she was only a cambion. Perhaps it would grow stronger, building with use, like a muscle. If so, he was screwed. Just as she would be.

She silently followed as he strode through the great room, past the hearth. The caretaker had lit a fire there.

So many memories . . .

He hastened toward the kitchen, finding it well-stocked with food—and liquor. For the second time in less than a week, Will thought, *Bless you, brother.*

Though tempted to chug from a bottle of whiskey, he found a highball glass and poured several fingers.

She retrieved a glass of her own, holding it up for him to fill.

Once he grudgingly did, she sipped. "Where am I supposed to sleep? I need a catnap."

She'd slept for most of the trip and craved more? How many hours out of twenty-four could she possibly sleep? What if she drifted off and never woke up?

The thought sent a jolt of panic through him, and he gulped down his drink. The bottle clinked against his glass as he refilled. —*Protect. Provide.*—

Crossing the great room, he said, "Your room's on the second floor." With leaden feet, he climbed the stone stairs.

What he found made him grind his teeth with frustration. None of the guest rooms had been aired. Nor had the brothers' childhood bedroom. Sheets still draped all the furniture, the windows sealed tight.

Grimly he ascended another flight of stairs to the master suite. Of course, it had been readied. *Munro, you prick.* Treating Will like he was master of the keep?

Chloe blithely entered, then turned in place. "It's beautiful," she breathed.

He understood her appreciation. Softly lit by another fire, the airy suite stretched from one side of the keep to the other and was elegantly appointed, though differently from days past. His parents' sleigh bed had been replaced with an enormous four-poster, and all the furniture had been exchanged for more modern pieces. The handwoven brocades his mother had favored for the window dressings and bed covering were gone, replaced by lighter textiles. The coverlet had a narrow border of plaid, the MacRieve tartan.

Chloe crossed to a curving bank of windows. "What's that forest called?"

"The Woods of Murk," he grated, fists balling. The woods where his mam had died. Ruelle's cottage lay inside that forest. *Remember, Will. Remember how weak you were.*

Whatever Chloe detected in his voice drew her gaze. She seemed to be noting his reaction.

"It's a place you will never go."

With a glare, she turned to the opposite wall, to another bank of windows. From there she could see the woods to the north and the courtyard below. In the center was a sera cherry tree in full bloom—like the one in Louisiana, except this one was much larger. It'd been there since he was a child.

When she saw it, she gave a little gasp. As if spurred by some invisible force, he joined her. No, not an invisible force—it had to be her strew. Was it getting stronger?

They fell silent, watching the breeze flutter petals. He knew both of them were thinking about that one perfect day.

Still gazing down, she said, "You really screwed yourself, MacRieve. Every day could've been like that. An eternity of them, just like you promised me. I suppose I should just be grateful that you haven't beheaded me yet." With a shrug, she padded toward the walk-in closet. "Oh, my God, it's full of new clothes! And they're ones I'd actually wear."

Draining his glass, he peered into the closet, saw jeans, long-sleeved T-shirts, no-frills button-downs, and blazers. There were running shoes and even tiny cleats. A new set of luggage stood by. As if Chloe would be traveling?

She turned to him, gazing up at him with eyes that flickered green with emotion. "Thank you. I wasn't expecting this."

Succubus green. A shock of anger hammered him. "I would no' do this for you. You'd best thank Munro." That bastard had provided her with things that Will hadn't.

She muttered, *"Such a dick,"* then began investigating the garments.

Had his brother picked out the lingerie she was now rummaging through? The red silks that would quicken any wolf's blood?

There was a piece of paper taped to the closet door. She handed it to him. "I can't read this. It's in either Gaelic or Wolf."

A printed out e-mail from Munro: *Calm down, you sodding jackass. Cassandra picked out all the clothes. Consider them gifts from you—for the new mistress of the keep.*

Mistress? Then that would make Will the master. This confused him mightily. Conall belonged to both brothers. Yet Munro kept giving hints that Will would live here with Chloe.

Probably to protect the clan. Will had already been shuffled to the fringe.

Chloe turned back to her new wardrobe, murmuring, "Not for the first time I'm wondering why I couldn't be Munro's mate. You both look the same—"

Will lunged forward, snatching her upper arm to yank her from the closet. "You push too far, woman!" Never had he been jealous of Munro. Now Will felt enough to stretch over nine centuries. He growled, "Is it him that you want?"

"Why wouldn't I? At least he's been decent to me."

As Will's grip tightened, he wondered why he was so surprised by this. It was only a matter of time before Chloe strayed. Munro would never touch her, but any other red-blooded male . . .

"Let go, MacRieve." When she couldn't budge his hand, she punted his leg. "Don't touch me!"

"Best get used to me touching you. Soon I will no' be able to help myself. You've started strewing. You're spicing the air right now."

"What?" Her face paled even more, highlighting her bruise. "No. No way."

"Oh, aye. I could barely concentrate on the road, coming in. My mind was in a fog."

"But you said it would madden you."

"It's getting stronger," he said, the truth—yet it was not so simple as that. Her strew was affecting him differently than Ruelle's had. Perhaps because Chloe was his mate.

Ruelle's had controlled him physically; Chloe's was

taking him over both physically and mentally, an even more shuddersome proposition. He was compelled not only to mate her, but to clasp her to his chest, to make her smile, anything to chase away the despairing look that was on her face right now.

He resisted it with everything in him. *My will is my own.*

"I wish I could stop," she said. "It's not consciously done."

"That's all you have to say? Do you have any idea what it's like to have no control of your mind? Your body?"

A flash of irritation crossed her face. "You're kidnapping and terrorizing me. I've got a clue."

"Kidnapping? Try *saving your arse*. I've brought you to an isolated location for your own safety."

She pinched the bridge of her nose. "You don't seem surprised that I've started this."

"I knew it was only a matter of time."

"If that's true, and you believed I couldn't escape, then you fully intended to be with me . . . sexually?"

"There were two scenarios for me to choose from: let another male have my mate, or take you myself. My Lykae Instinct and my beast would never allow another to fuck you, which meant there really was no choice. I'm compelled to claim you."

She sank down on the window seat, as if the mere idea exhausted her. "Compelled? You are the most hateful man I've ever met. I ask you again, what the hell did I ever do to you?"

He didn't have a ready answer. Yes, she'd pulled

him back from the brink, then pushed him back to the edge. But that wasn't her fault.

She'd been his dream female until she'd become one among his nightmares. Again, not her fault.

"You canna have it both ways, canna fill the air with your chemicals, then cry when the result is what you need. You've got my hands tied."

"You're cool with this? To have sex with someone who doesn't truly desire you as a person? Who only wants not to feel pain anymore?"

"My predicament exactly," he lied. He'd never desired another so fiercely. "It will happen tonight, Chloe. Prepare yourself. And gods help us both."

THIRTY-TWO

B *lech, blech.*

　　Chloe drew the wastebasket toward her, then spat out a mouthful of saltines as if they were radio-active.

Surrounding her on the floor was a moat of cracker wrappers and crumbs.

She remembered when one of her middle-school friends had fed her beagle some cheese-covered broccoli. The dog had been happily smacking away—until it got to the harsh broccoli center.

I feel you, dog. Blech.

Was food truly no longer an option? With shaking hands, she unwrapped another package, biting through two crackers. Anything not to strew. Chewing, chewing . . . was this mouthful going to do down? *Please go down—*

Wastebasket! She emptied her mouth, hooking a finger around her gums to get out all the offending particles. Then she tested the rest of her drink. Natch, the whiskey went down like silk. But she knew it wouldn't be nearly enough to sustain her.

Field position? Her body was failing her. She'd done everything she could to stay the course, but maybe it was time to admit defeat.

With each minute she suffered an empty stomach, her desire blossomed. Awakening? Oh, yeah. Like her libido had mainlined crank.

And it remained fixated on MacRieve.

Did that mean all his predictions were about to come true? Would she go crawling to him? Or plead as he denied her again and again?

She'd always heard that you remembered your first time forever. She didn't want to remember groveling for his dick—especially since forever, in her case, could be literal.

The idea of that made her more ill than the crackers.

Was she one of those women who got off on cruelty? Some spring-loaded dojo dummy, perpetually bouncing up for another strike?

No, she refused to believe that. He was simply the target of sheer desperation. When she was young, she'd gotten lost in the woods without water; she remembered being so thirsty that she'd eyed a stagnant puddle with serious consideration.

MacRieve was simply a big Lykae-shaped puddle.

Maybe she should just do it. He'd given her bliss once before, and if sex was supposed to be the most pleasurable act of all . . . Once she was stronger, she could escape him. Would it be so bad to feed and heal?

Her succubus half avidly recalled the energy she'd received from that blow job. If she felt like that again, she could jog straight out of this place, this country, away from him forever.

This would be the last night she'd ever have to see his hateful smirk.

Still, as desperate as she was, she balked at the "crawling to him" portion of tonight's program. She could handle anything but the begging.

Or his beast.

So much confusion. And trying to ignore her escalating desire wasn't working. Her panties were wet, her sex achy.

Could she release some pressure? Or even delay more strewing?

She rose, heading for the shower. As she undressed, she gazed into the mirror. She was slimmer from hunger, but her bruise didn't look too bad.

Her hair had almost grown out. Earlier, she'd thought about finding scissors, but was too tired to be bothered. Pulling it up in a ponytail would be quicker and easier than shearing off that thick mane each day.

Would MacRieve find the length more attractive? Did she care?

She turned on the shower, impressed with the array of toiletries. She stepped under the steaming water, then soaped up a cloth, starting with her breasts then letting her hands linger over her every curve. Her hips, her backside.

As she touched herself, she imagined MacRieve downstairs in front of the fire, his golden eyes lit by flames. She fantasized that his hands roamed her body. She cupped her sex as he had on the plane, massaging herself like that.

She was on the verge of coming, whispering his name, when a spike of worry that he'd scent her shattered her concentration. Visualizing his head between her legs, his strong tongue working her flesh, brought her back into striking range—but then she jumped at a noise, which turned out not to be him at all.

In the end, she was just too weak. All she'd done was leave herself even hornier.

She dropped her hand, leaning her forehead against the wall. With a groan of frustration, she slapped the tile with her flat palm—and it didn't even crack.

MacRieve had been right. If he came upstairs, ready to have sex with her, it *would* happen. Gods help them both?

And if he *didn't* come for her soon, would she go limping through the keep, chasing after him?

With a curse, she dried off, wincing when the terry cloth rubbed her swollen nipples.

Perusing her new clothes, she saw there was really only one choice for a night like this. . . .

Though the weather was mild by Highland standards, Will had stoked the fire in the keep's great hearth, forcing himself to sit before it, drinking for fortitude.

This was going to happen. He was about to bed a

succubus. Which meant he needed to get as numb as possible before he relived his nightmares.

No. He was a grown man. If he was to mate a succubus again, it didn't have to be anything like last time. He didn't even have to fuck Chloe—a tidy blow job would nourish her. He didn't have to claim her, didn't have to mark her as his mate.

With a perfect mix of misery and eagerness, he knew he'd be inside her tonight. He'd fall on that sword, letting her use his body.

Because that was what succubae did.

He'd heard water running in the master bathroom, unable to resist picturing her in the shower, streams cascading over her naked body. He'd imagined her soaping those glorious breasts of hers, gliding her fingers over sensitive nipples.

He swallowed, gazing down at his stiffening cock. Oh, aye, she was strewing more potently. He decided he would hold out as long as he could, testing his will against the force of her need.

Shaking as badly as he had the night his family had been ripped apart, he stared into the flames. Not ten feet from him was the spot where his mother had stood the last time Will had seen her alive. *Never one like her, my Uilleam.*

His father had sat before this very fireplace, telling his sons about how he'd met their mother, adoration in his tone.

When Will had predicted that his father wouldn't last the week, he'd been wrong. Da hadn't lived past the next sunset. No one in the clan had been surprised when he'd entreated a trusted comrade to deal his deathblow.

Nothing Will or Munro could say would change Da's mind. He'd been out of his head with grief, unmoved by their pleas, half taken over by his beast already. Will and Munro had just lost their mother and sister, and then their father as well.

All of that because of a succubus. *And there's one in our home.*

The shame of it! And in the midst of his turmoil, he *needed* Chloe. He needed her hand on his brow, a loving stroke against his face.

He needed to be inside her—because that was the only place in the world he hadn't yet tried to find peace.

He finished the bottle, setting it down too close to the edge of the whiskey service; it fell to the floor. Nothing left to spill. He collected another fifth, then proceeded to top off his highball glass repeatedly, chasing that numbness.

By the end of the second bottle, all he'd achieved was drunkenness.

When he'd heard her turn off the water, his pulse had quickened. Now he could detect the faintest scent of her arousal, making him quake, like a dog maddened by the scent of heat.

—*Claim!*— There was nothing preventing him from being inside his mate—nothing but his stubbornness. His battered pride.

He needed to accept that it was his fate to surrender and cede. He told himself that for the nine hundred years between succubae, his life and his will had been his own.

He should be grateful for those centuries at least.

Grateful? With a yell, he shot to his feet, throwing his glass into the fire. Before it shattered, he'd already sped halfway up the stairs, having no idea whether he'd throttle her, rut her, or just clasp her tight against him.

He'd made it all of *two hours* here before succumbing to her call.

Why did he always lose, when he so badly needed to win . . . ?

THIRTY-THREE

Chloe whirled around when MacRieve entered the room, then raised her brows in surprise. He looked wasted.

He had to get drunk before he could sleep with her? *And the dojo dummy takes a hit!*

"You look surprised to see me." He scratched his head, ruffling his thick hair. "Why's that? You know I'm in your thrall. You know nothing could stop my feet from taking me here."

Aside from being trashed, he seemed filled with rage. She felt like she was in the room with a bomb about to detonate.

His eyes flickered ominously as he raked his gaze over her. "A red robe," he grated with a bitter laugh. "Keen on seducing me? No need! I am thoroughly *bestrewed*—could never escape your clutches."

"It was the only one in the closet," she said defensively, but he wasn't listening.

"Come then, succubus." He spread his arms wide, his expression inscrutable. "Your dinner has arrived, awaiting naught but your consumption."

How was she supposed to reply to that? She guessed she should just be happy that he wasn't making her beg.

When she didn't answer, he shrugged, then started to undress. Unsteadily, he toed off his boots, dragging his shirt over his head.

Though she was wary of his current state, the sight of his muscle-packed chest elicited an immediate physical reaction in her. Her breasts grew even heavier, her heartbeats accelerating.

"Tell me how you're preferrin' your repast," he said, his accent so strong she barely recognized his voice. And his fury-tinged words sounded . . . old-fashioned.

He paused with his fingers on the button of his jeans, inhaling deeply. "Ah, I think Chloe craves what's in here verra badly."

God help her, she did. Her succubus half was clamoring to feed. *Don't reach for him—*

When he unfastened his jeans and his erection bobbed free, her gaze locked on its movements. A feeling like delight filled her when the head grew moist, as if begging for her tongue.

Once MacRieve stood before her naked, magnificent in the firelight, he spread his arms wide again, as if he expected her to fall upon him.

Part of her seriously wanted to fall upon him.

His broad chest heaved with breaths. Between those narrow hips, his shaft jutted proudly. His testicles hung heavy beneath it. "Is this no' what you want?" When he gripped himself with one big hand and began stroking, every fiber in her body tightened with lust.

She should be doing the stroking. *That's mine.* She clenched her fists, shaking with the effort not to rush him.

Watching this was at once erotic and *wrong*, like . . . punishment.

"How does my succubus mate wish to be deflowered? I could lie back on the bed, for you to straddle my cock. Least amount of contact that way. And you would no' muss your hair."

Huh? As if she'd ever cared about that.

"No kissing, naturally," he continued. "Would no' want to smear your lip rouge."

Lip rouge? "For real, MacRieve? I don't understand what you're talking about." She simply didn't know enough about sex to determine what his game was. Did he truly intend some kind of punishment? Was this domination? Some sort of role-playing?

In the past, she'd let him lead, guiding her, but now she didn't understand where he wanted to take them.

At her blank gaze, he stopped stroking.

"I'm here by *your* command." His gaze narrowed into a malevolent glare. "You tell me how you prefer this," he hissed between gritted teeth, "or I promise you, succubus, you will no' like what you get. I'm a heartbeat away from freeing my beast."

She pulled her robe tighter, protectively. "But you said it'd take me on my hands and knees. That it'd take me hard."

"Oh, it would."

She shuddered. "Have you forgotten that I'm a virgin? I don't want to see that thing again!"

"Doona want?" He crossed to her with a black look. "I gave you a chance to tell me what you want! You declined."

She quickly said, "Then I'd prefer not to have sex at all. We can be as we were before."

"'No' an option." When he stood before her, he said, "I've sacrificed myself on this altar. I stand ready to be harvested thoroughly—and one fuck closer to being envenomed. You're going to feed, succubus, and feed well."

She bit her lip, wondering if there was any play at all for her to make. "Then tell me what *you* want."

Control.

Will needed for this to be different from the sex he'd known with Ruelle, and craved for it to be different from the sex he'd had as a beast.

"The succubus would like to know how I'd have this?" he sneered, still surprised she hadn't sunk her claws into him yet. "Why? So you can deny me what I truly crave?"

He was close enough to spy the swells of her breasts beneath that damnable red robe. Close enough that her breaths ghosted over his chest.

—*Claim her. Provide.*—

He was bloody about to!

She gazed up at him with those big hazel eyes. "Just tell me."

Why no'? He was just drunk enough to be honest. "I want to kiss you till your lips bruise beneath mine. I want to swat your plump arse, simply because you belong to me and I can."

She swallowed and her nipples stiffened even more against her robe.

He peered hard at them, giving a harsh laugh. "And because I know you'll get off on it. I want you to come a dozen times, but only when I allow it." He reached forward to clamp her nape. "When I look down on you as I mount your little body, I want to know that you're as desperate to receive my cock as I am to give it to you."

Her lips parted, her lids going heavy.

"I want to say filthy words in your ear, because it gets me hard"—he tightened his grip on her—"and because it's a tool for me to use, like a third hand with which to pet you."

She'd begun panting, her breasts rising and falling so temptingly. Her nipples now *strained* against the silk. Yet her hands still remained by her sides.

Could this be different from before? Because Chloe was different? He shook his head hard, now wishing for clarity. "I want total control of this situation, total domination of you, until my beast wrests it from my claws." *And in exchange, I'll be giving you one-third of my soul.* "I want you on that bed, awaiting my touch." Now that he'd spelled out his wishes, imagining every one, nothing less would do. He'd feed her, on his own terms. "Have we an understanding?"

She shook her head.

Denying him! He dropped his hand with a growl. Why should he be surprised?

"I'd like my lips bruised from your kiss," she began, "and I want you to come as many times as I do. Because that's only fair. Right now, for some reason, the idea of you spanking me turns me on—as much as the neolithic idea of belonging to you. So I'd love for you to demonstrate what the hell that's all about. And I'm asking you to use every filthy word you can think of, but stop calling me succubus."

She climbed on the bed—awaiting his touch?

"Chloe?" His voice broke lower.

She removed her robe. Gods, her body took his breath away. She was thinner, but still so lovely. All curves and sweet hollows.

Yes, mayhap he'd find peace inside her.

When she was completely naked before him, she lifted her chin, as if daring him to come take her fire. "I'm waiting." Then she lay back, reaching out her arms for him.

His heart seemed to stop. *And* this *is why she's my mate.* In a daze, he joined her, passing the point of no return.

—*Claim her. Provide!*—

Nothing could keep him from doing both. Their fates were sealed.

THIRTY-FOUR

Lying beside her, MacRieve buried his fingers in her hair, holding her steady, his gaze on her mouth.

When he kissed her, he growled against her lips, "There's my Chloe. It's *you*."

He sounded a shade less drunk—and relieved.

Chloe was as well. He hadn't made her grovel, and they were in bed together. Waves of energy had begun to wash over her, like a fingertip rippling a still pool of water. Though she hadn't forgiven or forgotten, she was happy to return his kiss.

So he needed her to give over control and let him call the plays? *Lead the way, Coach*. Everything he'd promised had excited her.

They would have sex, apparently wicked sex; but it wouldn't *mean* anything.

Their tongues twined harder and harder until she was moaning into his mouth. His kiss was shattering. He'd wrapped his strong arms around her, holding her body captive against his, chest to chest, as he ravished her mouth.

He didn't break that kiss until she was light-headed—and her lips were good and bruised. "Mac-Rieve?"

His voice a rasp, he said, "It's you, Chloe. It's you I crave." He gave her another whole-body squeeze, as if he wanted to feel all of her at once. As she lay beside him, his hands dipped down to knead her ass, grinding her mound against his shaft.

She could feel the blood-filled heat of it, scalding against her. "Oh, God, oh, God." She threw her leg over his hip, wishing he'd put her beneath him, needing his weight on top of her.

"I'm goin' tae take you tonight," he said, his brogue thick.

"Yes, yes!" *Just keep grinding.*

"And I'll do it how I need tae."

Just as she was puzzling over his words, she felt his big palm land across her ass. *Slap!*

Her reaction shocked her. Sounds she didn't recognize left her lips. She writhed for more, bucking against him. A cool draft of air streamed across the heated skin of her bottom, making her tremble.

He grated, "Now do you understand what the hell that's all about?"

Somehow she found the presence of mind to cry, "Nope!"

Slap!

Her eyes rolled back in her head. She was all but levitating, dimly aware that she'd begun sucking on his neck. She tightened the leg over his hip, her foot spurring him.

But he was releasing her.

She blinked up at him. "What? Why?"

"Go tae your back. Keep your arms over your head."

She nodded, biting her lip, wondering what he was going to do to her now.

He rose to his knees, leaning over her. His lips scorched a path from her neck toward one nipple, closing around it. When he suckled her hard, her back arched sharply. He moved to her other nipple, tormenting the peak with another harsh suck, but she loved it, grasping his head to hold him to her.

He nipped her breast. "Arms."

She shuddered from his bite, a sexy reminder of who was driving tonight. Her arms collapsed over her head.

"Now part your legs."

She drew her knees up and spread them, welcoming him.

He grated, "Good lass," and knelt between them. He kissed down her belly, each thorough sweep of his lips making her hips rock. Once the backs of her thighs rested over his shoulders, he dipped his head down to nuzzle her thatch of hair.

"MacRieve!" She flooded with wetness when she realized he was inhaling her scent.

His eyes were heavy-lidded when he finally drew back. "Spread your thighs wider. Let me see what's mine."

She bent her knees, letting her legs fall wide.

His gaze was nearly palpable as he peered at her sex. And then . . .

He licked his gorgeous lips with such a possessive—predatory—look that she almost orgasmed at once.

* * *

When she'd spread herself in complete surrender, Will's mouth had watered for her honey. He'd been without it for days.

He clamped her hips and licked the length of her. His sharp growl of pleasure drowned out her cries. "Woman, your taste!" With his second foray, he found her even wetter. He'd be feeding her soon, but right now she was feeding him the sweetest mead he'd ever tasted. He couldn't lap it up quickly enough.

Between strokes of his tongue, he said, "Did you miss me licking your wet cunny? Tonguing it like this?" He delved deep.

"Oh, oh God . . . not fair . . ." She was on the brink.

Will wanted to tease her even longer, but his Instinct was tolling in his head like a bell:

—*Claim your mate.*—

His beast was already stirring. And Will felt certain his cock was about to explode.

"Going tae ready you for me, for the seed I mean tae give you." He slipped a finger inside her, groaning when her untried sheath clenched around it. The moment seemed unreal. He was going to be inside his virgin mate.

He could feel her delicate maidenhead, ready for him to claim.

He pressed his opened mouth over her clit to suck it till it throbbed between his lips.

Her hips tried to shoot up from the bed, but he kept her pinned. Her head thrashed, her drying hair streaming out over the pillow.

He wedged a second finger inside her. Brushing kisses against her swollen clit, he said, "Relax, my sweet, and open for me." As he probed his fingers, her core stretched around them, her folds swelling in welcome.

His beast wouldn't be denied much longer, was baying inside him to possess its female.

"Chloe, look at me."

She cracked open her eyes.

"I'll try tae stay in control as long as I can." He sat up on his knees, positioning himself. "If I look into your eyes, I might be able tae remain with you longer." He wanted to be above her like this, watching her expressions, mastering her, taking her like a man.

"And if not, I'll be looking into your eyes while you change." Her voice was miserable.

He had his mate in his bed, after waiting nine centuries for her, and she was miserable. Why wouldn't she be? She was about to lose her virginity to what she believed was a monster.

With his free hand, he awkwardly brushed her hair from her forehead, trying for tenderness, having no idea how to go about it. "I'll tell you when tae close your eyes. You need tae relax again." He fingered her entrance harder with shallow pumps, coaxing wetness. "There. That's it, baby. Give me more of that."

Her face was relaxing. Her nipples tightened into stiff little berries. He leaned down for a taste of each, earning a moan and more of her honey. It glistened on his fingers as he thrust them inside her.

When he drew his fingers from her, she gave a cry, twisting in the bed, undulating to be filled. His heart sang when she kept her arms above her head. "You're ready, Chloe."

Was he?

THIRTY-FIVE

With a shaking hand, MacRieve gripped his huge shaft, aiming it between her legs.

When he rubbed the crown up and down her sex, she was overwhelmed with the urge to claw his ass and draw him into her. Somehow she prevented herself.

Instead, she locked gazes with him, needing him to see that she'd never wanted anything more than this. She'd swear his eyes were telling her the same.

She felt pressure at her opening, the crown penetrating her, not to be denied.

"Tight, so tight," he groaned.

Then the head was inside, pulsing, stretching her. But those twinges felt necessary, right. *No longer a virgin, Chloe.*

"Good?" he bit out. The tendons in his neck and all the muscles of his torso were straining. He'd begun to sweat, his skin sheening in the firelight. How badly he must need to thrust.

"Good." She felt like she'd waited her entire life for that hot fullness. That feeling of puzzle pieces clicking together. She gazed up at him in surprise. "Really good."

"More?" he rasped, vulnerability in his gaze.

She nodded. Only to regret it immediately when a pinching sensation flared inside her. *More* was a little *much*. "It hurts."

His brows drew tightly together. "It'll pass, I promise."

As he pressed deeper, she tried to focus on anything but the pain. She studied his expression. He looked anguished. So much was going on inside his head that she couldn't begin to comprehend.

Yet she also saw his eyes flickering blue.

How much time did she have until she was supposed to close her eyes and let that thing have her?

***

Will was already fighting not to come inside her impossibly tight cunny—and fighting the beast, who wanted its turn with their virgin mate.

No, not yet! Will wasn't even all the way in. More hurriedly, he rocked his hips, pushing farther inside.

She gritted her teeth, but didn't say anything.

Pressure. Everywhere. From his rising beast. From the scorching clutch of her sheath. From his consuming need *not* to hurt her.

Pressure increasing with every inch deeper. Sweat slicked his skin, running down his spine.

Finally he was as far as he could go. Gazing down at her with pride, he bit out, "You've taken me." He reached forward to stroke her hair again. "Good girl." He drew his hips back so he could sink back into that moist heaven. His head fell back as pleasure bombarded him. "Ah, you feel so fucking amazing!"

No response. He gazed down. "Chloe?"

Her cheeks were flushed, her lips thinned. "It doesn't hurt anymore. But it's not . . . enjoyable."

Somehow he resisted the tight tug of her sex to pull almost all the way out. Keeping her on the tip, he put his palms under her back, scooping her up to suck on her sensitive breasts. His lips clamped onto a nipple, his arms crisscrossing her back, holding her for the taking.

"Ohhh!" The sound of her delight was almost his undoing. "Better!" She fisted the sheets beside her hips.

Will kept himself from thrusting until she was wriggling on the end of his cock, wetting the head for more. "You want it deep inside you?"

"Deeper!"

Laying her back down, he raised himself above her on straightened arms. Sweat dripped from his forehead onto her quivering breasts as he surged his hips forward between her thighs. Her core clenched his every inch, wresting a strangled groan from his chest. "Ah! Deeper still?"

"God, *yes*!" The rapture in her cry . . .

As he rocked his shaft home again and again, she tried to meet his thrusts. "MacRieve, I'm close! More!"

"Give you what you need!" He was satisfying her,

taking her like a normal man. Experiencing pleasure such as he'd never known. In this, he felt as much a virgin as she.

He was overwhelmed by how perfect she felt. *Waited my entire life to be inside her.*

"Don't stop, please!"

That was the plea he'd craved! "Say it again."

"*Please.* It's so good!"

When he increased his rhythm for her, his beast roared inside him, nigh frenzied to possess her.

Will gazed down, seeking the anchor of her gaze.

The sight sent an icy chill through him. Her eyes glowed with her arousal.

"Succubus green," he hissed.

Just like Ruelle's. Because Chloe was greedy to feed off his body. When he saw her claws flaring, chills swept over his damp skin. His breaths began to whistle.

As if he suffocated under pale flesh.

Canna get enough air! His chest heaved, his lungs burning for breath.

Ah, gods, he was losing his erection. No, no, he needed to perform, to provide. This was his mate, and she was hungry.

Yet just as he'd feared, he couldn't stay hard— as if his body was refusing to surrender what hers demanded.

"What's wrong? What's happening?" She rocked on him. Of course she could feel his erection waning.

And just like before, he would let his beast rise up to do the dirty work for him. "Chloe, close your eyes." His own claws began to lengthen. *To pierce her skin, to hold Mate steady for seed.* His fangs grew in his mouth. *To mark her flesh.*

"Already?" She squeezed her eyes closed. Her body trembled against him. "Will it hurt me?"

"No' on purpose." His voice was growing distorted, his impulses no longer his own. The beast inhaled deeply of his mate's scent, and his cock responded, swelling like a rod inside her.

"MacRieve, I'm scared."

"Know that the beast . . . aches for you," he choked out right before it took over.

Will watched in horror as it maneuvered Chloe to her hands and knees. It dug its claws into her hips, wrenching her back on his shaft, farther than Will had gone.

Impaled, she cried out as the beast seated itself deeply, positioning her to best receive its savage thrusts. With the beast at the fore, Will bucked into her again . . . and again . . . until he was riding his mate hard, growling over her with delight.

She was taking him, moaning. Was she getting wetter? Wishful thinking?

Soon he'd spend, soon it'd be over, this deed done.

The closer he got to coming, the more his fangs ached to mark her neck, to claim her forever—because his will was not his own. A thread of resentment grew, outdistancing the other feeling that was growing.

Obsession.

His semen had climbed, about to erupt uncontrollably. The beast tightened its hold on her to better deliver it to her womb, then leaned down to mark her neck.

Somehow, just before he ejaculated, Will exerted control for just long enough to prevent that claim—

A roar burst from his lungs as his seed jetted out of his cock, torrents so powerful that even the beast shuddered in awe.

Between heaving breaths, he bellowed to the ceiling as he filled her, over and over, plunging into his own hot spend.

Then came that last mind-scrambling draw. A succubus's extra pull. *So many years distant; yet so familiar.* He quaked violently, powerless as the last of his semen was wrung from him.

With a groan, he collapsed atop her shivering body. She was panting, pinned on his length, squirming.

He'd been close to satisfying her. Yet in the end, she'd found no release.

Not like he had. *That last indescribable pull . . .*

The beast receded reluctantly, Will driving it back. It was normal for a Lykae's beast to praise its mate after sex, licking and kissing her with abandon under the light of the full moon. *I'm no' normal, dark and twisted.* He felt sick.

He'd fed a succubus—was hardening inside her even now. No, not again. *Two times is too close to three.* One-third of his soul was enough for this night.

Without a word, he withdrew from her body, then rose. He dragged on his jeans, breathing deep to cage his beast completely. Her sweet succubus scent filled his senses until he was drowning in it.

Dragging me down . . .

He ran for the toilet to be sick.

THIRTY-SIX

That didn't just happen.

Chloe hadn't known what to expect for her first time. But she'd never imagined she'd get railed from behind by a werewolf—or that her first lover would dash to the bathroom to vomit directly after.

She lay stunned on the bed, trying to process everything that had just occurred. All she knew for certain was that he was sickened by sex with her, and that she would never repeat this ever again.

At first, she'd thought she could enjoy having him inside her. She'd even been close to orgasm, until he'd started to . . . flag.

He'd known it, she'd known it. And then she'd seen him gritting his teeth, endeavoring to get through it, as if sex with her was a grueling last lap to be completed.

When that hadn't worked, he'd tagged out with the

beast, letting it finish something he was too disgusted to do himself.

Fear had assailed her. But when the beast had turned her over and taken her, it hadn't been as bad as she'd thought it would be.

She'd even chanced a peek back at MacRieve's wolven face. It hadn't been nearly as terrifying as last time. And she'd realized why: the one time she'd seen the shadow of the beast before, it had been wavering over MacRieve's *mask of hatred.*

Tonight, the beast had gazed at her with possession, with yearning—as if she'd just become its entire world. It *had* ached for her, just as MacRieve had said.

Chloe had responded, reveling in its ferocity, because she'd known that *she* had provoked that intensity. She'd relished the way its claws had gripped her hips, knowing that it was frantic for her.

As frantic as she'd soon grown.

Once she'd relaxed again, the pleasure had returned, just harder, more jarring. She'd been smiling into the pillow because the beast of her fears had been fucking her straight toward the most intense orgasm she'd ever imagined. Just when she'd been on the verge of release, she'd felt wave after wave of its semen shooting inside her. She hadn't come, but that seed had been like a balm against her every ache—no pain anywhere, not her ankle or her bruised face. Her energy had been renewed. She'd truly *felt* immortal. Then it had ended. Then MacRieve had returned.

He'd just finished vomiting. She heard him filling a glass of water at the sink.

She'd always considered herself thick-skinned. Rub some dirt on it, right? But with this . . .

There was no upside.

Will lurched from the bathroom, trying not to notice as Chloe stared blankly at the wall, sheet clutched to her throat.

—*Allay, comfort.*—

How could he comfort her when he still felt like he was suffocating?

He descended the stairs, heading straight to the liquor cabinet. As he cracked open another bottle and took a generous slug, he comprehended the hopelessness of his situation. She would always be a succubus; he would always hate her kind.

Some part of him would resent his mate for eternity, blaming her for things she'd had no part in, blaming her whenever she needed to feed.

My will is no' my own.

He heard her scurrying to the shower. It sounded like she was frantically scrubbing herself. Not a good sign. And he thought . . . he thought he heard her *crying*, the sound echoing in the shower stall.

Just as Ruelle had made him cry during his first time, so Will had made Chloe.

She'd never spilled a tear in all those soccer clips, had never cried from his many insults. *I'm the villain. Slaoightear.* As Munro had warned.

How horrifying for her to be taken by the beast.

While Will had experienced unequaled pleasure. Another remarkable milestone for an ancient immortal.

Yet I'm no' sated. Already he wanted her again. Her strew must linger.

Another throat-burning chug. He sank down in one of the chairs before the waning fire, staring at the embers. He didn't *want* to hate her; she didn't deserve it.

So what to bloody do? Mayhap he needed to talk to someone. Naturally, his first impulse was to call his twin—but Munro would just rail over Will's treatment of his *deirfiúr.* So Will collected his sat-phone from the bag he'd left in the great room and dialed Nïx, having no expectation that she'd answer.

She picked up almost immediately: "Are you calling about the ad?"

"Ad?"

"For the gently used Bentley for sale. It has *zero* miles!"

Well, that explained the backward driving. "It's me, MacRieve."

"*You-lamey!* How good to hear from you! Scotland must be beautiful. I'm currently out with Mariketa, Regin, and Carrow. We're doing rescue work."

He swigged, not even surprised she knew his location. "Aye, collecting Order orphans. Malkom Slaine told me." In the background, Will heard what sounded like a multitude of bairns spatting—demonic wails, baby roars and hisses—and what he thought might be a van rocking on its shocks.

Nïx said, "I'm nodding. We've gathered demonlings, ankle-biters, and a couple of centaur foals, just to name a few."

"I need your help, soothsayer. You and I—we've definitely rebroken that bone, aye?" he said, his bitterness undisguised. "Yet it's still no' right. I've bollixed this up with my mate."

"I know," she said sadly.

"I doona want to treat her this way." He began to pace. "How do I keep myself from hating her just for what she is?"

"Why don't you work on her hatred of you?" Nïx asked. "Win her and perhaps *you* can be won over."

"How?"

"Lykae can be so smooth—charming tricksters who cajole what they want. *Woo* her, wolf."

"I doona believe she can be won by me." Just saying those words brought on a swell of despair.

"You haven't exactly made it easy for her."

The back of his neck heated. So Nïx had seen what he'd done to Chloe?

"Yes, I see all, wolf. And by *all*—"

"You mean *some*. If you saw enough, then you ken why she will no' want me again. My beast came out in full force. It was no' gentle."

"You need to talk to her, confide in her. Tell her what happened to you."

"Never." For Will—a Lykae male from a warrior clan and a line of Sentinels—the only thing worse than being . . . molested by Ruelle for four years would be to admit it to his mate.

How could he even introduce the topic? *We need to*

*talk about why I subconsciously despise you. When I came, you
see, your last greedy pull harkened back to a time when my seed
was taken by one of your ilk.*

*Because my disgust ruled me tonight, I withheld my claiming
bite from you.*

The sounds of the bairns' tiff grew louder, the rocking more pronounced.

Nïx told Will, "Lovely. Demonling horns just punctured the roof of our rental vehicle. Hold, please." Then to the children, she said, "I *told* you Bertil would bite if you pull his legs. Now, cut out that caterwauling or Auntie Nïxie will eviscerate you."

Will thought he heard the witch Mariketa saying brightly, "Ha-ha. Auntie Nïxie meant to say 'no ice cream.' " Then Mariketa snorted. "You might have overcommitted on younglings, Regin."

The Valkyrie Regin answered, "Dude. Don't you judge me. And where's the fucking fire extinguisher?"

"I've returned," Nïx said in a dry tone. "You have much to resolve for yourself, wolf. Don't make me regret placing Chloe in your care."

"Why did you? You're the one who told the witches about her, are you no'? To get her to the auction? If you could find her, then you can find Webb." At least he'd gotten some measure of revenge against the man—Webb's daughter had just been defiled by a Lykae beast.

He winced at his thoughts. *You sick prick, that's your mate you're gloating over!* He clasped his forehead, squeezing till he thought his skull would cave in.

"Webb has a role to play with the Bringers of Doom; he's not to be touched," Nïx said. "And I helped you because I trusted that you would find your feet with this."

"What if I canna?"

"Do you know what's so strange, *Uilleam*?" she asked, saying his name perfectly. "You have never, in your entire life, done something for which you should truly be ashamed. You think you have, but you haven't. Not until you hurt your own mate, blaming the poor girl for things she can't control."

His mouth went dry. "Will she change?" When Nïx didn't answer, he said, "She has spirit and courage. Will she change to become like Ruelle?"

"No. But you won't know that because she'll be gone."

His legs felt weak. "Nïx? No!" He sank back against the wall.

"Mark my words, wolf: bury your past, or it will bury you." Click.

THIRTY-SEVEN

An hour after his call with Nïx, Will found Chloe sitting on the floor in the pantry, trying to choke down an apple.

Whiskey bottle in hand, he sank down beside her, tugging the apple from her. "That time has passed for you, lass. Never to return."

Her eyes were puffy from crying, her nose red, but luckily no more tears fell. The mere idea of her crying had gutted him. To *see* her tears . . .

I could no' stand it.

"I can still drink." She reached for his bottle, swigged heartily, gasped.

"Aye, but you canna eat food."

"I can do a liquid diet. Or what about an IV? Something surgical?" With a *eureka!* expression, she cried, "Artificial insemination!"

Her panic set him on edge. She was this desperate because she'd hated sex with him. Yet another unsatisfied succubus. "Or mayhap you can do as nature intended you to. Your face has healed, your color's returned."

When he reached for the bottle, she absently relinquished it. "Nature didn't intend for sex to be humiliating like that. Some parts were unbearable."

Unbearable? Her words gave him chills. Any male, in a potentially eternal relationship, would react thus. *My mate hates sex.* He had no call to expect different, but still he said, "It was no' *that* bad. You got to feed. And I dinna mean to humiliate you." Surely, he hadn't. *Slaoightear,* his conscience whispered. "You will no' have pain next time. Things will go better between us."

"Next time? Are you listening to me at all?"

Probably not an ideal moment to remind her about the full moon in two nights. His beast would be even more powerful. If Will hadn't built up her strength by then . . .

"Th-there's got to be a way for me to forgo sex. If those witches can camouflage me, maybe they can fix me."

Fix? She felt broken. *Because of me.*

Ruelle used to blame all her failings on him; had he done the same with Chloe? He cleared his throat. "Mayhap you're no' the one who's broken." Other males would easily love her. If he hadn't been twisted by a succubus, he would have lost his heart to the lass beside him.

"Not broken?" she cried. "Now you're going to screw with my head? To survive in the Lore, I'm supposed to drug and rape men? You think I don't know how wrong that is?"

He'd never expected her to *agree* with him about the nature of succubae.

"When I started changing, my dad abandoned me. Remember? You were quick to remind me of that. You relished telling all of the Lore how he discarded me like trash." Her eyes watered. "Not to mention how *you've* reacted to my change."

"Chloe—"

"I lost *everything* that day. My career, my remaining family, my friends, my team. You were the only constant in my crazy life. But you did a total one-eighty, bullying and insulting me. You had to get Sheen-wasted tonight to take me to bed." Gazing up at the ceiling, she murmured, "I can't believe my first lover *vomited* after being with me."

Will scrubbed his hand over his face, embarrassment scalding him. "Your first lover and your *last*. And he will no' do so next time."

She faced him with an incredulous expression. "You can't control your reaction to me—any more than you can your beast."

"You'll get used to that part of me. You'll have to. It's inseparable from who I am, like a soul. I can understand why you might hate my beast, but you should no' blame it, for it does no' reason."

"You think that's the problem? At least the beast looked at me with yearning, with desire. It's *you* that's the problem."

"What does that mean?"

"Your beast has accepted me; you never will, and unfortunately *you come back*. If I ever have sex again,

I don't want to open my eyes to see your back as you beat feet for the toilet."

Could this get any more shaming?

"And I might not have any experience, but I know what whiskey dick is."

"What the hell are you talking about?"

"MacRieve junior took a tee-oh right before the beast substituted in."

Aye, it can *get more shaming.* He drank deep. "Chloe, just know this. Sex for me is . . . complicated."

She turned to him with owl eyes. *"Noooo."*

"Aye, smart-arse. It has no' always been pleasant or rewarding. Mayhap I thought of a past time. Mayhap it affected me."

"Then tell me about the past time."

"All you need to know is that I'm working through it. It will no' factor in the future."

"You're right about that." When she snapped her fingers for the bottle, he handed it over, watched her take a healthy gulp. "Because I will never have sex with you again!"

He stabbed his fingers through his hair. "Damn it, lass, you're a cambion. If you refuse to feed, I doona know what will happen to you."

Against the rim of the bottle, she murmured, "Maybe I'll die, and you'll be off the hook."

When Nïx had said Chloe would be gone, had the soothsayer meant gone, as in *left?* Or gone, as in . . . *lost?* His chest constricted, strangling his breaths for an entirely different reason.

"Whiskey," he bit out.

Frowning, she handed it to him. There they sat, passing the bottle, holed up together on the floor in the goddamned pantry. "You think I could be off the hook if my mate died?" He repeated her words: "Have you been listening to me at all?"

"Oh, yeah, because you think you'd have to follow me. But never fear, I'm sure that only applies to *beloved* mates. Since you hate me, you should get a pass."

"You belong with me," he said simply.

"Tell me why I should stay. Why shouldn't I run, now that I'm healed?"

His lips drew back from his fangs. "Because I will catch you."

"Ugh—you could not suck worse!" She was shaking beside him, her body filled with fury.

Wrong. Everything's wrong. He pulled on the collar of his loose T-shirt, puzzled by how tight it felt around his neck. *All my fault.*

"You know, sometimes I do this thing where I assess my life's field position, getting a lay of where I am," she said. "I've been in this pantry, evaluating my field position, the most important one of my life."

"And what have you determined?"

"That we can never be happy together. So it's in your best interest to cut ties with me." He opened his mouth to tell her that wouldn't be happening, but she continued, "Don't worry, I don't *expect* you to let me go. Because you're not a fair man."

No, he wasn't. So why did her words sting so badly?

"In that case, what do you plan to do with me? Keep me here, isolated until I go crazy?" She met his gaze. "You can keep me here for centuries, and at the first opportunity, I will blaze. Do you understand me? I will always look for a way out—because you will never change."

"You speak of change as if it's easy! I'm nine centuries old! I doona alter my course so easily as you might."

"At least it's possible for you—I *can't* change. Ever. I can accept your beast, but you can't accept things in me that I can't control?" She squeezed her temples. "And not only that, you're constantly treating me with scorn, making me feel like shit about myself!" Her irises glowed green with anguish. "I can't sit around here and let you convince me that I'm nothing but an evil, worthless succubus. I *won't* do that."

When her eyes filled with tears, his widened.

"You're . . . crying?" He gazed at her in astonishment. She was always so strong, seeming invincible. She'd acted unaffected by his barbs. "This is *twice*," he said inanely.

He'd never had a mate; he'd never had a mate cry. He and his beast were roiling. "Chloe, look at me."

When she buried her head in her hands and started *sobbing*, his stomach felt torn apart, as if he'd been stabbed and the knife was steadily turning in his gut.

Twisting with no end, like the second hand of a clock. *Tick, tick, tick.*

"Get used t-to me crying. Or *let me go.*"

MacRieve pulled her hands from her face. He looked as if her tears were wrecking him—and still, after everything, some part of her regretted causing him pain.

"I canna, Chloe."

She ran her sleeve over her damp cheeks. "Then at least t-tell me why you hate me. I'll figure out a way to make this situation better for *both* of us. But I can't shoot for a net that I can't see."

His eyes were stark. There was clearly so much going on in his head. Yet he'd rather let her dangle in the dark than share any of it.

"Damn it, answer me, what did I do to you?"

When he said nothing, she snatched the bottle from him and flung it from the pantry. It shattered in the next room. *"What—did—I—do?"*

"NOTHING!" he roared.

"Then for God's sake, why are you treating me like this?"

He gazed away.

"No, don't you look away!" Clambering up on her knees, she dug her hands into his hair, pulling him back to face her. They stared into each other's eyes, both out of breath. "Tell me!"

"I felt rage toward your species. I know I've been taking it out on you. But I doona know how to stop!"

Did that mean he *wanted* to stop? The tiniest spark of hope began to burn inside her. She released him, her tears drying. "What happened to you? Tell me."

With a wary nod, he parted his lips. He seemed to

be trying to answer her—but only his breath whistled out.

"MacRieve?" What was going on here? He was a powerful, courageous immortal. Yet he'd been rendered mute by whatever had injured him in the past.

He pulled on his collar. "I canna . . . breathe." His voice broke low. "I . . . canna."

Rising unsteadily, she murmured, "I've gotta have a net to aim for, MacRieve."

He said nothing.

That spark guttered out. With a last glance, she left him sitting alone.

I want my mate.

As Will walked the halls of Conall early into the morning, pacing like a resident ghost, that one thought kept surfacing.

He didn't want to sleep alone, to wake up alone. Chloe had gone to bed hours ago, all but passing out from the whiskey. When he'd gone to join her, she'd shaken her head warningly, as if to say *Do it and die.*

He'd been so busy thinking about how he'd been injured that he hadn't considered—or cared about—how vulnerable and hurt she'd been.

All those years ago, he'd categorized Ruelle's tears as antics. In truth, they'd been *tactics.*

Chloe's tears had been raw and real. And she'd told him to get used to them.

He assessed his own "field position."

—Watching Chloe cry had hurt him worse than his recent tortures, had taken more from him than Dixon had.

—He'd rather die than cause Chloe more pain. If her eyes glowed green again, it should be because of pleasure. Would he ever see that?

He returned to the hearth, stirring the embers. Short of being seared clean by flames, how could he get right? Nïx had said, "Bury your past, or it'll bury you." He knew burying his past wasn't possible. It was too much a part of him. But he could hide the worst of this, if it meant Chloe might accept a life with him.

Will would never be able to give her his *all*. Yet mayhap he could give her *enough*?

His phone rang then. Munro. Bracing himself, Will answered.

"I was about to take the lads out to Erol's," Munro said in a measured tone. "Thought I'd check in first."

Fearing the worst? "We arrived without incident. She sleeps now, or I'd let you talk to her. She enjoyed her new clothes and was grateful for them." He scrubbed his hand over his face. "I read your message. You think I should remain here?" *And where the hell will you be?* Will's recent imprisonment was the longest span they'd ever been separated.

"I may no' like living apart from you"—*that makes two of us*—"but mayhap that's the way, now that you've got your female? Besides, one of us should manage our family's lands. I've thought about this for years, figuring whoever found his mate first should live there. This is your chance to reclaim your home—and your past."

My past?

Munro asked, "Will, did you . . . ?"

"Aye." When Munro let out a relieved breath, Will admitted, "It dinna go well. There were, uh, some issues. But I want to get past them."

"Are you prepared to take her venom bond?"

Will swallowed audibly, hoping the sound didn't carry over a transatlantic call. "I've accepted that I have no choice but to do so. I canna lose her. Damn it, I need your thoughts on this."

"Tell me what happened."

Will was so desperate for help that he relayed everything that had occurred, stinting on few details. He told his brother what Nïx had said.

"You've much to make up for, Will. I agree with Nïx that you need to win Chloe."

"How?" He'd lost some serious ground tonight.

"It's verra simple," Munro began. "In the morn . . ."

By the end of the call fifteen minutes later, Will felt somewhat heartened. At least he had a plan. He made his way up to the master suite, back to his mate.

Pausing in the doorway, he watched the moon stream through the windows, bathing her beautiful face in silvery light.

Her nose was no longer red from crying. Her eyes weren't puffy. Unlike Ruelle, his Chloe did not cry prettily—because her grief was sincere.

He crossed to the bed, sitting beside her. When he brushed the locks from her forehead, she cracked open her eyes.

"What're you doing?" she asked, her words slurring. " 'S'not time for my *special shot* yet."

Not a promising beginning. "Chloe, what would it take to start anew with you?"

Hopelessness settled over him when she murmured, "More than you've got."

Yet then he reminded himself, *She has no' seen all I've got.*

THIRTY-EIGHT

I feel amazing, Chloe thought bitterly as she tromped down the steps that morning. She had energy again, wasn't even sore from the night before. Because of him.

Fucker.

After she'd vented in the pantry and returned to bed, the whiskey had hit her like a tsunami. Before she'd passed out, she would've sworn the entire keep had been spinning.

Later in the night, MacRieve had awakened her. She barely remembered what they'd talked about, but she thought he'd mentioned "starting anew." Then he'd stroked her hair and tucked her in, much as he had those first two nights at the compound. She'd missed it.

She'd missed the side of MacRieve she'd first known.

What would she encounter when she faced him today? Surly and abusive or charming and sexy?

She strode into the kitchen, then stopped short.

MacRieve was shirtless in a pair of low-slung, broken-in shorts, drinking orange juice straight out of the jug. Her lips parted, her gaze lovingly taking in all his rigid muscles, then sliding lower to that ink-black goody trail. She wanted to nuzzle it like he'd done between her legs last night—

No, don't think about that!

He finished his drink and swiped his forearm over his mouth. "We've got a busy day planned."

She blinked to attention. "Doing what?"

"You're to go running with me."

She arched a brow. "Running?" Exploring the Scottish countryside? Her new gear upstairs was just waiting for her.

Then she remembered her situation. Her next play wasn't running with him; it was running *from* him. "Why don't you go by yourself? I could kick back and watch TV." *Escape.* "Then we could meet up later." *Never see each other again.*

The thought brought on another pang. Did Dojo Dummy still want him?

"And leave you to flee? No' likely." He set down the jug, moving in closer to back her against the counter, until she could feel the heat emanating from his bare chest and bask in his tempting scent. His voice was husky when he said, "I'm never letting you go, lass."

His nearness piqued her desire, one that had nothing to do with hunger.

"Do you remember what I said early this morning?" he asked.

"Yes." Mostly.

"I want to try this again with you. I'm offering an olive branch. Will you take it?"

She shook her head, saying, "Fool me once. Mac-Rieve, you were all I had and you turned on me. What if you find out something else that you hate about me?"

"I was wrong. I am apologizing. I want a chance to win my mate back."

"Give me one good reason why I should trust this." Again she felt like she was running with a cleat and a climbing boot. Would she ever feel *on*-kilter with him?

He leaned down to say at her ear, "Because for a time last night, you liked me moving inside you verra much."

Her cheeks heated. "Right. Now, if only *you* had liked it, whiskey dick."

He drew back with a scowl. "Stop saying that, woman! I dinna have—never bluidy mind." He clamped the counter on either side of her, caging her in, peering down at her with intent golden eyes. "Doona mistake what happened. Being inside you felt incredible. And whether the beast was at the fore or no', I still came so hard my ballocks begged for mercy."

"Must've been nice. For you. Not so much for me. Out of those dozen orgasms you promised, you were twelve short."

A flush spread over his chiseled cheekbones. "I'm keen for a rematch tonight."

"Ha! Your last attempt at-goal went way wide. Not even close. As a matter of fact, you got red-carded out of the game."

With his smoldering gaze boring into hers, he grated, "I want—back—*in*."

Her lips parted at the double entendre. His eyes were promising her a hot, thorough taking.

She feared hers were begging for it. She darted her gaze away.

He tucked her hair behind her ear. "I've been up all night, thinking about us."

"Is there an *us*?"

"I want there to be."

"MacRieve, I haven't even agreed to go running with you, much less to being the verbally abused half of your *us*."

"I vow to the Lore that I will never speak to you that way again." He said this as solemnly as a groom would a wedding vow.

At length, she said, "I'll go, but only because I'm jonesing for a run." She ducked under his arm, then headed toward the stairs, muttering over her shoulder, "Need to change."

As she hurried up to her room, she wondered if she could trust his sincerity. One minute he hated her, the next he was offering her an olive branch with orgasms on top.

Why had he changed so drastically? She wished she could read his cues better. He was like a skilled opponent telegraphing fake plays to keep her running in circles. She sensed that anything he'd told her about himself was underscored with countless things he hadn't.

She frowned, remembering some of what he'd revealed last night, when she'd been too tipsy to analyze it. Sex for him was *complicated*, and it hadn't always been "pleasant or rewarding." What guy didn't find sex pleasant?

Right before he'd lost his erection last night, he'd said, "Succubus green," about her eyes. Later he'd confessed that the reason he'd flagged was because he'd thought of a past time. Because Chloe's succubus eyes had reminded him—

Oh, dear God.

Munro had told her that his family had been harmed by a succubus, so Chloe had figured someone they loved had been seduced by one. She now suspected that the victim had been MacRieve—and that there'd been no "seduction."

Do you have any idea what it's like to have no control of your mind? he'd asked. *Your body?* And then he'd told her that maybe *she* wasn't the one who was broken.

It wasn't a big leap to connect everything together.

No wonder he hated Chloe. No wonder he'd *vomited* after sex with her. For a man that big and strong to have reacted so violently . . . Her eyes watered with sympathy.

He hadn't even been able to speak of it, his breath hitching again and again. She sank down on the bed. MacRieve had been trying to tell her!

And physically *couldn't*.

Everything about Chloe must have reminded him of whatever bitch had raped him. Considering this, she was surprised he hadn't been even more hateful toward her. Oh, and added to that: *My dad recently had him tortured.*

She fell back across the bed, throwing her arm over her face, beaning her forehead with her new bracelet.

Despite all this, MacRieve had offered her an olive branch. So what should *she* do with this newfound comprehension?

Confront him? He might go ballistic again.

Start over? He might hurt her again.

That's my *man,* her heart seemed to cry. And now that damned hope-spark was back.

Soccer hadn't been easy, Stanford definitely hadn't, but she'd never given up on either.

Maybe she shouldn't with MacRieve.

She sat up. She still had feelings for him, still experienced that sense of connection to him. She liked his clan, actually missed them. She needed sex to live; sex with MacRieve had held such promise.

What were her other options? If she escaped, where would she go and how would she live? Would she be driven out every night, looking for sustenance, feeding on random guys? The thought made her skin crawl.

Compared to that, a life with MacRieve was the championship trophy. Why *wouldn't* she fight for it?

Because he detests my entire species? Oh, yeah.

So how to make him forget what she was? Before she'd boarded the plane, Munro had told Chloe that she was like an anti-succubus. Her personality was completely unlike the fawning, deceptive ones he'd known. He'd said, "Just be yourself with Will. If you feel the need to tell him he's being a prick, do so. If you feel the need to kick his arse, doona hold back. He needs you to be . . . you. With all your *attitude.*"

Chloe hadn't understood at the time, and more, she hadn't given a damn what MacRieve needed. Now she was starting to read between the lines. Munro wanted Chloe to continue being an anti-succubus to show MacRieve how different she was.

As she dressed in new gear—shorts, a jog bra, running shoes—she decided that she'd play this day by ear, reading MacRieve's cues as if he were a tricksy fullback, while keeping the trophy in sight. She pulled her hair up in a ponytail, then hurried downstairs.

When he raked his gaze over her, his irises flickered.

"What? What's wrong?"

He growled, *"Red."*

Yes, her shorts and bra were red. "So?"

Seeming to give himself a shake, he said, "Everything fits?" But his voice was rougher.

"Like a glove. It's nice having my own stuff again."

He scowled, rubbing his palm over the back of his neck. "You'll have more. We'll head to the city soon. I'll buy you new. Anything you want."

She blinked at him. "Did you not see that haul up there? I've got everything I need."

Deeper scowl.

Way to take cues, Chlo. So the guy needed to buy her stuff. "I could use a watch, though."

"Aye," he said quickly.

"And an iPad and a soccer ball."

"Done." Mood obviously improved, he said, "If you vow you will no' weaponize the latter. My stones were singing for hours after your last shot."

"Then don't say things that make me want to cleat you in the face." Now she understood *why* he had; didn't mean she'd ever let him get away with trash-talking.

"A fate to be avoided. I've seen you cleat someone in the face—and that was before you'd turned immortal." He pointed at her shoes. "You will no' need those."

"The importance of arch support can't be overstated. And what if I cut myself?"

"You're no' human, Chloe. There's no need for *anything* support. Hell, you could go without your bra."

She quirked a brow.

"So that's a solid '*nay*' on the bra removal?" He sighed as if he'd just missed a goal. "Verra well. As for cutting your foot, you'd heal nigh instantaneously." He seized one of her hips, dragging her close. "Today, I plan to show you our lands—and what you're capable of."

Cue taken, MacRieve. She gazed up at him. *Then hold on to your ass. 'Cause Chloe's about to lower the boom.*

THIRTY-NINE

"Your pace is impressive," Will told her. They'd jogged about a mile from the keep, taking a path toward Mount Conall, one of the higher vistas in the area. From there, they'd be able to see a good deal of the holding.

Important, since Will now felt the need to impress her. *To acquaint her with all I've got.*

"I've been holding back." She ran faster along the winding trail, tossing over her shoulder, "To show respect for your advanced age."

He raised his brows, treated to a view of her arse swishing in those tiny red shorts. He scrubbed his palm over his mouth. Her arse in motion was like catching a glimpse of the hereafter itself.

And she was teasing him to boot? He didn't know what had happened to her between the time when she'd gone up to change and when she'd returned, but something drastic had.

Her entire attitude had shifted from pissed to mischievous. Mayhap she was in a cheerier mood just to have renewed energy.

Oh, aye, he'd be getting back *in* that game. As Munro had pointed out the night before, it was indeed possible for Will to woo her—because he already had once.

The plan? Will was to do whatever he'd done on that day he and Chloe had shared.

So he intended to court, flirt, kiss, and touch, all while filling her ears with dirty words. And once he'd seduced her slowly over the day, he planned to take her in their bed again tonight.

Yet as his wolf gaze followed the back and forth swish of her arse, he feared . . .

I'll never make it back to the keep.

When he drew up beside her, he found her running with her face lifted to the sun, her lips curled with pleasure, and a shot of lust hit him like a punch to the gut. Her skin was just beginning to dampen.

In a casual tone, he observed, "Your eyes are bright, your skin glowing. Sex with me becomes you."

Her wee bare feet stutter-stepped, but she righted herself. "You don't look too shabby yourself. For a crypt keeper. Been meaning to ask you, how'd you keep warm before fire?"

So that's how she'd play this? "If you get hungry, just let me know." His gaze landed on her bouncing breasts. "We can stop for a bite."

"I don't *do* fast food. Not really into wolfing down my meals."

Ach, he liked her sass. "Nay, this meal will have many courses, a bounty *overflowing*. You can feast until you're . . . gorged."

Her cheeks went red again. She gave him a sidelong glance, as if she was seeing something in him for the first time. "So, MacRieve, how long has it been since you were here last?"

He let her steer the conversation back to tamer ground. "Hundreds of years." He'd enjoyed seeing the world and many of its planes, and building a colony had been rewarding. But now that he was back here, the land called to him.

"So this is truly a jog down memory lane."

He nodded. Memories had been arising, surprising him. Aye, he had tragic ones, but he also recollected picnics with his family—he and Munro fishing the river as their parents lazed in the sun, gazing at their boys with utter pride. He remembered their da teaching them to ride, their mam trying to teach them etiquette. There'd been snow fights with them and countless tales around the fire.

There'd been so much laughter.

Before, Will hadn't remembered playing as a boy. Now he recalled idyllic times with Munro—forts, hunts, chases. He understood Munro's words: *Reclaim your past*.

When Will and Chloe crossed a brook, an off-shoot of the Conall River, he found himself telling her, "Munro and I set up a toll on this bridge when we were seven. Clan members paid us in shells, telling us that they were akin to gold. We were convinced we'd become big-time merchants."

She smiled. "Was that before or after the wheel was invented?"

His lips were curling. "Nary a year after."

When they passed a flock of sheep, she cooed at the prancing lambs. "Wolves keep sheep? Doesn't that go against the laws of nature or something? Next you'll tell me fox shifters raise hens."

"Anything goes in the Lore. Look at us," he said, earning another appraising look from her. Was he gaining *any* ground with her?

Once they reached the base of Mount Conall, she said, "Race you to the top?" Before he could say a word, she charged upward.

He'd been so obsessed with her arse, he feared he'd neglected due attention to her legs and tiny waist. To her slim shoulders and graceful arms. To those flawless breasts currently highlighted by a bright red bra.

As he watched her body moving, so fit and sure, he was abundantly aware that he'd given her the energy she burned today. She was the picture of health, invulnerable to harm—because he'd helped make her strong.

Was there any real difference between how other males provided for their mates, and how Will would? Food versus sex?

His Instinct hadn't differentiated last night, commanding him at once to mate her—and to provide.

With Ruelle, he'd surrendered his seed, fully aware that she would have it from him whether he wanted to give it or not.

With Chloe, he'd had to all but force nourishment on her. Could he get her to take it again today?

Munro had asked if Will could handle the venom bond. If the other option was losing her, then he'd take on her bond like a sword thrust to the chest—with regret, but valiantly. . . .

After giving her a generous head start, he followed, his easy strides eating the distance between them. But at the last moment, he let her win.

When she cast him a triumphant smile, things became very simple.

I feed her; I get days like this.

Atop the peak, he dragged her back against his chest, draping his arms across her shoulders. She allowed it, eventually relaxing against him as they took in the view.

He inhaled deeply of the crisp air, smelling the land and his mate's scent. Like this, he was centered as he hadn't been in memory.

Mayhap he'd never been this centered—since becoming a man.

She shielded her eyes from the sun. "Why'd you stay away so long? It's clear you like it here."

"I dinna remember how much I liked it." Munro thought Will and Chloe belonged here, and as Will gazed out, he suspected his brother might be right. "When I was young, a village flourished near the keep over there." He pointed to the west. "My family were Sentinels here."

"What does that mean?"

"We were tasked with guarding the boundary of the Woods of Murk." He indicated the forest to the south. Just gazing at it made his jaw clench.

"What did you guard the boundary against?"

"It was once populated with all kinds of creatures. Evil ones." Understatement. "We kept those beings in, and kept our kind out."

"So that's why you tensed up yesterday when you gazed out at it. Are they still there?"

"Nay." Hundreds of years ago, his rage at Ruelle still burning hot, he'd yearned to make war on the Woods. Soon he hadn't been the only one. "When those beings got out of control—when Cerunnos were slithering into our lands to steal sheep and maidens—we gained permission from our king to venture into the Woods and hunt them down."

If Will had been molded early in his life, Munro had been fashioned during those grisly battles.

Fashioned by what he'd found in a warren in the woods.

"All of those beings died in the last Accession," he said. "Do you know what that is?"

"I read about it. Every five hundred years or so, fate forces different species to war. Lots of death. Scary stuff. And it's happening now, right? Makes me wish I'd taken up sword-fighting or knife-throwing or something."

She had zero defenses, no Fury killer instincts or Fey speed. She couldn't trace like a vampire or cast witchy spells. All she had was her strew, which she would never bloody use on another.

"Doona fret. You've got yourself a protector." A ruthless one. But on the off chance that something happened to him, he'd need to begin teaching her to defend herself. Plus, intensive training would provide her a distraction, might mitigate the worst of her grief over the Olympics.

"Good to know, protector," she said lightly, almost as if she doubted he could protect her.

Or doubted he *would*?

"So what did you do once your Sentinel gig was over?" she asked.

"When the Woods grew light once more, Munro and I were freed to leave, to see the world."

"Did you?"

"Oh, aye. Every continent, many times over." It hadn't been all travel and exploration. They'd loyally served King Lachlain for centuries. When Lachlain had been lost to the vampires, they'd futilely combed Russia searching for him.

With the loss of their king, many members of the clan had wanted to leave Scotland. Will and Munro had helped them, developing Bheinnrose.

"And now back you've come," she said.

He rested his chin on her head. "Munro expects us to live here."

"Aren't you the chieftain of the Nova Scotia clan?"

"He's far better suited for that job. I could step down. Then this could be our home," he said in a gruff tone, insecure with this. He'd never even asked a woman out on a date, much less to live with him. "We could be content here."

She tensed against him. "MacRieve, you don't have to say that. We don't have to talk about the future. Let's just enjoy the day. I don't want you to say something you'll regret later."

"In other words, you doona want me to make promises I will no' keep."

"Can you understand why I'm gun-shy here?"

She'd accused him of being a liar. Likely because he'd been such a twatting liar with her. Which meant she didn't believe him when he told her he would be her protector, or that they'd live here together.

"I understand your hesitation." And for the first time today, he began to sweat.

Seeming determined to avoid any deeper discussion, she asked, "What about the woods to the north? Are they empty too?"

"Legend holds that the Old Ones live there—primordial Lykae."

"What are they?"

"If Lykae are men who become wolven, primordials are wolves that become human. They never hurt our kind—indeed, there are anecdotes of them coming to our aid. But I have no' scented them here since we arrived," he said with a touch of regret. "They might have died out."

She pointed to a distant loch with a waterfall. "Is that part of Conall too?"

"Aye. Munro and I used to swim there."

"Can we go see it?"

"It's a good ways. Doona want to overtire you."

"Wolf, please," she scoffed. "I'm not the one who's eight thousand years old." She ducked out from under his arms, then took off down the hill, with him right behind her.

When they'd reached the loch, she craned her head to gaze up at the top of the waterfall.

"We jumped off that once." He expected her to express disbelief, because it was seriously high.

Instead, she said, "I want to see the view from up there."

He raised his brows. "It's a treacherous climb."

"For a mortal, right? I thought you were going to show me what I'm capable of."

He waved her forward. "Then by all means. Ladies first."

"Oh, you're a gentleman wolf now?" The sun was beginning to kiss her skin with color. "Or perhaps you just want to ogle my ass?"

"Suggested solely for my ogling pleasure. Off you go." He gave her a swat—and her arse did indeed move for a breathtaking split second afterward.

She shivered in reaction, because his lusty mate *liked* a good swat. She'd nearly climbed the walls last night. After clearing her throat, she said, "Behave."

And then the show began as she started climbing up the steep incline directly above him—in those tiny shorts. The outer fabric was little more than fluttering mesh, delivering ample glimpses of her arse, but the silky inner lining was like connected panties, taunting him as it covered her sex.

Up higher, the mist from the waterfall wetted their clothes. That lining was now *clinging* to her cleft.

Gods almighty. He followed her, cockstand pointed due north and showing no signs of waning.

When her foot slipped on a slick rock, he took the opportunity to palm her. Under the pretense of giving her a boost, he shifted his grip. With a tug of his thumb and a swift slice of his foreclaw, he rendered that inner lining crotchless.

Mercy.

"MacRieve! Why do I feel a draft? You cut my shorts?"

He grunted in answer.

"You think you're very sly, don't you?"

Somehow he mustered words: "Rewarded with this view, I *know* I'm the slyest of wolves."

"You can let go of me now!"

"Doona think I will. It's no' often a man gets a grip of hot, plump heaven in the palm of his hand." He squeezed the flesh in his grasp, delighted when he scented her arousal. "Ah, and there she goes. You like when I play with your arse."

In a strangled tone, she said, "I'd like to not fall."

"When I spanked you last night, your eyes rolled back in your head."

"Oh, yeah, and you didn't get your rocks off on that *at all.*"

"I doona deny it—" Words left him when she raised her knee and he caught a glimpse of the dip at her entrance. Jaw slackened, he began inching a knuckle toward it, rubbing his way to that maddening spot.

"Cut it out! I'm at the top. I'm serious."

With a sigh, he gave her a heft, sending her up and

over the edge to land on her feet. He joined her, found her blushing.

"You took advantage of me."

"Of the situation, more like," he replied shamelessly.

She cast him a look that promised comeuppance, then turned to take in the view. He knew she'd see the keep in the distance, the two forests, the river winding through green fields. He was staring only at her.

"This is so amazing." Her expression was awed. "Okay, you're forgiven. For my shorts."

When he stood behind her and rested his hands on her hips, her heart sped up. "You glad you came out with me?"

She turned to him, surprising him by saying, "I've had fun. When you're not mauling my clothes to grope me."

"Still no' hungry though? If you need it, you've only to tell me." At her stern look, he held up his palms. "Nay? Then mayhap after the climb down?"

"Climb?"

"It's too high for you to jump, lass."

"I thought you said I was all indestructible and everything."

"I'm no' worried about your body. I'm worried about how you'll react when you see the loch below you. It looks like it's from a bluidy circus high dive."

She put her hand on her hip. "I'm not the veriest pussy, MacRieve. I will be jumping."

"Uh-huh. We'll see."

"And I'll be doing it topless." Before his stunned

gaze, she yanked off her sports bra, sling-shooting it at his face. "That's a solid '*aye*' on the bra removal."

Those breasts kissed by sun . . . "Woman! My mouth waters—"

But she'd already whirled around, charged for the edge, then leapt with an excited squeal.

He put her bra between his teeth and dove in behind her, the quicker to reach her.

FORTY

Chloe hit the water with air-wrenching force, but she recovered easily, kicking toward the surface with a laugh.

Had she ever felt this alive? She'd pushed her body this morning, covering miles of challenging terrain. Bliss in itself. Add in a playful MacRieve . . .

He'd been opening up to her, showing his charming side—and his domineering one. It was official: she liked one as much as the other.

When she reached the surface, he was waiting for her.

"You dropped this." He held up her top with a darkening expression.

Shocking him had seemed like such a good idea at the time. Now she was topless with an immortal male who looked like he wanted to eat her for dinner.

In fact, that was what *she* would be doing when they had sex again.

When?

She held out her hand. "Gimme, MacRieve."

He tossed her bra on the shore. "Oh, I think no'." There was a threatening undertone to his voice, a sub-text of *Your ass is mine.*

She swallowed. No, she didn't spook easily in most situations. But this was a sexual situation; sex had been a mixed bag for her. So she began swimming backward away from him. He steadily pursued. She didn't think he would hurt her, but then, she'd never had a wicked wolf eyeing her like he was about to rail her into next week. At the thought, her nipples got even harder.

His gaze dipped. He could see them! She dove away from him, started swimming in earnest.

Yet he was right behind her. "Breaststroke?" he said in a rumbling voice. "Sounds like a great idea."

Not really. The water streamed past her nipples, turning her on even more. Her hair must've come loose because strands tickled across her breasts. She chanced a look over her shoulder. By the way his molten gaze narrowed, she got the sense that he liked the chase.

I think I might too.

Reaching the bank, she scrambled up the edge. He looked like he was about to lunge for her, so she dived, arcing over his head to start for the opposite shore.

As she surfaced, he was still groaning. "That image'll stay with me for the next nine hundred years."

She was gunning for land when he snagged her ankle, snatching her back to him. When they were face-to-face, he informed her, "Playtime's over, mate. I mean to be inside you." Then he looped his arm around her thighs, lifting her until she was forced to bend over one brawny shoulder.

"What the hell are you—"

Smack! Down came his palm across her wet bottom.

"MacRieve!" She wriggled over his shoulder, no longer surprised by how that turned her on. Her stiff nipples grazed his back with each step he took toward the shore.

"That's what happens if you make me chase you." Another *smack!* "And that's what'll happen if you *doona* make me chase you."

When he started kneading her there, she bit her bottom lip to keep from moaning.

He sloshed through the water to a grassy bank that dropped off to the lake. "Down you go." He settled her so she was sitting with her feet still in the water, and with him between her knees. Their faces were level, which meant her breasts were within easy reach of his mouth.

He inhaled deeply. "Rough play got to you again? How I'm goin' to enjoy discovering everything that pushes your buttons."

Busted. She lifted her chin. "And what pushes yours?"

He reached beneath the surface, pulled off his swim trunks, then tossed them on the shore. "Simple. Tawny-haired female footballers who like to have their arses swatted. Gets me every time."

Her lips parted around shallowing breaths.

He brushed a drop of water from the bottom one. "You're all wet. I told you that you'd never need a towel when I'm around," he said, raising his hands to cup both her breasts. He bent his dark head over them, lowering his mouth to one.

He alternated nuzzling kisses on her nipples. When he scraped his stubble over the tips, she gasped with delight.

Then he gave a loud suck on one peak, rendering it swollen red. He moved to the other one, repeating the process.

When he blew on them, she cried, "MacRieve!"

"You tortured me thus when you suckled on my cock." He rasped in her ear, "I'll do the same with your wee clit, sucking till it's throbbing, then blow on it."

She whimpered. Not fair, and he knew it! His brogue plus dirty words equaled Chloe about to orgasm.

He kept at her breasts until she was murmuring, "Please," over and over.

"Shall I make you come just from nursing your sweet tits?"

How about just from talking? He could make her come *from his voice*. She beat against his back, but he just chuckled against her skin.

Yet when he hooked his fingers into her shorts, she gave herself a mental shake and stayed his hands. She had an agenda—and a championship trophy at stake. "Um, wait. I don't know about sex."

He drew back to face her. "What's wrong?"

"MacRieve, twice is really damned close to three times." She gave a nervous laugh. "The succubus hat trick?" She wanted to win him over; they shouldn't be rushing into anything.

And what if she got pregnant from this time? Munro had said succubae had cycles throughout the year, but he didn't know when or how a cambion could get pregnant. Considering MacRieve's past, how would he react to part-Ubus kids? "I'm just saying it's a big step, and I don't want you to have any regrets."

"We're already bound by fate, Chloe. What if I would do anything to have you? Even something that . . . that I'd no' envisioned for myself?"

Of course he hadn't envisioned a bond with a succubus. But his admission seemed to carry a wealth of sentiment.

"Can't we just take this more slowly?" Today she'd glimpsed what life with him could be like, and she *wanted* it.

"I would dearly love to take you when you are no' hungry. When you would no' strew. When I could have control of my own actions." Though his tone was even, his bearing told her he was aching for this.

Her resistance was melting.

"I dinna want to make you nervous, but tomorrow night's the full moon."

"What does that mean?"

"My beast will rise. It'll seek to mate you all night, with much more power. I'll have no control over it."

"Remember, I don't have a problem with your beast. We got along great."

MacRieve's expression was disbelieving, like a wolf sensing a trap—because the bait was too good to be true. "Then you'll receive me under the moon?

If I feed you between now and then, you'll be strong enough to take me."

The bond would definitely be completed tomorrow; today would make no difference. Was she ready for this?

"You have tae feed, *mo chridhe*."

My heart. He hadn't called her that since the day of her turning.

He brushed a lock of hair from her cheek. "I canna be easy until you have fed at least once a day. Besides, you will no' want tae miss what I've in store for you."

The sinful look in his eyes made her stutter, "N-no?"

He kissed her neck, her jawline, her ear, telling her, "I plan tae lick your sweet cunny right up tae the point when it's quivering, about tae release right on my tongue. Then I'm goin' tae fit my thick cock inside your sheath, fucking you till you come all over me."

She moaned, "You're not playing fair." She was losing this battle—happily losing it. So why was she still wavering?

"Play fair?" He gave a husky laugh. "If you understood how badly I want you, then you would no' even expect me tae. . . ."

<hr>

Will's shaft pulsed, his ballocks full for her. He loved that Chloe responded to dirty words; now that he'd learned the power of them, he knew he was just going to get worse.

Sex as a man was infinitely more exciting than sex as a beast.

So stay down, creature. As if in answer, his beast started prowling.

When Will reached for her shorts, this time she lifted up to help him remove them. Once she was unclothed, he savored the sight.

Her vivid eyes were heavy-lidded, and sunlight glinted off the drops all over her supple body. He would never tire of seeing her breasts swelling for his greedy gaze, her nipples pouting for his mouth. Never tire of seeing her shapely legs trembling with anticipation. The way the tawny thatch of hair between her thighs sheened in the sun . . .

Leamsa. Mine. At that moment, he didn't feel cursed—quite the opposite.

Determined to make her come during sex, he decided he would take her to the very edge. She'd pay for all her talk of *whiskey dick* and uneven scores. "Spread your legs for my kiss."

When she dutifully did, her heart sped up.

"My wanton mate loves tae be tongued." As he bent down to her sex, her luscious lips were pink and glistening. He used his thumbs to spread her moist folds wide, then thrust his tongue inside her.

She mewed, arching her back and drawing her knees up around his head.

"Gods, you heat my blood!" he groaned against her. He felt like a race was on—to take her to the brink before he lost his battle with his beast. And with his cock. It throbbed to replace his tongue, was spilling pre-cum into the water. He grated, "Play with your breasts for me." Then he set back in, burrowing his tongue into her.

With a cry, she lifted her hands, cupping those full mounds. When she pinched her nipples, he growled praise against her flesh.

Between deep licks at her entrance, he said, "My seed's going right in there. Right where you need it. Do you crave it, hot and thick within you?"

"Y-yes!" she panted. Her thighs were tightening around his ears, her hands clutching her breasts.

Already close. He kissed up to her clit, rubbing it with his tongue.

"Oh God, MacRieve, oh God, I'm about to . . ."

Somehow he drew back.

"No! Why?" Legs still spread, she undulated for him with a breathtaking lewdness. So he speared her there with a thick finger. Slippery flesh clenched around it.

"Ahhh!"

He took his finger away. "Feels empty?"

When she could only moan low, he knew Chloe had given him her fire to tend once more. He was steering this encounter, he was leading them. He'd married his mate's will to his.

Now, if only he could govern his beast so well.

Will dragged her closer, so her arse was at the edge of the bank. With her spread even wider before him, he cupped her sex possessively. *"Is leamsa so."*

She mindlessly rocked to his palm.

"This is mine. Look at me and tell me that."

She opened her eyes. They were green—telling him she was about to orgasm for him.

"It's y-yours."

"And what are you?"

"I'm yours too."

"Good girl." He entered her with a swift thrust of his cock.

She came immediately, freeing him, lessening his nerves. As her sheath squeezed his length and wetness coated it, he rasped, *"Tapadh leat, aingeal." Thank you, angel.* Then he plunged into her come, yelling out to feel it. "Your honey's all over me."

Her head lolled, her mouth open on a soundless cry.

Keep the beast down. This was too powerful to share; Will wanted her all to himself. He wrapped one arm around her arse, one around her neck, lifting her to him.

With each thrust, some indescribable need seemed to awaken more and more, one that had nothing to do with his beast or his Instinct. He felt like he couldn't get close enough to her—though he'd clenched her body seamlessly to his.

He felt like he couldn't fuck her hard enough—though he was pistoning his hips between her thighs.

He was inside his mate, and yet he was *desperate* for her. Madness seemed to dance at the edge of his consciousness. How could he want her so . . . violently?

His heart thundered in his ears; his chest felt scored inside. Crazed, he drove in and out of her. Only one thing could make him this frantic for her! "Your strew, it's happening."

"How c-can you tell?"

He clamped her nape to meet her gaze. "Because I am"—thrust—"fucking"—thrust—"*ravening* for you!" His roar echoed off the rocks, louder than the falls.

When she whispered, "I feel the same," emotions he didn't understand overpowered him. Dangerous feelings. Demented. *Dark.*

I'll die without her. I'll bluidy die! He roiled with confusion, his thoughts tangled. Sometime in his frenzy, she'd come again. She was now limp in his arms, moaning with ecstasy, simply taking his manic shafting. He clasped her beautiful face, dipping his thumb between her lips. She sucked it with bliss, eyes rolling back in her head.

My lass, my lass. Love.

When his beast rose up with redoubled strength, Will was too dazed to fight any longer. He receded. *Tend her well, beast, she's yours.*

For now.

Never withdrawing, the beast maneuvered her body, flipping her so that her front lay on the grassy bank.

Pressing her head down and lifting her arse, it pounded into her from behind like the animal it was.

It moved her thick mane of hair to bare her neck, gazing at her flesh with longing, baying to mark her there.

Give her enough, but no' all. . . . Will reined the beast back in, denying its bite—allowing only the strongest ejaculation they'd ever known.

FORTY-ONE

Is it like this for other people?" Chloe asked. She and MacRieve were lying on the bank together, reclined on their sides, naked in the late afternoon sun. His smooth, damp skin was flushed from exertion, his muscles still bulging. His eyes were heavy-lidded and warm gold, his beast at rest.

MacRieve gave a short laugh. "I know I've never felt anything like it."

With a grin, she said, "Did your ballocks beg for mercy?"

"They still are."

She laughed. "I used to wonder why everyone was always thinking about sex. I couldn't understand it. Now I do."

And more, she'd been reminded today of how good it could be between them, her hope-spark flaring unchecked. To think she might've missed this if she hadn't given him a second chance!

"Hey, aren't you supposed to mark my neck?"

"In time." Had his gaze darted?

"If we're going to keep doing this, I need to get on birth control. Munro said he didn't know what my cycles would be like."

"You've no need to worry about that."

"How can you be sure? MacRieve, what if I did get pregnant? What would you do?"

There. A flash of anguish before he disguised it.

Her heart fell. She'd wondered how he'd feel about having children with her. Now she knew. She could even understand it, considering his past. That didn't mean she wasn't hurt.

She got up to dress. "Message received." Then she sucked in a breath. "Would something be wrong with them? Would they be monstrous?"

He sat up with a weary exhalation. "Monstrous? Nay. But they could be incubi or succubae."

She stilled. "You just so much as said, 'They wouldn't be monstrous, *however*, they could be like you.'"

"That's no' what I said." He ran his fingers through his wet hair. "You are the one who wanted to take this slow. The idea of children is a lot to wrap my head around."

She yanked on the wet shorts, searching for her bra. "What if it's already happened? It might have!"

"Rest easy, Chloe. The talisman you wear has been imbued twice. Once to keep you hidden, and again to keep you from getting pregnant."

"*What?*" She turned on him, draping her arm over

her breasts. "You put me on birth control without even discussing it with me?"

"Your eyes are glowing with anger? Do you *want* me to impregnate you?"

"No, but I hate that you made a decision like that for me! That shit might've flown in the eleventh century, but not today."

He rose as well, dressing with obvious irritation. "We were no' exactly speaking much when I was ordering the talisman."

"That was only two days ago. Yet you're acting like everything's been settled with us."

"It has! We intended to start anew, remember? I've accepted that you need to feed from me. I'll claim you once more, and then you'll be mine forever."

"I haven't promised you anything, and you're illuminating why that was a smart move on my part. Do you *try* to hurt me? Or is it just a talent? Because let me tell you, you've hit me with some sharp zingers over the last week. Hey, at least you didn't puke today. Progress!"

Between gritted teeth, he said, "This is getting blown out of proportion."

"Do you expect me to wear this bracelet for eternity? What happens when I eventually want kids? Hell, you'd probably just cut off their heads, right?"

"Doona be ridiculous," he said with a scowl. "If we had children, we'd have to remain away from my clan, for fear our offspring would prey on others."

"Maybe they'd be dormant like I was. We could find out if you ever let me talk to my kind!"

"Never!"

She saw him digging his claws into his palms, but was too furious to care. "Never? Because all of them—down to the last male, female, and child—are evil?" She started off in the direction of her bra. "I'm sure you've met them all!"

He followed. "You're making more of this than you should!"

"*I* am? So it's my fault that I'm mad—because *I* am overreacting." Again, she was one decibel away from screeching.

His eyes widened. "I doona want to assign *fault*. That's no' what I meant."

She found her bra, yanking it on. "I thought we had a shot, thought I could make you see I'm not like the succubae you've encountered before. That's not even possible, is it?"

She was no victim, but that's what she was acting like—a pushover, rewarding his hostility with softness.

That was a losing strategy in soccer—and in life.

He was beginning to look alarmed. "If you want offspring, even after I've expressed concerns, I'll give them to you!"

"You're missing the point. Until you can get right with what I am, until you can imagine having kids with me, there is no hope for us! The thought of having a little girl like me should make you happy, not fill you with disgust. Whatever *this* is"—she waved from him to herself and back—"it's doomed."

"Doona bluidy say that!"

"You're blinded by hatred, and I won't tolerate being treated like shit anymore; ergo, doomed! My God, MacRieve. Even I'll admit defeat when I'm down twenty points with two minutes left on the clock. Anything else is just delusional."

As Will watched her striding away, he chuffed with displeasure.

His mate was walking away from him—directly after telling him she thought they were doomed. This would set any Lykae's teeth on edge.

His beast howled inside, hankering to lope after her.

In an attempt to give her space, Will trailed her at a distance, keeping her in sight. Damnation, he was out of sorts, already wanting her by his side. Not surprising, considering that he'd just experienced some kind of strew-induced, transcendent sexual frenzy with her.

When sheep got in his way as he crossed a field, he gave a halfhearted growl, sending them scampering.

Yesterday when he'd felt her succubus pull, he'd been sickened. Today? He'd lost the ability to stand, collapsing over her back. When he'd finally opened his eyes, he'd leaned down to kiss the corner of her lips—because they'd been curling with a satisfied smile.

Satisfied! Gods, she pleased him.

Sex with her hadn't just blown his mind, it'd tweaked

his gray matter forever. What he'd known about bliss was now changed, the upper threshold ratcheted up to record heights.

Over this day, he'd had three realizations.

First, to possess Chloe as his own, he would let her feed from his body for eternity, allowing her to compel him with strew for just as long. He might not be happy about it, but he wanted her so badly, he would do *anything* to keep her. Every man had his own secret sorrows. So would he.

Second, he didn't know when—or if—he could claim her with his bite. Withholding it made him feel more in control. Keeping something back allowed him to rationalize all he was ceding.

And last: Though he didn't dread taking on her venom as much as in the past—it would tie her to him—he didn't relish the idea. *Regretfully, but valiantly.*

All his life he'd had a phobia about three times. Now it seemed his mate did as well.

No matter. It would happen with their very next time.

When Chloe entered the keep, she slammed the door behind her. All right, mayhap he should've told her everything the talisman did when she'd first donned it. Yet at the time he hadn't felt consideration for her. And aye, that was only two days ago, but something *had* been shifting inside him. He was adjusting to her species, making concessions.

Because today, he'd begun to believe they had a future.

Right when she'd become convinced they would

end? He needed to make some kind of gesture. Something to convince her he would try.

Will remembered when he'd been eight, he'd broken his mam's favorite vase. Filled with guilt, he'd charged out to pick her flowers, the only thing he could give her. With her gaze twinkling, Mam had ruffled his hair. "Ach, Will, now it does no' matter that I've nothing to put them in. . . ."

So what to give Chloe? His eyes widened. The attic of this place was full of treasures.

FORTY-TWO

Way to lower the boom on him, Chloe thought as she scuffed to the bathroom, turning on the shower in the oversize stall.

She'd meant to act like her old self, letting things roll off her back, rubbing dirt on it, rolling with the punches.

Instead, she'd lashed out at MacRieve. She didn't even want kids anytime in the near future! But when she did have them, she didn't want their father to gaze at them with that anguished expression.

Like the way my dad looked at me that last night.

Did MacRieve still gaze *at her* that way when she wasn't looking? She wished she could talk to his beast—and tell it to whip MacRieve into shape.

She peeled off her abused clothing, glaring at her bracelet. That bastard had put her on birth control, like she was chattel! If he had to take a business trip, would he strap her into a chastity belt too?

Under the steaming water, she winced at her sore muscles. She might have been fed, but she was still feeling the day. Her head ached and her stomach felt weird. She supposed too much running—and too much rough lake sex—had worn her out.

One of her breasts had a grass stain across it, and claw marks dotted her hips. *Hey, not much different from a soccer match, Chlo!*

When she was finished showering, the bed looked too inviting to resist. She changed into her new PJs, tossed a log on the embers in the fireplace, then crawled under the covers.

She stared at the ceiling, glad to have this time alone. All these new aspects of her life had been hitting her so fast that she'd barely had a moment to reason through them. For instance, it was now dinnertime; she would never eat dinner again. That was going to take some getting used to.

Also, she should probably accept her familial situation—as in, she didn't have one anymore. She'd told herself that as long as she continued eating, she might not be totally "detrus-ed out" to her dad. He might still accept her.

Now? The odds looked grim.

In time, maybe she could track down Fiore's family—but then, MacRieve would never allow her to see them.

Noises sounded above her, as if he was rummaging around the attic. For what exactly? It wasn't like there'd be scrapbooks or old yearbooks. No vids of MacRieve's first steps. . . .

She'd just closed her eyes when he opened the door and strode in.

"Why are you resting?" He wore a black T-shirt and beat-up jeans, and he had a smudge of dust on his cheek that made him look less intimidating, almost boyish.

She shrugged. "I'm tired. I think I overexerted myself today."

He tilted his head, surveying her face. "This will no' take long. Then I'll leave you to rest." He sat beside her on the bed. "Listen, Chloe. I know I should have told you about the bracelet."

Exhaling with irritation, she said, "No, you should have *asked* me about the bracelet before I ever put it on my wrist!"

"Aye, that's what I meant," he said quickly. "I regret no' asking you."

She sat up, almost grimacing when her headache intensified. "I need more, MacRieve. I need you to confide in me. I need to know why you hate my kind so much. Why even the thought of having kids with me makes you sick."

He rose to pace. "It's going to take more than a few days for me to work through my . . . issues. Can you no' be patient with me?"

"Tell me why you beheaded the last five succubae you encountered."

His nostrils flared, along with his claws. From the mere mention? "Over my life I've killed any I've come across."

A horrific thought arose. "Were you killing one a

little over two decades ago? Her name was Fiore, and she would've looked a lot like me."

"I dinna murder your mother. We've obstacles between us, I grant you that, but no' that particular one. I vow to the Lore I had nothing to do with her death." He sat beside her once more. "Here, lass," he said, drawing a polished wooden box from his back pocket. "I have a peace offering."

"What is this?" She opened the box to find jade-green hair combs, each intricately etched with Celtic designs.

"My grandmother passed these down to my mother. I thought you might like them, now that you've taken to wearing your hair long."

"You want *me* to have them?"

He ran his hand over the back of his neck. "Doona sound so shocked, Chloe. They belong to the mistress of this keep."

If he was giving her heirlooms, then surely he was starting to work past his hatred. She grazed her fingers over the engravings. "They're lovely." She set them on the bedside table, keeping them close.

"Patience, Chloe." He ran his knuckles along her jawline. "I'm an old dog, and all this is a verra new trick for me. I'm no' saying I canna change—just give me time. Can you do that?"

How much time? Maybe with enough of it, he could fall for her. Maybe if he loved her more deeply than he hated other succubae, he could see his way to having kids.

By that time, he might've snuffed out what she was

feeling for him. She just needed to think about all this. "I'm tired." She lay back down. "I'd like to go to bed."

His brows rose. She could tell he'd expected her to react differently.

When he shucked off his shirt and joined her, she didn't have the energy to rebuff him.

"Come, *mo chridhe.*" He reached for her, clasping her against his warm chest. "Sleep easy and rest. Everything will look better tomorrow."

The heat from his skin increased her drowsiness. Before she drifted off, she murmured, "Gotta be honest. This clock might've zeroed out, MacRieve."

His entire body tensed against her. She didn't care because sweet sleep was enveloping her. . . .

⁂

In the middle of the night, Chloe woke from an ache in her stomach and another in her head.

She found MacRieve sleeping restlessly beside her, his chest slick with sweat. Was this the first time he'd slept since they'd arrived? Since she'd turned in the first place?

His eyes darted behind his lids, and he moaned, obviously in the grips of a nightmare. As she watched, his fangs and claws began extending, his face growing more wolven. The beast was rising, even in MacRieve's slumber.

When he chuffed and whimpered, Chloe wondered which horror he was reliving tonight. Rape by a succubus? Battles in the dark Woods of Murk?

The shock of Chloe's transformation?

Then he splayed his hand over his chest, his claws embedded in his skin—around the spot she'd once kissed with all the tenderness she'd felt for this man.

He was dreaming about the torture her father had ordered done.

This is *doomed between us.* Accepting that grieved her so deeply. Chloe would be punished by MacRieve if she stayed, and punished by her heart if she left.

Because she might have gone and fallen in love with him.

FORTY-THREE

Will paced anxiously. It was well into the afternoon, yet Chloe still hadn't awakened.

The room was dimly lit. A storm raged outside, the sun obscured, the lands dark. Winds battered Conall's bricks, pelting debris against the windows.

He sat beside her on the bed to stroke her hair. "Chloe, love?" Why this fatigue again? He must've hurt her yesterday in his throes. She would need rest to heal.

Chloe might be immortal, but strength and endurance came with age; she was still so incredibly young.

Mayhap he should have thought of that before he'd rutted her with all his might.

In sleep, her brows drew together. With a huff of irritation, she turned from him.

He wanted to talk to her, to gauge her anger. The more he thought about yesterday, the more he recognized how cutting he'd been to her.

Aye, Chloe, I'll be withholding my parentage because of

your species. He cringed to think that he'd used a bloody witch spell to bind her fertility—without her knowing.

She'd told him they were doomed, and as he reflected on his behavior over the past week, he feared she was right. Some part of her *must* hate him. In her place, Will certainly would.

He shook Chloe's shoulder. "Wake, lass, I need to speak with you."

She groaned, pulling the pillow over her face. "Jesus, MacRieve, can it not wait?" she snapped.

He drew his head back. "Aye, then."

Soon her breaths grew even with sleep once more.

Nïx had predicted that his past would bury him. She'd told him he'd lose Chloe if he didn't change.

He hadn't buried his past, hadn't changed, and yet he'd still expected Chloe to accept him. He'd expected an infallible soothsayer to have made a mistake.

Will *was* delusional.

On Chloe's side table were the hair combs he'd given her. When he'd found them in a chest in the attic, he'd known they were for her. Last night she'd run her fingers over them as if he'd gifted her with a priceless treasure. They were so little compared to what she'd given him. Without her, he would've burned to death in a fiery pit. So why had he not claimed her fully?

Because I canna. Because I'm no' right.

As he stood to pace, he remembered Mam's last words more clearly. She hadn't said, "Never with a succubus." She'd said, "Never with one like *her.*"

Like Ruelle. A sick, child-molesting fiend.

His breath left him in a rush. Chloe was nothing

like Ruelle, but he'd treated her as if she were. He'd *mis*treated her, heaping insults on her, lying to her. And then he'd marveled when she was hesitant about a future with him.

Will had been trying to get revenge on a goddamned dead woman by hurting his mate!

As if on a movie reel, he replayed all his abuse. The day of the wall alone . . . he'd called her a seed-feeder, telling her she was trash. He'd terrified her with vicious threats, humiliating her in front of enemies.

The days to come had brought no improvement. Will had told her she probably craved getting gangraped by Pravus males. He'd all but told her she wasn't good enough to have his bairns. He'd withheld his claiming bite, reasoning that *enough* would suffice for her—not his *all*, but enough.

He'd vomited after taking her virginity.

And she'd borne it all, even giving him yesterday. Which he'd then ruined. *Slaoightear.* Villain. As all his actions sank in, he stood numb, incapable of moving.

Wrong. Everything's wrong. All my fault.

Sorrow, guilt, horror, hatred—all warred within him. The first three for how he'd treated Chloe, the last toward Ruelle.

And toward himself. As Will gazed at Chloe, his vision blurred.

I treated my innocent mate as Ruelle treated me. At the thought, he bashed his fists against his head, his face twisting. *What is* wrong *with me? Sick, sick!*

His beast tried to rise, to shield Will from pain. Yet Will wanted the agony, needed it.

Babes with Chloe? A new family between them? They'd figure it out.

All my fault. He chuffed, pulling at his hair. He wished Chloe would wake to hit him, wished she'd sink another shard into him.

Get right for her. Chloe was a fighter, scrapping for everything she'd ever gotten in life—Will would do no less for her.

Bury your past, or it'll bury you. He was ready to; he just didn't know how.

His Instinct urged: —*Wreak your vengeance upon those who deserve it.*—

How? Ruelle was long dead. Her memory alone lived on. And it was driving a wedge between him and his mate. Driving him nigh insane for hundreds of years.

Bury, bury, burn your past. . . .

One idea emerged from his chaotic thoughts. He strode to the line of windows facing south, staring out at the blustery Woods of Murk.

Burn your past, or it'll burn you. There was something he could do to tear down that memory.

—*Go there.*— his Instinct commanded. Suddenly, he was as desperate to breach that forest as he had been in his youth. He would leave Chloe snug in their bed, warm and safe within the impervious keep of his ancestors.

He'd lived for more than three hundred thousand days; he felt like his entire future rested on what the next few minutes would bring.

—*The answer lies within the forest. GO!*— He jerked at the Instinct's loudness.

He pressed a kiss against Chloe's hair, then turned to leave. At the doorway, he gazed back at his mate.

Some unknown emotion threatened to engulf him. It was primal and raw, disquieting him so much his beast stirred once more, protectively.

With a low growl, Will charged out into the storm. Running to an outbuilding, he ransacked it for supplies, then sprinted toward the Woods. The path to his destination was overgrown, but he would never forget the way.

Once Chloe woke, he wanted to greet her as a new man. One who could accept her strew, the venom bond, everything about her. As he ran, he identified that unknown emotion, owning it.

He imagined himself made whole, refashioned into a mate who could cherish her fully, giving her bairns and love.

He felt frenzied with the need to give her these things. With each step closer to his destination, his beast fought to rise. Will struggled to keep it leashed, to think clearly, to reason.

As the storm strengthened, shadows closed in on him, leaves swirling, trees shuddering. The winds howled, disrupting Will's hearing and sense of smell. Gusts brought confusing scents all the way from the sea.

Scents that would forever remind Will of that night.

His worry that he'd lost Chloe was so sharp, it was like pain coursing through his body. Will squinted through the tempest as he ran. He could make out the object of his hatred, the one he'd soon destroy. . . .

FORTY-FOUR

Something's wrong with me.

When Chloe woke she felt weak, as if she had the flu—with nausea, aches, and chills.

Her bones felt like they were breaking. Deep in her womb, she suffered what felt like menstrual pain from hell.

She roused and opened her eyes, gazing around the room for MacRieve, but he was gone. She recalled him sitting beside her earlier. She'd been half-awake, irritated that each of his words had sounded like a gong in her ears, worsening her splitting headache.

Hadn't he wanted to tell her something? She remembered peeking over from the bed to watch him standing at the window, his broad shoulders tense. She'd wanted to ask him what was wrong, but she'd drifted off again.

Chloe had dreamed that she told him she loved him, but he refused to answer her. He wouldn't look at her face for so many centuries that she turned invisible. . . .

Dragging herself to her feet, she crossed to the same spot where he'd stood, surveying that same forest to the south. When they'd first arrived, he'd gazed out in that direction, clenching his fists, tension radiating from him.

Now a funnel of smoke billowed from the treetops, deep within the Woods of Murk.

A fire? Was MacRieve there? The soughing winds carried that smoke and even embers against Conall's indifferent walls. Foreboding suffused her, a sense that he was in danger.

Tamping down her nausea, she pulled on jeans, a shirt, and shoes, then labored down the stairs. Each step jarred the bones in her legs, sending new waves of pain.

But she had to reach him. Panic overwhelmed her illness, giving her enough strength to cross the expanse of windswept fields. Dusk was deepening when she reached the boundary of the woods.

To journey within them? With night approaching?

That sense of foreboding only strengthened, until she could feel it in her aching bones. Fearing for MacRieve, she trudged on, following the smoke.

She hadn't made it the length of a soccer field before she had to lean against a trunk, resting her legs and catching her breath. She pushed on, the scent of smoke growing stronger and stronger. The acrid smell burned her nose and throat.

By the time she was close enough to hear the

crackle of fire, the trees had thinned. Was there a clearing ahead? She slowed, even more cautious—

The scene before her took her breath away.

A structure was burning. MacRieve stood in the firelight, staring at the flames. Ash streaked across his cheeks. At his feet was an orange can that read PETROL. He'd started this fire?

Apparently he hadn't scented her with the winds gusting toward her.

She watched as he twisted around to slash his claws through a nearby tree, then another. He gave a crazed roar, tearing at his hair. His eyes were blue—but the beast hadn't risen. This was just MacRieve, the man, seeming to go insane.

What was happening? What was this place? She stood stunned, unable to react.

When he turned back to his work, firelight reflected in his eyes. The color of ice and flame mixing. And she thought they . . . glistened *with tears.*

Yes, tracks coursed down through the soot on his face.

Before she could stop him, he charged toward the building, battering a fiery wall with his fists—as if it wasn't burning fast enough. Flames curled around his arms. He didn't seem to notice them.

"MacRieve!" She rushed forward. "Your shirt's on fire!"

He whipped his head around. "Why've you come here, Chloe?" Without interest, he peeled his shirt from his blistered skin, tossing it away. Then his expression tightened. "How long have you been there?"

Long enough to see his agony, to understand that this was the root of his pain—she just didn't know why. "Not long."

"You should no' be here. I have to take you back." His body was quaking.

So was hers. Though she felt like her legs wouldn't carry her much longer, she said, "I'm not going anywhere until you tell me what this is."

"Your face is deathly pale. You should be back at the keep."

"I draw the line here, MacRieve. Tell me what I want to know, or we end whatever is between us."

He gazed in the direction of Conall. "I'll tell you back home."

"Bullshit. You'll tell me *now*."

"If I do, will you let me take you back?"

She nodded, knowing she was finally going to learn his secrets. He was ready to tell her; did she have the strength to hear him out? She moved out of the path of the smoke, picking her way to one of the newly felled trees. Each step brought splintering pain.

When she sat on the trunk, he began to pace in front of her. He parted his lips to speak, then closed them, repeating this again and again.

"Please, MacRieve," she murmured.

He swallowed hard, his Adam's apple bobbing. At last, he began: "We were forbidden to go into these woods. But I went on a dare, and I caught the attention of a succubus who lived in this cottage. Her name was *Ruelle*." He spat the word, as if it was foul in his mouth. "She took me to her bed."

"A succubus . . . raped you?"

He swung a fist at the closest tree. "Doona put it like that!"

She sucked in a breath at his reaction. "Then did a succubus use her chemicals on you?"

A tight nod. "I knew it was happening, knew what she was. I thought I loved her. When she told me she was my mate, I believed her." Had his breath begun whistling in his chest again? "I was . . . still a lad."

"How young?"

He didn't meet her gaze when he muttered his answer.

Nine. Dear God. *Nine?*

"She had to use her strew on me. At my age, it was too . . . much. I'd feel like I was suffocating, like I was dying." His chest had started heaving, as if he was suffocating even now. "I learned later that she could've killed me by drawing too deep. Mortal men barely survive a taking, and I was no' grown. But my beast rose up to safeguard me each time."

Chloe was dumbstruck. He'd been just a little boy.

Still avoiding her gaze, he said, "I cried the first time. And the second, and so on . . . But the praise and the gifts kept me coming back. No' to mention her venom bond. She'd use the pain to punish me sometimes."

Chloe's eyes watered, but she fought not to spill tears for him, knowing he would hate that. *The male I love was abused like this.*

Between harsh breaths, he continued, "At that age, Lykae are learning to control their beasts. My family and members of my clan were teaching me to, but it rose every time I lay with Ruelle, any progress undone. After four years with her, I could no' imagine sex without my beast. It was all I knew. When it ended with Ruelle at last, I was no' . . . right. I dinna care to lie with another until I was in my forties. By then, the mold had fixed, and I knew I would be forever twisted."

She wanted to scream that he wasn't twisted, that he was *hers*, and that she wanted him so badly. This was the net she hadn't been able to see!

But she knew this was a precarious time for him. In as steady a tone as she could manage, she asked, "What happened to her? How were you freed of her venom?"

How could you ever even contemplate accepting mine? He'd been punished with it.

When he hesitated again—as if what he was about to tell her would prove even worse—a memory tugged at Chloe's consciousness. Hadn't Rónan said the twins were orphaned at thirteen? Four years with Ruelle would put him at that age.

"Ruelle had barred me from this place for days, and her venom hit me hard. I was sneaking out to go to her when my mother caught me. Gods, Mam could be fierce. She and my father squired me inside, and I confessed all." He ran his hand down his face, smearing more ash over it. "As if it was yesterday, I can remember how mystified I was by their disgust. I'd believed Ruelle was fated to me, that I was only doing as nature intended." He glanced at Chloe, then quickly away.

MacRieve was ashamed of this to this day.

"When my parents talked about killing her, I was

so confused. My da planned to set off in the morn to end Ruelle. But like I said, my mam was fierce, impulsive too. She could no' stand the pain I was in, so she slipped away into a blizzard. She came here."

Chloe could tell where this was leading.

"Munro, Da, and I followed, but we were too late. Ruelle was no' alone. To my bewilderment, she had another lover. A young vampire. He slew my mother."

"Oh, God, MacRieve, I'm so sorry."

Staring past her, he said, "Da beheaded the vampire and Ruelle. One day later, my father followed his mate."

She raised a tremulous hand to her forehead. She almost wished she had food in her stomach to vomit.

"On the last night of their lives, my parents must have thought me weak-willed, spineless. And I was. I got both of them killed. My mam was pregnant with a little girl." Another drop streaked down his face. "My entire family was destroyed because of my weakness."

"You weren't weak! You were still a boy! Blame Ruelle, *not* yourself. That bitch *groomed* you. I wish she was still alive—so I could behead her myself!" By the way he was looking at her eyes, she knew they were glowing with emotion. "MacRieve, you were so young."

"Mayhap then. But in the ensuing years, I grieved Ruelle's death nearly as much as my mother's." He peered hard at the ground as he rasped, "I knew it was wrong to do so, despised myself for it for so many years. Self-hatred like you canna imagine. It took me centuries, but eventually I accepted my lot in life. I'd never be right sexually. I'd never sleep with the same female twice. I'd never know a woman without the beast rising. So I just bided my time, waiting for another good war. War was comfortable for me. On the battlefield, everyone was happy to see my beast—everyone except the enemy. I was . . . managing."

"Then you were captured by the Order," she said in a deadened voice. "You were tortured. Vivisected."

He didn't ask how she knew that last part, didn't even seem to register it. "In the prison, we were made to wear collars that robbed us of our strength. But during the breakout, all the Pravus captives had theirs removed. Five starving succubae hunted me. They were so bluidy strong."

Chloe's lips parted. "Did they . . . ?" *Please say no.*

"Nay. Because allies helped me. But that night was like a straight blade slicing through a raised scar, resurrecting all Ruelle had done to me."

"How did you not kill me that morning? When you scented what I was?"

He finally met her gaze. "My beast would never have let me. It had accepted you. It adores you. Goddamn it, *I* want to adore you!"

"How could you ever?"

"I'm trying to move forward, to stop living in the past. But you have to understand, I was like a puppet with Ruelle." Again his breaths shallowed. "When I feel the effect of your strew, it unsettles me so deeply. There is no more wretched feeling than ceding your free will."

She couldn't hold back her tears as she said, "Then I'm harming you all over again. *I* am slicing the scar open!" And they only had one more time before he was bound to her forever. "MacRieve, I can't keep hurting you, can't let you take on my venom. You're going to have to let me go."

He fell to his knees before her, startling her. "Doona say that!" Wrapping his arms around her waist, he buried his forehead against her chest. He clutched her hard, sending new pain cascading through her. "I know I'm wrong in the head! I want to be . . . *right*. For you." When he nuzzled her neck, she felt more of his hot tears against her skin. "I kept this cottage standing so I would always remember what was done to my family, to me. Now I just want to forget. I thought burning it would fix me." He shuddered against her, the movement like a jackhammer to her aching head. "Help me be right for you, Chloe."

The pain was growing too intense, her vision dimming. "How?" she bit out. "Tell me what to do."

"I must have control of my own mind and body. Can you no' free me? I'll come back to you, woman! Just free me." He took her in his arms, now pressing her face against his chest. "I'll want you forever." His breaths rattled in his chest. "Just let me do it on my own."

"I can't free you. I don't know how. I would!" Those impassioned words drained away her last reserves of energy. Black dots swirled at the edges of her sight. "MacRieve?"

He drew back to gaze down at her face, his eyes widening. "What's wrong, Chloe? Have you hunger?"

"No, I-I don't know what's wrong. There's pain."

"I was too rough with you yesterday." He laid a palm on her forehead, his jaw slackening. "You're burning up? Does aught else hurt you?"

"My head. God, my entire body aches. My . . . bones hurt."

Voice gone low, he said, "Do they feel like they're slowly shattering from the inside?"

"Yes."

"Everything hurts you so badly, you canna distinguish areas of agony. The pain in your head is blinding."

She nodded, the slight movement bringing on a new wave of dizziness. "Please . . ." Words failed her; she went limp in his arms.

Just before her lids slid shut, she saw the building's walls collapse in an eruption of flames. A blast of searing air shot over them.

The cottage was no more.

FORTY-FIVE

Will leapt to his feet, Chloe unconscious in his arms, and gave a sharp howl. "No, no! Chloe, stay with me!" Nothing.

His beast was rising, along with Will's panic.

—*Protect.*— "I want to protect!" he bellowed to no one. He well remembered the symptoms of venom. Why the hell would *she* have them?

All he knew was that this was somehow his fault.

The witches could help her. Surely. He just had to get Chloe to them. But what if she worsened on the long flight back? Not to mention that mated Lykae did not fly under a full moon. Fuck!

Worry stabbing at him, he whipped around, about to sprint to the keep—

Two succubae were standing not twenty feet away. The pair he'd seen outside the wall at Glenrial.

"Where the bluidy hell did you come from?" One

looked to be in her mid-twenties, the other in her late teens. The younger one wore a sword at her hip.

His first impulse was to ward these two away from Chloe. He hated succubae—but he was frantic to heal his mate.

The older one said, "I'm Gisela, Chloe's aunt. Her mother was my sister. This is my daughter, Nieve."

Chloe had family besides Webb? She'd never spoken about her mother much. Not that he'd asked about Fiore—because Will hadn't wanted to be reminded of where Chloe got her succubus nature from.

All he knew was that Fiore had died when Chloe was still a baby.

He turned to Gisela, who at least looked sympathetic. Her daughter was presently slitting her eyes at Will. Was that succubus actually carrying a *weapon*? "Chloe's taken ill." Between gritted teeth, he said, "Do you . . . can you help me?"

Gisela said, "She's very sick, MacRieve."

"How do you know my name?"

"All the Ubus peoples know of you and your brother, of the Woods of Murk." Just as he was about to ask how, she added, "And, I have to admit, I listened to what you told Chloe. I did not know Ruelle, but you have my sincerest apologies in any case."

And pity—he could see it in her eyes! Fury raged inside him. "I doona want your goddamned pity!" With Chloe secure in one arm, he lashed out uncontrollably, slashing at a tree. "I want my mate well!"

Nieve murmured to her mother, "Didn't I say he was crazed?"

Gisela told Will, "She needs to come with us, her family. We might be able to heal her."

"Go with you? You must be bluidy daft! I will never let this creature out of my sight. Do you understand me? Never!"

Nieve said, "Do you want our help or do you want her to perish in your arms?"

"Perish?" *I canna lose her!* "She's immortal now. She canna."

Gisela said sadly, "I believe Chloe's dying."

He chuffed with fear. *My little mate* . . . "What will you do?"

"Take her to my home in the Ubus Realm. I'm a healer, and I have medicine there. Our portal lies just over there." She pointed to an area that looked like the rest of the forest.

But now he could scent a difference. The door to that plane was in his fucking forest?

It made sense—that's where Ruelle had come from.

And this pair expected him to allow his mate to travel through that same portal? He'd heard that men who went to the Ubus Realm did not return.

The least of his worries. Could he trust these females with Chloe?

"MacRieve, I have a good idea of what's happened to her." Gisela held out her arms. "Give her to me, and I vow to the Lore that I will do everything in my power to save her."

An unbreakable vow.

"There's not much time," she continued. "If I'm right, then she'll sicken further with each moment we delay. I need my tools to diagnose her."

"Lykae are stubborn, ignorant creatures," Nieve said coldly. "He won't do what's necessary to save her."

Will gazed down at Chloe. She had her wee hand pressed against his chest. Right over his heart. "Why must I give her to you?"

"Our portal guardians will not let you through on the night of a full moon, especially not in your condition"—*shirtless, burned, wild-eyed, a heartbeat from turning?*—"not unless we have some surety that you won't harm others. Chloe is that surety. You must entrust her to me."

—*Trust.*— his Instinct advised. But his history told him he should be running with Chloe.

The Instinct won. Will shuddered when he handed her over, wolven sounds erupting from his throat as he and his beast reacted.

Gisela clasped Chloe tightly, maternally. With a glare at Will, Nieve stepped through the portal, her mother behind her.

Though he might never return to his home again, Will was right on their heels, striding through without hesitation.

Where your mate goes, you follow. . . .

FORTY-SIX

Slave auction blocks, harems, chained sex servants . . .

Over the centuries, Will had pictured the Ubus Realm in a thousand sordid lights. As he followed the succubae through the portal, he braced himself, expecting to see all of his worst imaginings.

As with many planes, this was a hidden cubbyhole within the wider world, with the same temperature of the surrounding lands, the same time.

The same moon cycle.

Once they'd cleared the portal guardians—two stony-faced incubi whose feet hadn't been touching the ground—Will snapped his fingers for Chloe. "Hand her to me."

Gisela tucked a curl behind Chloe's ear, then reluctantly returned her to Will's arms. "My home is just there." She pointed out a row of large hilltop homes on the other end of a shop-lined street. The architecture could've been found in any quaint Highland hamlet.

They started toward the hill. He didn't want to take his eyes from Chloe, but he forced himself to pay attention to his surroundings, in case they needed to leave in a hurry.

The shops they passed were no different from those of any typical European town, the street like so many main streets, only without cars or electric lights.

He scented species of all kinds, not just the Ubus peoples. He even smelled . . . another Lykae? A tart scent tickled his nose. Apples? What must be orchards of them. Why the hell would they grow food?

Just before the hill lay a grassy field. Will did a double take.

A lacrosse game was under way?

Lads about twelve years of age were playing an aggressive, no-holds-barred game. Will blinked when he spied more than one young succubus taking part as well. Parents were cheering from the sidelines.

Nieve noticed his bemusement. "What? Ubus can't play sports? Humans didn't corner the market on lacrosse."

For the last nine centuries, if he'd thought about Ubus children, he'd imagined them in some dimly lit school training to ruin lives and prey on the unsuspecting. . . .

Fountains lined the edge of the field. Picnickers laughed. Bairns flew kites.

Goddamned *kites*.

Nieve said, "We're not much different from Lykae."

"We've quite a big difference between our kinds. So why are those Ubus spreading out banquets of food?"

Nieve frowned at him. "Why wouldn't they?"

Gisela said, "As with vampire young, our children eat food from the earth right up until they freeze into their immortality—females usually in their twenties, males in their thirties. Before then, *that* need is dormant."

Just as Chloe's had been.

Nieve was still frowning. Then her eyes went wide. Under her breath, she hissed, "He is *vile*, Mother. Who thinks like that?"

"Outsiders rarely understand our ways," Gisela murmured back. "Just remember, he's one of the *twins*."

What did that mean? He shifted Chloe in his arms, drawing her closer to his chest.

Nieve shot over her shoulder, "I'll bet you expected chained slaves and whip-carrying masters? Orgies on the street?"

Exactly what he'd expected. Judging by the banners hung over the street, the next public gathering was . . . the Cider Fair.

He felt a trickle of embarrassment that flared into anger. This Nieve witch did not need to push him on this day. "How could I expect anything different? My encounters with your ilk informed my opinions!"

Gisela cast him an apologetic look. "Yes, well, any Ubus in your realm were most likely . . . exiles from ours. Or the offspring of them."

"What?" He hadn't heard her correctly.

"Centuries ago, if any of the nobility were convicted of an unconscionable offense, they were cast out."

"Into *my* family's lands?" Inhale, exhale. *Doona kill Chloe's blood kin.*

Nieve said, "There were not that many."

"It only took one!" Picnickers turned to stare at him. Children looked up at him with owl eyes—and they looked no different from Lykae bairns.

He tightened his grip on his mate, gazing down at her. *Chloe, I've been so bluidy stupid.*

"Let's discuss this inside," Gisela said.

He held his tongue as they climbed the hill to her house.

He crossed the threshold. The second succubus home he'd ever been in.

This was vastly dissimilar to Ruelle's. Here were trappings of obvious wealth—crystal, a gilded chandelier, plush rugs, intricate woodworking. The colors were understated. It was, he was loath to admit, a home he could live in.

As he followed the two females up the stairs, medicinal scents grew stronger.

"Here's my office." Gisela ushered him into a room with a single bed, surrounded by shelves of vials and bottles that rivaled any olden apothecary's shop. Incense burned, yet it wasn't cloying.

Gisela indicated he should lay Chloe on the bed. Will took a seat beside her, fighting back his beast and his own protectiveness to allow a succubus to examine Chloe.

"I'm going to draw her blood." Gisela's tools looked antiquated but clean. She pushed up Chloe's bracelet, then made a small incision in her wrist, dripping blood onto a waiting dish. "I sense power in this bracelet. I need to know what it does."

"It keeps her hidden from enemies." He scrubbed his palm over the back of his neck. *Go on, then, Will.* "It keeps her from conceiving."

Gisela nodded. "I believe that was a wise decision on her part. At least until she can figure out her new life."

Hadn't been Chloe's decision. He'd foisted it on her. *Slaoightear.*

Nieve crossed her arms over her chest. "I'll say. She's probably keeping her options open. We don't know for certain that you're her fated male."

"Fated," he choked out. "You're saying Ubus have . . . mates?" Wouldn't that get in the way of their trolling for countless victims to violate?

Nieve gave him a look that said *duh.* "We're as committed as mated Lykae. Most of those parents you saw at the field are incubus and succubus couples."

"That's no' even possible." If they were both energy sucks, they would need an outside source. "Two negatives doona make a positive."

"Actually, that's not quite true," Gisela said. "If a succubus and incubus are fated, they become even stronger with their union. But then, all Ubus receive— and *give*—strength each time they join with their fated one."

Had Will been stronger after taking Chloe? The first time, he'd gotten drunk. The second time, he'd been growling at sheep, feeling like an imbecile for hurting her.

His eyes darted. What if she was his—and he wasn't hers?

Nieve said, "I know what I'm hoping for with my cousin." In a lower voice, she asked her mother, "Can you imagine birthing a litter of Lykae?"

"You think I canna hear you?" he snapped, more angry at himself than at her. Being here, learning about these people wasn't . . . comfortable. He felt like his prejudice was being dismantled—with a wrecking ball.

It called to mind a long-ago battle when he'd sustained a mace blow to his favorite breastplate, the dented metal gouging his skin throughout the melee. Afterward, he'd watched the smithy hammer and hammer it, pounding it back to its original shape.

Aye, Will had been twisted by Ruelle . . . but mayhap he *could* be wrought anew, one pounding blow at a time?

Mayhap I'm on the smithy's anvil right now.

Once Gisela had collected a few drops of Chloe's blood, she added a white powder to them. "Now we have to wait fifteen minutes for the test results." She reached for the smallest of five sandglasses, then turned it upside down to start the counter.

"What do you think is wrong with her?"

The woman glanced away. "I hesitate to say. Let's wait for the results."

"Why have you no' come for Chloe in years past?"

"We had no idea she existed until a succubus escaped from an Order prison just a few weeks ago. She returned here with word of Chloe and Webb. I believe you're familiar with the Order."

He cast her a cruel smirk. "I'm surprised any succubae from that prison lived to tell tales—since I beheaded five of them."

Neither Gisela nor Nieve appeared upset by that. "Actually, a succubus named Dehlia escaped with a guard, one who'd been planted there to spy on the Order. Do you remember Calder Vincente? They're wed now."

Out of all the guards, Vincente had been the single one Will might've considered sparing. "Wait, why would you be talking to that succubus? Was she no' an outcast? And for that matter, was no' Chloe's mother?"

"I said Ubus in your realm were *most likely* exiles from ours. There are also hunters tasked with executing those exiles. Dehlia was one. As was Fiore. My three brothers roam the outside world even now. Aside from me, our family is comprised of hunters."

Confusion churned. He stroked Chloe's forehead for calm. "So you're telling me that her mam hunted evil succubae?"

"Yes. With much success." Gisela was unmistakably proud of her late sister. "She was the best of them all, aggressive and unrelenting."

So that's where my mate gets it from. "But why cast out criminals, only to dispatch hunters after them?"

"Ages ago, we had little concept of your world," Gisela said. "We're self-sustaining here, had no reason for a portal. Back then, our leaders believed the rift was solely to dispose of those who would harm others. But after the Murkian Wars—"

"Murkian?" He pinched the bridge of his nose,

having a feeling he didn't want to hear what was coming next.

"The creatures from the Woods of Murk grew in number, discovering our portal," Nieve answered, sounding like she recited from a textbook. "Bent on seizing females and resources, they attacked, overrunning us. We fought them back with greater numbers, but we only had so many trained soldiers. Our foes were vicious, kept coming until we knew Ubus would fall."

"And? What happened then?" he asked, still flummoxed that Ubus had not only guardians but hunters and soldiers. And hard-hitting lads and lasses who liked sports.

For some reason, Nieve pursed her lips, so Gisela answered, "We were saved by you and your brother, when you led forces to rid the Woods of Murk of evil."

You're bluidy kidding me. "We aided you?"

"Our realm would have been lost. Once saved, we realized how unfair our exile system had been to your family and people. No one had any idea you'd been . . . personally affected."

Will repeated, "We *aided* you?"

"You regret your actions?" Gisela queried in a stern tone. "If not for your assistance hundreds of years ago, Fiore would never have been born, much less sent out into the world to hunt. She would never have been imprisoned by Commander Webb, would never have given birth to your mate. Chloe wouldn't exist."

Will sank back, stunned to his core. Because he could take the chain of events back one more step. Will would never have suggested raiding the woods if he hadn't been filled with rage—toward Ruelle.

That bitch had set fate in motion. Without her, there would be no Chloe.

Without his *torment*, there would be no Chloe. *Fate is our faith.*

He recalled how her eyes had blazed when he'd told her about Ruelle. Chloe had been wracked with fever—yet in every line of her body, he'd seen her fierce need to fight.

For me, he'd thought in bewilderment. *She wants to fight for me.* It had humbled him—and given him hope. Now he knew that everything was fated, he would suffer his torment again just to see that look from his mate.

How the hell had he ever associated Chloe's expressive glowing eyes with Ruelle's malicious gaze . . . ?

"What happened to Fiore?"

"She must have been forced to use her strew on Webb to try to escape, or because she was starving," Gisela said. "We steer clear of mating with humans because of the inherent weaknesses of cambions."

"What weaknesses?"

"A cambion can die from hunger." As Will registered that with a new spike of alarm, Gisela added, "And yet she can't strew."

"This one can." There'd been times when he was out of his mind with lust for Chloe. Yesterday, he'd roared to her, "I am fucking *ravening* for you!" while he'd thrust with all his might—as feral as the beast that had followed him.

Now he said, "You will no' convince me differently."

"Check her lips," Nieve said. "There should be an opening there." She held up her own upper lip, pointing out a slit within, just above the top edge.

Will checked Chloe's. All smoothness.

And down came the hammer once more. He gave a crazed laugh. How many times had he abused her, then blamed her strew? He'd taken her virginity like a monster, then railed at how much control she had—over him. When he'd felt tenderness toward her, when he'd wanted to hold her . . . it hadn't been strew.

No, he'd been falling in love with her. All on his own.

I love her. I love Chloe MacRieve.

Nieve said, "Without that ability, she is very vulnerable."

His head whipped up. "You consider the fact that she canna rape to be a negative? A lack to be avoided at all costs?"

Gisela's tone was indignant. "Understand me, wolf, the only time a decent Ubus would use strew is if she was starved. Ideally, we would use it only on whoever was starving us."

"I doona understand."

"Succubae are abducted and held captive more often than any other species. Don't forget—Chloe's own mother was a captive. If Chloe's abducted from you and can't attract nourishment, then she could die before you ever found her. Period."

He swallowed. "How did Fiore die?"

"We learned from Vincente that she tried to escape with Chloe shortly after her birth. Webb caught her and killed her. He was going to kill Chloe as well, but her blood tests indicated she was human—"

"My dad was going to kill me?" Chloe said weakly, just as the sandglass emptied.

FORTY-SEVEN

"**C**hloe, lass, stay with me! Stay awake."

She was in a bed, felt like it was spinning. Her pain was worse, her nausea unbearable. She could barely process what she'd just heard.

MacRieve knelt beside her, clasping her hand in both of his. Before she'd passed out earlier, he had appeared crazed. Though he seemed more in control now, underneath he still seethed with *something*. "We're at your aunt's. In the Ubus Realm. We're about to get you fixed up."

In a bleary voice, she said, "I don't have an aunt."

He slid one hand under her head, gently lifting it so she could see two women standing at the foot of the bed. She recognized them from the wall at Glenrial! They were so beautiful; both looked to be about her age.

"You do now, love. This is your aunt Gisela"—he pointed out the black-haired one—"and your cousin Nieve," he said, indicating the brunette.

"I-I have family?"

"By all accounts, it's . . . extensive," he replied, but she couldn't read his tone. He didn't sound disgusted. After what he'd told her earlier, he should hate all succubae.

"Um, hi," Chloe murmured to them. She tried to wave, but couldn't lift her arm.

"Rest easy," Gisela said, and again Chloe was struck by how caringly these two looked at her. So far from malicious and evil. "You're safe here. When you're better, we'll tell you all about Fiore and Webb."

Had she really said Webb had considered killing his own daughter? Even more hazily, Chloe thought she'd heard that Fiore had died by his hand.

Gisela glided over to a counter, peering down at a shallow dish. "For now, you must concentrate on getting better."

"I feel even worse. What's wrong with me?"

"Good question," MacRieve said. "We're about to find out."

Gisela gave a sidelong glance toward her daughter. "The odium curse."

MacRieve swallowed audibly, his hands tightening on hers. "What does that mean?"

"She's gravely ill. As I suspected, she's . . . at a critical point."

"Critical p-point," Chloe said through another wave of shudders. "Dying?"

When Gisela didn't deny it, MacRieve said, "Nay, I doona understand this! She's no' injured. She's no' wasting away."

"No, she's received nourishment," Nieve snapped. Even in Chloe's condition, she could tell Nieve didn't like him. "Indeed, it's poisoned her."

He exhaled a shaky breath. "I *knew* it was me who caused this, but I doona know how."

Nieve said simply, "Some part of you must've hated her."

Given his history, of course MacRieve hated me.

Gisela frowned at her more blunt daughter, then said, "In the Lore, most powers are tempered with weaknesses. Yes, succubae—and even cambion—have the ability to bind a male to them with venom. That's one of our powers. But the male must want that bond as well."

"I doona understand."

Makes two of us.

"The venom reverses itself if one of us was to mate an unwilling man more than once. Once might be forgiven, might be the difference between life and death. But after that, every time she takes from him, she'll sicken in the same way males do after taking on venom."

"That's why she has the symptoms I had when bound to Ruelle."

These women knew he'd been envenomed? Had they heard his earlier confession?

"Exactly. A male sickens from withdrawal, a succubus from excess. The odium curse prevents males from becoming enslaved by strew and envenomed against their will."

"This dinna happen with Ruelle."

Gisela cast him a pained look. "Because back then, you believed you loved her, did you not?"

A strangled sound rose from his chest. "So I poisoned Chloe." He absently brought Chloe's hand to his face, brushing it over his cheek.

Longing for his mate's touch? She wanted to stroke his jaw, to tell him that everything would be okay. But she was too weak.

"Considering what you suffered, you were understandably averse to your mate," Gisela said. Then she turned to Chloe. "The good news is that you'll make a full recovery, if we act quickly. We have consorts here to help you, some who've proven most potent. Rest easy, niece, all you need is untainted nourishment."

"Consorts?" Chloe looked at MacRieve. She didn't want to sleep with another man; surely MacRieve would stop this!

His jaw slackened as Gisela's words sank in. "You want me to sit back and allow another male to take my woman?" His head suddenly jerked as if he'd been slapped; probably his Instinct yelling at him.

She could imagine what it was saying right about now. —*Fuck no.*—

"It would be a great honor among the consorts here to mate Fiore's daughter. Chloe could be well with her first taking. If not, then certainly by her second."

Twice?

MacRieve shot to his feet, inserting himself between them and Chloe. "Have you lost your minds?"

Nieve said, "If you loved her, you'd do this for her. You've gotten her sick, and you're too selfish to do what's right. Think, wolf—if nothing's changed, you'll simply poison her again. She won't survive it."

Gisela said, "It would likely kill her."

That gave Chloe pause. She didn't want to die—partly because she didn't want *him* to die. And after what he'd told her tonight, she couldn't imagine him wholeheartedly, unreservedly having sex with her, taking on her venom. In a faint tone, she said, "MacRieve, I don't want another man. But I don't . . . I can't take any more . . . poison. And I feel like . . . I only have so much time left on the clock."

He turned back to the bed to gently cup her face. "Let me see you well. If this is how I keep you alive, then no man could be more willing. I will do *anything* to keep you."

Nieve added, "Even if you've neutralized the hatred, your beast would kill her on the night of the full moon. She's too weakened to withstand it."

Chloe gazed away. Her bones still felt like they were shattering; what had been a pleasurable romp with his beast before would be torture now. "I can't . . . too much."

"Chloe, my beast will no' rise. I know you have no reason to trust me in this, but I'm asking you to believe in me anyway."

Gisela shook her head. "The moon is dawning even now. A mated Lykae can't suppress his beast through sheer will alone. It's simply not possible."

He bared his teeth at her. "Just because it's never been done before? Tonight, I'll do whatever it takes."

"You gamble with her life."

"First of all, it's *our* lives. If she dies, I'll follow her. Second of all, you've never seen a Lykae with more cause to be gentle with his mate." As he tenderly collected her in his arms, he appeared haunted with regret.

What had happened when she'd been out?

"Mother, you're not considering this?" Nieve's hand landed on . . . a sword hilt? "Your brothers will be furious." She moved to block the door.

"I believe your people *owe* me this," MacRieve said. "I'm taking my mate home. Now, get out of the bluidy way."

Undaunted, Nieve said, "Chloe needs to decide." In a flash of movement, she unsheathed her sword, pointing it at him. "This is her life, *her* decision."

"Aye. It is." He drew Chloe close to his warm, bare chest, pressing her against his heart. When he gazed down at her, it sped up. His eyes were gold and filled with an emotion she'd never seen in him. "It's no' my responsibility to feed you—it's my goddamned privilege. Let me do this."

"But my venom. You'll have to take it this time."

"Listen to me, *mo chridhe*. I crave *any* bond with you, will scour this earth for more. I want my body bound to yours, my soul chained to yours. Any tie I can find, I'll bind us even tighter. We'll have marriage, bairns, a new line between us!" In a hoarse voice, he said, "I can do this. For us, I can. I'm pleading with you, lass. Believe in me . . . ?"

FORTY-EIGHT

Will charged past the incubi guards with his barely conscious mate secure in his arms. He leapt through the portal to hit the ground running in the Woods.

Chloe had trusted him, putting her life in his hands. If he weren't besieged by panic, he would howl to the world about such a female.

—*SAVE HER!*— Hundreds of years ago, his Instinct had commanded him thus. But he hadn't been able to save his mother. He gazed down at Chloe's limp body. "Just hold on, love!"

As he ran for Conall, the moon broke through the dispersing clouds, and its light began filtering through the treetops. If he was going to be the first Lykae to deny his beast on the night of a full moon, he needed to avoid its seductive light. He dodged beams if he could, each one like a sizzling ray of sensation.

Just get to the keep. Gisela had given him a potion for

Chloe that would alleviate the worst of her pain, but only for a brief window. *Get her to the keep, use the potion.*

Then make love to her. Gently. Though he never had before.

When she moaned with pain, he doubted himself, his decision. *I've done wrong.* He'd known he was somehow to blame for this. His Instinct certainly had known. It had been guiding him to destroy Ruelle's memory, before Will destroyed his mate with his own poison.

Even now, he scented the lingering smoke from the cottage. The next rain would wash that stench away.

Right before he shot from the Woods, he thought he smelled another scent—the faintest hint of . . . the Old Ones, far in the distance. Not died out? They would hold no menace for Will or his mate—*if* she was claimed and marked with Will's bite.

Soon . . .

The keep was in sight. He'd have to cross the fields under the light. Could he prevent himself from turning and taking her in the grass?

Some benevolent fate smiled down on him, cloaking the moon with drifting clouds. "We're almost there, Chloe."

He bolted through the doorway, up the stairs with one great leap. In their room, he laid her on the bed, then dashed to the windows. Those bays were positioned to catch the moon's rise and set.

As he stretched out his arms to clasp the drapes, the moon emerged from the clouds; light blasted him like a spotlight.

He shuddered, his beast stirring. Will snatched the

curtains closed, shaking his head hard. *No, no' tonight! Stay in your goddamned cage!*

Back to his mate. As gently as he could, he removed her clothes, slashing off his own, then grabbed the potion bottle.

Her shakes were growing worse, her teeth beginning to chatter. "MacRieve, it hurts so bad."

"I know, baby, I know exactly. Here." He opened the bottle. "You need tae get this down." He cupped the back of her head, raising her to drink. Some spilled down her lips. His chest twisted as he tenderly brushed the liquid away.

Now, waiting.

"What happened while I was out?" she asked in a hushed voice. "You're so . . . different."

He brushed her hair from her forehead. "I'll explain it all tomorrow. For now, just know that I meant what I said—I want *everything* from you."

Her eyes grew a touch brighter. "But how can you forget what I am? Once I feel better, surely I'll strew—"

He cut her off with a quick kiss. "You doona have that ability. A wee cambion like you has no control over me. You never did."

"What?"

"Imagine my shock, after I blamed everything on your strew. Ah, lass, I've so much tae make up for. Starting tonight." *Just let me be her mate.*

"Can you truly keep the beast caged?"

"I've avoided the moon as much as possible. I can do this for you, Chloe. For us."

"The pain's lessening. I feel a little stronger." The first move she made was to stroke his cheek. *Heaven.*

He'd fallen head over heels; he began to hope he could claim her heart as well.

If he could save her. Reminded of the clock, he began kissing her neck, trailing to her breasts. "This first time must be quick, before the potion wears off." All he had to do was be quick, yet gentle, and keep his beast at bay.

What could possibly go wrong?

As he took a nipple between his lips and started to suck, he dipped his hand between her thighs to sink a finger inside her. Gods, her silken sheath was so hot as it clenched his finger. Even in his panic, his cock went rock-hard for that tightness, moisture welling atop the crown.

By the time he'd moved to her other breast and wedged a second finger inside, she was rocking her hips, riding his fingers. Responding so perfectly.

"Is this better, lass?"

She nodded. "I'm ready. I think."

He would've liked to prepare her more, to take her to the very edge. They had no time. He moved between her legs, fisting his cock, aiming it against her opening. With a shallow roll of his hips, he began inching his length inside her. "Am I hurting you?"

Her eyes widened. "No, but something's different. . . ." She bit her bottom lip. "I, uh, just got a hint of what's to come, so to speak."

His pre-cum. "I imagine those hints are no' in short supply. Even now, you've got me crazed for you."

She moaned, wriggling on his rod to get him deeper. "It's pure energy—like adrenaline. Stronger than I've ever known."

Because it's no longer tainted. Pressing wet kisses to her swollen breasts, he rocked between her taut thighs. When Chloe gripped his shoulders and met him, the beast gloried in her wellness and wanted its turn inside her. This was the first full moon with their mate; the night was the beast's by right.

And the beast wanted its due.

Will refused it. He skimmed his fingers down Chloe's side, then reached between them to stroke her clitoris. He groaned to find that little bud so firm and sensitive.

She moaned, undulating her hips for more touch, for more of his shaft.

"Ah, your eyes are glowing!"

She promptly closed them. "Y-you hate that color."

"No longer, because I can see them clearly now." He kissed one lid, then the other. "I find them so beautiful, Chloe. I need tae see them. If your eyes glow, I'll know you're getting better."

She peeked them open. Whatever she saw in his expression made her relax, the corners of her lips curling.

Aye, he needed to see her eyes—and he needed to feel her succubus pull. He knew what he felt for her, knew he would nourish her well. And the more she fed, the stronger she'd be. Only when he experienced that last pull from her would his worry ease.

He lay fully atop her, forehead to forehead, his

hands snaking behind her to clamp her arse with splayed fingers. He held her in place beneath his body, so that her stiff nipples raked along his sweating chest, so that the root of his erection ground her clit with his every thrust.

Though he scarcely knew how, he was controlling his beast. Yet the need to mark her neck lashed him. She was still too weak; he could defeat that urge.

For now—

A beam of light from the rising moon slipped through a crack in the curtains and shone directly into his face.

Light illuminated his ice-blue eyes. "MacRieve?" Though Chloe was already stronger—each time his shaft throbbed inside her, she got a hit of adrenaline—she wasn't ready for the beast's ferocity.

And the pain medicine had begun wearing off. "I-I need you to stay with me."

He pinned her wrists above her head, his face just above hers, his gaze boring into hers. "I'll give you whatever you need. I've wrested control of it, Chloe." With a stunned expression, he said, "I'm in control. Of it, of *everything*."

For the first time in his life.

"I'm goin' tae be right for you." He leaned down to take her lips.

Between kisses, she murmured, "You are . . . you are."

He continued surging his big body over hers, covering her completely. With each thrust, his hips stroked against her thighs. Beneath her calves, his muscled ass flexed to drive his cock deeper, penetrating her to the hilt. His chest rubbed over her breasts, while the base of his unyielding shaft hit her sensitive clitoris.

She was about to come for this hot, lathered male. And the dizzying intensity of her building orgasm was . . . frightening.

With his voice rough and his accent pronounced, he said something in Gaelic.

"What did you say?"

"You've let me tend tae your fire, and tonight it's searing me clean. I can be what you need." At her ear, he rasped, "I'll feed you well, mate. Give you everything I have in me. Always." He circled his hips, grinding his thick shaft against her. "All for you."

"Oh, God, oh, God . . ." More thrusts, more grinding. More MacRieve. That dizzy intensity kept mounting until she was whimpering, bucking beneath him, two slick bodies roiling.

She was insensible, a slave to pleasure, to whatever this man wanted from her.

Rapture struck. *"MacRieve!"* Pounding waves seized her as she screamed, "More!" In a wet rush, her sheath contracted along his length, hungry for his heat to flood her.

"Chloe, ah, gods! You're milking me so hard. . . ."

She'd clenched him so tightly, he stopped thrusting—

His back bowed. "Woman! It's *strong!*" he bellowed

in disbelief. "Take it from me!" he roared as streams of hot seed shot into her.

She was still writhing with her own orgasm as his semen filled her, pulse after scorching pulse.

At the last instant, his entire body jerked. "There's your pull, baby. That's it." Jaw slack, eyes rolling back in his head, he grated, "Take it deep for me. *Take my seed so deep. . . .*"

⁂

When Will's brain could register thought once more, one realization was foremost: *I'm her mate.*

Chloe had strengthened him. Indeed, his new power was so staggering, he feared hurting her. She lay still with her eyes closed. When he started hardening again, he forced himself to withdraw and roll his weight off her.

"Are you better, lass?" He thought he'd been gentle with her. Tonight, he'd leashed his beast so totally, he knew he could handle it as well as any Lykae. Better than! Still, he must have hurt her. "Chloe, did I—"

She suddenly arched her back, arms falling over her head. When her palms slapped the headboard, the solid wood *cracked.*

Will bit out a short, shocked: "Whoa."

She reared up, eyes alight. "You're my mate?"

"Oh, aye." He beat a fist over his chest. "I could stop a locomotive right now."

"Good. You're going to need all the strength you can muster."

"That so?" He rose to open the drapes. When he faced her, she was on her hands and knees crawling across the bed to him.

"I've got the moon on my back, my beast in submission, and the hottest piece of cambion arse feeding me power. I can take anything you can dish out. And your neck's about tae bear my bite."

When she visibly shivered, he said, "I'm back in the game with my bonny mate, no? I believe I just scored a hat trick."

"You're officially off the bench," she breathed, "cleared for play. With a fangirl who fell for you—"

He lunged for her; she leapt for him. He caught her in midair, twisting to pin her against the wall as he shoved his cock home. "Ahhh, Chloe!"

She took his mouth with her own so hard their teeth knocked together before they found each other's lips. Both their tongues thrust, both their hips rocked. Deep kisses, hard fucking.

She locked her legs around his waist, holding on for dear life because he was plowing her cunny like a piston. Bliss ratcheted to another record height.

When she sank her claws into his back, he howled with satisfaction—and did the same to hers. Though his beast remained dormant, Will's fangs lengthened to mark his mate.

He and Chloe bounced from one wall to the next, shaking the entire structure.

Between kisses, she said, "I hope your keep's sturdy!"

"It's *our* keep, *our* wolf's lair, and we're about tae

find out." He took her mouth once more, and she licked his tongue, sucking it.

Mercy me.

But then she broke away with a breathy plea: "Mark me hard, MacRieve."

"You want my bite?"

"I love you. I belong to you, and I want everyone to know it."

Just stopping himself from roaring with triumph, he gripped her hair, tugging till her neck was bared to him. "*Is leamsa so,* Chloe MacRieve. And I'll be marking you as hard as I'm lovin' you." With a snarl, he sank his fangs into the tender skin of her neck, biting the ever-living hell out of her. . . .

FORTY-NINE

On into the early morning, long after the moon had set, Will still hadn't gotten enough of Chloe, was stiffening inside her yet again.

But his lass's lids were heavy. After their exertions, his young mate had inevitably grown sleepy. Not from sickness—from a well-earned need for rest.

"I'm signaling for a tee-oh." Her voice was throaty from her screams of pleasure.

He'd been insatiable, taking her repeatedly, determined to satisfy her in every way. They'd both been so much stronger that at one point, he had indeed worried about Conall.

Their new home had proved as enduring as time.

"Perhaps when you reach my age, you will no' peak so early." He tucked her hair behind her wee ear, marveling at his female. *Adorable and sexy, all at once.* "I'll grant you a reprieve. But know that it's reluctant and verra temporary."

"Good." She was dreamily running the pads of her fingers over his chest.

He'd sought peace with her, and he'd found it. Will felt right with the world for the first time. He could recognize that feeling just by virtue of how long he'd felt wrong.

Chloe had given him this. He'd conquered and claimed. And, gods, so had she.

"I still can't believe you kept your beast on the leash."

He shrugged modestly, though he was damn proud of himself. "You'll only see it on the night of the full moon, if that's your wish."

"Can it hear me?"

"Aye." He let it stir. "Try now."

She cupped his face, gazing into his eyes. "You were so good tonight. In one month's time I'll have the sweetest treats for you."

Putting the beast to bed, Will said, "And what treats are those? A Lykae's curiosity is a powerful thing."

"I *know*," she murmured with a coy grin, even as her lids were growing heavier. "You'll have to wait to see, MacRieve."

He curled a finger under her chin. "Will."

"Hmm?"

"I want you to call me Will."

His name on her lips and a smile on her face, she fell asleep, with him still inside her.

FIFTY

"You're deft at this," MacRieve told her as they practiced attacks and parries with swords.

For the last four days, he'd been training her to use various weapons, so she could protect herself. Though he'd had to admit, "You're so strong, you could probably just crush your opponents."

Chloe had never in her life felt so powerful—or so connected to another being. If she thought she'd been energized from sex before, she'd seen nothing. Evidently, now that her big Scot was in love with her and they were mated both ways, he was providing only the highest-grade energy. If she were still playing sports, his stuff would be banned.

And MacRieve—or rather, *Will*—was stronger than he'd ever been. She was trying to remember to call him Will, but it would take a while.

He thrust his sword with a quick jab.

She easily deflected it. "Sword-fighting is just like

soccer. Read opponent, adjust tactic, misdirect. I am going to be so bad-ass at this."

He scratched his head with one hand while he twirled his sword with the other. "You kind of already *are*."

"So are there any Lore competitions I could enter?" Today would've been check-in for the Olympics training camp. And even though a fascinating new life was opening up for her, she still missed aspects of her old one.

"There's one competition. We old ones like to call it *survival*."

She laughed. "Smart-ass."

He grinned. "Doona worry. If you've got a skill in the Lore, there will be someone around to test you. Especially during an Accession. But then, I have a feeling you'll enjoy war. It's like sports, though sudden death actually means *death*." He subtly telegraphed to the left, then struck to the right.

She blocked and misdirected with a two-handed strike upward—only to change it midair to a one-handed sweep.

MacRieve barely blocked it, raising his brows again. "You vow you've never held a blade in your hands?"

"It's in my blood, remember?" With a saucy grin, she brushed off one shoulder, then the other. "Raw talent. Rookie phenom. At least I won't embarrass myself with the new sword-fighting fam."

He'd relayed all that had occurred in the Ubus Realm. She'd been amazed by the developments, convinced, as he was, that everything had been fated.

That littlest hope-spark? Now an inferno, never to be extinguished.

The morning after the full moon, she'd wanted to let her new kin know that she was okay, but there'd been no need. They'd found a note from Nieve affixed to the front door:

Judging by the shock waves originating from Conall Keep throughout the night, we assume you've made a complete recovery—and that Uilleam MacRieve, Lord of Conall, is indeed your fated mate. Please do us the honor of joining us for our Cider Fair. . . .

The fair was this weekend, and MacRieve had readily agreed to take her: "They healed my mate. For that, I'll even be civil to Nieve."

In truth, she was a little embarrassed to see them again. By now everyone in that realm would know she'd been hauled off by a ravenous werewolf for Richter-scale sex under the full moon. That was probably scandalous, even to the Ubus.

She shrugged. *Oh, well, I'll be sure to wear red.*

Only a few things marred her honeymoon with MacRieve. One was his unrelenting remorse over the way he'd treated her. She made sure to jank him continually for all his misconceptions, which seemed to ease his guilt.

Yesterday he'd drawn her close, saying against her hair, "I canna get enough of you, Chloe. Gods help me, I know I never will."

"I'm sure it's just my strew—oh, *wait* . . ."

He'd nipped her neck, making her squeal with laughter.

Her confusion over her father was another source of worry. When she and MacRieve talked late into the night, they'd discussed his childhood and Ruelle, his parents—and her dad.

By clinging to some tenuous belief in his goodness, was she being loyal—or willfully blind? MacRieve had been grievously harmed by him. Immortals all over the Lore had. Her relatives believed Preston Webb had killed Chloe's own mother. Yet she didn't feel right passing judgment until she'd heard his side of the story.

Which might never happen.

For MacRieve's part, he'd relinquished his urge for vengeance, explaining, "I canna kill my mate's sire. I'm too much in his debt. Without him, no Chloe."

Now MacRieve said, "I doona understand why Munro has no' rung me back."

Another worry. He couldn't get in touch with his brother.

MacRieve had left his first message for Munro the day after the full moon. She remembered him placing his phone on the bathroom counter just before they'd taken their first shower together.

She shivered to recall that shower. MacRieve had knelt before her, placing a hand over her belly. "When you're ready, I'm goin' tae put a babe in here." His hand had been so hot, even in the water. "Mayhap even twins." He'd gazed up at her, his eyes flickering. "Honor me so?"

Breathless, she'd only been able to nod.

"*Tha gràdh agam ort,* Chloe. I love you. And I'm about tae show you how much." Then he'd leisurely—*lovingly*—washed her from head to toe, still learning her body. When she'd done the same to him, one thing led to another.

By the time he'd finally released her to get dressed, the water had grown cold and she'd been grinning ear to ear like she'd just medaled. Since then, they always shared showers. As he'd repeated, "We like to conserve water around here."

And so it went with them.

"Has Munro ever gone this long without calling?" she asked.

"Since telephones were invented, Munro has *never* no' returned my calls. I worry." In a gruffer tone, he said, "Feels strange to be apart from him again."

She couldn't imagine how it must feel to be separated from one's twin, wondering if he was safe and well. "Let's give it to the end of the day. If no one at the compound has seen him, then we'll return to Louisiana."

He lowered his sword. "You'd miss the fair with your family?"

"Munro's my family too," she said, making MacRieve's brows draw tight with feeling. "Why don't you go try him again? I'll chill for a bit."

He nodded. "Doona leave the immediate grounds, no?" After giving her a sweet kiss, he jogged off.

Alone, she strolled through the courtyard, treading upon cobblestones where countless MacRieves had walked, long before Will was born.

God, this place was so beautiful. Over these four days, he'd drilled into her head that this was her home. "Conall belongs to you as much as to me. You're Chloe MacRieve, lady of this keep." She could invite whomever she wanted, could decorate it however she chose.

She wouldn't touch a thing, already found it perfect. Finally, she lived in a home with character. No McMansion here!

She and MacRieve had even talked about reviving the area, bringing in more sheep, inviting clan members to resettle in the old village of Conall.

As she walked, she ran her fingertips along the cool stone wall. She could feel the history here, and it grounded her. No longer did she feel like her world had been upended. She'd landed on her feet.

Here. With MacRieve.

Maybe the lads could come and stay for the summer? She missed them. But then, she might be seeing them directly. She'd meant what she'd said earlier: she and MacRieve would be on a plane tonight if he didn't hear from his brother—

"Chlo . . ."

She whirled around at the strange voice. Standing not ten feet from her was the same towering, cloaked demon that had been in her father's study.

"You!" She raised her sword. "What do you want from me?" She didn't expect a real answer; last time, it'd barely been able to speak.

It surprised her by saying, "You don't recognize me?" Its words were still rough, though much clearer than before. It stepped closer.

Recalling this creature's strength, she choked up on her sword. "Should I?" Chloe was first and foremost a fighter. But she wasn't above calling on her ally. She drew a breath to scream a heads-up for MacRieve—

The creature pulled its hood past its horns.

Her scream died on her lips. Her sword hand went limp, the blade clattering to the ground. *"Dad?"* It was him, but he'd been *altered.*

When she'd seen him before, he'd been obscured in shadow; now every feature was sharp in glaring day-light.

He had unnaturally pale and flawless skin, age-less. Tapered fangs had replaced his teeth. Matte-black horns rose from his head like an old-timey devil draw-ing. His irises were so dark, they brought to mind the bottom of an abyss.

Yet he was arresting, with the air all Loreans seemed to possess. "Dad? Wh-what happened to you?" She rushed up to him, tentatively touching his face. "You were the one in our house? Why didn't you talk to me?"

With a claw-tipped hand, he brushed a curl of hair from her face. "I was trying to ask if you were still mor-tal, but I'd only recently been transformed. I've had to relearn how to speak, how to move, how to think."

"Transformed into what? You need to explain this before I freak the hell out." *And before MacRieve scents you.* She lowered her hand, reminded of what her dad had done to the male she loved. "Start spilling."

A hint of Dad's old smile rose. "I see you haven't changed—even with your own transformation."

She bit out, "Talk."

He inclined his head. "I was being hunted by one of the most fearsome vampires in the Lore, Lothaire the Enemy of Old. I knew sooner or later he would find my hideout. But I was prepared. Just before he drained me to death, I popped a capsule full of blended immortal blood. Though he did kill me, I was resurrected."

"As what?"

"The blood contained a mix of several creatures. My powers will be endless, once they've all manifested."

She crossed to the courtyard's low wall, sinking down on it. "Why didn't you warn me about the Lore and what I might be? Why didn't you tell me about the Order?"

"I thought I could keep you separate from all this. God, I wanted that! Your life was uncomplicated, so focused. I never wanted to take that away from you."

"You could've told me what I was turning into before you left. You gave me zero explanation. Just left me an encyclopedia—of creatures you hated."

"That night I was . . . dumbfounded." He sat beside her. "Your blood had tested out as human, again and again for twenty-four years. Even our most advanced arrays picked up nothing."

"I was so alone, and you just disappeared for weeks," she said, hating how weak she sounded.

"I forced myself not to contact you, fearing that would put you in Lothaire's crosshairs—a place you *never* want to be. Only after I'd turned did I come home for you, but you disappeared that night."

"Yeah, the witches found me."

Irritation flickered over his uncanny face. "I was betrayed by a former ally."

"Wonder what that feels like."

He reached for her, but she drew back.

"Chlo, please—"

"Did you do all the things I've heard? Torturing Loreans, killing them in front of their children?"

He let his hand drop. "I did what any general at war would do to his enemy. I did whatever it took."

Admitting it so easily? Even . . . proudly? The fears about her dad that she'd barely allowed herself to entertain all came crashing down on her.

"I believed those creatures were subhuman, which meant they needed to be destroyed."

Though she felt even more stunned, she forced herself to her feet. "And now what? You've switched teams? You're a detrus now."

"Precisely. We in the Order knew we would need stronger soldiers to defeat immortals. To fight the monsters, we would have to become them. So I headed a project designed to blend Lorean blood for human use. When my death was imminent, I decided to test it on myself." He scrubbed a palm over one horn. "The transition has been . . . challenging."

She could tell this. His fangs had cut his lips. Blood trickled from the corner of his mouth, but he didn't seem to notice.

"With each day that I come into my powers, I've recognized that immortals will always prevail. You've felt the strength—you must understand that humans have no chance against us."

"Who the hell is fighting against humans?"

"A war is inevitable, and I've been on the wrong side."

She sensed a growing tension inside him, as if his veneer of calm was fracturing.

"After a lifetime of working to defend humanity, after all the sacrifices I made, I've finally comprehended that I was protecting the weak—when I should have been championing the strong!"

"Dad, no! Why does it have to be one or the other?"

He floated to his feet with an eerie fluidity. "It's become so clear to me." His abyss eyes gleamed with an unnerving light. "They have to be destroyed!"

"Listen to what you're saying! Destroy mankind? Don't be like this, just . . . *don't*."

As if he hadn't heard her, he said, "There are only two people in the world that I love, and now you are both immortal. This is all meant to be!"

She was almost too afraid to ask: "Who's the other one?"

"Declan Chase, the Blademan. He's a son to me. I found him when he was just a scared teenager, knew he had Lorean blood in him." In a fond tone, he said, "I raised him to hate immortals, to battle them, but he saw the light before I did. Now he's a champion of the Lore: I'll take you to him. I want you to meet."

"Why would I ever?"

"With you by my side, he might not kill me on sight."

When she gazed blankly at him, Dad said, "Before

my epiphany, I had his female . . . studied." A bloody, sheepish grin. "He was violently displeased."

"You think?" MacRieve too had been *studied.*

"But that was before I discovered the true path!" He was getting worked up again. He of the stiff upper lip was unraveling. "With your help, we can convince Declan to join us. To start a new Order! My daughter and my son will be my first generals."

Who are you? "I don't know what's scarier—your insane plans or the fact that you think I'll be on board with them."

"I will convince you. I must." He rubbed his hand over his mouth, smearing blood all over his chin. "The three of us will lead the charge—to purge the earth of the weak!"

Insane. As she stared at his semi-familiar face, she realized her dad had ceased to be the last night she'd seen him as a man, the night he'd given her the book.

It had been his deathbed gift.

This being was not her father, not Dustin Todd, the devoted dad who'd cheered her pattering around the yard with a miniature soccer ball. Her eyes watered. This was Commander Preston Webb.

My dad's dead.

"With these new powers, I can usher in a new era," he said with maniacal fervor. "I'll have a Lykae's senses, a vemon's strength, and a fey's speed. I'll be able to harvest nourishment from lightning like a Valkyrie. I already have a vampire's strengths. I can reap power— and a being's memories—from blood, but have no aversion to the sun. I can trace over the entire world."

"You must be very proud," she bit out, wondering how to get away from him. But first, she had to know one thing. "Did you kill my mother?"

His expression didn't change, even as he nodded. "I loved Fiore, more than anything. Yet she filled me with doubt, made me question my mission." In an absent tone, he murmured, "Guarding the monstrous ones was relatively easy. It was far more difficult to guard the innocent-faced ones, the beautiful ones. They called to our sympathy." He shook his head. "And then she tried to take you from me."

"Probably because you would've killed me if I'd tested out as a Lorean!"

"No! I wasn't ready to accept the Lore for her—but I was for you. Part of the reason that I chose to take that capsule was because I knew you were going to transition."

That hyped-up blood. Even with MacRieve's new strength, he might not be able to match Webb's. Which meant she needed to get this being out of here before MacRieve returned. "You have to go. Do you understand whose home this is?"

"It belongs to the Lykae from my prison. I drank someone with that knowledge—not to the death, of course; we're going to need all our numbers." He grinned with ravaged lips. "How do you think I found you?"

FIFTY-ONE

We vowed no' to tell you anything."

"What the hell?" Will snapped, wishing he could throttle Rónan over the phone. "My brother's *missing*?"

The boy said, "Munro heard about these warlocks who were turning humans into Lykae and enslaving them."

Will cursed. There was a reason Lykae never turned humans into their kind. *Turned* Lykae were violent, unthinking creatures. "The warlocks are called Those Best Forgotten, no?" He was familiar with that sect. Around each Accession, they created armies of Lykae on their home plane of Quondam.

"That's them! Some real bad dudes. They sacrifice nymphs. Talk about a waste. I mean, what are they thinking—"

"Boy!"

"Right. Anyway, so Munro and Madadh and six

others were going to raid the lair and free some new wolves. They had a nymph informant who knew of a limited-time weak spot in the Forgotten's defenses. It was the night of the full moon, so it should've been a snap. Before he left, Munro told me and Ben that you already had more on your plate than you can handle. We were no' to tell anyone of this—but especially no' you—unless they didn't return by today."

Will had known something was wrong with Munro after there'd been no response to his last message: *Munro, I need to speak with you. Where the hell are you? I went to the bluidy Ubus Realm! No shite, can you believe it? Chloe has relatives there. They've honor, and they're strong. Ach, brother, you'll no' believe the things I've seen and learned. Call me back.*

"Then this was a set-up." To what end? Why risk an eight-Lykae raid?

Rónan said, "Lachlain, Garreth, and Bowen are all meeting here at midnight to organize a full-scale assault. No' less than a hundred. Happy Accession, you know what I mean?"

"Tell Lachlain and the others that I'll be there tonight."

"You bringing Chloe?" Rónan asked.

"If I can help it, she'll never leave my side."

"Good man! See you later."

Will hung up the phone and bellowed, "Lass, we need to leave. Now! Munro's in a spot!"

No answer.

"Chloe?"

He inhaled for her scent, past the fragrance of the sera tree and the damp of the old stone—

Caught it. *Wait, that canna be right.* Will smelled myriad beings: Lykae, vampire, demon, even Valkyrie.

He took off in a sprint, barreling headlong for his mate.

Now, beast. Now we earn our keep.

❖❖❖

Chloe gave a cry when the double doors to the courtyard blasted open, flying off their hinges.

MacRieve charged out, fangs bared, claws flared. An awing sight.

With a deafening roar, he lunged through the air at Webb. Impact! MacRieve tackled him so hard that the two males crashed over the cobblestones, plowing them like a tiller.

Stone rained in all directions.

Webb might be coming into his strength, but MacRieve was protecting his mate. He pinned Webb, one hand crushing his windpipe, his other hand raised.

Webb dug his claws into MacRieve's arm, flailing, unable to budge a Lykae's hold.

Just as MacRieve was about to swipe his glinting black claws through his prey, Chloe cried, "It's *him*, MacRieve! It's . . . Webb."

MacRieve stayed his hand midstrike. With a hard shake of his head, he began caging his beast before her eyes. Voice rough, he said, "I doona understand this."

She answered, "He's turned himself into a mix of creatures."

"Tell me what you want me to do. It'll be done."

He'd said he would give up his quest for retribution against Webb, but to see him shake off his hatred and ferocity like this for her . . .

Chloe's eyes watered once more. MacRieve was giving her the choice.

Though she'd accepted her dad's death and knew this wasn't her father, she didn't want MacRieve to ever regret killing her "sire."

"Let him go."

With a shove, MacRieve released him, then hastened to stand in front of her, shielding her.

Webb rose with that creepy grace, rubbing his throat.

"He's leaving, for good," she said. "Isn't that right, Webb?"

He narrowed his eyes at MacRieve. "Mercy from a Lykae? And after everything I had done to you? I remember you were one of Dixon's favorites. She loved to talk about your experiments over biscotti and coffee."

Not my dad, not my dad.

MacRieve tensed even more, but his tone was steady when he said, "Aye. A small price to pay. If no' for my time in prison, I would no' have found Chloe."

She moved beside MacRieve, taking his hand.

"You think you're good enough for my daughter?" Webb asked.

"I think she's chosen me. Now, get the fuck off our lands."

Webb offered his hand to Chloe. "Come with me, daughter. We can start our own kingdom."

With a growl, MacRieve clutched her closer, pressing her against his side.

"I'm staying here," she said. "Where I belong. And if you ever cared about me at all, you'll leave and never come back."

As if she hadn't spoken, Webb said, "I can trace, Lykae. Do you think you can stop me from snatching her away if I want to?"

"*She* can stop you, old man. You underestimate your daughter at your peril."

At that, Webb told her, "I'll go. But know that you'll always have me, daughter. I'll forever be in the shadows watching over you." He smiled a macabre grin. "In time, you'll change your mind. It might take a hundred years or two, but you will."

"You keep to those shadows, Webb," MacRieve grated. "Emerge from them, and I vow to the Lore I'll take your goddamned head."

"Good-bye for now, Chloe," Webb murmured, just before he vanished into thin air.

Her knees gave out, but MacRieve caught her, pulling her to his chest.

"I'm so sorry, lass. I know how much this must hurt."

She rubbed her watering eyes. "It does, but I don't consider that man my dad. That was Webb. Dustin Todd died two months ago."

"Ach, *mo chridhe*, please doona cry."

MacRieve had told her how he'd felt to see her tears, so she tried to stem them. "It's going to take a while for me to come to terms with this."

He pressed a kiss against her hair. "I'll help you. I'll be there for you."

"I know you will. But I can sort out my feelings later. Did I hear you yelling that Munro is in trouble?"

"Aye. Can I tell you while you pack a bag?"

When she nodded, he took her elbow to squire her inside.

As she stuffed clothes into her new carry-on, he explained everything Rónan had told him, a tale of warlocks, and raids, and sacrificial nymphs. . . .

He finished by telling her, "Munro was most likely captured."

"How are you handling this?" she asked. His eyes were golden. No beast raging?

"I'd know if he'd died," MacRieve said simply. "My beast would be in a howling frenzy for its brother wolf. Which means Munro's likely in a warlock dungeon, spitting mad. Or . . ."

"Or what?"

"Chloe, they enslave our kind, building armies of Lykae, as mindless as revenants or ghouls. The warlocks call them *vassals*. We doona know how they control born Lykae. Now *turned* Lykae? That I can understand."

"Why? How are they turned?" She zipped up her bag.

"A human must be bitten by a Lykae whose beast is fully risen. With the bite, the Lykae transfers part of his beast into the mortal."

She blinked at him. "Different from a claiming bite?"

"Aye. And more, the catalyst for the change is death."

Her eyes narrowed. "So all those turned humans had to die first?"

"And few will rise. There's no guarantee. All we know is that in turned Lykae, the former mortal has zero control over the beast that's been shoved inside him."

Like MacRieve had once had little control. This must be hitting him hard.

"It takes years of work to get them even into the realm of civilized. Munro, being Munro, would have been ready to adopt a legion of noob Lykae. I'm no' surprised whatsoever that he led that raid."

Bag in hand, she started for the door. "We have to go break him out."

"We?" He followed, collecting the bag from her. "You think you're ready to tussle with warlocks?"

At the top of the stairs, she said, "I've been preparing for this all my life—I just didn't know it. I won't cower from a charge, won't panic under pressure. If eleven of them bear down on me, I can run circles around them. Think about it, Will, I'd make a helluva wingman."

"I'll scout the field of play"—he brushed his knuckles over her face—"but T-Rex's spot on first string is looking solid. I pity unsuspecting warlocks."

She tilted her head. "I thought you'd react differently." But then, she'd thought *she* would react differently to seeing her father.

"Expecting me to lose my shite? I've got my mate,

and she's healthy and hale. My brother's in trouble, but he will no' be for much longer. You could say I'm as close to Zen as a werewolf can get."

And his calm fueled her own. *Connected.*

"This is no' the first time a battle's been needed. And it will no' be the last. Chloe, I'm hankering for this."

Then so was she. Excitement began filling her, anticipation. "Hotter's eager to go free Hot?"

His lips curled. "Now you've got the idea. Of course, we'll have to recharge on the flight over."

"If we do that, then we're gonna *win ugly* against these warlocks."

"Is my fierce female directing me to lower the boom?"

"Oh, yeah." She grinned up at her new mate, and he was already grinning at her.

Because they were about to pull off a coup. . . .

EPILOGUE

Dungeon of the Disremembered
Quondam, Realm of Those Best Forgotten

Madadh's bloodied fist slammed into Munro's face, the sound of cracked bone echoing in the dank cell.

Munro had long since stopped trying to reach his mindless friend. The man had been *vassaled*; Madadh's beast was fully risen, his eyes ghostly blue—and vacant.

Since Munro's right eye refused to open, he narrowed his left one at the warlock controlling Madadh. Had other Forgotten called this tormenter *Jels*?

Jels had ordered Madadh to torture Munro nigh continuously—neither Lykae had slept for days, with scant lulls in the violence. Madadh's fingers were broken from raining blows, the skin over his knuckles raked clean to the bone from Munro's teeth. But the Lykae seemed to feel nothing.

The warlock wouldn't allow Madadh to stop until Munro released his own beast.

Though Jels's purple robe covered him from neck

to heels, Munro could tell his frame was spindly. He was bald of hair, his face sunken. So easily broken. Yet Munro was in no position to attack—or to defend himself.

He was on his knees, arms stretched tight above him. His manacled wrists were connected to a chain that descended from a pulley in the ceiling. All the metal was mystically forged, unbreakable even to one like him.

"Give it up, Jels," Munro bit out between bloodied lips. "Nothing you can do . . . will make me loose my beast. Nothing." His head had been beaten to a pulp; his brain felt like it rattled inside his cracked skull. Thoughts were foggy, but he held on to the knowledge of one critical fact he'd learned: the warlocks couldn't enslave a Lykae until his beast had risen. Once it did, they used their dark magic to leash it. But they had no arcane power to compel the beast to rise.

During the Lykae raid on this dungeon, Madadh had unknowingly freed his beast and been vassaled by the warlocks. Then those bastards had used the massive Madadh to attack Munro and the rest of their crew, catching the others off guard.

The warlocks had spent the last several days trying to torture Munro's beast to the surface—doing everything they could to add his feral howls to the ones constantly sounding up and down this corridor of cells. Yet after living with Will's volatile beast for nine centuries, Munro had taken great pains to control his own.

He could resist any torment, especially when he

knew another raid would come soon. The clan would send in powerful reinforcements—Garreth, Bowen, the great king himself. If Munro stayed lucid, he could warn them to keep the beast caged.

Would Will accompany them? Part of Munro was desperate for a warrior like his brother to come; part of him dreaded it. His brother's beast would be so easily claimed.

Another punch took Munro across the jaw, nearly dislocating it. His head snapped around, blood and sweat spraying the hem of Jels's robe. His arms were all but wrenched from their sockets. "Bluidy hell, Madadh!"

The man's scarred face was blank. No reaction.

The legendary Mad Dog of the Highlands was now an obedient dog. Munro shuddered at the thought. *No, I'll no' be giving them my beast.*

Jels tilted his head, seeming genuinely confused. "Why do you resist our thrall so totally? To be vassaled is to be at peace. I never expected it to take this long."

If Jels was finally going to talk, Munro had questions. "Why no' just kill me?" he asked, but he feared he knew. The few times Madadh had been commanded away from this cell, he always returned with his fangs bloody.

"Kill?" Jels blinked. "The purpose of this entire trap was to secure an elder like you. We ensured that a new Lykae vassal would get much attention at a public event, knowing a white knight like you would raid us."

Exactly why Munro had come; he'd heard a newly turned Lykae had been beheaded, slaughtered for no reason other than blindly following the warlocks' commands.

"Then we dispatched a nymph to guide you in. Poor girl thought we'd release her sister if she cooperated."

He'd had no reason not to trust the nymph. Atop all Munro's pain, foreboding whispered through him. "A lot of trouble. Why would you want me so bad?"

"We could have searched a thousand planes and dozens of eras for a beast so strong as yours."

Munro knew this ancient faction could move through time, creating portals and even entire planes.

"We will use your beast to seed all of our newling vassals."

They wanted Munro to bite humans? To give innocent mortals years of insanity—or death? "Fuck that, Jels! Never." The perversion of it! "You can take your beastly 'seed' and shove it up your warlock arse."

"One Lykae can only produce so many newlings. Madadh here has bitten fourteen; two have risen. You might have heard their screams?" Jels asked, his tone deceptively pleasant. "He's had his fill of human necks, is nigh tapped out. He's only a couple of centuries old, but you . . . we believe you could turn even more! Many more!"

Munro's bloody mouth split into a grin. "The next bite I make will snatch clean your throat."

"You have no idea what's coming, do you?" Jels's smug look briefly faltered. "The Bringers of Doom are soon to rise—the threat that will end all of us, if we can't fight back. The Forgotten won't stop until we've amassed an army. Until we've sacrificed enough beautiful females to appease enough dark gods. And in the end you'll be glad we have."

"You're crazed, little man. Tell yourself whatever you need to."

A nod at Madadh set the man into motion; his claws slashed down Munro's face, plowing through his skin and obliterating his right eye.

Biting back a yell of agony, Munro told Jels, "Tickling me? You'll have to do . . . better than that."

Another nod, and Madadh gripped Munro's thigh in two places, readying to snap his femur. *Motherfucker!*

A second warlock slinked inside the cell, calling out to Jels in their unintelligible language. Whatever news the messenger brought pleased Jels. He turned to Munro. "Do better than that, you said? It seems I just have." He crossed to the wall, unhooking a chain there.

As the pulley above squeaked, the tension on Munro's arms ebbed until he could lower them in front of him. The searing pain of blood rushing into his limbs rivaled that of his maimed face and eye. He fought to remain kneeling, keeping Jels in his limited sightline.

There was no way to defeat Madadh without freeing his own beast. But he could at least peel Jels's head from his neck. Munro tensed to attack—

Two beings appeared not five feet from him, another warlock and a raven-haired female who looked barely out of her teens. She appeared dazed, trembling beside her captor. Mortal? Yes, and utterly lovely with her olive skin and bright irises the color of new pennies. Flowers decorated her mane of wild black curls. She looked like a wee *traveller*, a gypsy.

She was dressed in an ornate white gown. It was either of olden design—or a wedding dress. Or both.

At her ethereal scent, Munro's body shot tight, spine straightening.

—Yours.—

Shock assailed him. "No, no," he grated, "what trickery is this?" She was like a vision, an angel come to take him, far too beautiful to be in this fetid place.

"No trickery," Jels said. "Meet Kereny. *Ren* to her extended family. You wouldn't believe where—and when—we had to go to procure her. Suffice it to say that the mystical expenditure to find your female was costly."

My female? Yes. *The hands of gods.*

Her wide eyes were glassy, unseeing. She tottered on her feet. Injured? Munro saw no blood marring the immaculate white silk of her gown. Yet he scented something like . . . poison.

Munro bellowed, "What the fuck did you do?" He lunged for her, but Madadh clotheslined him, choking him to the ground. How badly was she hurt?

As Munro thrashed against the man, his Instinct screamed, *—YOUR FEMALE DIES.—*

Dies?

His beast howled inside to fight for her, but somehow Munro resisted. If enslaved, he had no hope of escaping with her, much less of saving her life.

When the second warlock drew away from her, she

sank to her knees, forearms upraised along her thighs. Her fragile fingers were limp.

With utter glee, Jels shoved up her sleeves, revealing black veins that stretched from her wrists to her elbows. "Behold. Her lifeblood turns to stone. Wait until it reaches her heart—I'm told there's no worse agony."

They'd bespelled her. Rage reddened Munro's vision.

"She has only a couple of minutes before she succumbs," Jels said. "Such a distasteful business."

Her expression twisted to one of utter agony, and she cried out, those fragile fingers knotting with her pain.

"What do you want, warlock? I'll do it!" Dread squeezed his heart, a great icy fist around it. His remaining eye watered. "Anything!" His beast clamored inside him, but Munro fought it.

Jels made a tsking sound. "If only you had cooperated, then we wouldn't have had to steal her from her own wedding."

Wedding? Munro couldn't worry about that right now! "Bluidy tell me what to do to save her!"

"You have little time, Lykae. She fades like night douses sun." Jels snapped his fingers for the others to depart. "I'm sure you'll figure out what needs to be done. But if not . . . might I suggest death by bite over the stone blood spell? Much less excruciating."

Rage. Haze. *No, fight it! Think!* Before the cell door clanged shut, Munro had lunged for her once more. "Doona be frightened of me, Kereny. My name is

Munro MacRieve, and I mean you no harm." He could only imagine what his mutilated face looked like. When he looped his bound arms over her quaking body, she stared blankly. *Shock.* "Just stay with me! I'm going tae help you."

As another wave of pain hit her, she shuddered. Her brow grew damp, her breaths panting.

Have to get her out of here! She was so delicate and young, her skin clammy. *Am I to lose another mortal?* His eyes darted wildly. *They perish so readily.*

No. "I will no' let you die!" There was no time to escape the dungeon with her, to take her off plane for aid. His mysterious female was going to die in moments.

Munro had only one hope of saving her—as the warlocks well knew. He drew her in closer, desperately trying to warm her.

To *prepare* her. And himself. He rubbed his chin over her slim shoulder, breathing deep of her scent. It helped to temper the rage and panic he felt.

She finally spoke in a hushed voice. "Do n-not do this to me." Her words were English, accented. With difficulty, she turned her head toward him, the movement plainly agonizing to her. "Defy this evil." Once they faced each other, she gave a cry at his injuries.

"I will do anything tae save you." *Even become a slave myself.* "You're my mate, little one."

"Mate?" Even so weak, she still sounded aghast. "Then how can you even think of abusing me like this?"

He began to relinquish control to his beast. *Save her, beast, bite her fiercely.*

"I know what you are," she whispered between ragged breaths. "Please don't infect me . . . with that thing inside you."

Unmoved by her pleas, he used his ruined face to nudge her curling hair off her shoulder. She tried to resist him, but had no strength left. "I will take care of you, teach you tae control it."

"My kind revere freedom." She started crying. "You would turn your mate . . . into a warlock's slave?"

"You will no' be a slave! I will free you."

"Leave me to an honorable death."

He rasped, "I canna, Kereny. You will resurrect—do you understand me? You must return tae me!" Only two of Madadh's victims had. *But my beast is strong; it will roar to life inside her.*

So much so that this young female would have no chance of controlling it. *Figure that out later.*

"If you do this . . . I will hate you. My family will curse you . . . you'll still have no mate."

"Then I'll spend eternity earning your forgiveness." And punishing those who'd done this to Kereny. *His* Kereny.

"It will go unearned. You would transform me into an animal . . . making me an outcast from my people . . . enslaving me to those I long to see dead? There is *no* forgiveness."

Munro's claws and fangs began lengthening, his body morphing against hers. "Close your eyes for me, my love."

"I-I'm *begging* . . . no." Instead of closing her eyes,

she trained them on his face. She whimpered at the sight of his emerging beast.

Voice gone guttural, Munro choked out, "And I'm beggin' you tae return tae me, little one."

With a primal roar, his beast took over completely. Munro could only exist in the background, perceiving his head whipping forward, fangs sinking into the sweet skin of her neck. Perceiving her writhe and sob with anguish.

Perceiving her heartbeat slowing. *Beat—beat . . . beat—beat. . . .*

The beast snarled against her cooling flesh, frantically injecting its essence, a part of itself, through a vicious bite.

As Kereny shuddered with death throes, the beast pawed her closer to his body, rocking her, spilling tears and blood over her wedding gown.

The beast drew back, but only to sink its fangs into her again. And again. Howling between each furious bite.

Dimly, Munro was aware of Jels's laughter outside the cell, of the warlocks' power coiling around him, overtaking him.

How can I protect Kereny as a mindless slave? And he wouldn't be the only one under their sway. What would they do to a beauty like her when they controlled her utterly?

Thinking of the hell he might have condemned her to, Munro prayed his twin could sense his turmoil. Before, he'd dreaded Will coming to this place. *Now I fucking demand it!*

Be smarter than me, Will. Be stronger.

Free me, so I can free my mate.

Kereny's body fell limp. *Beat . . . beat . . .* silence. When his mate's heart went still in her chest, Munro threw back his head and roared until the entire goddamned dungeon quaked, quieting only when her lips parted.

Her final breath escaped her, carrying her last words: *"I . . . hate . . . you. . . ."*